Into the Light

Immortal Hearts, Volume 1

Katherine Hastings

Published by Flyte Publishing, 2019.

INTO THE LIGHT

Copyright © 2019 by Katherine Hastings

For information contact :
http://www.katherinehastings.com
Ebook ISBN: 978-1-949913-16-3
Paperback ISBN: 978-1-949913-17-0
First Edition: October 2019
Editing: Tami Stark
Proofreading: Vicki McGough
www.katherinehastings.com

CHAPTER ONE

Emilia

"TWO GIN AND TONICS. More gin than tonic, darling."

The forced smile on my face looked no more authentic than Lizzy Dillon's when she got back from her "vacation" in Scottsdale, looking twenty years younger and like her face had been stretched within an inch of its life. Frozen, fake, and lacking all emotion. An expression I'd mastered since taking this crappy job as a cocktail waitress.

"So, you'd like a double?" I asked.

"No. A single, just heavy on the gin." He winked and flashed a smile so white the airport could have used him to guide in planes. Either those were veneers, or he brushed with bleach every day. Judging by his spray-tanned skin and the perfectly coiffed grey mustache, I'd put my money on veneers.

"Coming right up," I said through gritted teeth. I wanted to say *piss off*.

Anyone who has ever worked as a server knows that there should be one of those conversation bubbles over our heads displaying what we are *actually* thinking when we nod and smile.

Of course you can have a double for the same price as a single. You can also have a kick in the face.

These regular responses clamored for attention in my head to the constant stream of ridiculous requests these Chicago people bombarded me with the five nights a week I worked here.

I turned and moved through the dimly lit club, sliding between tables and trying to avoid bumping the swanky guests in their designer clothes... the ones I couldn't afford even if I worked here a hundred hours a week. The new Birkin bag two tables down caught my eye and for a moment I considered a life of crime. If I grabbed it and ran, I could live a pretty happy life sleeping on the street with it until the police ripped it from my hands and dragged me off to jail. Glancing at it again I seriously considered it.

"Emilia, behind you." Sharon startled me from my visions of running screaming through the street clutching the beautiful red leather bag with a dozen police tearing after me.

"Sorry." I stepped forward allowing her to pass. "Gin and tonics," I mumbled to myself as I got back on task.

A loud woman in a pink velour track suit with diamond earrings as large as my now-widened eyes stood at the small spot marked "server station." She flapped her money in the air while shouting out a drink order to the bartender, Eric, who continued ignoring her. The fastest way to not get served involved waving your money in a bartender's face. That was rule number two, right behind don't whistle at them like they're a dog. Rule numero uno.

"Excuse me," I said with no attempt to mask the irritation in my voice, "this is the server station."

She glanced at me and shrugged then returned her attention to Eric as he shook yet another specialty craft cocktail in his metal shaker. "Yoo hoo! Bartender! Two cosmopolitans straight up!" she shouted into the abyss. He didn't even glance in her direction, continuing his ruse of pretending she didn't exist.

"Ma'am, you can't stand there. It's for employees only," I said, pointing to the mat on the bar marked in bold letters 'Server Station: Employees Only.'

"I'll only be a minute; I think I'm next."

"Ma'am, I need to get in there," I said through gritted teeth, irritated she took up my time... and in cocktail waitressing time equaled money.

With an exaggerated groan, she shot me a look. I matched it and raised her a pair of arched eyebrows.

"Fine." She spun around and pushed her way past me. I stumbled into a hipster as he took a sip of his craft beer. The overpriced ale sloshed over the edge of his glass when I bumped him and rode its way down his beard, making a beeline for my cleavage. I cringed when the cold liquid slipped between my breasts and pooled in a place I couldn't reach until I could get to the bathroom later.

"Damn!" I wiped the trail it left behind. He shrugged an apology and turned back to his conversation.

"Having a good night, Emilia?" Eric's voice startled me as I stood with my fingers pushed down between my breasts wiping up the beer as best I could.

"A real doozy," I answered with an accompanying eye roll.

He laughed and handed me a cocktail napkin. "I've been shaking the same shaker for over a minute waiting for that Housewives of Chicago wannabe to get lost. Did you see the freaking velour tracksuit?"

Of course, I had. Every middle-aged, bored housewife in the city sported them, attempting to look young and casual. "The rhinestone 'Juicy' across the ass when she stomped away was the icing on the cake," I snorted.

"Nothing but class." He laughed. "What do you need?"

"Chomps Houlihan over there needs two gin and tonics, more gin than tonic, *but* he's only paying for singles."

"Chomps Houlihan?" he asked.

"He has these freaking veneer chompers that are literally hurting my eyes. Like Chiclets. It's not even right."

Eric laughed and craned his neck to see him across the crowded room. "Doubles for the price of singles? So, you're saying to pour even less gin than a normal single for Mr. Chomps Houlihan?"

"You know it."

We exchanged smiles and a fist bump. Since Eric had been at this for years, he rolled with the punches better than me. Every night while we counted our tips and sipped on our one free shifter, he'd tell me it got easier with time and gave me advice on how to control my temper when the customers shredded my sanity. But it had been three months since I'd accepted this second job and I swore it got harder each day not to lose it on my customers.

"Two really weak gin and tonics." With a wink, he set the drinks on the server mat in front of me.

"Thanks, Eric." I grabbed one in each hand and surveyed the best way to get back to my table. Friday nights always proved tricky as the place filled up with over-paid, over-worked business types looking to blow off the stress of the week. The group of gold diggers in six-inch stilettos and skintight dresses moved like a school of fish toward the booths and left me an opening. If there was one thing you learn as a cocktail waitress, it was evasive maneuvering. I spun my way through the crowd toward the opening, but it filled with bodies before I could make it.

Damn. New plan. I jumped in behind the Glamsquad, letting them break the path to get me closer to my table. Their high-pitched squeals nearly shattered the glasses I guarded as I looked for an opening.

"He's gorgeous!" one cooed.

"He's mine!" another said.

"He's looking at me. Suck it, bitches," the one with the legs up to my ears argued.

Who are they looking at? Craning my neck around I searched to get a glimpse of the man they still bickered about. The thick crowd and the Glamazons blocked any chance I had of sneaking a peek. No luck. Oh well, not like I could do anything other than stare anyway.

"Waitress! We're thirsty!" It was Chomps Houlihan. He waved his hands like a man stranded on a desert island trying to hail an overhead plane. I rolled my eyes and gave up my quest to see the man causing an all-out girl war in front of me.

Holding my breath, I squeezed between two lawyers debating who had argued their case better today. They made no attempt to move or acknowledge my awkward maneuvering trying to get two full drinks and my ample breasts between them. Rubbing your boobs on strangers all night while you squeeze between them was a part of the job I would never get used to.

I made it through with both drinks still intact, but when I turned the opposite way to begin my next military-style maneuvering the last ten feet to my table, I ground to a stop and growled. The Glamazon pack had managed to get there before me and once again blocked my way.

Son of a...

"It's him. That's Henry Cavill. Swear to God!" The tallest of the girl squad peered over the heads of the others.

Henry Cavill is here? He's so hot. Okay, this I need to see.

I saw a parting in the pack and took the opportunity to sneak a peek. Standing on my tiptoes, I craned to see the corner booth where they focused all their attention.

And then I saw him.

Holy shit.

My jaw slackened while I soaked in the sight of him. He looked the other way, but it gave me a great profile view of his chiseled jaw and straight, perfect nose. His dark, thick hair was swept back into a style that would send Ken Barbie into a jealous fit. A designer suit flowed over his broad shoulders and tapered to a set of perfectly chiseled abs hiding behind the table. At least they were in my mind's eye. Now I could understand all the fuss.

He was talking to someone I couldn't see because the redhead in the black Prada dress I had eyeballed in this month's Vogue blocked my way. His head turned back, and blue eyes the color of ice passed over the crowd and found their way to mine.

Sweet Jesus, he's looking at me.

But he wasn't looking *at* me. He was looking through me. My skin prickled and my spine shivered with the intensity of his gaze. I knew I shouldn't stand there gawking at him, but my feet and my eyes both ignored my pleas to move. I stood there clutching those gin and tonics for dear life while arguing with my jaw to stay shut. As I soaked in the sight of the gorgeous man at the booth, my breath stalled in my lungs. Not Henry Cavill after all. Similar, yes, but this man was even more striking. He was... beautiful.

The girl with the legs up to my neck wobbled on a too-tall heel and stumbled back a step. Her lanky arm swung for balance and collided with the bottom of the gin and tonic in my right hand. It tipped backward, and ice cubes and liquid chased the path the beer had laid between my breasts.

Shit!

I broke his gaze and looked down at my breasts that were now covered with gin and tonic. Another glance at the glass showed it only half full. The smell of junipers mixed with beer wafted from my breasts to my nose and I choked down a gag.

You've got to be kidding me.

To add insult to injury, she didn't even turn around to apologize. My cheeks flushed with heat as my blood heated to scalding. Would this shitty night ever end?

"Oh, come on! Waitress!"

Chomps Frickin' Houlihan.

"I'm *coming!*" I snapped at him loud enough he could hear me over the din of the crowd.

A quick glance at the man in the booth showed the pair of icy eyes still fixated on me. As much as I wanted to continue drinking him in, there was no time to dream about men out of my reach. There were bills to pay, and I wore half of a drink that should have been to the table a while ago. At least one gin and tonic had survived. While I tried to gather up the last shreds of my composure, I pushed my way through the crowd to Chomp's table.

"Here you go," I said, setting the drinks down in front of Chomps and his equally ridiculous-looking friend. Maybe I should find the Juicy tracksuit lady and introduce them. They seemed like they would get along famously. "That will be twenty-two dollars."

"What is this?" He pointed to the half empty drink.

"Someone bumped me. I'm sorry."

"I'm not paying for half of a drink."

My body quaked with rage. He wasn't wrong, of course, but he had no idea what I had been through just to get him that drink.

"Fine. Just pay for half. We'll call it fifteen."

He took a sip. "This isn't Beefeaters."

The temperature of my blood rose from scalding to near boiling. "You didn't request Beefeaters, sir."

"Yes, I did. I said two Beefeaters and tonic. Isn't that right, Harry? You heard me, right?"

His friend, presumably Harry, nodded in agreement. "I only drink Beefeaters. I'm not paying for these. Run back and get me two *Beefeaters* and tonics. Did you get it this time?"

Despite my exploding head, like a good waitress I nodded and bit my tongue instead of spitting out what I wanted to say.

You said gin, douchebag. At no point did the words Beefeaters pass between your horrifyingly blinding teeth.

I reached for the glasses to take them away, but he caught me by my wrist.

"Whoa, there!" He laughed. "You can leave them here. No need for them to go to waste!"

My eyes moved from the glasses to the wrinkled fingers holding my wrist. The moment I felt his weathered hand touch my skin, my near-boiling blood started to bubble. "If you're not paying for them, you're not drinking them. Let go of my wrist."

"Ah, come on, sweetheart! Don't be such a sour puss! Just give me a little smile." His blinding teeth offended me once again as he beamed.

That. Is. It.

Unwritten server rules number three, four and five. Don't touch me. Don't call me sweetheart. Don't tell me to smile. As my blood hit a rolling boil, I knew I was so far gone rage was no longer visible in my rear-view mirror.

"You want me to smile?" I said, my voice rising with each syllable. "Why in the actual fuck would I smile? Should I smile because I just wasted all this time dragging the two gin and tonics you ordered across the club only to have you tell me they're wrong, *which they're not?* Should I smile because my boss makes me wear this ridiculous black dress with my tits popping out, my tits that are now covered in not only beer, but beer *and* your gin and tonic? The one you're refusing to pay for that I will get docked for tonight? Should I smile because I already worked an eight-hour shift today crammed in a cubicle in my dead-end career? Should I smile because my piece of shit husband walked out on me six months ago for a twenty-two-year-old stick figure and left me with a mortgage and thirty-five thousand in credit card debt, hence why I now work here as a mistreated cocktail waitress five nights a week *on top of my full-time job*? You tell me, Chomps... if you were me, would you fucking smile?"

He stared at me blinking, his veneers now hidden away. A quick glance around confirmed that my overdue outburst had not only reached the ears of Chomps and Harry, but everyone in the near vicinity. Another glance revealed the stranger with the icy eyes had been listening as well. His lips weren't smiling but I could swear his eyes were.

I rarely indulged in tears, but the non-stop work, the exhaustion, and the stress of rebuilding my life after Jeff walked out all built up in my tear ducts. Turning on my heel, I pushed my way through the crowd to the storage room behind the bar. I could feel the man in the booth's eyes on me all the way. He must think I'm a freak.

This is so embarrassing. I can't believe I snapped.

I slammed the door to the storage room and with it, shut out the music and voices that had resumed since my outburst.

"Damn it!" I pushed back the tears and exhaled a cleansing breath.

You've got this, Emilia. Get it together. No. Tears. We had a deal.

The day Jeff walked out I had given myself seven days to cry. Seven days to wallow in self-pity and curse myself for all the bad decisions I had made since the day I met him. After seven days, no more. No more tears would get shed because of that lying, useless, cheating asshole. Another deep breath and they slipped back away to the recesses I had forced them into. It wasn't so much Jeff I was ready to scream and cry about, it was the situation he had put me in. The situation I had allowed myself to get into.

A soft rapping on the door startled me back to my senses. "Emilia?" Eric asked. "Are you okay?"

"Yes," I lied. "I'll be right out."

I stood up straight and smoothed my ponytail. A quick swipe with my fingers under my eyes confirmed I had won the battle against the tears. With a deep breath I opened the door, cringing at the wave of sound that assaulted my ears. I would kill for a hot bath, a good book and silence.

You need the money. Get your shit together and get out there.

I closed the door behind me and walked over to the serving station. All eyes were on me as I tried my best to pretend the unfortunate incident was just a figment of their imaginations.

Eric leaned on the bar. "You sure you're okay?"

I nodded. He was the closest thing to a friend I had in this town. Considering I never saw him outside of work that wasn't saying much. The girls at the office were catty and still treated me like an outsider. The other waitresses here were all in college and into partying. I was the only "adult" of the bunch. At twenty-nine, I had left that life years ago when I'd agreed to support Jeff while he pursued a singing career.

I had worked all the time. He'd played music and partied. And since he'd left just six months after we'd moved from Milwaukee to Chicago, I'd had no time to make friends. Now I worked two full-time jobs and didn't have the time or the dime to go out and meet new people. Eric was it... my one sort-of friend.

"Excuse me." I felt a tap on my shoulder and turned to see the face attached to the voice.

A man about my age stood in front of me. Blonde streaked his light brown hair that he'd tousled into trendy spikes. His eyes, soft and brown, reminded me of the loyal Labrador, Barkley, who'd lived down the street during my childhood. He wasn't as attractive as the man I'd seen earlier, though honestly, I'd never seen his equal. But this guy was well above average in the looks department. On top of his impressive looks, he also sported tailored designer clothes that fit his athletic build like they were custom made. He was walking style.

"Hi, I'm so sorry to bother you. I'm Mark Atwood."

"Hi Mark," I answered with hesitation in my voice. *What does he want?*

"This is going to sound terribly high school, but my friend would like to meet you." He smiled, his eyes dancing with an almost childlike enthusiasm while he awaited my answer.

"That does sound very high school," I responded, not sure whether to be flattered or annoyed. "Tell your friend I'm sorry to disappoint but I'm working."

"He knows you're very busy and on the clock. Here, he will happily pay for your time." He pulled out a wallet and I noticed the Versace logo stamped into the smooth black leather.

Yep, walking style.

"Five hundred enough?" He fingered the hundreds that seemed to go on forever. My eyes widened as I eyed the wad of money.

"Five hundred? To talk?"

He nodded, seemingly unaware of his unusual request.

"Jesus! Take it!" Eric said, now leaning over the bar eyeing up the dough.

Glancing over my shoulder my eyes connected with Eric's. My face asked for permission to take the money I really, really needed. His enthusiastic nodding said go for it.

"Five hundred. To talk. Here. In the bar." I said it as more of a confirmation I wasn't agreeing to leave with anyone.

"Great!" He slipped the money into my hand. I shoved it into my cocktail apron and pushed it down deep so it wouldn't fall out. "This way."

He placed his hand on the small of my back and guided me through the club to... wait a minute. We were going to the corner booth. To him. That incredible male specimen.

Him? He wants to talk to me?

I kept moving but my pace slowed. The Glamazons still preened in front of him, laughing too loud and talking with exaggerated hands in obvious attempts to get his attention.

Why me? I wasn't unattractive, but I certainly wasn't of the caliber of those leggy thoroughbreds. They didn't even have a dimple of cellulite. I hadn't been able to say that since I put on ten pounds eating my weight in ice cream when Jeff left. *Those* girls were the ones he should talk to... not me.

Mark encouraged me forward. My eyes locked with the man in the booth.

Good God is he gorgeous. That's not even right.

He stood up, one hand clasping the button on his grey designer suit shut while his other hand gestured to the padded leather chair across from him. I smoothed my black dress under my butt and slid down into the seat. He stared at me for a moment before slipping his coat button back open and sitting back down.

"Hello."

Even his voice is beautiful. A deep tenor with a hint of grit. Not so deep he sounded like a muscle head, but deep enough he sounded all man.

"Hello," I squeaked back.

"This is Aiden McKay." Mark stood beside him now. "I'm so sorry but I didn't catch your name."

"Emilia. Emilia Charles."

Mark nodded and turned back to Aiden. "Aiden, please meet Emilia Charles."

What the hell? Why is he introducing us instead of this guy just telling me his name? This is so weird.

"Pleased to meet you, Emilia." His jaw ticked and then tightened, inhibiting any chance of a smile. It almost seemed like he was clenching his teeth.

We sat in silence for a few moments as Mark's eyes darted between us. I waited for Aiden to speak, but he only clenched his jaw tighter, causing the muscles in his neck to twitch.

Enough of this cryptic nonsense. I wanted to know what this hottie wanted with me. "Why did you want to see me?"

After taking a deep breath, he cleared his throat. "Can I offer you a drink?" His gaze drifted to my cleavage before lifting to meet mine. That ten pounds I'd put on may have given me a few dimples in my ass, but it had done wonders for my tits.

"No, thank you. I'm working. I'm not allowed to drink."

"Very well." He gestured for Mark to sit. Mark didn't hesitate and slid into the booth beside him. As I sat across from them, I shrank under their penetrating stares. The last time I had felt this uncomfortable in a chair was sitting in Principal Smith's office back in tenth grade when I got caught cheating on my math test.

"Tell me about yourself," Aiden said.

"Like what?"

"Do you have any family?"

What kind of question is that? "No. My parents died and I'm an only child."

Something resembling approval flashed through his eyes. "Husband? Boyfriend?" he continued.

"No and no. I'm sure you, like the rest of the bar, heard my husband walked out on me six months ago."

"Yes, I recall that."

Okay, he may be gorgeous but he's fucking weird. What is with these inappropriate personal questions?

"Would you say you have an active social life?"

"I'm not even sure what you mean by that. If you're asking if I have friends, the answer is no. I work over eighty hours a week between two jobs. I don't have time for friends."

Wow. No boyfriend, no family, no friends... I'm starting to sound pretty pathetic.

But as pathetic as that admission felt, his eyes flashed more of that approving look.

"I also overheard you are having financial difficulties?"

Pathetic *and* broke. This conversation stole my already shredded self-confidence.

I nodded. Ordinarily I would have told him it's none of his business, but I had already announced it to the whole bar.

He glanced over to Mark. The two exchanged a look, and then turned their attention back to me.

"I have a proposition for you, Emilia," Aiden said. "A very lucrative one."

Whoa. What is this, "Indecent Proposal"?

"I'm not a hooker!" I shouted, the nearest heads all snapping to look at me. I leaned forward and quieted my voice. "I'm not a prostitute! I can't believe you think I would take money for sex!"

It appeared again. A flicker of mirth inside those frozen eyes.

"I'm not propositioning you for sex. It's a business opportunity."

"What kind of business opportunity?" My question didn't mean I trusted him or would entertain his crazy proposal, but he'd piqued my curiosity.

"I cannot explain that now, but if you meet us tomorrow, we can tell you how you stand to make a considerable amount of money."

Considerable amount of money? This must be illegal. I may be broke. He may be beautiful. But hell. No.

"I don't know what it is you think I would be good for and why it is you think it, but I'm not meeting you any-where. I've seen enough movies to know this doesn't end well for me."

His face didn't change. A frozen gaze remained fixated on my eyes.

"Emilia," Mark's soft voice interrupted the stare down. "I promise you, there is nothing illegal or dangerous for you. This is an incredible opportunity. I wish we could tell you more but not here. Trust me... you're going to want to do this."

His eyes were honest and kind, unlike the straight preda-tory gaze of his companion. Aiden made me feel like a fright-ened gazelle; Mark eased my tensions. Still, this reeked of nothing but bad ideas. I'd made enough of those in my twen-ties with Jeff, and I wasn't going to start into my thirties down the same crappy path.

"I'm sorry but I'm not interested. If you'll excuse me, I need to get back to work." I pushed back my chair and rose. Both men stood in unison, Aiden opening his coat button again before giving me a nod.

"I hope you will reconsider. In case you do." He nodded to Mark who whipped out a white card with only a number on it. No name, no logo, just a number. I took it and turned around.

"Emilia!" A shrill voice sent shivers up my spine, and not the good kind. My boss, Carol.

Son of a...

"Are you still clocked in?" she asked as she stood with crossed arms and an eyebrow arched so high it nearly touched her hairline.

"Yes, but I—"

"You're on the clock and have been sitting at a table with customers. Unacceptable! I also heard you yelled at a customer tonight? He complained about you at the desk. Is it true?"

"Yes, but he—"

"We have a reputation here, Emilia! I cannot have you behaving this way. I'm sorry. There is no excuse. You're fired."

Fuck.

Watching her walk away I considered begging. I needed this job. Without it I was certain to lose my home. Even with both jobs I wasn't sure if I could make it. I started after her, prepared to toss myself on the ground and cling to her ankle while I pleaded, but I stopped myself. Carol didn't believe in second chances, so I'd just end up fired and with my remaining dignity in tatters.

I looked over at the bar to Eric who mouthed the word "sorry" and stuck out his lower lip. With a shrug, I slipped my hand into my apron and touched the wad of hundreds. This would have to stretch out until I could find another job.

Or would it?

My slow turn brought be back around to face Mark and Aiden. Mark's eyes held sympathy while Aiden's flickered with pleasure. With a breath, I spun and marched back.

"Promise me you're not a rapist, serial killer, or criminal." I stared Aiden straight in the eye.

"If I was, do you really think I would admit it?" A smirk lifted the corner of his lip for a beat.

"Promise," I demanded.

"I promise," Aiden said.

"Mark." My attention shifted over to him, "Do you also promise neither of you are serial killers, rapists or criminals nor will you be asking me to do anything horrible like prostitution, drug running or anything of that nature?"

I realized the futility of my dire situation, and as Aiden pointed out, even if they had nefarious plans for me, they would just lie. Yet I found it necessary to ask before I did what I couldn't believe I was about do.

"Emilia. I promise. This is a *good* thing and you will be safe."

I gave them a sharp nod. "Fine. Where am I going?"

Mark grinned a goofy grin and clapped his hands together. Aiden stood unresponsive, his face never moving. No wonder he remained wrinkle free, yet he had to be in his thirties.

"Wonderful!" Mark said as he pulled out his cell phone. "What is your address? I'll send a car tomorrow at four."

"I'm not telling you where I live." At least I had enough sense left in me not to do *that*. "Where am I going?"

Mark glanced at Aiden for direction and got a brief nod from his stoic friend. Mark pulled a pen from his pocket and took the card with the number I still held in my hand.

"Here. Uber to this address. We are so excited to see you tomorrow, Emilia. Please, don't be worried. This is going to be fun!"

I returned his contagious smile with a small one. Aiden must have been immune to Mark's charms because his face remained frozen. In fact, I still didn't even know if he had teeth.

"Very well, we will see you tomorrow, Emilia," Aiden said, maintaining his formal tone.

With a nod, I turned and walked away to grab my purse and leave this godforsaken job. Eric gave me a hug and said he would call but I knew I wouldn't see him again unless we bumped into one another on the streets. We weren't that good of friends.

I glanced back to the booth before I left. Aiden sat in stoic silence, his eyes watching my every move.

Well, if I am about to be murdered at least I've got one hot ass killer.

He nodded to me as I walked out the door.

What the hell have I gotten myself into?

CHAPTER TWO

Emilia

THE COFFEE POT SPUTTERED and wafted out the smell of the one thing that made mornings bearable to me. If I could wake and sleep as I chose, I would never rise before ten o'clock. But I rarely got to sleep in because of the chirping birds, honking horns, and people shouting outside our little Chicago apartment.

Our. I cringed. I was still getting used to not saying that. "My" was the new "our". My apartment. My car. My life. The word "our" shouldn't still cause such a shock to the senses yet there it was slapping me in the face once again. I hadn't been able to use that word since Jeff had walked out leaving me saddled with the mortgage on this apartment we had bought together, and drowning in half of the credit card debt he'd hidden from me. There was no "us" paying that off. It was all me.

At least that meant the coffee was all mine. I took a sip and stared at the business card sitting on my little farmhouse table. Sleep had evaded me last night while visions of Aiden kept flashing through my mind. Panic over my financial status followed just behind, rounded off by the horror of being

fired last night. Those three things had played on a continuous loop through my mind all night long.

The card on the table with the address and phone number continued to taunt me as I downed my second cup of
coffee. It was eleven o'clock. In five hours I was supposed to
arrive at the address written in sloppy scribbles on the back
of the card. In five hours, everything could change.

*Or I could end up dead when they turn out to be murderers
who torture and kill me.*

My senses returned, and I shoved off the idea of going
on this stupid adventure. Last night, in the heat of my panic
over the loss of my job, I had thought it a promising idea.
Like most things, in the light of day, it looked very different
now. It looked dangerous and stupid. I may have made some
bad decisions over the last decade to get me to this
place—friendless, no family, broke and divorced—but at
least I was still alive to tell the tale. Going to this address
might change my life status if they turned out to be serial
killers.

No. Nope. No way. Not going to do it.

Walking my coffee mug to the sink for its bath, I looked
at the card one more time before tossing it in the trash.

There, it was settled. I watched it flutter down and land
on the wet coffee grounds. Brown liquid spread and stained
the little white card, the number fading as it took on a dark
shade of brown. As the number faded away, so did my hope
of finding a better solution to my money problems than
working eighty hours a week for the rest of my life.

Son of a bitch.

Plunging my hand into wet coffee grounds, I yanked out the card and gave it a once over. The phone number was gone, but the address was still visible. I was broke, alone, and without any real options. This was a life-defining moment. Would my luck finally change, or was I heading toward my impending doom? But in the end, what did I really have to lose?

Your life. You can lose your life, dumbass.

But desperation drove me on, and I silenced my inner voice and walked to the closet. What does one wear to a clandestine meeting with two handsome potential serial killers? Little black dress? Business casual? Perhaps something more spy-chic like a headscarf and large sunglasses?

Though I didn't have as many outfits as I'd like, I loved every item of clothing in my closet. I picked through them with the care one takes when handling priceless art. They weren't the expensive designer clothes I drooled over, but they were mine and I loved them. There were a few thrift store designer scores mixed in with Target and TJ Maxx as the heavy hitters. My closet reflected that fashion didn't have to be expensive to be stylish and pretty. Quality took a hit at my price point but who really wore an outfit more than a few times?

I pulled out a white summer wrap dress and grabbed a thick black belt. Paired with the Coach black sandals I had snagged on eBay for thirty bucks, it would be the perfect outfit for... whatever lay ahead. Casual yet dressy.

The perfect outfit to wear to my own murder.

Several hours of pacing and getting dressed, then undressed, then dressed again had culminated in my final decision to go. I clasped the black leather strap of my shoe around my ankle and stood up, admiring my outfit in the mirror. I'd been right. The little black heels made the look.

After pulling a brush through my hair one last time, I made a mental note to buy a box of hair dye from Walmart the next time I shopped. My mousey brown color had revealed itself again. A few shades darker with a hint of auburn red was my preferred color, but lately I couldn't afford to keep it up. Mousey brown and straight would have to do.

A sweep of bronzer, a dab of lip gloss, a bit of mascara and I was set. I was going to... wherever it was. Google Maps showed the address took me to a parking lot. Probably abandoned and covered in tarps where they would chop me up when they finished murdering me.

Several times I thought I should bring someone with me or tell a friend about the meeting. Several times I concluded there was no one to tell. Even my beloved cat, Mittens, had left me a few months ago when old age forced me to kiss his nose one last time and hold him while the vet slipped him the pink stuff. That devastating loss came not long after Jeff had left. Alone hadn't come close to describing how I felt coming home that night. No husband. No cat. Just me and this stupid apartment I broke myself to pay for and couldn't sell. The neighbor two doors down had shot his wife and with that tragedy dropped any chance of me getting it sold soon. Every miserable inch of it belonged to me, leaving me stuck here. Alone.

I looked at the clock. Three thirty. If I was doing this, it was time to call an Uber.

Good things didn't usually happen to me, but I always managed to remain an optimist. And today would be no different. Lifting my chin, I tried to summon my inner strength.

I was going to this meeting and my life would change for the better.

I hoped.

Either that or I would meet a terrible and grisly end.

Okay, so maybe I wasn't a *total* optimist.

A few swipes and taps on my phone and the Uber was on its way. Grabbing my Coach purse, another eBay score, I headed down the steps to wait for him on the street. A sleeping homeless man inhabited the familiar little bench I sat on most days. Not liking to be woken myself, I decided not to disturb him. I paced on the street twirling my handbag while staring at the little icon on my phone that showed my driver coming around the corner.

When the grey Ford Taurus pulled up, a bearded man hopped out and ran around to open my door. I took two double takes to confirm it wasn't the hipster whose beer I'd worn down my dress last night. Same beard, same plaid shirt, same curled hair twisted into a knot at the top of his head. It wasn't the same man, but they could have been twins. Actually, most of the hipsters in Chicago could have been clones these days.

Confident this was not in fact last night's bearded man, I hopped into the back of his car. I rattled off the address on the back of the card and watched as he punched it into his GPS. Only ten minutes away based on the estimated arrival time.

"Where are you off to?" he asked, guiding the car down the busy streets.

"Honestly?"

"Only if you feel like it." He chuckled.

"I'm off to meet two strange men I met at a bar last night. They offered me a job."

"Oh, yeah? Doing what?"

"I'm not sure. They offered me money and told me to meet them at this address."

Watching his face in the rear-view mirror, I saw his eyebrows stretch almost up to his hairline.

"I'm not a prostitute. I made that clear to them. No sex and no illegal stuff."

"I see." He nodded. "Then what do you think the job involves?"

"I have no idea."

It was the truth. I really didn't.

"Wow. Ballsy. Are you worried?"

"Definitely."

"Do they seem safe?"

"One seems safe. The other is a little intense. You're probably driving me to my death."

He didn't answer, but the horrified look on his face told me he felt mighty uncomfortable right about now.

"Don't worry, I'm sure I will be fine," I said, trying to convince him and perhaps myself.

He nodded and kept driving. His silence indicated he regretted asking such a basic question like my destination. I had scared the Uber driver. That was saying something. These guys had seen it all.

A few stoplights, some turns and a short stint on the freeway and I watched the arrival dot growing closer. Peering out the front window I saw an empty parking lot sprawled out in the warehouse district.

Empty parking lots. Abandoned warehouses. Yep. I was going to die.

"I don't see anyone," he said, and double checked the address. Our little car icon sat directly on the purple dot on his screen. This was the place.

"Thank you," I said as I opened the door. "I'll just wait for them here."

"I think I'll wait with you." His voice dripped with concern.

"Really? You would do that?"

"Of course." He turned back in his seat. "This sounds like a terrible idea. I will sleep much better tonight if I make sure you're safe."

What a sweet guy. A kind, sweet Uberman I was lucky had answered my call. I felt much better with him being here although ironically, I knew him about as well as I knew Aiden and Mark.

"Thank you. I really appreciate it. I don't do things like this but desperate times and all. It's not often you meet such a generous Chicagoan."

"I'm from Wisconsin."

Figures the nicest person I had met in a while was from good old Wisconsin. I laughed and nodded. "Me, too. Go Pack Go!"

"Go Pack Go!" he cheered back.

A loud *thump-thump-thump* sound coming from above cut our little Wisconsin reunion short. We opened our doors and peered out to see a helicopter descending to the parking spot a dozen yards away.

"Holy shit," he muttered as it touched down.

"Holy shit is right," I responded, though the thumping of the blades likely made my response inaudible to him.

The black helicopter landed with ease, the blades slowing down as the door opened. Mark stepped out; his stylish look had changed but didn't disappoint. White linen pants topped by a tailored blue button-down made up the perfect outfit for this warm summer day. He slipped off his trendy shades, and his eyes smiled as big as his mouth.

"Emilia! You made it!" He clapped and waved for me to join him.

I looked over at my Uber driver. Equal parts of concern and awe met my eyes.

"What's your name?" I called to him over the car.

"Jake!" he shouted back.

"I'm Emilia Charles! Thank you, Jake! Remember my face... and remember his! If I turn up dead on the beach, you know what to do!"

"I'll be watching the news! Good luck, Emilia! I hope it's everything you wanted and more! Try not to get killed!" He waved as I scrunched down and fought the wind to arrive at Mark's side. He met me with a warm embrace.

"I'm so glad you're here! Come with me! The world awaits!"

I took his hand and stepped into the helicopter. It had posh leather seats with two mimosas poured and ready on the table between them.

"Grab a mimosa and hold on to it tight. Based on your record with spilling drinks last night, I probably shouldn't have worn white next to you." He winked and flashed his warm smile.

I couldn't help but laugh as I strapped myself in and took a swig of the fresh squeezed orange juice and champagne.

"Ready!" he called up to the pilots.

The sound of the blades sped up, and the thumping reverberated through my body as the speeds reached full height... though it may have been my pounding heart. I looked out the window at Jake. He leaned over the top of his Taurus, watching as we ascended into the air. I raised my hand and waved before pressing it to the window. He returned the wave with a concerned smile. Down there, my Uber driver Jake was the only person who knew I had left in a helicopter with a total stranger. I wondered if he'd be combing the newspapers for weeks looking for stories of dead girls and wondering if any of them were me. We held eyes until the helicopter spun him out of sight.

"It's not a far ride from here," Mark shouted over the whirring of the blades. "Just enjoy your mimosa and relax. We'll chat when we get there!"

I nodded, too nervous to shout back. Snuggling into my seat, I enjoyed the beautiful view of Chicago below. I'd been over several times in a plane, but it looked different hovering past in a helicopter. Soon the city disappeared, and the houses got farther and farther apart. The city turned to suburbs, then the suburbs turned to towns, and then less than an hour later we drifted over wilderness. There was nothing below but trees and cornfields.

Mark reached forward and touched my arm. He gestured out the window to my right. Down below I saw hundreds of acres of manicured property nestled in the center of a thick forest. Tall trees formed a border around the lush, mowed lawn. A mansion sat along the west edge of the property, and several other matching buildings speckled the impeccable landscape. The helicopter began its descent and my stomach dropped with it.

We touched down on the helicopter pad just across the lawn from the mansion. Mark tugged my hand and helped me to the ground. Ducking low, we made our way past the whirring blades before he turned to wave them off. The *thump-thump-thump* sped up as the helicopter lifted away. Fear gripped me as I watched my only escape veer out of sight. I hoped my Uberpal Jake had a good memory... he would be the one identifying my body and pointing out Mark in a lineup.

"Where's the helicopter going?" I asked, swallowing hard over the growing lump in my throat.

"The hanger is just down the road at the other end of the estate. Don't worry, they aren't far if you need a lift back."

Biting my lip, I nodded and watched it disappear behind the trees in the distance.

"I'm so glad you're here," Mark said, practically bubbling with joy.

"That makes one of us. Can we just get to the part where you kill me and chop off my limbs? The anticipation is the worst part."

Mark doubled over with laughter.

"You're spunky! I love it! No one is going to murder you. I gave you my word, remember? Let me give you the tour of Aiden's estate."

Aiden. This belongs to him?

I followed Mark along the brick path around the house. He creaked open a tall wrought-iron gate that led to a pool out back and I followed behind him.

"Wow." Not a very creative response to the lush sight, but there weren't any words to capture the incredible oasis surrounding me. An infinity pool hovered on the rock ledge landscaped around the area. Tall trees, palms it seemed, dotted between the stone pathways that followed the winding pool around the corner. I walked along the path, noting the tropical plants and trees that shouldn't have been able to survive here in the Midwest. Bright pink flowers and green foliage decorated every rock and crevice.

"Impressive, isn't it?" Mark beamed.

"Very."

We walked over the stone bridge suspended across the narrowest part of the pool. A set of stairs descended into a hot tub surrounding a fire pit built into the center that burned hot with tall flames.

"Apparently he doesn't like to be cold?" I said, pointing to the fire within the hot tub.

Mark just chuckled and continued the tour. The sounds of the waterfall reached my ears before I saw it. Maybe fifteen feet high, it cascaded water down into the end of the pool below it. Another hot tub was built into the side of the waterfall, causing the water to flow from one to the next.

"That's pretty cool."

"I love it out here," Mark said on a sigh.

"How does he keep all the tropical plants alive? Are we still in Illinois?"

"Yes. He has them shipped in every spring. When the weather gets too cold, they get shipped back to the heated warehouse."

"Shipped? Trees?"

"Yes."

He says it like it's normal. This is not normal.

"Interesting," was all I could manage to say.

"Do you like horses?"

"I love horses. I used to ride every summer at camp."

His eyes lit up. "Follow me."

Mark led the way out of the pool area and down a stone path to a beautiful stable at the bottom of a hill. Lush green pastures surrounded by pristine white fences housed a dozen horses of varying colors. They grazed unaware of our presence. The bay with the blaze nipped at his neighbor and sent him trotting away.

"It's gorgeous, Mark, but what am I doing here? You haven't said much since we arrived and I'm pretty freaking nervous."

"You're right, Emilia. I just wanted to show you how amazing this place was before we met with Aiden. I know he can come off a little—"

"Weird? Scary? Mean?"

Mark chuckled. "Intense. He can be a bit intense. But you need to realize how incredible this place is. You haven't even seen the half of it yet. It's paradise."

"So, what is this high-paying job you have for me that doesn't involve prostitution or drug running?"

Mark glanced over to the setting sun. Oranges and yellows streaked across the sky as it started to dip below the horizon.

"Follow me to the house. We'll fill you in soon."

It was a long but beautiful walk to the house through lavish gardens and past pristine sculptures. We arrived at the front doors that stretched up well above our heads. Mark pressed them open without a knock.

I struggled to keep my mouth shut while I soaked in the sights of the opulent home. A grand staircase stretched out through the ivory and marble room. The single set of stairs split and parted directions to wrap into a balcony surrounding the entire space. Looking up, I saw the crystal chandelier suspended above me while we made our way across the gold detailing on the cream tile floor. It felt like walking into the lobby of a ritzy hotel. A bit gaudy for my taste, but impressive nonetheless.

"This way." Mark ushered me toward a red carpeted hallway.

Historical paintings and artwork dotted the hall as we made our way to the doors at the end. Art had never been my forte, but I didn't need an art degree to know these paintings were authentic... and expensive. I bet one of them could have bought my apartment ten times over.

We reached the doors at the end of the hall. Mark glanced back to the window behind us. The sun had just set, and darkness settled in. He knocked on the door twice, pausing to listen for a response.

"Enter."

Aiden. I'd know that gritty voice anywhere.

Mark turned both handles of the wooden doors and pushed them open simultaneously. I looked to him for direction. He nodded and reassured me with the warmth of his smile, and we stepped into the room side by side.

Even though I could only see his back, I knew it was Aiden leaning against the mantle of the fireplace. I stepped off the dark wood floor onto the oriental rug that stretched almost the width of the expansive room. We passed between two high-backed red chairs with carved armrests as we continued walking toward Aiden.

Candles and dimly lit lights illuminated tapestries hanging from the wall. Everything about this place said old school. Expensive. *Creepy.*

"Hello, Emilia, welcome to my home," Aiden said.

He turned around, his icy gaze landing squarely on me and it sent a shiver slithering up my spine. He seemed to have that effect on me, and whether it was fear or attraction causing it I wasn't sure. Probably a little bit of both. I cracked a nervous smile and stepped closer to Mark as we moved to the couch facing the carved fireplace.

Aiden wore a suit again, but this one looked more casual than the one he'd sported last night. Equally impressive in both style and fit, yet this black one lacked a tie, and the top two buttons of the ebony shirt beneath peaked open.

He may be creepy, but sweet Jesus is he gorgeous.

"Please sit." Aiden gestured to the couch.

Mark nodded and helped me down. Crossing my ankles, I fidgeted with the bottom of my dress. Anticipation surged through me. Stabbing? Strangling? How were they going to off me?

I hope I'm still recognizable so UberJake can identify me.

"Can I offer you a drink? Bourbon perhaps?" he asked.

"No, thank you," I responded. Drinks would dull my wits and I needed them.

"Something else?"

I shook my head.

Aiden and Mark slipped into the chairs facing away from the fire and directly across from me.

Again with the principal's office scenario?

"You have nothing to fear. You are safe here." Aiden started.

I didn't feel safe. A lamb at slaughter came to mind. My eyes searched his for answers, but none revealed themselves.

"Emilia," Mark said, leaning forward and placing his elbows onto his knees. "We are going to tell you something but please, there is no need to panic or be frightened."

Sure. Because telling someone that they're getting scary news isn't going to scare them more.

Mark looked over to Aiden who urged him with a nod.

"So I'm just going to rip it off like a Band-aid, okay?"

Biting my lip, I waited.

"Aiden is a vampire."

He paused to let the words resonate with me.

What the fuck is he talking about?

"A vampire?" I asked, disbelief heavy in my voice. Vampires didn't exist.

"Yes, a vampire. But he's very safe I assure you, so no need to be scared." Mark beamed as if assuring me the snarling dog he held on a leash was safe to pet.

My eyes moved to Aiden. He sat in stoic silence. If one believed the myths in movies and lore, he certainly fit the bill that all vampires were gorgeous. But, in the real world, we all knew vampires weren't real.

"So you're what, one of those weirdos who stick on fake teeth and drink people's blood? I don't understand what you mean."

My mind drifted back to a news story from several months ago about real-life "vampires" who file their teeth to points and take turns drinking sips of each other's blood. Thinking I sat in a room across from one of these delusional freaks made me even more uncomfortable.

"No, Emilia. A real vampire. Not the poser wannabe kind. I know this is a lot to take in," Mark said with a sympathetic tone.

"Mmmhmm." I nodded my faked agreement and looked back toward the door. It might be time to find an exit. Things had gotten weird. "Well then, I guess it's time to get me home. This has been swell and all but—"

Aiden leaned forward and parted his lips, revealing straight, white teeth. With a twitch, his lips curled, and two white fangs popped down.

"Holy shit!" I pushed back on the couch trying to get as much distance between us as I could.

What the hell are those?

With another twitch they disappeared into his gums. He sat back in his chair. "I won't hurt you," he said, his eyes studying my shocked face.

"Are those real?" I found my voice.

"Yes. As Mark told you, I'm a vampire."

"Like a real one? A real freaking vampire? No." I shook my head. "Where is it?"

"Where's what?" Mark looked at me with concern as my eyes darted around the room.

"The camera. Where is the hidden camera?" This wasn't real. I was on some TV show where people would laugh at the stupid girl dumb enough to climb into a helicopter with a total stranger. I wasn't going to fall for this and give them something else to laugh at... the girl who believed vampires were real.

"Emilia." Mark reached forward and touched my arm. "There is no camera. This isn't a joke. It's unbelievable, but I can assure you... Aiden is a real, bonafide, blood-drinking vampire. I was just as surprised as you when I found out. It takes a minute to sink in."

My eyes searched their faces for any trace of lies or amusement. They found none.

"Do it again," I said and turned back to Aiden.

His lips snarled and out popped his fangs. I leaned forward tentatively to get a better look.

They seriously look real.

"Satisfied?" Aiden asked.

I nodded. He snapped his fangs back out of sight.

"They could still be fake," I said, my rational thinking still not allowing this to be reality.

Aiden glared, as if annoyed, then a smug look crossed his face. With a whoosh he stood on the other side of the room as if he'd teleported there. My jaw dropped. Another whoosh blew my hair as he reappeared back in the seat in front of me.

"Any explanations for that?"

Holy. Shit.

I shook my head. My wide-eyed stare moved back to Mark, my security blanket. He only nodded, and the look in his eyes confirmed the grim reality. *Vampires* existed.

And one sat across from me.

"Are you one?" I gulped and stared at Mark.

"No. All human." With a smile showing only straight white teeth, he pinched his skin. "Though hopefully some-day..." He wiggled his eyebrows at Aiden who rolled his eyes in return.

"What... what do you want from me?"

Mark jumped right in. "The job we have for you is five million dollars for five years of letting him feed on you."

Five. Million. Dollars? Wait... to do what?

"To feed on me? What does that even mean?" My eyes darted between them.

Mark answered first. "With social media, smartphones, security cameras and technology it's gotten difficult for vam-pires to feed out in the real world. The old "snatch and erase" feeding technique has gotten quite dangerous. Aiden also doesn't like the taste of fear in his blood. It's intoxicating to some vampires, but Aiden thinks it tastes—"

"Sour. It takes away the coppery sweetness," Aiden said the words like they were normal. Like *he* was normal.

I nodded a slow, stunned nod.

Mark continued. "The perfect solution is to find one co-operative donor who agrees to live here with us and feed Aiden as needed, generally once a day. After five years, your experience will be erased and replaced, and you will be sent home with five million dollars."

Five. Million. Dollars.

The different outcomes and options swirled in my head colliding periodically with the "vampires are real" realization that kept popping in.

"You can erase my mind?" That little doozy just sank in as well. "Why even bother paying me then? Why not just keep me hostage and erase my mind?" It only took a second for me to realize the stupidity in putting that idea in their head.

"The fear thing. Captives still taste like fear. Women getting paid shed the fear surprisingly quickly," Aiden said.

Captives?

"So, you've done the captive thing before?" I swallowed around the growing lump in my throat.

"Once. It wasn't pleasant for either of us. This new situation has worked out quite well."

I couldn't decide whether his callous and honest answer reassured me or increased my already mounting terror.

"Why me?"

"Your blood is different. Sweeter," Aiden said. "A rare delicacy a human could compare to that lobster or prime rib you all seem to love so much. I could smell it across the room last night."

"Aiden? The creepy factor... tone it down a bit." Mark cringed, gesturing with his hands to dial it back. "Sorry, we're still working on it." He smiled back at me. "It's like this. I smell like a Subway sandwich... most of us do." Mark shrugged. "It gets the job done but is not gourmet. You smell like the most perfectly cooked steak paired with lobster in drawn butter. As you can see Aiden only likes the very best of everything. You, my darling, are the best. For five million dollars, you'll live here in the mansion, eat the best food, swim in the pool, and want for nothing. You'll commit to five years. As you can imagine, it's quite a task finding an appropriate woman, revealing his identity and getting her to agree. We don't want to do this every year. After five years, memory replaced, we no longer exist, and you wake up five million dollars richer with wonderful memories of how you got it. Your choice, of course."

It sounded simple enough. It's not like I had a lot of other options. Still... a live feed bag? The thought made me shiver.

"And if I decline?"

"Your memories will be wiped, and you will awaken in your bed."

My eyes moved to Aiden's. The thought of him clamped down on my neck both enticed and terrified me. The lure of the money called to every cell in my body. I had nothing to go back to or anyone who would miss me.

Am I seriously considering this?

"The only catch is that to protect his secret, you won't be allowed to leave. No phones. No computers. No contact with the outside world. Not until your memories have been erased. You don't need to decide tonight," Mark said, interrupting my thoughts. "Why don't you stay the night, explore the mansion and see your room. Take some time alone to think this through. Tomorrow you can let us know."

Mark's plan made sense. My head started nodding though I wasn't sure I was in control of the agreement. A sigh lifted my shoulders. What was one night sleeping in a mansion? Things could be a lot worse.

Unless he sucks me dry in my sleep. Decapitation, strangling, stabbing... those were all deaths I imagined as possibilities from this encounter. Getting drank to death by a vampire? Nope. That one never occurred to me.

"Come with me. I'll show you your room... and your closet." His smile grew with his eyes.

Wait... clothes are involved?

"I have a closet?"

"Oh sweetheart, you have no idea what awaits you." He practically shook with excitement.

"Okay, let's see it."

Mark hopped up and tugged me to my feet. Aiden sat unmoving in his chair as he watched us go. I looked over my shoulder one last time at him before we left the room and those translucent blues met mine.

He's gorgeous. Creepy... terrifying... but gorgeous.

And a vampire.

Mark skipped up the stairs with me in tow. He got to the last door on the left and smiled when he pushed it open. "This is your room."

My mouth dropped as I stepped inside. The warm tones of the wood floor matched the posters of the bed towering to the top of the vaulted ceiling. White scarves twirled down around the crisp white bedding. Egyptian... had to be.

Silk drapes dangled from the windows and added to the elegance dripping off every expensive piece in the room. It was a bedroom fit for a queen. It was also bigger than my entire apartment.

"Ready?" Mark bubbled as he stood in front of a closed white door.

I nodded, excitement gripping me tight. He whipped open the door.

"Ta da!"

My mouth dropped further, drool threatening to leak out. I walked past Mark into the closet twice the size of my bedroom at home. Couture outfits of every texture, color and fabric rolled out in rows up and down each wall. Walking in stunned silence I pulled a tag dangling from a red dress on my left. The tag flashed me the price. Sixty-four-hundred-dollars. My eyes popped wider.

"Is this... Carolina Herrera?"

"Gucci and Prada and Chanel, oh my!" Mark sing-songed behind me. He seemed as excited about this as I was. I'd known he was all style when I'd first seen him. His appreciation for beautiful clothes had been apparent. That knowledge also secured the certainty I wouldn't have to worry about him sneaking into my bed at night. His door didn't swing my way.

"Shoes!" I squealed and raced forward to the wall at the end. Dozens of pairs of designer shoes glowed in the lit cubicles.

"Wait for it," Mark said as he stepped up and pressed a button on the wall. The wall rotated, revealing more and more shoes as it spun around.

"Holy. Shit." Further words stalled in my throat.

"It's like the mother ship has called you home." Mark stood in open admiration as the shoes spun before us. "I think you could be happy here with us, Emilia. I really do."

I nodded. Who wouldn't be happy here? Hell, I was just going to live in the closet. He could take all my blood in exchange for one night in those Manolo's.

"Everything you have ever wanted is yours for the taking. Think about it. I'll have something sent up for dinner. What would you like?"

"Anything?"

"Yes. Anything."

The concept of unending luxury loomed before me, strange and tempting. "Spaghetti and meatballs? Do you have that?" It was my go-to at home.

He furrowed his brow. "Out of anything?"

"Um, okay. How about seared ahi tuna with a wasabi sauce?" Knowing that pushed the envelope, I started to prepare another answer.

"I'll have it up here in an hour along with a bottle of wine. Relax, enjoy yourself. I'll give you some time but just push this intercom if you need anything." He pointed to the device on the wall to the door.

"Thank you, Mark. I've got a lot to think about."

He nodded and left me standing in the closet.

The beautiful closet filled with clothes I'd never dreamed I'd be this close to... and get to wear.

Yeah, I could get used to this.

I had a big decision ahead of me and all night to think about it. I decided it was a decision best made while wearing that Prada dress I just spotted, and those Stuart Weitzman pumps. Yep. I could get used to this.

CHAPTER THREE

Aiden

THE SMELL OF HER BLOOD still lingered in my nostrils even after I awoke from my sleep tonight. Knowing she hovered just out of my reach all night and day proved challenging, because I hadn't tasted her yet. I needed to get just one sip of her intoxicating blood. Despite my steely self-control, the aromas she exuded made my fangs prick the skin, begging to be released.

"She had a good day here," Mark interrupted my thoughts as he burst into the room uninvited.

"Please, come in." I shook my head. For a while, after he arrived six years ago, I thought him incapable of learning as he seemed to forget my every rule. Soon I realized he just didn't care. At first it irked me, but now I hated to admit I rather liked his carefree ways.

"We pet the ponies, swam in the pool and she was reading a book when I left her."

"And?" I asked, hoping to hear her answer to my proposal was a yes.

"She wants to see you again tonight before she decides." Mark pushed the button on the wall causing the light-tight drapes to roll up from the windows in my bedroom. "It's a beautiful night. You should get some fresh air." He cranked the windows open, and the sweet summer breeze wafted into the stuffy room.

"What do you think she will say?" The suspense strained me.

"I'm not sure," Mark said, sitting down on the chair in the corner of my bedroom.

"Why? What makes you unsure?"

He tented his hands in front of him and then touched them to his lips. "Well, for one. You've creeped her out."

"How?" The answer offended me. I had been a perfect gentleman to her.

"Aiden... we've talked about this. You need to lighten up. Catch up with the times. What was once considered appropriate and gentlemanlike back in the day, women now consider creepy and weird."

A jolt of unease rocketed through me. One that said I might not get what I wanted. "I'm not creepy or weird."

"I know that. You know that. But she doesn't know that. You definitely didn't do yourself any favors with the whole 'captives' thing, though." Mark's face scrunched up in disapproval.

I gave him a steely look, but it didn't faze him. The man's calm tenacity kept him by my side. That and his exceptional skills as my personal assistant.

He crossed his legs and settled back into the chair. "Just try to be a little more, relaxed, when you see her tonight. Not so, 'I'm going to suck your blood, muwahaha'. You know?"

"I *don't* know," I said as my brows snapped together.

"Just smile. Laugh. Try not to be so serious." Mark slapped his leg and stood up. "Put on some clothes, not a suit, that makes you look stuffy. Preferably something with color, and come down to the living room. I'll have her meet us down there. We'll laugh. We'll talk. We'll all fall in love. It will be stupendous."

"Fine. She had better say yes."

"Just don't be so doom and gloom and I'm sure she'll be sprawled out offering you her neck in no time. She's seen the closet. What woman could say no to that closet?"

With a deep breath and a nod, I walked to my own closet. It was imperative I impress her. The temptation of her blood compelled me to put my best foot forward. It lured me enough I was sure it would taste delicious even laced with fear if push came to shove.

Mark popped his head back in the door. "Do you want me to pick out the outfit?"

"I can dress myself, Mark."

"Colors. Something with colors," he said before he disappeared around the corner.

What is so wrong with suits these days? I happened to like wearing them. I liked nice things, and I liked looking pristine. And I thought I looked quite dapper in them. Men these days looked more and more like peasants each year—the scraggly hair, ripped up clothes, and rough fabrics. Having been alive for many centuries, I had seen the fashions come and go. One couldn't even call the garish choices of this century fashion. At least Mark hadn't fallen victim to the grungy look. I'd throw him out if he did.

Colors. Looking through my closet I saw dark suit after suit. A few sweaters and casual button downs had found their way in over the years, including a light pink cardigan. Mark's doing, of course. Settling on a pair of grey pants and a white button down, I got dressed. The outfit as casual as I was comfortable with. Grey was a color, right?

The pang for blood squeezed at my throat. Fighting it back strengthened my resolve to convince this girl to stay.

Emilia.

An odd creature. By no means unpleasant on the eyes, she had a spunk about her that intrigued me. Her blood wasn't the only thing I found fascinating about her.

Mark and I had been hunting for a new donor for weeks in clubs all over Chicago since completing the deal with my last girl, Jenny. I'd made this arrangement with her five years ago. The first one of its kind. It had worked out quite nicely and now I looked forward to a new one. Though Jenny had lived in the house, I'd rarely seen her aside from feeding time when I woke up and before she went to bed. I pictured her sitting on a beach sipping cocktails with the millions she now had and the story of winning the lottery I'd left her with.

Our only mistake had been parting with her before we had another girl lined up. It had proved more difficult to find a replacement than we'd thought. The blood bags I'd been sucking on the last few weeks didn't even come close to the satisfaction I got from blood fresh from the vein. We had learned a lesson and would find a replacement before the contract with Emilia ended.

If she'd accept.

She'll accept. She has to.

The moment I smelled Emilia in the bar my heart had flipped over in my chest. I'd wanted her with every second, every breath. Watching her tongue-lash that strange looking fellow entertained me and only increased my desire to bring her home. I needed *her* blood, but something else about her drew me in deeper. Only seconds after seeing her stomp away from the table last night, I'd told Mark I wanted her.

Mark reappeared in the doorway. "She is done with dinner and would like you to join her."

"Very well."

He gestured to my outfit and placed a hand on his cocked hip. "I thought I said colors."

"Grey is a color."

"Grey is most definitely *not* a color." With a huff, Mark turned and left my room.

I followed behind him, and the smell of her blood strengthened with each step. It had nearly caused me to jump across the room and drink her on the couch last night, only moments after I'd had a blood bag. I hadn't eaten yet tonight.

We entered the sitting room. Emilia rose from where she sat on the couch. Her long brown hair curled into soft spiral waves that ended just beneath her full breasts. A black cocktail dress clung to her curves and I followed her shapely legs right down to her sparkling pink shoes.

Beautiful.

Soft doe eyes filled with uncertainty met mine, and her full black lashes fluttered. Her skin flushed at the sight of me, the pink hiding the faint freckles that dotted her ivory cheeks and small nose. The soft lighting of the crystal chandelier overhead illuminated her translucent beauty.

"Good evening," I said as I entered the room. Mark shot me a censuring look. I sighed and tried again. "How are you doing tonight?" Better. Casual.

"I'm doing good. Did you sleep well?" Her voice had a soft innocence to it you didn't hear much anymore.

"I did. It's a beautiful night."

"It is."

Mark eyeballed me to perk things up.

"Mark tells me you two had a good day? What did you do?"

"Well, let's see." She walked over to the bar to pour herself a glass of wine.

"Allow me." I stepped to her side. Cautious eyes watched my every move while I refilled her glass. When I handed it back to her, I noticed the slight tremble in her hand as she grabbed the stem.

"Thank you," she said, then gestured to the other empty glasses. "Are you having one?"

I cleared my throat. "I don't drink but thank you."

"You don't drink alcohol?"

"I don't drink at all. Liquid that is. Just blood."

Her eyebrows rose in surprise before she shook her head. "Of course, of course. The whole *vampire* thing."

"I'll just leave you two to get acquainted," Mark said as he backed out of the room. I wasn't sure if he left because he had confidence I had this under control, or if he just couldn't stand the awkward exchanges between us any longer.

Emilia sat down in the oversized chair and took a sip of her wine.

Following suit, I sat on the couch across from her. "You were going to tell me about your day," I reminded her.

"Oh, yes! Well, let's see. First off, you have a beautiful home. I mean, wow... it's awesome. My room last night? Perfect. And the closet? Incredible. You and Mark certainly know fashion."

"Mark," I spit out, then realized my reaction had been abrupt. I forced a smile and cleared my throat. "He is the one with all the fashion sense. I wouldn't know a Prada shoe if it kicked me in the face." Her face softened with a smile. Mark was right... this helped. *Keep it light. Smile.* "Then what did you do?"

"Well, Mark took me down to the stables to pet the horses. They're so beautiful. After that we relaxed by the pool, which is also, beautiful. A nap, a book, dinner and now I'm here with you."

"I'm glad you are."

Another smile from her. It's working.

She tugged her lower lip between her teeth. "Aiden, can I ask you a question?"

"Of course."

"How old are you?"

Ah, the question everyone wanted to know.

I leaned back in my seat. "Well, I was thirty-five when I turned."

"And when was that?"

"1348."

Her wide eyes answered. "*1348?* As in, you're..." She started counting her fingers, then stopped. "Over six hundred years old?"

I nodded.

"Holy shit."

The cuss words were cute coming from her small, pink mouth. Looking at her innocent face, you wouldn't readily expect them. Her mouth, pouty and full yet smaller than most, was another feature on her face I found quite pleasing.

"I've been around a very long time."

"Where are you from?"

The question sent my mind back to days long gone. A life I barely recognized. "The Scottish Highlands. The kingdom of Moray."

"Wow. Scotland. I've always wanted to go there."

"It's beautiful."

Tipping her head, she furrowed her brow. "You don't have a Scottish accent."

"I haven't lived there in over six hundred years. I lost the accent centuries ago."

She bit her lip and I wondered what it tasted like. "Oh, I suppose that makes sense."

"And you? Where are you from?"

"Milwaukee. I only moved to Chicago eleven months ago."

"I see."

She pursed her lips and kicked her foot while she glanced around the room. She made me feel something I hadn't felt in ages... longer than I could recall. Nervous.

She's food. You don't need to impress her. Just convince her to stay.

I did want to impress her though, at least connect with her somehow. A connection was another thing I hadn't had in ages, nor cared much for it. Connections meant loss when you lived forever. I'd realized centuries ago the constant grief felt over burying those around you marred the joy of eternal life. Humans were no longer on my list of companions. Mark was an exception but only because I'd promised him immortality after several more years of service. He'd be around long after I grew weary of his constant insolence.

"Will it hurt?" Her voice quaked with the question.

"When I feed on you?"

She nodded.

"The first time hurts for a few moments. I'm told after that it can become quite pleasurable, euphoric even for some."

"Just like sex," she noted.

Her brazenness sat me back, but I appreciated it.

Biting her lip, she shifted in her chair. "Can we try it once before I decide? And if I don't like it, I can still go?"

She didn't know that the chance of me letting her leave was unlikely after I tasted the sweet red juice flowing through her veins. If she decided to go, I would try to respect her wishes, of course, but even now her scent stirred something deep within me, deeper than any thirst I had ever felt before.

A thirst I hoped I could control.

"Of course." The lie rolled off my tongue with a hope that I could maintain my honor and respect her decision.

"So how do we do it? Do you like, just bite my neck? Do we use an IV? How does this work?"

"I prefer to feed from the vein. Your neck is preferable. I will be careful and quit long before you are at any risk."

"You can control yourself?" she asked, a worried look on her face.

I liked that she thought things through. She was smart. Careful.

"Yes," I said, hoping I wasn't lying. It had happened to me many times in my youth, an unfortunate side effect that left casualties from time to time, but it had been decades since I had slipped. Another glance at the delicate lines of her face and I steeled my nerves. I wouldn't allow harm to come to her. I couldn't.

"Let's try it. I'll see if I can handle it," she said.

"I think that's a wise plan."

"Do we just do it here? Is there like, a special room?"

I flicked my wrist. "Here is as good a place as any if you're comfortable."

She raised both eyebrows. "I wouldn't say I'm *comfortable* in this situation, but I don't think a change of room is going to change that."

Smile. I reminded myself.

When I did, I could see the tension in her face soften. It pleased me to see her warm up. Jenny's happiness had meant nothing to me as I fed on her over the last five years, but seeing Emilia happy moved me. I liked it.

"Here will work just fine. Come. Sit by me on the couch."

Emilia looked to me and then her glass of wine. "Liquid courage," she said before she downed it in a huge swig. The act made me smile. This time it came naturally. That didn't happen to me often. She was certainly amusing.

"Let's do this." She hopped up and slipped beside me on the couch. I heard her pulse speed up as it thrummed through her veins, and my fangs begged to spring forth. As I leaned closer, her eyes met mine. They were blue with a hint of brown rimming the iris, like a warm sunset glistening off the ripples of a lake. Blues and greys swirled together in a dance that pulled me into their depths. But sadness crept across me when I saw the fear flash through them a moment before they fluttered closed. I didn't want to cause her fear. Though I didn't understand why I cared, I only wanted to bring her joy.

She tipped her head, exposing her long, creamy neck to me as she pinched her eyes tight. My gaze fell to the vein that whisked the nectar through her body and caused my fangs to pop before I intended. The sound made her jump, and I heard the deafening drumming of her heart speed to racing.

I couldn't blame her for her rising terror. Most donors reacted the same way their first time, but soon I hoped her fear would subside and I could enjoy the sweet tang of her fear-free blood. Fear tainted blood and gave it a taste like soured milk. Like a wine that hadn't been allowed to breathe. Some vampires needed the fear to feel powerful, in control. I *was* powerful and in control and didn't need to control a weak human to prove it. I preferred to drink my blood like one would sip a fine, aged wine. It was worth the time and the money to eliminate the fear and sip the sweet, pure juice from the vein. Even though fear coursed through her now I was certain I would still savor every last drop that tantalized my tongue.

I slipped my hand along her neck, brushing her hair behind her shoulder. The warmth of her skin invigorated me as I leaned down. Her body tensed when I slid my hand behind her head and lowered my readied fangs to the skin burning below me. Her flesh gave way as my fangs slid inside, and she gasped and grasped my shirt, clutching it tight.

The first drop of blood touched my tongue. Her sweetness slid down my throat, and my body pulsed with ecstasy as I bit down harder. She gasped again and clutched me tighter. Never had I tasted anything so pure, so complex, so intricate. Her blood flowed into me and awakened my every sense, stirring something deep within I had never felt before.

I could almost feel her life force blending with mine, and the sensation brought on a euphoria I'd not yet experienced in my centuries on this earth. Though I knew it was time to stop, my fangs remained deep within her neck as I begged them to release. Despite the frantic pleas of my mind, my body, my primal urge, refused to let go. I heard her whimper. The sound of her distress rocked me back to my senses.

Don't hurt her. Please, don't hurt her.

It took all my resolve to slide my fangs from the depths of her skin. She gasped again as I withdrew. Leaning back I studied her with concern. Had I gone too far?

The two red punctures on her neck began to close. Her eyes blinked open and found their way to mine. But this time the fear in her gaze had gone. In its place resembled something akin to bliss.

"Are you all right?" I asked, surprised by the question I didn't remember asking anyone in centuries.

A slow, dazed nod tipped her head up and down. "That was... I don't even know what that was."

"I didn't hurt you?"

"Only at first." She started to regain her senses, her lazy speech speeding back up.

"Good." I blew out a long breath. At first, I only wanted to ensure she had a good experience so she would stay and supply me with that liquid gold, but now... now I wanted to know she'd had a good experience because I wanted her to be... happy.

She reached up to feel the holes on her neck, but they were gone. "Cool," she said as she looked at her bloodless fingertips. "But how?"

"Our fangs puncture flesh, but our saliva repairs it."

"Incredible. That was... I don't know what that was, but it's a deal." She looked up at me, no question or fear left in her eyes. "Five years. Five million dollars. I'm in."

A smile tipped the corners of my mouth. She returned it. Something resembling joy, I think, rippled through my core.

"It's a deal," I responded with an outstretched hand. She grasped it and we shook.

"And I get to keep the clothes. And shoes."

"As many as you want."

"Holy shit, this is crazy. I need more wine."

A glance to the bar showed the almost empty bottle. "Mark!" I shouted toward the kitchen.

He appeared a few moments later, his face pulled tight in concern. "What is it? Is everyone okay?" He knew I would have a hard time controlling myself with her. Poor boy thought I drank her dry.

"We are wonderful. Emilia here needs more wine to celebrate the fact she has agreed to join us."

Mark's cheeks swelled with his huge grin. "She's staying? You're staying?" He looked to her.

She smiled and nodded.

He tossed up his hands and clasped them together. "Hallefrickinlujah! We're going to have so much fun! This calls for the good stuff! I'm going to the wine cellar. I'll be right back!"

He hurried off down the hall, his excitement causing Emilia and I to exchange another smile.

"The good stuff? Yay! I get the good stuff!" she chimed.

I looked at her and sat back. I already had the good stuff. And I couldn't wait to have more.

CHAPTER FOUR

Emilia

I TOUCHED MY NECK AGAIN. No holes, no bumps, nothing to indicate a vampire had been feeding from my vein just minutes ago. The skin didn't even feel bruised or sore. It was as if nothing had happened.

But something did happen.

Aiden had drunk from me. I had sat on the couch while a man... a vampire, drank my blood. The immediate sensation had been intense pain, fiery and hot, as if his fangs were made of molten lava. It had seared only for a moment and then... I can't even describe the feeling that came next. I'm not sure there is a word for it. Ecstasy? Euphoria?

No... it ran deeper than that. Different. I'd felt him pulsing with me as if our beings had somehow merged and breathed as one. Our blood had pulsed together while sensations I'd never knew existed raced through me. I'd felt the same blissful release as a full body orgasm, but somehow different... better.

Aiden stared at me now. His arctic eyes watched my every move. He seemed different now. Softer, maybe? His awkward attempts at smiling had been painful to watch. I wasn't Suzy Sunshine but smiling at least came naturally to me. It looked like the most unnatural thing in the world to him every time he attempted it. Except the one time at Mark's expense. That time he'd almost seemed human.

While Mark was off getting wine, Aiden and I sat alone in silence. What does one say to the man who'd just sucked on her neck? Was it good? Do I need a different diet? How's the weather? I thought I could hear crickets if I really tried.

Aiden just sat quietly and stared, making no attempt to fill the silence between us.

So flipping beautiful.

Honestly. The vampire lore had gotten this one down pat. Vampires are mythical, otherworldly beautiful creatures. Then another thought occurred to me... he was the only one I had met. Maybe he'd looked like this even before he'd turned? Maybe other vampires were overweight with bad hair and zits. Now I wanted to know, but I didn't want to come out and ask if he was naturally this hot or if it was a welcome side effect from vampirism. A little part of me wanted to see him without his clothes to confirm that physical perfection lay underneath them.

Okay, so a big part of me.

Continuing my silent studies I wondered what other traits I had seen in the movies were real. He had super speed. I'd seen that with my own eyes. Mind control. They'd said he could erase me, so we'll put a check inside that box. What were the rest? Hearing? Smell? Sight? Mind reading?

Mind reading! Son of a! Did he just hear all that? Did he hear me thinking about him naked? Is he hearing me thinking this, too? Can you hear me, Aiden?

I stared at him with widened eyes waiting for him to say, "yes, I can hear you." He continued to watch me but didn't answer and confirm my fears. With a swallow I decided to ask.

"Can you hear my thoughts?"

He scrunched his brow. "What?"

"My mind. Can you read it? In movies some vampires can read minds. Can you do that?"

Amusement flashed across his face. "Is that the cause of the big eyes and frozen face? You're worried I can read your mind?"

"Yes," I admitted. "Can you?"

Aiden shook his head. "No."

"Good." I collapsed back, the tension releasing from my shoulders.

"Why? What were you thinking about?" He tipped his head, a curious expression accompanying it.

"What? Nothing," I lied. Heat flushed my cheeks.

A smile.

There. His lips curled slightly at the corners. His eyes joined them in the gesture. My heart squeezed in my chest.

"You were thinking about something you don't want me to know about. What was it?" he asked, a sparkle flashing in his eye.

You naked.

"Nothing. Really. I was just curious about some... things."

"Mmmhmm." He laced his fingers together and set them on his lap, his eyes searching mine for an answer. The heat in my cheeks traveled to my chest. I cursed the splotches that started to form. A trait I had inherited from my mother. Anytime I felt stressed I broke out in a very glamorous speckled rash across my chest.

His eyes fell to it. It embarrassed me more and deepened the color.

"Are you all right?" he asked as he looked me over.

Shifting uncomfortably beside him I tried to brush my hair forward to cover it.

"Where is my wine?" I fumbled with my dress and diverted my eyes from his curious gaze. He made me feel like a bizarre animal at the zoo.

"I've got bubbly!" Mark shouted, entering the room holding a bottle of champagne and two long-stemmed glasses.

"Oh, thank God." The words slipped out of my mouth and I jumped up to meet him. I practically ripped the glass from his hand.

He looked at me, his confused expression questioning my antics. His next glance went to Aiden. I swear he scolded him with his eyes. Aiden returned his look with a shrug and his gaze wandered away.

Their silent exchange complete, and my embarrassment at epic levels, I eyeballed the bottle. Mark caught my eyes pleading with the champagne to uncork itself and fill up my glass. Hell, I wanted to break the neck and drink straight from the bottle.

"Step back," he said with a smile. His fingers slipped to the bottom of the cork and pushed. We both cringed waiting for the familiar *pop* that meant backup was on its way. Unlike us, Aiden sat unconcerned that the cork might break loose and take out an eye

I bet he can't be hurt by flying corks. Another vampire trait I must confirm.

Pop. The cork shot out and flew toward the ceiling. The height of the vaulted ceiling forced it to fall back before contacting it. Bubbles exploded out the neck and rushed down, making a small pool on the tile floor.

Mark glanced over at Aiden who gave the liquid on the floor a look before moving it up to Mark.

"Don't give me that look. I'll clean it up," he challenged right back. Aiden crossed his arms and sat back. Mark certainly knew how to handle him. Noted.

He filled up our glasses and raised his in the air.

"Here's to a wonderful, profitable, fabulous five years together. All of us."

I raised my glass to meet his and followed his gaze to Aiden. He tipped his chin in a nod as we clinked glasses. I downed that champagne like I might never get another drop.

"Atta girl!" Mark filled my glass again. This time I only slammed half.

"I swear I'm not an alcoholic," I said, licking the bubbles from my lips. "It's just been a strange few days."

"No judgement here, sweetheart. Isn't that right, Aiden?"

"None at all. Do whatever makes you happy."

Whatever makes me happy? This was starting to feel like an all-expense paid vacation to paradise. No bills. Anything I want to eat. A huge pool. No mortgage.

Wait. My mortgage!

"Question." Aiden and Mark both turned to me as I walked over to the overstuffed chair and sat back down. "When I got divorced, I ended up with the apartment... and the mortgage. It may be a crappy apartment, but they aren't going to leave it sit unpaid for five years without the bank taking it back."

"Yes. You're right. How much do you owe?" Aiden asked, his chin resting on his hand while his elbow perched on the side of the couch.

"Thirteen hundred a month." I winced at the large amount of money. At least large for me. Our rent in Milwaukee before we'd purchased in Chicago had been only seven hundred a month. With a pounding heart, I hoped we could find a way for me to work off my mortgage somehow. Shirking my responsibilities and debts didn't sit right with me.

"No. How much do you owe *total?*"

"Total?" I hated even thinking of it. Jeff had insisted the apartment was a good investment. An up-and-coming neighborhood in Chicago. Buy low, sell high. And after he'd left me, I'd been thrilled to get it in the divorce settlement. I'd sell it myself and at least recoup some of the money I'd invested over the years. Then Mr. Bradley had to go and shoot his wife. *Asshole.* "Just over two hundred thousand." The number still made me cringe.

My credit card debt! I almost forgot about that little parting gift from Jeff.

"I also have thirty-five thousand in credit card debt I need to keep paying on thanks to my dead-beat ex. He ran up seventy-thousand dollars without my knowing it, and thanks to the lovely state law about division of marital debt, I got to keep half of it." I rolled my eyes. "Those collectors would find me even if you take me to Antarctica."

"Mark?" Aiden said, his eyes still fixated on mine. "Pay off her bills and take care of her mortgage tomorrow. Make sure it's all tidied up and in her name. Hire someone to check on her place twice a month and keep it cleaned."

"On it!" He practically sang back.

"You're shitting me." I nearly spit out my champagne as I choked out the words. "My mortgage? You're paying my mortgage? *All* of it? Right now? *And* my credit card debt?"

Aiden's mouth pulled into something resembling a smile. With one slow nod he confirmed it. He was buying me my apartment.

"I don't... what? Really? Why?" Complete sentences hovered just out of reach of my brain.

"Consider it a signing bonus," Mark said with a smile.

My eyes remained locked with Aiden's. There was a warmth about him now... and not just because he just bought me an apartment. He regarded me with a look that no longer made me feel like dinner. He seemed pleased to see my excitement. It surprised me.

My head suddenly felt swirly. It might have been the champagne. Or the shock of the apartment and my new lack of credit card debt. Maybe the blood loss. Probably a combination of all three.

"Are you all right?" Aiden sat forward, then shot a concerned look to Mark.

Mark jumped to his feet and reached my side in a matter of seconds.

"I'm fine," I said, pressing my head between my fingers. "I'm just a bit woozy."

"You've had a lot of excitement tonight." Mark rubbed my back.

"I think I just need to lie down."

"Good idea. Just get some rest," Aiden said, concern threaded through his words.

With a nod, I pushed myself out of the chair and onto my feet. "Goodnight, guys." I turned to Aiden. "And thank you. Really. You have no idea what this means to—"

My knees buckled and my ears rang. I collapsed toward the floor as my legs gave out. I didn't even see Aiden move across the room, I only felt his arms wrap around me, stopping my impending collision with the floor. He lifted me up against his chest and my head settled on his shoulder as I blinked at him through black, speckled vision.

"Emilia," he breathed. "Are you all right?"

My vision came back into focus. He stared at me, worry seeped out from the depths of his cold, hardened eyes, threatening to break through like a storm brewing on the horizon. Emotions swirled just below the surface, his eyes fighting to keep them there hidden beneath the thick layer of ice that had held them down so deep. The ice cracked now, and I could see him in there. I could feel him emerging from the depths of the frozen water. I could feel him gasping for breath and scraping for freedom. I swear I could see into the depths of his soul.

"I'm fine," I whispered, my voice still quaking, though I didn't know if it was from the dizzy spell or the emotions flashing through his eyes. They penetrated me.

"Mark," he barked. "Get her orange juice, water and food. Now."

Mark jumped and hurried out of the room.

"I think it's time you laid down."

A nod was my only response. He started with me to the stairs, the muscles in his arms unflinching beneath my weight. He made me feel small, fragile. Even, dare I say, safe? Safe in the arms of a vampire... that had to be an oxymoron.

He carried me to my bed and set me down on the sheets with great care. His arm slid out from under my head as I lay it back on the pillow.

"I'm sorry," I said as I stared up at him while he sat crouched at my bedside.

"For what?"

"For being so, 'damsel in distressy', or whatever."

Damsel in distressy? What the hell am I even saying? Ugh.

The concern on his face wavered and made way for another one of those almost smiles. At this rate I might get a smile with teeth by the time my five years ended.

"No need to apologize. Just get some rest. Please, let me know if there is anything you need. Anything at all."

"Thank you."

He nodded and slid his arm the rest of the way out from under me. I hated to feel it go. He walked out of the room and glanced over his shoulder before turning down the hall. His blue eyes were so light they nearly glowed in the shadow of the dark room.

I stared at the empty doorframe and still pictured him standing there. I could still feel the coolness on my skin where his arms had been. He was cold, but not freezing. His skin felt like he had been out for a walk on a brisk, fall day. I snuggled down into my feather comforter. I had been right, Egyptian. Sleep rolled over me before Mark had even made it up with my snack.

"GOOD MORNING, SLEEPYHEAD."

Mark stood above me blinking and... oh, that smell.

"Coffee." I searched for the source through hazy eyes. My fingers found the cup and pulled it to my lips while I sat up.

"Careful, it's hot."

"Just how I like it."

The scalding liquid stung my lip, but I pushed through the pain. The pounding in my head had but one nemesis... coffee.

"How are you feeling, sweetie? Are you all right? You almost took a tumble there last night."

Mark felt like a mother as he stroked my hair. I liked it. Mine hadn't been around much or very attentive when she was there. It felt nice having him with me. He was a welcome sight and a comfort while I assessed the intensity of my headache.

"Damn, my head hurts."

"Here. Ibuprofen. Take these." He slipped them into my hand and tugged the coffee from my other one. I resisted, furrowing as if he was taking away my favorite toy.

"Let. Go." He chuckled and gave it one last tug, almost splashing the liquid as he ripped it from my grasp. "Pills with water first. Hydrate. *Then* you can have your bubbie back."

Following orders, I swallowed my pills and guzzled my water. Cotton mouth tattled that a hangover was part of my problem.

"Shower. I'll get breakfast. Then what do you think... you, me, pool?"

"I'm down with that." A dip in the pool sounded amazing. "What about Aiden? Will he be joining us?"

Mark shook his head. "No, sweetie. It's daytime. He's locked in a light-tight room resting those baby blues."

"Daytime. Right. That whole vampire thing."

"Yeah. The vampire thing. Kind of a downer for daytime pool parties. The whole smoking and bursting into flames isn't the best way to start the day."

Laughing, I pushed myself up and out of bed. I still wore my dress from last night, and my shoes with it. Realizing I had slept in a pair of pink, sparkly Jimmy Choos may have been the highlight of my life.

"I'll see you by the pool." Mark left me to get my bearings and try to regain some sort of humanity.

I'd been too freaked out to shower in a house with a vampire yesterday. All I'd had were visions of the shower scene in *Psycho* flashing through my mind, so I'd skipped my morning shower and opted with a sponge bath in the sink. Now that I felt more comfortable, I stumbled to the oversized marble bathroom and dropped my dress on the floor. Kicking off my shoes I stepped into the glass shower the size of my kitchen back home.

Glancing around, I couldn't find the shower head. I saw the valve I assumed controlled the water, but nowhere in this big, grey tiled box did I see the shower head. With a twist of the knob I stood off to the side, wondering what it would do. Warm droplets of rain poured down from the stainless-steel ceiling. I gasped as it rushed all around me.

Hell. Yeah.

A rain shower. I'd never even heard of such a thing. Steam enveloped me as the hot rain washed away some of the hangover that gripped my head tight. I spent too long in it before drying off, throwing on a suit and coverup and heading down to meet Mark.

"Out here!" he hollered from the patio out back by the pool.

I walked through the kitchen, noticing no dirty dishes and no aromas of eggs or bacon filling the air. My nose wrinkled from the disappointment over the lack of breakfast. Hangovers made me hungry... and cranky.

Stepping out into the warm late morning sun I found Mark sprawled on a chaise lounge poolside. I strode across the large flat stones that paved their way through the entire oasis.

"Come, sit, eat, drink, be merry." Mark peered over his shoulder from behind his designer sunglasses.

There sitting on a tray atop the small table between two chaise loungers was a pile of bacon, a croissant, coffee and two Bloody Marys.

"Good God, I love you," I said, flopping in my chair and eyeing up the spread. "Like, really, really love you."

"Right back at you." He blew me a kiss.

"I don't even know where to start."

"I suggest the Bloody Mary followed by bacon, but please, do as you must."

Leaning back in the chair I reached for the Bloody Mary. One long, slow sip and already I felt my hangover subsiding. Bacon would send it to an early grave.

"Where does this all come from?" I asked, realizing the kitchen hadn't been used, but the food looked freshly cooked.

"Nancy and Mary."

My eyebrow rose. "Who?"

"A few years ago I was complaining that since Aiden wouldn't let me keep a cook, I was going to starve to death. I can seriously burn water."

"Oh my God, me too."

"Aiden doesn't allow staff, you know the whole vampire thing, so for my birthday he bought a house down the road and hired two cooks, Nancy and Mary. They live there full time and the place is stocked better than any restaurant in the Midwest. Seafood, steak, pasta... you name it, it's there. All we need to do is call and they whip it up and deliver it. He even got them this little catering truck complete with food insulators and warmers, so my food arrives hot and delicious. Greatest gift of all times."

"Wow. That's impressive. He's very good to you."

"Nah, he was just sick of hearing me and Jenny bitch about it. But it worked and now we have our own twenty-four-seven gourmet delivery service." He clasped his hands behind his head and waggled his eyebrows at me.

One part of that story snatched my attention. "Who's Jenny?"

"Jenny was the last you."

My brow plunged into a deep furrow. "What?"

"Oh, she was nothing like *you*," he said noticing my reaction. "She was Aiden's donor. Our first, actually. She just finished her five-year contact a few weeks ago."

It felt like jealousy gripping at my chest, but I shouldn't feel jealous, right? I'm a donor. She was a donor. A hired hand. But jealousy flared up again as I pictured him latched on to her neck, sharing the same connection I had felt with him last night.

"What was she like?" I asked, though I instantly regretted it. Images of a young, leggy brunette flashed through my mind. Just like the one who'd resulted in my ex's betrayal.

"Awful. A total bitch. The personality of a flounder." His face twisted as if he'd caught scent of something foul.

"Oh." I tried to hide the smugness in my voice. Good. I didn't know her, but I hated Jenny. If Mark had held affection for her, I would have inexplicably felt betrayed. I would have felt sick if Aiden had. The thought surprised me.

"She was stunning to look at it. We found her just after she'd finished a photo shoot downtown. Legs up to her ears and perfect blonde hair." He cupped his chest and bulged his eyes. "And huge knockers. *Huge!* Not that I'm into those things." He puckered his face like he'd sucked on a lemon.

Beautiful? Now I really hated her.

"She may have been beautiful, but she was like having a fancy housecat around. Just lounging about with her pert nose in the air. Since she never interacted with us, we basically treated her like one. We fed her and kept her in the house and pretty much all ignored each other." Mark laughed.

"How was she with Aiden?"

"Oh, he hated her. Loved how she tasted so he just woke up, drank from her and she went to bed. They rarely saw one another besides feeding time."

Like a jolt, it appeared again. The flash of her, beautiful Jenny, with Aiden clinging to her neck. Did she taste better than me? The thought of it gave me another burst of jealousy. Knowing he hated her eased the blow just a touch.

"But now Jenny is gone, *finally,* and you are here. This situation makes me much, much happier. Aiden thinks so, too."

"He does?" My head snapped around as I chomped down on my piece of bacon. "Why, what did he say?"

Mark eyed me up, wise to my game.

"It's not so much that he said anything, it's how he's acting around you. He's different. I can tell."

"Really?"

"Really. Why, do you like him?" His eyes flashed like my middle school girlfriend, Alissa, when we used to hide under the covers with flashlights and admit to our lovesick crushes.

"I don't *like* him like him!" I blushed. "He's weird! And a vampire."

"He's gorgeous." Mark waggled his brows again. "Don't tell me you didn't swoon when you saw him."

I scoffed. "Okay, yeah, he's gorgeous. But that still doesn't mean I *like* him. It just means I'm not blind."

"You'd have to be not to appreciate a man like that." He blew out a puff of air.

"How did you meet him?" I asked, trying to divert the attention from me, though curiosity over how two such opposites could meet tickled my brain.

"I hit on him at a club." Mark laughed.

"No! Really?" I stared at him over the pickle of my Bloody Mary.

"Yes. Really." His laughter deepened.

"Tell."

Mark rolled over onto his side and slid his sunglasses up onto his head.

"It was six, or is it seven, years ago? I'm out at a club and in walks this six-foot-two, pale eyed, chiseled jaw, ripped muscles... well, you've seen him."

I nodded along.

"The group I was with were fighting over him and I said, 'screw it' and marched over to him while they squabbled."

"What did you say?" Aiden terrified me, so the thought of approaching him made my heart race.

"I said..." He doubled over in laughter, struggling to form words. "I said, to *Aiden* mind you, 'Do you know what my shirt is made of? Boyfriend material.'"

"No!"

"Yes!"

We both fell backward, rolling in laughter. My whole body shook at the thought of Mark bravely marching up to Aiden and hitting on him with the worst pickup line in history.

"I can't believe he didn't kill you right there!" I said between gasps.

"I know!"

"So then what happened?"

He struggled to contain his laughter. "He ignored me, obviously. But I kept at it. I may have had a few martinis before this so let's keep that in mind. So a few more cheesy pickup lines and he finally left. Not long after, I went out to hail a cab and saw him by the alley. The alcohol forced me to stumble over for one last go. I mean look at him, can you blame me for trying?"

I shook my head. "What did you say this time?"

"Oh God. Are you ready?"

"Ready." He hadn't even told me, but a stream of giggles escaped.

Mark snorted. "Do you work at Starbucks because I like you a latte."

"No!"

"Yes!"

We both collapsed again and laughed until tears poured down our faces. Breathing became near impossible now while I gasped for breath.

"So then, he yanks me into the alley and slams me up against a wall. I think, he's either gonna kill me or kiss me, preferably the latter. Turns out he was quite amused by me. He gave me an address, much how it happened to you, and when I arrived, he told me he needed a new assistant. Lots of money, great clothes and I made him sweeten the deal to do all his bidding."

"With what?"

Mark speared me with a knowing look. "He'll turn me after ten years of service."

The statement made my heart stop. "You're going to be a vampire?"

Mark nodded eagerly. "Yes. Immortality here I come! And I hope before I get any more wrinkles. I've got a line right here between my eyebrows starting and I don't want any more for all eternity."

Shock didn't quite cover my whirling emotions. "You *want* to be a vampire?"

"Who wouldn't?"

"Me. I don't think I would want it."

"Give it time. You'll be begging him to turn you one day."

I shook my head in amazement. "Wow. That's crazy!"

"Only a few more years left. Then you'll have two vampires to live with!"

The thought of immortality scared me. I couldn't even comprehend the reality that it could actually be a possibility, much less something I may want.

Me? A vampire?

"Oh, before I forget. We need to put your bracelet on."

"Bracelet?" He pulled me out of my Vampire Emilia daydream.

"Don't freak out, but to ensure the safety of Aiden's identity, we need to put an alert bracelet on you that tells us if you leave the property."

"What?" Shock sat me upright.

"It's not a big deal, and it's diamond so at least there's that!" He tried to lighten the blow.

"You want me to wear a bracelet like a dog inside an invisible fence?"

"The moment a human gets fed on or sees a vampire they are erased. The memory removed. Because Aiden needs your fear gone, he can't erase you after every feeding. Your fear would come back each day when you discovered he's a vampire over and over again. Like that movie, what's it called?"

"*Fifty First Dates.*"

"Yes! That one. So the only way is to keep your mind free. Your fear will leave soon, and Aiden can enjoy fear-free blood... his lobster. But we can't risk you or anyone running off and telling the world. Hence, no phones, no internet, and... a beautiful diamond perimeter bracelet."

This revelation didn't sit well with me. For the first time since arriving I felt like a prisoner.

He pulled out the bracelet from the small leather satchel at the side of his chair. The diamonds glistened in the sunlight. Though admittedly beautiful, the implications dimmed the radiance of the diamonds.

"We put it on, I lock it up, and it's over. Okay?"

I scowled and stuck out my wrist. "Fine. But I don't like it."

"I know, sweetie. But it's for Aiden's safety."

He snapped the tennis bracelet on and secured the lock with a small golden key.

"You owe me another Bloody Mary." I furrowed my brow and clanked the ice around the empty glass, the bracelet shaking with the movement and sending reflected rays of light all around us.

"Coming right up!" He hopped up and disappeared into the house. I looked at the bracelet and then reminded myself... five million dollars. This was a small price to pay. The tan line it would leave behind was another story.

CHAPTER FIVE

Aiden

MY EYES SNAPPED OPEN as they did most evenings the moment the sun set. Pulling back the sheets, I stepped out of bed and stretched. I felt energized upon waking, more so than I could recall in recent history. My body buzzed with an energy that heightened all my senses. Though diminished from last night, it still left me feeling better than I had in years. It was her blood moving inside me that was causing this euphoric feeling... it had to be.

The feeling intrigued me almost as much as the woman who'd caused it. Emilia. Memories of her flooded my mind. Her laugh. Her smile. Her eyes. There was something about those eyes, as if she saw deeper inside me than anyone had in centuries. Since Isobel.

Pain seared through me while I forced Isobel's memory to the dark corner of my mind where it resided. If I let her creep into my thoughts, pain overwhelmed me. It had taken a hundred years just to get her memory to stay there and still took considerable effort every day to keep it at bay.

Mark would be waiting outside my room, part of our evening routine, handing me a newspaper and chattering at me incessantly about his day. He was bored; I understood that much. Being a social creature, my isolated life left him empty. He took a few days off each month to kick up his heels on the town, but most of his time he spent here with me. I had hoped Jenny might keep Mark entertained, but in his opinion she had turned out to be, as he would say, an epic fail.

She was cold and callous. Not unlike me, I suppose, but Mark had held high hopes for her. It seemed all she'd done was ignore him all day and offer me her throat with a sigh each evening. That was the deal, so nothing to complain about on my end, but Mark had been disappointed. This time I hoped Emilia would make a better companion for him.

I opened the door and reached out my hand, waiting for him to place the paper in it. I didn't care much about the musings of mortals, but I liked to check on my stocks. As I stood with an outstretched hand, no paper landed in my palm. Poking my head out into the hall I furrowed my brow. Mark was nowhere to be seen.

That's peculiar. Where is he off to?

Pricking my ears, I listened. No sounds came from inside the house except a dripping faucet upstairs I noted needed repair. I focused in harder, my keen hearing now pushing out to the areas surrounding the house.

Laughter.

Mark's. Another laugh shook my eardrums. Emilia. They were doubled over in stitches near the pool from the sound of the water splashing accompanying their giggles.

My questions over his whereabouts put to rest, I went to my closet and reached for my favorite suit. In my head, I could hear Mark scolding me to grab something more casual. There, folded above the rows of suits were several pairs of jeans Mark had grabbed for me on his latest shopping spree. The tags still dangled from them since I found them to be rather distasteful and crude, but he had assured me they were the best jeans money could buy. I could seize this opportunity to try them out.

After sliding on the rough material it surprised me how comfortable they felt once I had secured the button. Interesting. I started to understand why he preferred this particular fashion. A dusty blue button-down shirt caught my eye.

Colors. Wear colors. Mark's voice echoed in my head.

It wasn't pink or anything but provided more color than the greys and blacks I usually wore. I pulled it from the hanger and slipped it on. When I glanced in the mirror, it surprised me to see how good I looked in this outfit. Hope that Emilia would feel the same flashed through my mind followed by shock that I cared enough to wonder about her reaction.

Heading down the corridor, I followed the sounds of continuous laughter to the glass doors opened to the pool area. The crisp evening breeze carried the sounds of Mark engaged in an animated story, and Emilia chuckled at his antics. I saw them laying side by side on blowup rafts as they floated across the aqua green water that glowed from the underwater lights.

"No. Way. Stop the presses!" Mark said, his eyes wide when he caught sight of me. "Are those jeans? You're in *jeans?* It's a miracle!"

I narrowed my eyes at him. He had told me to dress more causal to put Emilia at ease and now he had the audacity to tease me about it... in front of her. As I stood in front of them, his taunts made me feel uncomfortable. Another emotion I had almost forgotten existed.

Her eyes scanned my body before settling on my own. "I like it. A lot. You look great."

Her opinion mattered to me, I realized only after she'd offered it. Mark continued beaming, giving me a thumbs up with the hand not clutching a margarita. He'd indulged in too much liquor, which would explain his inability to see he was making me look like a fool trying to impress a girl. He wasn't incorrect, but I didn't need Emilia to know it. Even though his behavior irked me, it was nice to see he'd made a friend he could enjoy. I suppose I could forgive him.

"How did you sleep?" she asked as she drifted my way.

"Good, thank you. Did you two have a nice day?"

"The best!" Mark chimed. "Breakfast and bloodies by the pool, afternoon naps, Nancy whipped up cheeseburgers and chocolate lava cake for dinner, now we're back in the pool. She's so great, Aiden! Can we keep her? Forever?"

Emilia laughed and splashed him with water. He returned the favor and fell off his raft pulling his margarita under with him. His head popped up first, then his hand clutching the cactus glass now filled to the top with pool water.

"Boo!" he said with a fat lip protruding.

"Oh! That sucks!" Emilia laughed, Mark following suit. The two seemed thick as thieves already. A flash of jealousy tightened my stomach. He was so natural around her, and she was so relaxed with him. I wished she felt that way around me.

"Care to join us, Aiden?" Emilia asked.

"Good luck with that," Mark spluttered.

"I don't swim." Emilia searched my face for more. I had been too short again. "I've never been in the pool. I haven't been swimming in decades."

"Centuries I think," Mark said.

"Why not?" Emilia asked.

"It serves no purpose. I don't need exercise to stay in shape and it serves no benefit. I only swim when the need arises."

"Oh," she said, her eyes falling. "I love the water. I love swimming in it, floating on it, looking at it. I'll probably be in this pool for most of my stay here."

"I'm glad you will enjoy it."

I shifted my weight while silence settled between us. After a few moments, Mark broke it by pushing to the edge of the pool and hoisting himself out.

"I'm getting another margarita."

Grimacing, I shot him a look. He had spent all day with her and now it was my turn for some alone time. She intrigued me and I wanted to learn more. He caught my look and even the margaritas hadn't clouded him so much he misunderstood.

"On second thought, I just got a terrible headache. Would you two mind if I took a breath and laid down?"

"Not at all," I said, thanking him with my eyes.

"Of course not. Feel better!" Emilia called to him after finishing her sip of margarita.

"Good night, Emilia. Good night, Aiden." He flashed me a wily smile and headed into the house.

Emilia looked up at me, her head now resting on folded arms that lay across her purple raft. "I guess that means I should head in?"

"Please, stay. No need for you to end your fun."

"Don't you need to feed?"

"Later. Please, enjoy yourself." Generally, I would have already fed by now. My throat scratched and my fangs throbbed at the smell of her. Though famished, I didn't want to disturb her. She looked so peaceful floating about. Beautiful, too.

"Are you sure? I don't mind. It's getting chilly now that the sun is down."

"I don't mind at all. Please, take your time. Just find me when you're done. If you're chilly, might I suggest a swim over in the hot tub? Mark tells me it's, how did he word it, awesomesauce."

Emilia burst into laughter. The sound of it brought me pleasure.

"I can't believe you just said 'awesomesauce.'"

"I'm only repeating what Mark told me." We exchanged a smile.

"If you won't swim, maybe you'll sit with me?"

My head nodded yes before I even thought about an answer.

Emilia grinned. "Good. I'll meet you by the hot tub."

She slipped off her raft and under the aqua water. Her body shimmered in light as she glided beneath the surface. Her admirable curves became illuminated when she resurfaced, causing something in me to stir. It wasn't her blood this time, and it wasn't my fangs begging to spring forth.

She followed the curves and channels of the pools while I walked beside her. My eyes remained glued to her every move as she dove and twirled, cutting through the water with ease. We arrived at the hot tub together, and she pulled herself over the ledge and slid into the steaming water.

"Oh, man. That's nice."

I enjoyed watching her pleasure, and the way her head tipped back exposing her neck as she let her arms drift to the top caused another surge in me. This one belonged to both my fangs and my member below.

"Here. Mark had this installed," I said, referencing the fire pit that formed a circle inside the hot tub like the center of a tire or those donuts everyone raved about. I pushed the button on the pole beside me and flames erupted. Her face lit up from both the flames and from the wonder of it all.

"Awesomesauce is right," she said as she swam in circles around the fire.

"I'm glad you like it," I said, her enjoyment increasing mine.

"Love it. I love it. I love everything here. It's paradise. It's too bad you won't join me."

"I don't even have a swimsuit," I said, realizing I'd never owned one.

"At least stick your feet in?"

Her puppy dog eyes pleaded with me and I felt compelled to obey. With a nod I kicked off my leather shoes and rolled up the bottoms of my jeans. I sat at the edge of the pool and slipped my feet into the bubbling water. It pricked my skin, the heat uncomfortable at first then soothing. Her smile warmed even more.

"There? That isn't so bad, is it?"

I shook my head and looked at her face, aglow in the cool blue lights. She reminded me of the beauties from days of old. There was no makeup or contouring back then to trick the eye and improve a plain face. You were either beautiful, or you weren't. She was. Stunning, really. In the most natural way.

"Tell me about yourself?" she asked, trailing her fingers through the bubbles.

"What do you want to know?"

"You were born in Scotland, right?"

"Yes. Dùthaich MhicAoidh, Durness, Sutherland to be exact."

"That's a mouthful."

"So is the spelling of my real name."

"Now I'm intrigued, what is it?"

"Aodhagan," I said before spelling it out.

"Aye-gawn." She sounded it back.

"We changed it to Aiden when we left Scotland."

"What was your life like back then? I'm so intrigued."

It was so long ago, it should have been hard to remember, but I recalled every detail of my life. "I was part of Clan MacKay. We worked the fields, tended the herds, and some of us, like me, were warriors."

"You were a warrior?"

I nodded.

"Did you have a family?"

That was a loaded question. "Yes. I still do. A brother and a sister."

"Wait, still? Are they...?"

"Vampires? Yes. Lothaire and Annella. We were all changed at the same time."

"How... how did you become... you know?"

"You can say it out loud." I chuckled. Pink flushed her cheeks. "How did I become a vampire? That's a long story."

"I've got time. Five years to be exact." She tipped her head and urged me on.

A sigh rode my shoulders, and I struggled for where to begin. "The short version is that the Black Death, a deadly plague, was coming our way, and my clan were descendants of Picts."

"What are Picts?"

I tried to find a way to describe them. "The Picts were a tribal people in Scotland, similar to Native Americans here when foreigners first arrived on the soil. Pict means 'painted people'. They were tattooed and painted, very primal. Even in comparison to our simple ways. They fought hard, but clans slowly pushed them from their lands, forcing them into seclusion and hiding. They were thought extinct by the eleventh century. But a small tribe of them survived, and only a handful of descendants, like my clan, knew they still existed."

"Where did they go?" She blinked rapidly as she hung on my every word.

"An island. Hidden by magic."

"Magic?" She sat back and clutched her chest. "There's magic? It's real?"

"Yes. It's rare. But it's real. It's the reason I am still standing here hundreds of years later."

"So, what happened?"

"With the Black Death sweeping the country, our chieftain, who was also my uncle, was one of only a handful of people who knew their whereabouts, and he sought them out. Knowing this small tribe also possessed magic, he asked them to grant our clan protection from the plague. Since we were their descendants, they agreed on the condition we would use our newfound powers to protect them from the invaders seeking to destroy them. Our chief made the deal and they cast a spell over my tribe. It granted us immortality, strength, speed, hearing, and fangs for weapons. We needed no food or drink. Sleep was optional. But, only some of us survived the transformation."

She watched me with bated breath. "People died?"

"Yes. My father and mother, along with one brother, didn't make it."

"I'm sorry," she said, genuine concern heavy in her voice.

It had been painful at the time, but the centuries had eased the pain, though I appreciated her concern. "Thank you. It was a long time ago."

"So, now you were all vampires?"

She finally said the word. "No. Not yet. As part of the deal, the strongest of the warriors were promised to live on the island, immortal soldiers to keep them safe from invaders. But our chief lost his wife in the transformation. Furious and grief-stricken he refused our end of the deal and our immortality was ripped away."

"Then how are you still here?"

"During a battle only a week later, our chief ripped the throat from an invading clansman. As he swallowed the blood, he felt all his powers return. He commanded us to do the same. We drank the blood of our enemies and with it stole their life force and embedded it with our own."

"Whoa."

"As long as we continued to drink fresh blood, our powers and immortality remained. Furious he had found a way to keep the gift and unable to fully retract it, the Pict leader, a very powerful witch, cursed us to walk the dark for all eternity. We became unable to stand the sunlight after."

"So, you are essentially the first vampires?"

"Yes," I said, swirling my feet in the water.

"Wow. That's so hard to comprehend."

I nodded. It had been awhile since I had talked about it. My life as a human was a memory now, and I didn't stop and think back on it very often, used to my new reality.

"Mark tells me you're going to change him into a vampire?"

I saw the flash of judgement in her eyes when she looked up at me from the bubbling water below. The fire crackled and sent embers floating up into the night sky. I watched them flutter about like fireflies for a moment before answering her burning question.

"Yes. That is our arrangement."

"How do you do it? Does he have to die? What happens? Is it safe?"

She fired off questions as she leaned forward on the edge of the stones just beside me. Her face rested upon crossed arms, inquisitive eyes searching mine for answers.

"We discovered, quite by accident, that anyone who dies with our blood in their system awakens a vampire."

"So, you're going to kill Mark." She scowled.

I shook my head. "No. I'm going to grant him eternal life."

"But you need to kill him first. So, he'll be dead."

"Only for a few moments."

"But you didn't have to die to become what you are, did you?"

It was a good question. "The transformation had been excruciating for all of us. I had passed out during a particularly painful moment and awakened transformed. We all sometimes wondered if we had indeed died, and some of us just never returned. None of us can be sure though. So, answering your question, I don't know. My heart beats. I breathe. For all intents and purposes I seem to be alive... just a different kind of alive."

"So, to be a vampire you just need to drink blood every day?"

"Yes."

Her eyes narrowed. "And no sun?"

"No sun."

"Ugh. I would hate that. I love the sun. Do you miss it?"

"I hardly remember it. It's been six hundred years since I've seen the sun."

"Can you be killed?" She arched a curious brow.

"Contrary to the stake through the heart theory, we can only be killed by beheading. And considering no human is strong enough to strike the blow, we can basically only be beheaded by another vampire."

"So, you're pretty much invincible."

"Pretty much."

"Wow. That's a lot to digest. What about your family? Where are they now?"

That question caused a pang inside my chest. Rifts and pain followed when it came to talking about my family. It had been a decade since we'd parted ways. "Your turn," I said dodging the question. "Tell me how Emilia Charles ended up sitting in my hot tub?"

"Oy. Where do I begin?"

Everything about this fascinating and beautiful woman intrigued me and I longed to know every detail. Where she grew up, what she loved, what she hated... everything. These thoughts never occurred with Jenny. She represented food, nothing else. Asking her about herself would have been as strange to me as Mark asking his milk where it was pumped just before pouring it into his coffee. It was different with Emilia. She wasn't just food to me. She was already so much more.

Emilia sat back in the hot tub, her eyes meeting mine. "I grew up in Wauwatosa, Wisconsin, just outside Milwaukee. Only child. Two parents. No other family that I ever heard of. My parents both worked two jobs to keep us afloat, so I rarely saw them. When I did, they were too tired to do much but stare at the wall and try to recover."

"You must have been lonely," I said, sadness creeping in as I pictured her small and alone.

"I was. I had a few friends but by high school they had moved away. My senior year, my parents went out for a very rare date night. It was January. They hit a patch of black ice. I'm told they didn't suffer. Their deaths were instantaneous."

Pain flashed in the depth of her eyes. She had suffered the same loss as me. I understood how it felt although at least I had been older and surrounded by family and my clan. Emilia had been left alone. I fought an urge to reach out and touch her, comfort her, take away all her pain.

"I'm sorry," I choked out. She nodded and continued.

"Since I was almost eighteen and without family, the courts emancipated me. I had a hundred thousand in life insurance and a few months before I had to move out of the duplex we rented. One night I saw a flyer that my favorite band was playing at a place called The Rave in downtown Milwaukee. I bought myself a ticket and went to the show. During the second opening act, I locked eyes with the lead singer. Jeff." She rolled her eyes. "I was going through my bad boy stage and fell head over heels for his long hair and black eyeliner. He found me after the show, and we hooked up."

Jealousy pumped through me, and I couldn't mistake it. The thought of her wrapped up in the arms of a dirty, wannabe rockstar twisted my gut in knots.

"So young, naïve me falls in love and moves into his duplex the day I had to move out of mine. I was supposed to go to college that fall, but Jeff convinced me to postpone one year and work to support us while his band 'hit it big'. Once he was a millionaire, I could go to school and he would support me. He blew through my parent's life insurance building a recording studio in our basement. I was so in love it never even occurred to me to stop him from spending the money and use it for college."

She tapped her head in disbelief. "Flash forward a few years, I'm still working as a receptionist to support us, he's still promising this is the year he'll make it big and I can pursue my own dreams. I threatened to leave, finally coming to my senses. He slapped a ring on my finger and like an idiot I tromped down the aisle with him. A few more years of me working, him partying and playing, he says he's got a huge opportunity in Chicago. We spent the rest of my savings on a down-payment on an apartment he insisted was a great investment. I got a new crappy job in Chicago and he continued to play music and party. Finally, he does it. He actually fucking does it."

"Does what?"

"Makes it. His band, the same one he's been with since high school, gets a hit single. It's on the radio, they have record labels banging on their door and we are on our way. I'm *finally* not going to be the sole income. Finally we catch a break."

"So, what happened?"

"Sheena. Sheena fucking happened." Daggers shot through her eyes. "I come home to find Sheena in my bed shagging my husband. I told him to get out and he barely even apologized. He left that day and has been with her ever since. I only found out during the divorce mediation that he had racked up seventy thousand in credit card debt. Since it's marital debt, it's *half* mine even though I didn't buy anything with it. And because I couldn't afford a fancy lawyer or legal fees, do you know what isn't half mine?"

I shook my head while I watched her face scrunch up in anger.

"The record deal. He waited until after we got divorced to sign it, so I didn't get a penny. Not. One. Penny. And right before he signed, Sheena and the label convinced him to ditch his band and get a new one so they don't get a damn thing either. Now Sheena gets to enjoy all the fruit of the career that *I* made... and that his *band* made! Ugh!"

Rage flashed through her. Who could blame her? "What an asshole."

My words stopped her in her tracks. She turned toward me and stared with wide eyes. "Did you, Mr. Prim and Proper, just say asshole?"

I shrugged. "It seemed fitting."

Emilia laughed. "*So* fitting! Thank you! He *is* an asshole!"

I joined her in exasperated laughter. This Jeff character would potentially be the first casualty I'd caused in decades if I ever stumbled across him.

"So that's my long, sad, pathetic story. And the reason I'm here. Though, I'm not complaining. This place is amazing. You might have to throw me out after five years. I'm not going to want to leave." She laughed.

I don't want you to leave either.

Not wanting to admit that illicit thought, I quickly changed the subject. "Can I get you anything?"

"No. I'm fine but thank you for asking. I feel bad. You must be starving and I'm just going on and on in here."

I *was* starving, but I also loved hearing all about my new, intriguing guest.

"Here," she said, slipping out of the water and settling at my side, her feet touching mine as they splashed beside them. "Eat."

She tipped her head, offering her neck to me. It pulled me in and drew my fangs from their resting place. She didn't jump this time when they made a sound as they popped out. Sliding my hand behind her head, I let them sink back into her warm flesh. The fire danced beside us as I sucked her sweetness and felt it tangle with my own. Her hand pressed against my chest, an instinctual touch as she moaned a soft tune.

Once again not just the exquisite taste of her blood flooded me with ecstasy.

She did.

Her touch that caused my heart to race and match her own.

Her warm breath ghosting my cool skin.

Her scent. An intoxicating blend of vanilla and lavender.

And once again I felt our bodies connecting as her blood coursed through my veins... thrumming through me and awakening every inch of my body.

And my soul.

When I realized I'd drank too long, I forced myself to break our connection. She settled back and eyes shielded by heavy eyelids met my own.

"Are you all right?" I asked, examining the neck that showed no sign of my presence.

"Better than all right. It really is as good as they said it was. It puts sex to shame," she said, her voice still dazed.

Her hand stayed splayed on my chest. Emotions long thought dead flooded my body under the warmth of her touch. Like the embers of a smoldering fire I'd extinguished centuries ago, they crackled and sparked as she dragged her fingertips across my chest. My emotions had been buried along with Isobel when her mortal nature had ripped her from my life. I had begged for death, desperate to rid myself of the pain her loss had seared into me. I'd mourned for a century, and then I'd mourned even more.

Emilia evoked a feeling in me that no other had ever awakened. None but my Isobel. But like Isobel, Emilia was mortal. I couldn't bear the thought of mourning another woman when old age ripped her from my arms and my life.

No. These feelings for her can't happen. I won't let them.

"Thank you. I hope you have a good night," I said as I pulled myself to my feet, her hand slipping off my chest as I rose.

She frowned, confused eyes searching mine. "Did I do something wrong?" She sat back on her hands.

"No. It's not you. I'm sorry. It's just..." Words eluded me. I barely understood my own roiling emotions, let alone explaining them to the woman who'd caused them. "Goodnight."

Without another word I spun and hurried off, closing myself behind my heavy bedroom doors. I wanted to go back out there, grab her and pull her into my arms, drink more of her blood, and listen to her stories. And then I wanted to do something else I hadn't done in centuries.

Kiss her.

At times over the centuries, my grief and loneliness had driven me into the bed of a woman that I'd used to ease the ache Isobel's loss had left behind. But I'd found nothing but more loneliness awaiting me in their arms. And even though I'd tried to find solace in their bodies, I'd never allowed their lips to touch mine. My lips, my kiss, belonged to Isobel and Isobel alone. But for the first time in five hundred years I longed to touch them to another.

Emilia.

Though I knew I couldn't submit to my growing feelings for her, I had been rude tonight. Tomorrow I would make it up to her. Tomorrow I would do better.

CHAPTER SIX

Emilia

"DESSERT?" MARK ASKED, pushing back his plate.

"No way. I will be five hundred pounds by the time my contract ends if I keep eating like this."

We had just dined on another one of Nancy and Mary's incredible creations. Butternut squash ravioli. It was to die for, and I had eaten way too much.

"You're probably right. I need to keep my abs in check, so they stay with me for the rest of my eternal life. I worked my ass off for these things. No sense in seeing them go to waste now." He patted his washboard stomach.

"My abs were much flatter before Jeff left. I swear I did nothing but eat ice cream and watch *The Notebook* every night for a month straight. The only thing that stopped me was lack of funds. I was so broke, I couldn't afford all the ice cream and then I had to get that stupid cocktail waitressing job." I groaned.

"Lucky for us or you wouldn't be here. And you look great. I wouldn't change a thing."

"Thanks, Mark."

"Only an idiot would walk out on you. And I still can't believe Aiden called him an asshole." His eyes tripled in size before he sputtered out laughter. "He really said that? *Asshole*? It's so not Aiden! Hoodlum or scoundrel, maybe even rapscallion, but asshole? Man, I would have killed to hear it."

I threw my hand up in the air like an oath. "*What an asshole.* True story."

"Well, that closes up that short mystery. He definitely likes you."

"No," I said, shaking my head, "I got all swirly and a little too handsy after he fed on me and he freaked out and ran away."

"Trust me. He likes you. Being weird, that's just Aiden. He's a strange bird."

"I think he thought I might kiss him or something, which I *wouldn't*. It's just after he feeds on me, I feel... I can't explain."

"Please. Please try." He lurched forward onto his elbows, expectant eyes wide with anticipation. "Jenny just shrugged when I asked. I need to know. I'm living vicariously through you. I would kill to have that man sucking on my neck... or on my... sorry, go on."

I giggled and shook my head. "You know that feeling that builds right before you have an orgasm?"

"I know it well."

"It's like that, but everywhere. Not just down in the happy bits."

"Happy bits?" He bit his lip to suppress a smile.

I shrugged off his inquisition. "Whatever. Anyway, it's like the orgasm is pulsing through my blood, my muscles, my everything. There's no release like the other kind of orgasm but the peak is ten times higher. It's... amazing."

He sighed. "I'm so jealous. It sounds like tantric sex. I've never had the patience to withhold an orgasm, but it's supposed to be mind-blowing."

"If it's anything like this, it's awesome."

"He'll be up any minute. Almost time for your orgasm." Mark wiggled his eyebrows and pushed up from the table.

The thought tightened my stomach. I began to wish he had to feed more than once a day. It had crossed my mind to put it out there that I'd be game if he got hungry again. Hell, he could live attached to my neck and I would be just fine with that.

When the sun dropped behind the horizon Mark grabbed a newspaper and headed off to Aiden's room. Apparently, he did this every night. Not because Aiden asked for it, but because before I came, Mark's loneliness made him resemble a puppy waiting for his owner to come home from work.

While waiting for Aiden to come feed, I wandered into the study just off the main sitting room and I walked over to the large tapestry covering the wall. Embroidery of a large circle with a hand and a dagger emerged from it.

"My clan's badge." Aiden's voice startled me, and I spun around clutching my chest. "This, over here, is the white banner of MacKay." He gestured to a large flag hung on the opposite wall. A blue X formed across it. A gold and red lion emblem sat dead center. "We flew it when we charged into battle."

I tried hard to picture Aiden, so formal and well-spoken, draped in a tartan, hair flying behind him covered in mud charging into battle. The not-at-all-unpleasant vision now invaded my mind and it caused me to stare at him and try to envision him in nothing but a kilt.

Yep. That worked for me.

"Were you in a lot of battles?" I asked, my mind still undressing him and putting him in different barbarian clan outfits.

"It was a way of life back then."

With a shake of my head, I broke the fashion show and forced my eyes elsewhere. "What are these?"

Carved wooden sculptures covered shelf after shelf along the end wall. They ranged in size from peanuts to one the size of a football. The beautiful, intricate pieces mesmerized me. Animals and statues of women and warriors dotted each shelf. I reached for one, a horse rearing, his mane blowing in the breeze, but jerked my hand back, realizing I shouldn't touch it without permission.

"It's all right, go ahead." He nodded and encouraged me to pick it up.

Pulling the tiny figurine off the shelf, I turned it over in my hands. "It's beautiful. Where did it come from?"

"I made it."

My head snapped back. "You? *You* carved this?"

"I carved all of them."

Stunned at the skill and the beauty in each piece, I looked back to examine him again. A wild Scottish warrior with a gifted artistic side lied buried beneath that cool exterior. I had seen glimpses of him and now I really wanted to see more.

"Where did you learn to do this? They are incredible."

"My father. At night when I was a young boy, we would sit by the fire and he would teach us how to whittle wood."

I had a hard time picturing Aiden as a child. It was easier to think he'd popped out of the womb a full-grown man already brooding. But at one time he had been a child. Carefree and wild, racing through Scottish fields and likely pulling his sister's hair. The thought of it made him a little less intimidating.

"I'm sorry for running off last night. It was rude and I apologize."

"Oh, please. It was no big deal. I was a total bore just whining about my pathetic life choices."

"No." He stepped forward, his tone startling me. "No, you were not a bore. I... I enjoyed our talk. It's just that, I'm not good at this whole socializing thing. I haven't done it in a very long time. I just wanted to apologize."

"No apology needed. Being a social butterfly and catering to my need to talk wasn't part of the bargain."

He looked worried, nervous. Like Jimmy Higgins the day he'd asked me to prom and then promptly threw up on my new shoes.

"Allow me to make it up to you?"

"There's really no need..."

"Please." His eyes pleaded with me.

"Okay."

He drew a deep breath through his nose, exhaling his relief quickly. "Good. Meet me back down here in three hours. Wear pants."

Wear pants? What the...?

He didn't wait for an answer. He flashed out of the room before I could blink. It still made me gasp every time I saw him move that way.

DONNING A PAIR OF DOLCE & Gabbana skinny jeans that had been calling to me, I left my room three hours later and headed for the den. Not sure what he had in mind, I had also tossed on a plain white tank top and a pair of Frye boots. Cute, comfortable and ready for anything.

Aiden stood in the den with his back turned toward me. The first thing I noticed were the shiny black riding boots pulled over tight, white riding breeches. My eyes moved up to his ass. Those breeches weren't hiding a thing and there would be no complaints from me.

Pure ass perfection.

He held the little horse carving I had picked up before. It looked even smaller as he turned it over in his large, muscular hands.

"That one's my favorite," I said, announcing my presence.

Turning around, his gaze raked my body. Seeing him in full formal riding gear and a crisp white polo, I questioned my outfit choice.

"Mine, too." His gaze met mine.

"I'm sorry. I think I should go change. You said to wear pants, but I missed the part about formal."

"No. Please. You look perfect."

He smiled at me. A warmth slid behind it, like an open hearth on a cold, winter day. The icy shell around him fractured even more.

"Are you sure? I don't mind changing," I said while I looked him up and down. The front of those pants didn't hide anything either. Again... no complaints from me.

Damn. That thing needs its own zip code.

"I'm positive. You're perfect."

It didn't go unnoticed that he'd said, 'you're perfect' this time. I tried not to read too much into it.

He's a vampire, Emilia. This is going nowhere. No. More. Bad. Boys.

My promise to myself after Jeff had been no more tortured artists and no more bad boys. A brooding vampire who sculpted beautiful wooden pieces of art was about as bad as it got when referring to my rules.

Do. Not. Fall. For. Him.

Not that he would want me anyway. He may be warming up to me, but he certainly wasn't going to be falling in love with me. Billionaire vampires like Aiden didn't fall for simple girls from Milwaukee.

"I have a surprise for you. Follow me."

He set down the little horse carving and walked past me out of the room. I couldn't help but stare at the muscular lines that came and went on his ass with every step. The breeches hid nothing, and I was certain I could chip a tooth on that thing.

I followed him out through the house and down through the garden to the horse stable below. I stuttered to a stop when I came over the hill and saw them. White twinkle lights draped between the trees glowed against the black sky. My mouth fell open as I saw row after row of twinkle lights crisscrossing the sky, twisting from tree to tree and continuing into the woods farther than I could see.

"Oh, my god," I sputtered out. The beauty of it gripped me and held me tight.

Aiden didn't respond. He turned the corner to the barn. Mark stood in front of the stone entrance to the barn aisle holding a white horse in one hand and a black in the other. He grinned so wide I worried his teeth might fall out.

"What... what is this?"

"Allow me to take you for a ride?" Aiden asked, turning now to look at the astonishment I struggled to conceal.

"Yeah... yes. Yes, of course," I mumbled back. In addition to the twinkle lights, candles in white bags flickered in pairs, creating a path that wound under the lights down a trail into the forest. All of it together created a romantic atmosphere, causing the surrounding air to light up in a warm, golden glow. "What is all this? How did this get here?"

Mark huffed an exhausted breath. "Helicopter ride, cleaned out stores, and one—"

Aiden stopped Mark with a look. Mark cleared his throat and straightened up like those soldiers who stood in front of Buckingham Palace.

"You told Mark you missed riding. Since you don't have my night vision and I can't ride in the sunlight, I thought this might be a good compromise. Mark got the supplies, I hung them up."

He hung them up? Himself?

"You did all this? For me?" It felt like someone had shoved a sock in my mouth. All my saliva dissipated at the thought of him out here stringing lights and lighting candles... for me.

"One of the perks of vampirism is my speed, as you've seen. This would have taken Mark weeks. No sense in missing out on this beautiful night waiting for Mark to break his neck climbing trees all week."

Aiden's newfound smirk turned into something that resembled a full-blown smile.

"The white mare is yours. Her name is Belmira. She's a Lusitano. Born and bred in Portugal, I had her shipped here two years ago. Beautiful, isn't she?"

Beautiful didn't cover it. Gleaming white with a mane curled down past her broad chest, her forelock was so thick it covered her face, one I could imagine was elegant and refined. A long, thick tail glimmered in the candlelight. The summer camp horses I rode every year at Camp Mondocky were nothing compared to the mare pawing before me.

"This is Alfonso, my mount. He's been with me for eight years, haven't you boy?" He stroked the black gelding's neck. "Shall we?"

My head nodded but my arid mouth refused to talk. Aiden took Belmira from Mark and led her over to me. Before I could slide my foot in the stirrup, Aiden lifted me as if I weighed nothing, and in the blink of an eye I sat in the saddle.

The quick movement caused me to gasp. My stomach dropped like I had plummeted down the arc of a roller coaster. It settled back to its usual resting place as I centered myself in the saddle.

"Thank you," I sputtered. Aiden nodded and flashed to the top of Alfonso. The fact it didn't startle the gelding was a testament to the time they had spent together.

"Have fun!" Mark's eyes twinkled like the little white lights suspended above.

Biting my lower lip, I glanced back at him as Belmira stepped in line behind Aiden and Alfonso. She followed them between the glowing lights on the ground. Mark waved and then crossed his arms and watched us disappear into the woods. A knot formed in my stomach when he disappeared from sight. He had become my security blanket, and I already felt insecure alone in the woods with Aiden without him.

Belmira followed them through no cue of mine and we wound beneath the lights down the worn wooded trail. The surrounding silence felt as heavy as the cool, summer air only broken by the snapping of twigs as the horses made their way deeper into the woods. I struggled for something to say, which was odd because rambling in the face of awkward silence was my usual go-to. Another trait I inherited from my mother. I fought the urge to go off on a tangent.

"Do you ride a lot?" I asked, keeping it short.

"Almost every night. It is one of my favorite activities. I can see in the dark and Alfonso is very surefooted."

"You can see in the dark? Like night goggles?"

Aiden chuckled. "I've never tried them so I can't attest to the comparison, but yes, I can see as clearly in the dark as I can in the light."

"What other special abilities do you have?"

"Well, mind reading is not one of them, so you're safe there," he joked, and it set me at ease.

"Seriously, what else can you do?"

He rode in silence for a moment as the horses continued down the trail. "I can hear exceptionally well."

"Like how?"

"It's hard to explain. I can focus my hearing at different levels and distances. I don't hear everything all the time, but when I choose, I can hear the smallest things hundreds of yards away."

"So everything isn't loud all the time?"

"No, nothing like that. Everything sounds normal right now but if I want, I can listen to see what Mark is doing back at the barn."

Aiden's posture stiffened as he tipped his ear in the direction we had come from. A moment passed before a smile crept across his face.

"What is it?" His expression piqued my curiosity.

"He's walking back to the house and singing."

"Singing?" I laughed. "What is he singing?"

"I'm not sure what the song is."

"You can't leave me hanging. What does it sound like?"

Aiden frowned for a moment and tipped his head toward the sound. I waited for him to respond.

He cleared his throat then began to sing in a stunted, awkward tone.

As I listened to the familiar words I'd sung in front of the mirror while shaking my ass on more than one occasion, I choked down my laughter. "*Bootylicious*? He's singing *Bootylicious*?" The amusement I'd suppressed exploded out and nearly caused me to tumble off Belmira. Aiden joined in and our laughter combined and echoed through the woods. "Bravo by the way. An excellent rendition of Beyoncé."

"Why thank you." He waved his hand and took an informal bow.

"So, you can move quickly, you're strong, you hear really well... and you can sing. What else can you do?"

"That's about the extent of it."

"Well, that and the eternal life part, I guess. That's pretty cool."

"Pretty cool? Just pretty cool?" He turned around to look back at me, his scowl questioning my statement.

"Yeah. Pretty cool. I don't think *I* would want to live for eternity in the dark. But it's cool if you're into that sort of thing."

My statement caused his eyes to widen. "Doesn't everyone want immortality?"

"Not me. No thanks. Not at the expense of sunlight and food. I really love sunlight and food."

He stared while waiting for more of an explanation.

With a shrug, I continued. "You've been alive for how many years? Hundreds? And honestly, what do you really do? You live alone in a huge house, you come out at night, drink blood and wander around on your horse. Besides Mark it doesn't seem like you have any other friends or companionship. I guess, no offense, I just don't understand the attraction. I would rather live one short, really full life, than an eternity of being alone in the dark."

Shock and pain flashed on his face and I realized I had insulted him.

"I didn't mean that to come off so cruel. I'm sure immortality is great, and you enjoy your life. It's just... not for me. I want to be human. I want to experience everything."

Aiden turned forward and rode for a few moments in silence. "I wasn't always alone," he said, his voice quiet, pained. "I was married once."

"You were married? To who? When?" My questions poured out.

The path opened into a huge field. All the twinkle lights disappeared as we stepped into the darkness. My eyes adjusted and found Aiden again. He rode along the edge of the field and Belmira followed close behind.

"Her name was Isobel. We met in 1514," he said, and sadness weighted his words. "I used to pay prostitutes for their services but feed on them instead, erasing any memories of the feeding before I left. I walked into a brothel one night and there was a beautiful woman with hair and eyes as dark as a raven. That night I fed on her. She was fearless, and when I drank her blood, it almost excited her. It was the first time that had ever happened. My first time drinking fear-free blood. After feeding on Isobel she looked elated. Intoxicated. It intrigued me. Instead of erasing her memory, I lay in bed and spoke to her. She was filled with questions about me. My life. My condition."

I nodded along even though he had turned forward and couldn't see me. The thought of Aiden in the bed of another woman caused a twinge of jealousy, but pain for his loss quickly replaced it. You could hear how much he cared for her in the tenor of his voice.

"I told her everything. We talked all night and before I knew it, the sun was peaking up. There was no time to get home, so she hid me in her closet. I thought about erasing her but every time I looked into her eyes to do it, something stopped me. So, I went into the closet convinced she would whip it open an hour later with a horde of angry villagers prepared to burn me in the sun. But the door didn't open until darkness fell. There she was, eager to spend more time with me. She didn't look at me like I was a monster. She looked at me like I was a human again."

Aiden paused for a moment, his mind reliving that moment again, no doubt.

"She offered her neck to me that night. And once again I drank fear-free blood. Again, we laughed and talked into the night and when the sun came up, I went back into her closet. The next night a customer demanded her as his lady for the evening. Jealousy tore me up when she told me I would have to go. I asked her to come with me, to join me in my life. I had money, means, and the world at my feet. She hesitated but for a second and then smiled and said, 'Let's go.' I took her away that night, and we never looked back."

Aiden's voice faded off. I rode behind him in stunned silence. "What happened?"

"A week after we met, I proposed and we married in Venice. We traveled and laughed. We saw the world. Life was wonderful having her at my side. Things were good for many years. I offered her the gift, but like you, she declined. She loved being human. She got older, more beautiful in my eyes. Lines formed on her face and her black hair became streaked with grey. Some years later she got tired easily and her breathing became ragged. I could feel her slipping away. I begged her to take the gift, and she agreed, but she wanted just one more day as a human. She wanted to breathe the warm air, eat her favorite foods, and dance one last time in the sunlight. She died that night in my arms." His voice cracked and trailed off.

My breath caught in my throat. The vision of Aiden holding his beloved in his arms while her life slipped away tore at my heart.

"I thought she was sleeping until I heard her heart stop. I tried to feed her my blood, but it was too late. I've never forgiven myself for not forcing the gift upon her. She should still be here. She died of what I think now, with more knowledge, was cancer. A waste of a life."

"It was the life she wanted, Aiden. A full life with you. You were right not to force immortality on her. Being human was what she wanted. I'm so sorry for your loss. I can't even imagine."

"I made a pact with myself never to feel that again. To honor her memory by never loving another. You think I am lonely and cold, and you are not wrong. I live in a prison of my grief and loss and I deserve to be here."

"Aiden..." My chest clenched tight as he revealed this other side of himself, the reason for the distance and the darkness. It was a broken heart that had formed the layer of ice I had seen slowly melting away. "You can't believe that. You can't believe this woman who loved you, who valued life and choice so much, would wish you to suffer in eternal grief and darkness. I don't know her, but from just the small amount you have told me, it sounds as if she would want you to live. To really live and to experience the most this life has to offer... well, what eternity has to offer."

I held my breath, scared for a moment that he would respond with anger that I had overstepped, but his silence gave away his inner reflection.

"Perhaps," he said, though the word lacked the weight of conviction.

"You should honor her life by living yours to the fullest, Aiden. I know if it was me that is what I would want. If you can't live the human life she wanted, then live the best vampire life you can live."

"I could live a human life if I wanted."

We were outside, but it felt like the oxygen got sucked right out of the air. "What?"

"It's possible, not that I would ever choose it, but I could become human again, or so I'm told."

"How?"

"A century ago I heard a story about a vampire of the original clan that was tortured and deprived of blood. The process was said to be excruciating and took a month of starvation, however it ended with him human again."

"Human?"

"Yes. Human. Able to walk in the sun, eat food, live a normal life. Human."

"What happened? How long did he live?"

"About a week. They cut his head off when they realized starving an original vampire of blood doesn't kill him."

"Oh," I said, my face crinkling in disgust. "No one else has tried?"

Aiden snorted. "Of course not. Why would a vampire choose to become a human?"

His reaction sent a wave of warm anger though my cheeks.

"What the hell is so wrong with being human?"

Aiden laughed, a full and hearty belly laugh. "Where do I even begin?"

"Try me."

"Mortals are fragile, slow, clumsy, defenseless, and most importantly... killable. No thank you. I'll stick to my immortality."

My mouth twisted and my eyes narrowed. Despite my lack of superpowers, I liked being human. "So, you're saying that my existence is worthless?"

"That's not what I meant." His tone softened.

"It's what you implied," I growled.

"Isobel chose to stay human. She died. I chose to be immortal. I'm still alive. I'll let you come to your own conclusions."

"She may have passed away, but who lived the better life? You or her?"

He didn't answer.

"What do you say we go for a gallop? These two haven't been out for a run together." He changed the subject.

"I haven't ridden since I was sixteen. I'm afraid my skills aren't quite up to a full-speed gallop. In the dark."

"You'll be fine, trust me."

"I think you're forgetting my fragile *mortal* status means that if I fall off, I could break my neck and end up dead or paralyzed. I think I'll stick to walking today. Maybe another time," I said back, only half joking.

"Lucky for you my *immortal* status means I'm fast enough to get off my horse and catch you if you start to come off. Your pretty little head won't have a chance to hit the ground. I will never let you fall."

His words, while said in jest, resonated deep within me.

I will never let you fall. There I was, feeling safe again because of a vampire's arms.

"Well? What do you say, human? You want to take advantage of my immortal gifts?"

"I say... you're on!"

Belmira felt my energy shift and danced for a step before Alfonso leapt into a powerful gallop. I grabbed her mane and smiled wide when she surged after him. The wind whipped through my hair and tore at my skin as we raced across the field. I had never ridden at speeds like this because of my fear of falling. Tonight I felt safe knowing Aiden would never allow harm to come to me. I kissed to Belmira and smiled as she pushed on.

We pulled up when the horses were puffing. Aiden smiled wide, his perfectly coiffed hair blown into a haphazard heap that looked surprisingly modern.

"Well?" he asked as Alfonso danced beneath him.

"You didn't need to save me, so I'll call that a win."

"Did you enjoy it?"

"Every second." My smile had already given it away.

"I'm glad you enjoyed yourself. I certainly appreciate a good run, as does Alfonso."

Alfonso yanked the reins and snatched a bite of grass. "Manners, Alfonso. You can eat when you get back to the stable."

Eat!

During the exhilaration of the ride, I had forgotten my whole reason for being here. And I hadn't fed Aiden since he woke up.

"Aiden. I just realized you haven't eaten yet tonight. You must be starving."

"No need to worry. Just enjoy the ride."

"I'll enjoy it much more if I know I'm holding up my end of the bargain." With a cluck I urged Belmira to Alfonso's side. She stood obediently hip to hip while I slid my hair from my neck and looked up into Aiden's eyes. Just moments before he fed, they took on a certain glow. Those eyes made my pulse quicken every time I looked into them.

The now familiar *click* of his fangs caused my heart to flutter in anticipation. His hand, smooth and muscular, slid behind my head, grasping me tight as he leaned down. The coolness of his skin was a stark contrast to the heat I radiated from the run and from the desire he evoked in me. His breath caressed my neck as he leaned down, pausing for a moment while I begged his fangs to enter me. My skin tingled in anticipation.

Scalding heat flashed through my neck as he slid them deep inside of me. My eyes rolled back, and my breath hitched in my chest. My body pulsed, a rush sliding over every inch of me as he held me tight. I dissolved into him, the intimacy of it leaving me completely exposed. The peak of pleasure heightened in my body, hovering there and washing over me in wave after wave of exquisite delight. Raw desire and passion flowed through me and into him. I could feel him, all of him, as he drank me in.

The moan escaped my lips as his fangs slid out.

"Are you all right?"

His voice pulled me back into my body. Every feeding was intense but this one contained an extra level of intimacy that deepened the pleasures and heightened the ecstasy.

It took me a moment to regain my senses enough to speak. "Yes, I'm fine."

"I don't want to hurt you," he said, his eyes searching mine.

"You don't hurt me, I promise." Hurt was the opposite of what he did to me.

"Good. Feeding on you reminds me of..." His voice trailed off, but I could anticipate his words. Feeding on me reminded him of Isobel. An honor I wasn't sure that I deserved. "We should get back. Is that all right?"

I smiled and nodded my head. "I'm ready for a soak in the hot tub. My muscles aren't used to riding and they are all screaming at me already."

"Then let's get you back."

With a cluck our mounts picked up a trot and headed back toward the stable. I touched my neck and found the absence of fang marks. Despite no external proof of his feeding, the internal proof still raged on. The buzzing in my body continued all the way back to the barn and I started counting the hours until he would feed on me again.

CHAPTER SEVEN

Aiden

EMILIA GAVE BELMIRA one last scratch before she stepped out of the barn. As I had hoped, the ride had invigorated her. She glowed pink, a mixture of windburned cheeks and flush from the exercise.

We walked in silence while we headed back to the house. It wasn't that I didn't want to talk with her more, but the words she'd said on our ride continued to bounce around inside my head and resonated in the pit of my stomach.

Is she right? Would Isobel be ashamed of this shell of a life I live?

It startled me that the thought hadn't occurred to me before. I came from a time where loyalty and honor still meant something. My love for Isobel had been a promise I never intended to break. It was absolute. Unwavering. Honoring her meant never allowing the memory of her fade. Never allowing my heart to heal and move forward.

As much as moving on pained me, Emilia had struck a chord. Isobel had been full of life and laughter. It had dripped from every pore, radiated throughout her entire being. It had been intoxicating and contagious. When we were together, she'd made me feel alive as well. Thinking of Emilia's accusations conjured a vision of Isobel in my mind.

Quit wallowing, my love. Go. Live. Suck every last drop of joy from this world. Fall in love again. That is how you will honor our time together.

Even though she'd never said them, I knew in my heart if she'd had a chance, those are the words she would have said. Whether I could bring myself to listen presented another problem entirely.

When we arrived at the front door of the house, Emilia's voice shook me from my thoughts. "Thank you for the ride."

"You're welcome. I hope you enjoyed it."

"I did. A lot. But I'm not tired yet, so I'm going for a swim. Join me."

It wasn't so much a question as a statement.

"I don't swi—"

She rolled her eyes. "Yeah, yeah. You don't swim unless it's a necessity. Try it. Try having some fun. What the hell is the point of your immortality if all you're going to do is stomp around and brood? Hmmm?"

Her blue eyes coaxed mine as I struggled for a defense.

"I don't have a suit."

"Borrow one of Mark's."

"Borrow a suit? From Mark? You must be joking."

She challenged me as she arched a brow and propped a hand on her hip. "Why not?"

"Men don't share trunks. It's just not right."

"Don't be such a prude. I'll ask him."

Prude? That was a word I'd never heard myself called before.

She continued the stare down. "Well?"

Go. Live. Enjoy your life. Isobel's voice flashed again in my mind.

"Okay."

"What?" Her voice echoed the shock I felt in saying the words. "You will? You're coming swimming?"

I nodded, and before I could change my mind, Emilia popped open the front door and stepped inside. "Mark! Where are you?"

"In here!" he called back from the den. He appeared a moment later, his eyes searching us both for some description of the ride. "Well? How was it?"

"Wonderful," Emilia said before I could respond. "The evening is still going. Aiden here would like to borrow a pair of swim trunks and join me in the pool."

Mark's eyes grew to rival the China plates that sat in the hutch behind him. "Aiden? Swimming? I must have bumped my head. I'm passed out somewhere on the property hallucinating while I slowly bleed to death, aren't I? Damn it! NO! I can't die before I become a vampire!"

Emilia giggled and shook her head. "Nope. He agreed to swim, didn't you Aiden?"

Both sets of eyes turned expectedly to me. A heavy sigh and a slow nod answered them both.

"Holy shit," Mark said. "Let's go pick out a suit. I only have a few clean ones, but they are all yours!"

Emilia turned back to me and her eyes danced with excitement. It seemed I was going swimming, because being the one to take away that joy on her face wasn't something I ever wanted to do. "Let's go before I change my mind."

Mark gestured for me to follow him.

I can't believe I'm going swimming. For fun.

I followed Mark to his room. Coming to this part of the house seemed odd as I didn't make it into this wing often. He pushed open the door to his room and I followed him in, realizing I'd never been in here before. It looked very different from the rest of my house, with modern lines and bright colors splashed throughout the fabrics and paintings on the wall.

The vibrant décor screamed Mark.

He opened a drawer in the mahogany dresser and pulled out a stack of folded swim trunks in a rainbow of colors.

"You can wear any of these." Before I could open my mouth, he lifted a hand. "I know, I know... before you say it, they aren't your style. But they will work, and I will head out first thing tomorrow and get you a pair that are 'Aideny'. AKA black and dowdy."

I ignored his jab and picked through the pile trying to find the least offensive fabric.

"I'm proud of you, Aiden. This is a good thing."

"What?" His words and his brazenness stunned me.

"You like her. I can tell."

I opened my mouth to respond, but again he lifted a hand to silence me. "Now before you go saying something cold and mean, just hear me out."

I narrowed my eyes but stood silently in front of him.

"She makes you happy, Aiden. I can see it. You laugh. You smile. You light up when she's around. I've known you going on seven years and I have never seen you like this. So just try not to get in your own way. She likes you, too.

The energy buzzing between you two is enough to cause this house to explode. Go have fun. Try, for once in your eternal existence, to just let go and enjoy yourself. You deserve it. Now choose a pair of fabulous shorts and go out there and change your life."

He didn't give me a chance to respond. He held up his hand until he had safely backed out the door. My jaw hurt from clenching it so tight but, hard as it was to admit, he was right. So was she.

What is the purpose of living forever if I'm eternally miserable?

With both their words ringing around in my head, and Isobel's imagined speech joining them, I got undressed and grabbed the least offensive pair of shorts of the lot and slipped them on. With a whoosh I stood outside in the pool area in front of Emilia and Mark. They both turned and eyeballed me in unison.

"Don't laugh." I arched my brows in warning.

Emilia continued staring at my shorts, and her eyes grew wider as she took in the vibrant pattern. "Are those... hot pink crabs all over your shorts?"

"They are," I said, trying to retain my stoic demeanor while I stood before her wearing pink crustaceans set against a light blue backdrop. "They were the mildest of the selections."

"The Vineyard Vines crab shorts! Good choice. I love those." Mark nodded his head in approval.

My eyes left hers and turned to meet his. "Tomorrow. New shorts. No animals. No pink. Got it?"

Mark nodded enthusiastically. He leaned over and kissed Emilia on the cheek. "You kids have fun. I'll be upstairs if you need me."

"Goodnight, Mark," she said, reaching out and squeezing his hand.

Mark shot me a look and mouthed "have fun" before disappearing into the house. My attention turned back to Emilia. She stood before me in a black one-piece suit. The halter top plunged low between her full breasts. Cutouts on the side showed the soft curves of her waist and pulled my eyes down to the hips that filled out the suit perfectly. She shifted on her long legs and wrapped her arms around her waist when she noticed me drinking her in.

"Hot tub or pool first?" she asked.

"You decide."

"Hot tub it is. I got a little chilled on our walk back from the ride. We'll warm up and then cool down. Deal?"

"Deal." I nodded.

She turned and started toward the hot tub. The already lit fire danced amidst the turquoise blue lights that radiated around it. Her hips swung with each long, deliberate step and induced desires in me that surpassed just wanting her blood... and left their proof in my pink crab shorts. I followed her into the warm water and concealed it beneath the bubbles before it gave me away.

"Well?" she asked, looking over at me where I sat chest deep in the warm liquid.

"I have to admit, it feels pretty incredible."

"Right? Relaxing! It's awesome!"

"It's awesomesauce," I added. Her face lit up and her laughter filled my ears. It was quickly becoming my favorite sound.

"Just kick back, relax, and enjoy. This is all yours. You should enjoy it."

The tiny bubbles tickled my skin, creating an interesting sensation not at all unpleasant. My shorts filled up with air and I could feel them floating toward the top. Furrowing my brow, I pushed the air out of them. A large bubble exploded out of the water and splashed me in the face.

Emilia doubled over with laughter as I wiped the water from my eyes. Her contagious laugh consumed me, and I joined her.

"Well I wasn't expecting that," I said, my laugh breaking up the words.

"It's a hot tub hazard." She chuckled. "How do you have all this?" She gestured to the house and the pool area. "I mean, where do you get all your money, if you don't mind me asking?"

"Not at all. One of the powers I have is mind control. I can 'persuade' people to do whatever I ask of them. All I have to do is look into their eyes and they will do whatever I say and never realize it came from me. Let's just say over the centuries some very wealthy people who didn't deserve their money simply decided to hand it all over to me."

"You thief!" She smiled.

I shrugged and matched it. "They weren't exactly the best people. I have no regrets about leaving them penniless. They had it coming."

"So, you can just look me in the eyes and make me do anything?"

"Yes."

"Do it. Try to make me do something."

"I don't think that's a good idea." I shook my head.

"Come on, I trust you. Something funny. I'll try to resist you." She baited me with her eyes and leaned forward, staring into mine.

"Very well," I said, and I closed the distance between us. I fixated on her pupils while I pushed into her mind. "Emilia, you will bark like a dog and scratch your head until I say stop."

Emilia began barking and scratching her head. She looked adorable sitting there yapping away. "Stop." She stopped immediately.

"Whoa. Okay. So that power works," she said, her eyes wide. "That was amazing. I didn't even question it."

"It comes in handy."

"I'll say! Wait, you can mind erase as well, right?"

"Yes, that's a little more complicated but essentially I can wipe out your memory and tell you what to replace it with. Your own mind fills in the blanks. It's necessary to keep the secret that there are vampires out in the world drinking people's blood. We drink and erase quite regularly. Well, I did until I got donors."

"Have you ever wiped me, and I just don't know it?"

"No. Your mind is entirely your own."

"Good." She sat back against the side of the hot tub. "So you have money because you just tell people to give it to you and then you can make them forget the whole thing?"

"That about sums it up. Although, now I have money because of the stock market and changing out my identity every few decades or so. I often need to do some compelling of the folks at the IRS when they get curious."

"You're amazing," she said. "Well I'm glad you spent some of it on this pool area. It's incredible. Ready for a swim?"

The casual words set me back. I wasn't a monster or a creature to her. I was... amazing.

I nodded, and she slipped over the edge of the hot tub and into the connected pool. When she slid beneath the surface, ripples of the glowing water's reflection washed over her figure and illuminated her perfect curves.

Her head popped up, and she wiped the water from her eyes. "You coming?"

I followed her lead and dove into the water, shocked by the cool temperature after being in the hot tub. When I emerged just beside her, she was lying on her back, hands outstretched while she floated over the soft waves my presence had created.

"Lay back, try it," she said as she reached for my hand. Sensations so far gone I had forgotten they existed washed over me when she tugged on my hand. I squeezed hers back before it slipped from my grasp. I lowered myself backward beside her and let the water lift my body and float me to the top.

We floated side by side, and her fingers brushed mine. It took every ounce of my willpower not to slide her small, fragile hand back into mine. She tipped her head toward me and her eyes met mine. The lights reflected in them and caused beautiful blue ripples to dance across her irises. We lay side by side staring at one another, and I could hear her heart racing as she looked past the wall centuries of pain and agony had constructed.

She saw me. All of me.

Her gaze drifted to my lips for a moment, and when she looked back up, I saw the desire in her eyes. When she noticed it hadn't gone unseen, she cleared her throat and looked away. "I love swimming; I find it therapeutic. I'm glad you joined me."

"Yes, I can see why. This is quite wonderful, I must admit. You have good ideas, Emilia."

"I'm glad you think so." She flashed me a quick smile, and the tension between us eased. I saw mirth flicker in her eyes just before she rolled over and disappeared beneath the water. When she popped up a few yards from me, she rose with a wide grin and slid her arm across the water as she twirled, causing a waterfall of spray to wash over my head.

Her laughter echoed around me as I sputtered water out of my mouth and wiped it from my eyes. When I opened them, I matched her mischievous look and I used my strength to push a blast of water that enveloped her completely. With a squeal, she splashed me back.

We choked out laughter through mouthfuls of water with every playful attack. I whooshed behind her and splashed her again. She turned to respond, but I was already on her other side. Again, I splashed her and continued the dance as she giggled and tried unsuccessfully to hit me.

"No fair! You're too fast!" she cried between splashes. Laughter rolled effortlessly from my body, a pure joy I had forgotten was possible. I flashed through the water and grabbed her by her waist, tossing her with ease high into the air. She screamed her surprise as she arced through the air, her arms bracing for impact as she came down. I appeared beneath her, catching her in my arms before she plunked back into the cool liquid.

Her face glowed with delight and she ceased her struggle in my arms. Wet hair clung to her face, and she pushed it aside. Her gaze dropped to my lips before she looked up at me, and my smile faded as her eyes locked with mine. The weight of her look consumed me.

No strength existed in the world that could stop the pull from her lips. Resistance proved futile, and I felt myself give in. My hand slipped behind her head as her arm slid behind my neck. I allowed my lips to close the distance to hers, a spark igniting between us when they touched. Her tongue slid past mine, hungry and curious as it tangled with my own. My stomach twisted as long-forgotten pleasure radiated through me while I devoured the lips I'd been so desperate to kiss. I grabbed her hair, pulling her in tighter as we clung to one another. All my agony, all my fear, it all melted away with the softness of her touch.

As if frozen for centuries, my heart started up again. It rattled against my chest, racing faster with every brush of her lips against mine. Like a light breaking through my eternal darkness, Emilia reawakened me and enveloped me in her warmth. I inhaled her breath and felt her breathe me back to life.

And once again I felt... alive.

"I heard screaming. Is everyone all right?" Mark's voice shocked us back to reality.

She pulled from my arms and stood standing in front of me, shock worn plainly on her face.

"There you are! Everyone okay? You didn't eat her did you, Aiden? She's my friend too, you know."

Our eyes remained locked as Mark appeared around the corner. Never had I wanted to snap a neck more than I did at this moment. I waited for Emilia to look away, but her eyes remained fixated on mine, her mind likely reeling as hard as my own.

"We're fine, Mark," I said, barely containing a growl.

"Good. I was on my way to the kitchen and heard Emilia screaming. What were you two doing?" he asked, his eyes moving between us, his face now registering his faux pas. "Oh. I'm sorry. I just... I'll head in. Good night."

He spun on his heel and started back to the house.

"No! Mark! Stay!" Emilia called after him, her gaze finally breaking from mine.

I scowled. Why would she want Mark to stay?

He looked to me for direction, fear widening his eyes. My own narrowed, but I nodded my head he should do as she asked. He walked tentatively to the side of the pool and slid his feet in the water. "So?" he asked, as he sucked his cheek and nodded his head staring up at the sky.

Emilia glanced over to me. Confusion filled her eyes. "So..." she said, her voice fading off.

"Emilia? Didn't you say you had a birthday coming up soon?" he asked, breaking the uncomfortable silence.

"Yes. It's tomorrow. Or if it's after midnight, I guess that means it's today."

"What?" Mark and I said in unison.

"Mmmhmm." She slid to the edge of the pool.

"It's your birthday? Why didn't you say so?" I asked, feeling guilty I hadn't known and didn't have a gift for her.

"It's not a big deal. I haven't really ever celebrated my birthday. It just comes and goes each year." She shrugged.

"Not a big deal?" Mark slapped his leg. "The birth of Miss Emilia is a *huge* deal! How can no one have celebrated your birthday before?"

"My parents didn't have a lot of money for presents and they worked so much we didn't get time for many parties. Then Jeff was always off touring or busy practicing, so I just kind of never really cared. It's no big deal guys, really."

"Happy birthday, Emilia," I said, my eyes searching hers. She said it was no big deal, but I heard her heart beat faster with the lie.

She smiled back at me with pursed lips. "Thank you. I... I'm getting really tired. I think I'll head off to bed if you don't mind?"

"Of course not." I tried to contain the disappointment in my voice. I wanted her to stay, for us to pick up where we'd left off.

"Happy birthday, Emilia," Mark said while he watched her pull herself from the pool and grab a towel from the chair.

"I'll see you guys tomorrow."

Watching her leave filled my heart with pain. I didn't want to be away from her. Something had happened here tonight and, while I couldn't explain it, I knew she felt it too. After she was out of earshot, I turned my attention to Mark. "I'm going to need you to do something for me."

"It had better have something to do with celebrating the birth of that amazing creature."

"Of course, it does."

"Then I'm all in."

"Do you have your phone handy?"

Mark pulled it from his pocket and nodded.

"Start Googling."

He typed away as I told him my plan. Emilia would have a birthday she would never forget.

CHAPTER EIGHT

Emilia

MY EYES POPPED OPEN one at a time. The world hadn't even come into focus yet when last night's events flashed through my head. I sat up with a gasp.

He kissed me. No, I kissed him. We kissed each other. Holy shit. We kissed.

Aiden and I had kissed. I couldn't even tell you who'd started it. It might have been me. Not like I hadn't thought about it a few, or dozens, of times. Maybe it was him? We were laughing. We were playing. We were...

Kissing.

A world-shattering, earth-moving, life-changing kiss. One that eradicated any man who'd come before him. A kiss that had flipped my world upside down and still left me struggling to figure out which way was up.

I sat immobile, clutching my sheets to my chest, eyes wide as the moment replayed in my head on repeat. My stomach flip-flopped every time my memory reached the part where his lips first touched mine.

Flip-Flop. There it goes again.

What did it mean? Something happened when our lips touched. Something similar to the connection I felt when he drank my blood. Had the power of the kiss affected him like it had me? Did the kiss mean he liked me?

I shook my head against the notion. No. Most likely he just wanted a quick screw. I may not know much about Aiden Mackay, but he didn't seem like the kind of guy who did the whole girlfriend thing. He was a bad boy... the ultimate bad boy, if fact. And even if that kiss meant something to him, I reminded myself of my number one rule...

No more bad boys.

Falling for Aiden would be a big no-no. Sleeping with Aiden would be an even bigger no-no. Kissing Aiden would lead to sleeping with Aiden which would lead to falling for Aiden. All three... no-no. Luckily for me Mark had intervened, and I'd run for my life. It's not that I didn't want to keep kissing him. Sweet Jesus, did I ever. I'd wanted nothing more in this world than to feel those arms wrapped around me again. Those eyes burning into my very soul. Those lips pressed against mine.

No, Emilia! Get it together! No. More. Bad. Boys!

My head collided with my pillow as I collapsed backward in bed, my teeth biting hard onto the comforter while I tried to force out the feelings still reverberating through me. This couldn't be happening. And all of it on my...

"Happy birthday!" Mark's voice chimed on the other side of the door. "Rise and shine birthday girl!"

Mark. Should I tell him about the kiss? No. Not yet. I needed some time to process this before involving anyone else. Forcing the confusion from my face, I replaced it with a smile. "I'm up!"

My door burst open and Mark stepped inside with a flourish holding a cupcake with a pink candle flickering from the top. "Happy birthday, Emilia!"

"Thank you, Mark. You didn't need to do this."

"It's not from me. It's from Aiden." He beamed at me while he put the cupcake in one hand and a note in the other.

Aiden. The kiss. Oh, God.

If all he wanted was sex, would he have sent up a birthday cupcake? Probably. I was over thinking this. He'd just got done telling me about the great love of his life that he'd lost. Making out with me was probably just some way to dull the pain, a way to pass the time since I was available. It was a kiss of convenience. Mystery solved.

"Emilia? Are you all right?" Mark had noticed my attention drift away. Little did he know where it had gone and the steamy memory I was reliving.

"I'm fine," I said with a sigh. "Thank you for the cupcake. It looks delicious. And what's this?" I looked at the note.

Mark beamed and gave me a sly smile. "It's from Aiden."

"He wrote me a note?"

He nodded his head. "Now hurry up! Make a wish and blow out your candle before it burns down and you miss out!"

I closed my eyes and made a wish. I wished that I could find true happiness. It wasn't very specific, but it was all I could think of as my little candle got shorter and shorter. With a deep breath I blew.

"I hope it comes true." Mark plucked the smoldering candle from the frosting. "Now, eat your cupcake, put on a robe and come meet me in the living room. It's time for *my* present."

"You got me a present? How? You only found out it was my birthday in the middle of the night?"

"Oh, sweetie, have you not met me? There's a reason Aiden keeps me around. I'm really good at getting shit done." He winked and walked to my door. "You. Robe. Downstairs."

It only took a few oversized bites to consume my cupcake. My chocolate-covered fingers stained the white paper from the folded note when I picked it up from my lap.

After looking at my name written on the outside of the thick, formal vellum, I flipped it open.

Happiest of birthdays to you. Please, enjoy your day with Mark. I have a special surprise for you this evening. I look forward to seeing you tonight.

-Aiden

He had written me a birthday note. And a surprise tonight? This was too much to process before I had coffee. Hopping out of bed, I tossed on a white terrycloth robe and I headed downstairs. Mark stood in the living room wearing a giant grin and a lady on each arm.

Furrowing my brow, I let my expression ask what the hell was going on and who were these strange women in the house.

"Emilia, this is Rosie and Lucy. They will start off your birthday morning with a massage. It's a couple's massage." He grinned and placed his hand beside his mouth, whispering, "Hint: I'm the other half of your couple. I'm getting one, too."

I had never had a massage before, at least not a professional one.

"Well, are you coming or not?" he asked.

A grin spread across my face as I nodded my head, then I skipped the rest of the way down the steps. I threw myself into his arms and wrapped by arms around his waist. "Thank you, Mark. This is the nicest thing anyone has ever done for me! A massage? I can't believe it!"

"Oh, sweetie." He kissed the top of my head. "You've been so sheltered. We're just getting started."

"What—"

He didn't let me finish. Instead he yanked my arm and led me to the garden where Rosie and Lucy had two tables set up, side by side. Lucy placed a mimosa in my hand and helped me down onto the table. I took a few swigs before handing it back to her and lying face down.

"Just relax and enjoy," she said while she took off my robe and covered me with the soft, white blanket. She worked magic on my body between sips of mimosas and coffee. Mark and I barely spoke as we spent an hour and a half having every ache and pain removed by very talented hands. I tried not to be sad when it ended, but Mark assured me more fun awaited us.

With a thank you, we hopped up, and he pulled me to the poolside. There stood two men with reclining chairs and bubbling foot baths in front of them.

Mark held up two fingers. "Two words, Emilia. Mani. Pedi."

"Really? I've never had one of these before either!" I squealed.

He pulled a face. "Seriously? I thought you grew up in Milwaukee, not St. Olaf with Rose."

"Shut up, Mark." I jabbed him in the shoulder.

After we settled into the chairs side by side, the two men massaged our feet and hands. I moaned and sighed as they buffed, oiled, clipped and painted. When they finished, we sat back and stared at our perfectly manicured fingers and toes. Red decorated mine while Mark had opted out of polish.

Mark's signature saucy grin lifted his lips when he turned to me. "Ready for round three?"

"There's more?" My heart skipped a beat. Already overwhelmed by the pampering, I couldn't fathom what else awaited me.

With an eyeroll, he huffed. "Of course, there's more. Yesterday you asked me to stop by Walmart the next time I was out and pick you up a box of your favorite hair color. Remember that?"

I nodded my head.

"I still can't believe you asked me to go to Walmart. As if I would ever." He scowled and shuddered. "Follow me."

Mark pulled my hands and hoisted me up to my feet. I didn't resist as he tugged me back into the house. There in the kitchen stood a gentleman and what appeared to be a hairstylist's chair.

"Emilia, meet Rocko Delboa. He is the colorist to anyone who is anyone in Chicago. He's also the genius behind keeping me looking like a natural sun-kissed blond year-round in the Midwest."

"It's a pleasure to meet you, Miss Emilia. I hear a happy birthday is in order?"

"Wow, I can't believe you came here just to do my hair. And yes, thank you. It's my birthday. Thirty today."

"Dirty thirty," Mark said with a smile.

Rocko strode around me, flipping through my waves of dull-colored hair. "Tell me, what color would you like?"

"Well, I normally go for a little deeper color than my natural mousey brown. But why don't you just color my hair however you think it will look best. You're the expert, right?"

"Oh, be still my heart!" Rocko clutched his chest and glanced to Mark. "Free reign? I should only charge you half... but I won't, of course."

"Of course," Mark joked back. "Now, get to work on my girl."

It took a few hours for Rocko to complete the coloring. With no mirror and Mark refusing to give me a hint, I could only wonder what I would look like when I saw my reflection. Rocko finished with the large barrel iron and I saw a glimpse of the deep shades of auburn and a rich ebony brown twirled at the tips of my hair.

"Now can I see?" I begged when they stepped back and admired me side by side.

"You have one more treat. Delia!" Mark shouted.

A leggy blonde strode into the room, a big duffle bag dangling from her arm.

"Emilia, meet Delia. She's here to do your makeup."

"She's doing my makeup?" Another thing I'd never experienced. Though I appreciated the thought, I wondered for what purpose. Once they left only Mark and Aiden would see me.

Aiden.

The kiss.

Oh, my God.

It flashed through my head for the umpteenth time that day. After an entire day being pampered, darkness threatened to return, and with it my awkward reunion with Aiden. Seeing him again meant he'd latch those beautiful lips onto my neck and drink my blood. And I'd have to fight the euphoric feelings that would inflame my already burning desire to kiss him again. Nothing but pure torture awaited me after he awoke. Happy birthday to me.

Delia made quick work of my face. Mark instructed her to keep my natural beauty but to just accentuate my eyes and lips. She put the last touches on my face, then stepped back to examine her work.

"Perfect," Mark said while he rubbed her back. "She looks perfect."

"Can I see now?" I asked, nerves and excitement bubbling inside my belly.

"Almost." Mark held up a finger. "Just one more thing. Thank you everyone! Please escort yourselves out. We appreciate you being here!"

I thanked them as they left, then Mark led me up the stairs to my room where he'd laid out a beautiful dress on the bed. Black lace covered the bodice which blended into the white skirt blooming below it. A pair of black strappy pumps sat balanced beside it.

"Mark," I gasped and hurried to touch it. "It's beautiful." The soft fabric felt heavenly on my fingertips.

"Go ahead. Put it on. When you're all done, we'll do the big reveal."

He turned his back and I slid my robe to the ground. It was a bit awkward standing naked in a room with Mark, but I knew he wouldn't peek. I pulled the dress over my head and tugged it down past my hips.

"Mark? Can you zip me up?"

He turned around and tugged on the zipper. The black lace bodice hugged every curve like a second skin, and the fabric fell off my shoulders, leaving them bare. The white satin folded into large, soft pleats around my hips and fell to just below my knees.

"The shoes. And then you're nothing short of perfection."

He didn't need to tell me twice. I pulled the black Louboutin's onto my feet and secured the silver buckle at my ankle. I stuck my feet out to admire them. Black leather crisscrossed its way around my feet coming to a stop just above my ankle. My red nail polish popped from the open toe and matched the bottom of the shoes to perfection.

"Those are the *Malefissima*. They are pure shoe perfection." Mark placed his hand over his heart while we both stared at them in awe. "Come."

After pulling me to my feet, he led me to the tri-fold mirror in the corner of my room. When I stepped in front of it, the air refused to release from my lungs. My reflection startled me. Classy and sophisticated, beautiful and powerful. I hardly recognized myself. Not because of the perfectly applied makeup or the professional hairdo, but because I radiated something from inside... something I hadn't felt in a long time. I felt beautiful.

My auburn hair fell in dark barrel rolls past my shoulders. Hints of red twirled along the tips. Dark kohl shadowed my eyes and my lashes looked significantly larger than my natural ones. The fiery red lipstick contrasted with my ivory skin and made my lips look plump and full.

Mark stood behind me and placed his hands on my shoulders. "You. Look. Perfect."

Tears threatened to spill from my eyes.

"No crying! You'll ruin your makeup!" Mark laughed and shook my shoulders.

"Thank you, Mark. This has been the most incredible day!" I turned and tossed my arms around his shoulders. He hugged me back before stepping forward and grasping me by the arms.

"The day isn't over yet. The sun is setting in just a few moments. When it does, come downstairs and Aiden will have his surprise for you."

Aiden. The kiss. Oh, God.

"Mark, he kissed me."

Mark's eyes saucered when he turned back around. "What?"

"He kissed me. Last night. Or maybe I kissed him. No, he kissed me. We kissed. I'm freaking out. I don't know what to say when I see him. I'm not going to be his fuck buddy. After my ex, I promised myself no more bad boys. This is so awkward. Help. I need help."

Mark stood unmoving and silent, not a natural response from him. It made me nervous as he stared at me in disbelief. "He kissed you?" he asked, as if he hadn't heard a word I just said, his mouth falling open. I couldn't tell if shock or anger caused his face to turn red.

"Yes, we kissed," I whispered, searching his face for the answer to his emotion.

"As in your lips and his lips touched?"

"That is what a kiss is, Mark."

"Emilia, he hasn't kissed a woman since his wife, Isobel, died. You're the first."

My stomach plummeted to the floor. The height of the heels gave it all the further to drop. "What?" I swallowed hard.

"Honey, those succulent lips of his have never touched another woman's since he last kissed his wife... centuries ago. He kissed you. He kissed you?"

I nodded my head, words refusing to form. What did Mark mean Aiden hadn't kissed a woman since Isobel? That shocking tidbit of info didn't indicate he only wanted me as a quick lay as previously thought.

"Emilia, this is a big deal. Huge. Gargantuan. Mammoth. He doesn't kiss women. He's slept with a few since he lost Isobel, because, well, hello... no one can be abstinent for eternity, but he has *never* kissed one of them."

"So, what does it mean? What do I do? I don't want to get hurt again, Mark. I can't."

"I don't know what to tell you to do, sweetie. All I can tell you is that if he kissed you, then there is something much deeper than just sex happening here. And I say go for it."

My head spun. Tonight would be awkward enough when he fed on me and I had to have the "I'm not going to sleep with you" talk. Now while he fed on me, I would know I was the only woman he'd kissed in hundreds of years. My head threatened to pop.

"Oh, my God, it's time. He'll be waiting for you."

"For what? What's happening? I'm freaking out, Mark!"

Mark shook his arms as he hopped up and down, then stopped and blew out a breath. "Okay, the kiss definitely is a big deal. I wish you would have told me about this earlier, so we had time to talk. But there's no time now. Aiden is waiting. He hates waiting. Just go downstairs and enjoy your night. Okay?"

My heart raced at the thought of seeing him again, but I nodded and followed Mark out the door to the top of the stairs. He gave me a tap and sent me on my way. I felt similar to how I imagined arranged marriage brides felt when they headed down the aisle. Total terror and no idea what to expect.

One step at a time, I made my way around the bend to the center of the stairs. Aiden stood at the bottom, his arms clasped behind his back. He wore jeans that fit impossibly well, and a white shirt popped out from behind his opened grey suit coat. Casual but dripping with sexy style. He'd styled his hair into a rough tousle, much more casual and trendier than his usual smoothed back style. The sight of him looking that good nearly sent me tumbling ass over teakettle down the stairs.

He smiled wide as I got closer. Another new look for him. I stepped off the last step and moved toward him, the pull between us so strong I couldn't have stopped if I'd want-ed to. As I closed the distance between us, he pulled his hand out from behind his back. A single red rose extended with it.

"Happy birthday, Emilia. You look..." He scrubbed a hand across the five o'clock shadow on his jaw. "There are no words in any human language I have heard to capture how incredible you look. We'll go with beautiful, but it is a vast understatement."

Flip-flop. There went my stomach again.

"Thank you, Aiden. You look..."

Perfect? Sexy? To die for? Incredible? Other worldly? So good I want to toss you on the ground and kiss you again? In-stead, I finished with "Really good" then took the flower and inhaled its sweet scent.

"Are you ready?" he asked, his eyes sparkling a brighter blue tonight.

"Ready for what?"

"You'll see. But first, I need to take something from you." He reached out and took my hand, exposing my diamond perimeter bracelet. He inserted the key. It clicked and slid off my wrist, falling into his open palm.

"I think this one suits you better." My gaze fell to the black velvet box. He opened the lid and I gasped when I saw the beautiful bracelet. Row after row of diamonds stretched out against the black pillow inside. The unique design and more than twice as many diamonds as my original bracelet made this one exquisite in every way.

"It's vintage. I thought it suited you better," he said, pulling it from the box. "The best part about this bracelet? No perimeter alarm."

My head snapped up. "What?"

"It would be difficult to have a perimeter alarm going off all night while we're out. Also, I trust that my secret is safe with you now."

"Out? We're going out?"

Aiden smiled and nodded. "Ready?"

"Where are we going?"

"It's a surprise."

He offered me his elbow. With a deep breath, I slid my arm through his and let him lead me out of the house. Looking back over my shoulder, I saw Mark leaning on the edge of the balcony. He grinned as he waved goodbye.

The helicopter sat silent on top of the grassy hill just outside the yard. Two men in suits stood on opposite sides of the doors, and their intimidatingly rigid poses caused me to slow my steps. Aiden must have felt me hesitate. He slid his hand over mine and smiled down at me, easing my fears with the softness of his gaze.

Once we settled into our seats, I looked over and caught him staring at me. An almost childlike excitement bubbled in his eyes.

Tipping my head, I asked, "Where are you taking me?"

"It's a surprise," he said, his voice getting louder over the thumping of the blades as the helicopter started.

As we lifted off, worry crept back into my gut and I fidgeted with the bottom of my dress.

Aiden glanced at my hands and stopped my fidgeting with his soft smile. "Don't be nervous. You're safe with me."

Just hearing the words, seeing the softness in his eyes, soothed me. My apprehensions disintegrated beneath his gaze.

I would go anywhere with you, I thought while I tumbled into their depths.

And in fact, I was.

CHAPTER NINE

Aiden

THE WHEELS OF THE JET shrieked when they touched down on the runway. After a short helicopter ride to Chicago and just over an hour on my jet we had arrived.

Emilia barely spoke during the flight. She seemed nervous. I wasn't sure if she was nervous about the flight, nervous about the trip, nervous about being alone with a vampire, or nervous about the kiss. Perhaps a little bit of everything. Several times I'd attempted to strike up a conversation, but the right words never came. Instead of the apex predator I normally was, I'd felt like a pimple-faced teenager asking a girl on his first date.

She stared out the window as we taxied down the runway, her red lips pursed while she tried to figure out our location. Little wrinkles formed on her nose as she surveyed the dark surroundings out the window. The plane slowed to a stop and my flight attendant knocked and then pulled open the door to the secluded private lounge.

"We've arrived, Mr. Mackay."

"Thank you, Sheila," I responded.

She walked over to the exit door and twisted the handle. A whoosh of air cut through the cabin when the door swung open. With the push of a button the stairs whirred while they telescoped out and settled onto the tarmac.

After standing, I turned to Emilia. Her eyes fixated on mine, searching for answers and assurance.

I extended a hand. "Coming, birthday girl?"

Without a word she reached up and slid her hand into mine. Though the sparks weren't visible, I could swear I saw electricity crackling between us when we touched. I could certainly feel it. With a gentle tug I pulled her onto her feet and guided her to the open door. Stepping behind her I paused when she stopped at the door, staring out at the limo waiting for us.

"Welcome back to New York, Mr. Mackay," my driver, Cyrus, called up with a smile so bright it nearly lit up the night. It was a stark contrast to his black suit, dark skin and mocha brown eyes.

"New York?" Emilia spun to face me, almost toppling down the stairs. My hand shot to her lower back to kept her from tumbling backward. "I'm in New York?" Her face lit up with excitement while she regained her balance.

"The city awaits." I smiled. A gentle nudge on her back started her down the stairs. Cyrus hurried to open the door when we arrived at my limo.

"Pleasure to meet you, Miss Charles. I'm Cyrus, Mr. Mackay's driver in New York City. And I hear happy birthday is in order?" he said, ushering her into the back seat.

"Thank you, Cyrus. It's a pleasure to meet you!"

I slid into the seat beside her and caught Cyrus' approving wink before he closed us inside the car.

"Bubbly!" Emilia squealed when she noticed the corked champagne bottled chilling on ice beside the solitary champagne flute.

Her enthusiasm made me smile. "It's for you. May I pour you a glass?"

"I'll never say no to champagne," she said and smiled while I filled her glass.

Cyrus climbed into the driver's seat and started off to where Mark told him to go when he'd arranged our excursion this morning. The car wound through the airport to the private exit. Emilia sipped on her champagne and glanced to me before quickly diverting her eyes out the window just as she had done the entire flight.

"Have you ever been to New York?" I asked, another attempt to break the silence.

"No, but I've always dreamed of coming here. I still can't believe I'm in New York! Thank you, Aiden."

Her rigid posture softened when I smiled back at her.

"Where are we going?" she asked.

"Another surprise."

She shook her head. "You certainly are full of them, aren't you?"

Honestly, I wasn't. I couldn't remember a time I had planned a surprise or adventure for any lady in my life. They had all been one-night stands since Isobel left me. Their happiness didn't matter much but seeing Emilia light up had quickly become a major driving factor for me. I craved her smile, her pleasure, and her happiness. And I would go to any length to see them. Her joy brought me joy. More than I had felt in centuries.

We made our way through the city. The lights and energy kept Emilia glued to the window while she took it in with awe in her eyes. Cyrus navigated his way to the first part of her birthday surprise. He pulled the limo up to the curve and hurried around to the door, pulling it open with a bow.

I stepped out first, turning then to offer Emilia my hand. She downed the rest of her champagne before taking it and stepping out onto the street. She spun in a circle, wonder radiating her already glowing face lit from the lights of the city still buzzing with life.

"I'm in New York! This is amazing, Aiden!"

"I'm glad you approve."

"This way, Mr. Mackey," Cyrus said gesturing us toward an alley.

Emilia's face scrunched up in confusion, but she followed me down the alley to the modest white door on the side of the massive building. Cyrus knocked twice, and in moments it opened, and I saw the familiar face of Rachel, a stylishly dressed brunette woman, appear.

"Good evening, Mr. Mackay. Welcome back," Rachel said and waved us in. I nodded my reassurance to Emilia and held the door for her to head inside. One tentative step at a time she moved down the grey concrete hall where only a few flickering lights illuminated the darkness. Rachel lead the way until we reached the silver door at the end. With a twist of the knob, she opened it and stepped out of the way. Emilia gasped when she stepped through the doorway.

"Welcome to Barney's," Rachel said.

Two rows of salespeople lined up to greet us in the fully lit store. Having closed to the public hours ago, we had the place to ourselves. Row after row of designer clothes, purses, and shoes glimmered in the lights, all pulled out special for Emilia's tastes per Mark's instructions. She stared in awe at the fashions, her eyes wide while she surveyed the scene. I barely noticed the assortment of fashions, being far more interested in the joy radiating from every inch of her face.

"Please, take a seat," Rachel said, gesturing us over to two plush chairs positioned right in the center of the spectacle. A dazed Emilia stumbled behind her and I followed just a few steps in tow. We took our seats and two gentlemen dressed in tuxedos presented two glasses of champagne to us. Emilia took hers with a thanks; I shook my head and watched the champagne whisked away from my sight.

It was such an odd-looking liquid the way it bubbled and fizzed, and I had to admit I was curious what it tasted like... what all the fuss was about. I'd had ale and wine before I had turned, but it had been six hundred years since anything other than blood had passed my lips. Ever after all this time I still could remember the taste. It paled compared to Emilia's blood, but there was something about it I still craved. Perhaps it wasn't the taste, but the feelings it evoked when I remembered drinking it.

It brought me back to nights sitting around the fire, my family and friends laughing and singing, telling stories of days long past and adventures that kept us keen to listen. My little sister, Annella, would dance to the music, and my mother would sit on my father's lap, her fingers stroking his long hair while she listened to his tales and laughed at his jokes. I remembered my first sip of ale, my oldest brother, Caleb, had slipped it to me when I was only ten. Having idolized him my whole life, sharing in that moment was a memory I would cherish for all of eternity. He had laughed when I'd choked, struggling to force the bitter liquid down. His death had hit me hard, losing him and my parents to the curse within hours of each other had torn through me and left wounds that would always ache.

"Mr. Mackay?" a gentleman asked, snapping me from my thoughts.

I cleared my throat and straightened up, realizing everyone looked at me expectantly. "I'm sorry, what was that?"

"Shall we begin?"

"Of course," I said. The salespeople jumped into action, each rushing to the racks and pulling out pieces of clothing and lining up in front of us.

"Aiden, I can't believe you did this," Emilia leaned over and whispered, her breath brushing against my ear. A shiver snaked up my spine, startling me more than it should... it wasn't the first shiver she'd caused me.

I turned to meet her gaze. Those soft blue eyes shimmered beneath the lights and the joy dancing in them made every second of this evening worth it. "It's your birthday. Please, choose whatever you like."

"I can pick something out of anything here?" she asked, her voice tentative and soft.

"Whatever you want."

"It's going to be so hard to choose one! This is so generous of you, Aiden. I've never celebrated my birthday before and this... this is just too much. Thank you, Aiden. For everything."

Her gratefulness shone through her eyes, and she reached out and touched my hand. I inhaled a sigh, holding it fast in my chest while I savored the warmth of her skin. Placing my other hand over hers, I squeezed. She didn't pull back, but left her hand resting on mine.

"I think you misunderstood." A smile tugged up my lips. "You don't have to pick just one thing. You can have as many things as you like. In fact, you can have it all if that's what will make you happy. There is no limit to what you can leave here with."

Her face dropped and her mouth fell open. I watched while she struggled to form words.

"To start, we have this lovely pair of Louboutin's that are not yet released to the public," the first salesman started, stepping forward to present a pair of sparkling silver heels. Emilia remained frozen, searching my face.

"Anything and everything you want," I said, gesturing to the glimmering shoes. Her head slowly turned toward the stilettos, and a dazed nod tipped her head up and down.

"Those are a yes," Rachel said, rushing the salesman off the floor to make way for the next gentleman in a tux. He held an elegant black evening gown with a plunging neckline that dusted the floor when he stepped forward.

"May I present you with this one-of-a-kind Versace gown?"

Emilia looked to me and searched my face once more.

I glanced at the gown and then back at her. Tonight was about her, but I'd love to see her in that dress. "We'll take it," I said.

"That's a yes," Rachel repeated, the salesman scurrying after the first one with the dress in tow.

"Are you serious, Aiden?" Emilia asked while the next salesman stepped forward.

"Joking isn't really in my repertoire." I shrugged.

"Aiden, this is too much. I couldn't possibly accept all this."

"You can, and you will. You said yourself that you've never had anyone celebrate your birthday. We have a lot to make up for."

Her dazed smile transformed into a grin that could illuminate even the blackest night. It certainly lit up my heart, the one I long since thought to be the darkest thing on Earth.

"Don't hold back, Emilia. Mark won't forgive me if I don't come home with a jet full of new clothing. You don't want to see Mark upset with me, do you?"

She shook her head.

"So, do me a favor and don't hold back. Mark is already upset enough I didn't let him come to witness this. He did this to me here once, hence how they already know me, and he made me promise to bring him back with us another time. But tonight... tonight is just about you. Now... pick."

She squeezed my hand tighter and nodded before turning to the red pantsuit displayed before her. She shook her head, and the salesman jogged off in the opposite direction of the first two.

Wave after wave of shoes, clothing, and purses came at us. Emilia squealed with delight when she saw things she loved, and the sound of her pleasures warmed a part of me I long thought dead. Her delighted noises made me wonder what she sounded like in bed, and I pictured her squealing beneath me while I took her over and over again.

Glancing at my watch I noted soon we'd need to go. In the hour we had been in the store, we'd created a considerable collection of couture. A collection that would please Mark and I wouldn't have to endure his disappointed scowl coming home without a proper wardrobe.

"Well, Emilia, we are about to move on to the next part of our evening. Do you feel like you have enough to bring home?"

She spun in her chair to face me. "Are you kidding?" she squeaked. "This is beyond amazing. This puts *Pretty Woman* to shame!"

"*Pretty Woman*?" I quirked a brow.

"A movie. Julia Roberts? Richard Gere? Never mind. Just... yes! Yes, I have more than enough! I can't believe you did this for me. Thank you, Aiden."

"Your smile is all the thanks I need," I said, and I meant it. Once again joy washed over me under the glow of her grin. "Rachel?"

"Yes, Mr. Mackay?" she responded, stepping to my side.

"We have other plans this evening, so please have that packaged up and sent to my jet."

"Of course, Mr. Mackay."

"Could you also bring out the final present?" I asked.

"Final present?" Emilia asked, turning toward me with eyes wide. "There's more?"

Rachel snapped her fingers and a young woman came around the corner with a red purse propped up on a silver platter. Emilia's eyes nearly popped out of her head when she caught sight of it.

"A Birkin bag? *The* Birkin bag? I can't believe it!" she screamed.

Her enthusiasm exploded out of her as she shot out of her chair and hurried toward it. "Can I?" she asked, stopping before grabbing it.

"Of course, Miss Charles," Rachel said, gesturing for her to take it. "It's yours."

"Oh, my God," she mumbled and pulled the bag into her arms. Closing her eyes, she hugged it and inhaled the smooth leather. "It smells like magic."

My chuckle shook my shoulders while I stood up, watching her sniff and fondle the leather bag. "Mark told me you were ready to go to jail over that purse the night we met. Now it's yours, and no jailtime is needed."

With a goofy grin she spun to look at me. In three big leaps she was in my arms, her own wrapped around my neck while she squeezed me tight. "Thank you, Aiden. Thank you, thank you, thank you!"

For a moment I stood frozen, stunned by her response and affection. My arms finally responded and wrapped around her waist, pulling her in closer. Closing my eyes, I inhaled her sweet scent and held her close, letting her warmth envelope me and soothe even my deepest scars. My affection for her exploded into a feeling I couldn't identify but I didn't want to let go. I stifled a groan when she slid back to the ground, pulling from my embrace. If I could have my way, my arms would never have released her. I wanted more of the feelings she evoked in me... the draw becoming even stronger than my lust for her blood.

"You're welcome, Emilia," I said while she stepped back and grinned at me. "Are you ready for the next phase of your birthday?"

"I can't believe there's more!"

Little did she know just how much more I had planned.

"Your ride awaits," Cyrus said, stepping in through the door. We turned to meet him before I extended an elbow to her. She giggled and slid her arm through mine.

"Thank you all so much!" she called over her shoulder to the sales associates who lined up again to see us off.

"It was our pleasure," Rachel said, waving us goodbye while we headed out the back door.

Stepping out onto the street, Emilia gasped when she saw the carriage with the gleaming white horse pawing his impatience. The driver stood waiting, his top hat in hand while his coat tails blew in the warm summer breeze.

"Good evening," he said, bowing.

"Are you serious?" Emilia said, her excitement barely contained. "Is this for real?"

"Your carriage awaits," I responded.

She held my hand while I helped her inside. I slid along the burgundy velvet seat and settled at her side.

After returning to his seat, the driver turned and placed his top hat back over his thinning grey hair. "Are you ready?"

Emilia nodded and I waved him on. "We are."

The driver clucked his tongue, sending the horse trotting off. The carriage turned onto Madison Ave and headed toward the entrance to Central Park. She sat beside me in silence, taking in the sights and sounds of the city until they disappeared into nothing but the chirping of crickets and the soft crackling of branches as we made our way into the park. The clip-clop of hooves kept a soothing rhythm while the horse pulled us toward our destination. He veered left onto the smaller path and soon we arrived at Gapstow Bridge.

Candles lined the entire stone arched bridge; another flourish Mark had arranged. It glowed in the warm lights and illuminated the soft flowing water beneath it.

"Aiden... it's so beautiful," she said, staring at the impressive sight. "Is this for me?"

"Of course," I responded, climbing out of the carriage and helping her down.

I walked her along the bridge until we reached the small table draped in white linen and topped with two candles, a small flower vase, a glass of wine and a silver lidded platter.

"Please, have a seat," I said, pulling out her chair.

She smiled up at me when she sat, and her gaze followed me until I took my seat across from her.

"What is it?" She examined the silver dome that shone in the candlelight.

"Open it and see."

When she lifted the lid her eyes popped open and flew to mine.

"Seriously?" she exclaimed. "You have all my favorite foods here! Pizza, sushi, *and* spaghetti?"

"Only the best from New York's finest restaurants. Please, enjoy your dinner."

"I don't know which one to start with." She laughed before settling on a piece of sushi, moaning while it slid past her lips. It was another sound she made that sent visions of her writhing beneath me flashing through my mind.

With each bite she closed her eyes and savored the tastes from the best selections in the city. Before, when she had told me how much she enjoyed food, I didn't realize just how much she appreciated all the flavors. Her pure and raw enjoyment of them made me long to taste them with her... to experience things as she experienced them. For the first time in centuries, I craved something other than blood.

"Oh, my God!" she said, her mouth still full of food. A powerful swallow cleared her throat, and she sat forward in her chair. "Your dinner!" She lowered her voice and glanced around us. "You haven't fed tonight! I've been so caught up in this experience I just realized that we haven't done our thing."

"I fed on a bag when I woke up so you could have the night off," I whispered back.

A look of disappointment washed over her face. "Oh, I see."

"Does that upset you?" I asked. Her discontent surprised me. I thought she would enjoy an evening not forced to be my live feed bag.

A non-believable shake moved her head. "No, it's fine. I'm just surprised is all."

I heard her heart race when the lie came out. A trait shared by all humans. It upset her that I hadn't fed on her. I scrunched my brow in response.

She wants *me to feed on her?*

"I'm sorry, I assumed you would appreciate the vacation."

"I don't mind doing it, you know," she said. Her eyes conveyed the surprising truth. She truly enjoyed it.

"Perhaps later," I said. Her eyes twinkled for a moment and she nodded. She enjoyed it more than I realized.

After finishing her last bites, she sat back and pushed her plate forward. "This dress and that much food may have been a bad idea." She puffed out a long breath.

"Did you save room for cake?" I pulled the piece of cake from where they'd hidden it beneath the table.

"Is that Boston Crème Pie?" Her eyes grew as wide as the small plate.

"I heard it's your favorite."

"You have no idea. You haven't lived until you've devoured an entire Boston Crème Pie in one sitting!"

"So, you have room?"

A child-like smile stretched across her face. "There is *always* room for cake. But we may need to go back to Barneys and get me some fancy sweatpants."

Her clever wit made me chuckle. "Then cake it is." I pulled out the small pink candle from my pocket and tipped it into the flame dancing on the table. The little wick sizzled before lighting up. After pressing it into the cake, I passed it across the table. "Make a wish."

Emilia closed her eyes and then blew, the little flame dissipating into a puff of smoke that drifted up into the dark night sky.

"What did you wish for?" I asked while she took the cake.

She flashed me a staying look and a smile. "I can't tell you or it won't come true."

"We don't want that now, do we." I sat back and watched her devour the little dessert, again taken by how much joy the taste of it brought her. Her moan reverberated in every cell of my body, setting them all on fire. I'd never had chocolate before and couldn't even imagine what it resembled.

"Aiden," she said, scraping the last bit of chocolate off the plate, "tonight has been more than I could imagine. More than anyone could imagine. I... I can't believe you did all this for me."

"There's one more surprise for you."

"There's more?" she said, the chocolate-covered fork still wedged in her mouth, mumbling her words.

I chuckled. "There's more. Are you ready?"

She licked the last bit of chocolate from her fork and set it back on the plate. Moving to her side, I took her hand and lifted her from her chair. Together we walked arm in arm across the glowing bridge back to where the carriage awaited. Cyrus would be waiting for us back at the limo to whisk us away to her final birthday surprise... and the one I was most excited about.

CHAPTER TEN

Emilia

"WE'RE HERE," AIDEN said, startling me from my trance induced by the bright lights and activity that still lit up the city even though it approached midnight. Everything about this place was incredible... the fact that Aiden had given me my very own Cinderella evening made it even more special. In my wildest dreams, I could never have imagined such an amazing birthday. To say his thoughtfulness made up for all the non-existent celebrations before would be the understatement of the century.

I turned to look at him. That impossibly perfect face still glowed with the same excitement he had worn on it all evening. Secrets and surprises still danced behind his eyes, and I knew from the glint of mischief in them that this part of my birthday excited him the most. I didn't dare even try to imagine what he had in store for me next.

Cyrus opened the door, and I squinted against the marquee lights illuminating everything around us.

"Miss Charles," he said, offering me his hand. I clutched my new Birkin bag against my chest and scooted along the leather seat to climb out beside him. Aiden followed just behind and soon the two of us stood beneath the giant building towering over us.

"Are we at Madison Square Garden?" I asked. The thumping of the music from within caused me to raise my voice while I tipped my head back to take in the building glowing with colored lights.

"You are correct." Aiden flashed me his most charming smile.

"Text when you're ready for pickup," Cyrus said before sliding back into the driver's seat and pulling away.

"Is it a concert?" I listened closer to see if I recognized the band.

"It's a benefit concert featuring some of the country's top bands. It's been going on all night, but there are still two acts left. There is one I am most excited to see."

I had a hard time picturing Aiden fist-pumping at a concert, but the delight in his smile told me he was ecstatic about this next stage of my birthday surprise. "Sounds great. Who are the bands?"

Mischief flickered through his eyes. "That's the fun part."

He placed his hand on my lower back and guided me around the corner. I looked up to see a sign with the band names, impressed by the talent listed as I read. "Wow! Kings of Leon, Imagine Dragons, Thirty Seconds to Mars..." My voice trailed off as I saw the next name on the impressive list. "Is that my ex-husband's band?" I gulped.

Aiden's smirk pulled into a full-blown grin. Even though his fangs were safely tucked away, the deviousness of his smile may as well have had them out in full display. He looked positively scheming.

"Wow," I started, unsure of what to say next. Tonight had been pure magic and he'd catered to every single desire I never knew I had. But why he thought I would want to see my ex-husband living out his dreams, actually *our* dreams, eluded me. Jeff's presence, playing amongst the country's top bands, made me sick to my stomach. He had achieved his dreams using me as the steppingstone he squashed on his way to the top. Seeing him standing on a stage singing for tens of thousands of people made me want to vomit. "I... I don't know what to say."

"When Mark discovered the line up here tonight, I knew exactly what I wanted to give you for your birthday."

I nodded, still not sure how to tell him I didn't want to go inside. I didn't want to see the success of the man who had betrayed me and used me. The man who'd achieved that success because of my funding and my support, and yet he had tossed me aside the moment he'd made his break. Even seeing his band's name in lights made me want to poke my own eyes out.

"Follow me and I'll get us in backstage."

"Aiden." I sighed. "Tonight has been incredible. Amazing. Perfect. I don't want to hurt your feelings, but I can't go in there and watch that piece of shit live out his greatest dream. I especially don't want to go backstage and risk running into him. Never seeing him again would be a better birthday present."

Much to my surprise, Aiden's smile grew. "Oh, I'm so sorry, Emilia. I wasn't clear enough with my intentions here." He placed his hands on my shoulders. "I have no desire to see that... asshole, succeed either. Tonight we are here to get you some much needed revenge. Tonight you and I will end the ill-conceived career of the man who betrayed you."

"What?" I stammered, still spinning from the twist in my evening.

"It all ends tonight," Aiden said, a malicious glint bubbled to the top from the depths in his eyes.

"You're going to kill him?" I struggled to keep my voice down while I felt the ground move beneath my feet. A healthy thirst for retribution was one thing, but killing him? I didn't think I had the stomach for that. No... I knew I didn't have the stomach for that. "Holy shit, Aiden—"

Tossing back his head, he bellowed out laughter, and the deep, true laugh shook his whole body. I knew he was a vampire, but sweet Jesus, seeing him so nonchalant about *murder* made me take a step back.

"Aiden, while I appreciate your intentions, we are not murdering anyone tonight," I said while his laughter continued.

"Oh, Emilia. Again, I was not clear. I'm sorry you thought I was here to rip out your ex-husband's jugular. I'm not... unless you want me to?" He quirked an eyebrow.

"No!" I shook my head.

"Just checking," he said with a shrug. "I have plans for him using my other talents that will leave him alive and safe when we're done. Do you trust me?"

Biting my lip, I nodded my head.

"Good. Then just relax and follow me. I won't kill him tonight, though he deserves it," Aiden said, scowling. "Unless you want me to. If you do, just say the word and I'll part his trachea from his body before you can blink an eye." He flashed his devious smile.

I chuckled and shook my head again. "Tempting, but no thank you."

"Let me know if you change your mind." He winked. "Now, follow me."

He reached out and took my hand; a spontaneous movement, one normally seen between couples much more intimate with one another. I didn't even know what we were, yet holding his hand felt natural. The coolness of his touch still startled me, though not at all unpleasant. We both glanced to our entangled fingers. His expression reflected my same shock at the involuntary touch, almost as if his hand had reached out for mine before he'd even realized it. I could see the uncertainty in his eyes, so I squeezed his hand in return, reassuring him that touching him was fine with me.

More than fine from the way my stomach did cartwheels.

He gave me a smile and tugged me forward toward the back of the building. We walked hand in hand up to the bouncers standing guard at the backstage entrance to the building. Roadies carted cases of instruments in and out from the trucks parked just down the way. Aiden walked up like we belonged there, and I waited for him to present the backstage tickets I assumed he had bought.

"I need to see your passes," the bouncer said, his arms crossed tight against his massive chest.

"I don't have any," Aiden stated.

"Then get the fuck out of here," the bouncer growled.

Aiden stepped forward and locked eyes with the giant of a man. "You will let us in and then you will forget you saw us."

The bouncer stood frozen, his face entranced for a moment before he blinked and spoke. "Of course, sir. Enjoy your evening."

My mouth fell open when Aiden turned to look at me. He waggled his eyebrows and pulled me into the backstage area of Madison Square Garden.

"Unbelievable!" I laughed and trotted to keep up with him. "Why do you even bother paying for anything when you can just do that?"

"I try not to mess with people's minds when I don't have to. Don't get me wrong, I do it when necessary, like tonight because they were sold out, but I have more money than I could spend in a hundred lifetimes. I figure it's good for the economy that I pay when I have the opportunity."

"Aren't you just a pillar of society?" I chuckled.

"Come on, this way."

Following him down the halls, we wound through the roadies, musicians, and groupies. Scantily clad women lined the halls, each no doubt waiting for their turn with the musicians. I figured Jeff lived the good life now with this arsenal of women to choose from every night. I hoped he and that ho Sheena were still together so this time she could be the one getting cheated on every night. It served her right. Payment for her shitty morals in sleeping with a man she knew had a wife. Pure karma.

The music grew louder as we made our way closer to the stage. The energy buzzed around us and I felt it moving into me. For a split second I wished things were different. That I'd be standing at Jeff's side for this moment to see all our hard work, tears, and money pay off. An unexpected flicker of sadness shot through me that I hadn't been invited to experience the end of the ride; the exciting plunge downhill at breakneck speeds.

It reminded me of a sledding hill I visited every winter during my childhood. Getting to the top was exhausting, climbing one slow step at a time through the snow until I reached the peak. But the exhilarating ride back down made the climb all worthwhile. With Jeff, I'd been the one pulling him up the hill, sweating and crying while he sat in his little sled twiddling his thumbs and asking me, 'are we there yet?' over and over. Then came the fun part, where we reached the top and I got to climb in the sled and feel the wind whipping through my hair as we rode at breakneck speeds down the hill, screaming our excitement. Instead, once we reached the top, he had pushed me down in the snow and threw some skank in the sled with him, leaving me to climb back down all on my own, without the thrill of the ride.

Anger started churning in my gut, but one look at Aiden and my stomach flipped over. Sometimes life had a funny way of working out for the best. Alone at the top of the hill, I'd turned Jeff's betrayal into a golden opportunity. If I had ridden the sled down with him, I never would have met Aiden. And when comparing the two men, if Jeff was an apple, Aiden was a fucking apple orchard. He dwarfed Jeff in every way imaginable, and the thought made me squeeze his hand tighter. Jeff may have gotten the career, but in the end, I beat him down that hill and ran him over, leaving him laying mangled in a pile of snow. At least I would when Aiden finished with him tonight. I giggled to myself and wondered what malicious plan Aiden had to help me get my revenge.

"Emilia?" His voice sent a shiver up my spine, and not the good kind like Aiden's touch did.

"Jeff," I ground out the name. Aiden's hand tightened around mine as we both turned to see Jeff standing behind us holding his guitar.

"Emilia! You're here! I can't believe it!" he shouted and stepped toward me with open arms and a clueless smile. Of course Jeff would be oblivious enough to think I'd be happy to see him.

Aiden stepped forward, eyes lowered while his chest expanded, and he seemed to grow in size. Even though Jeff wasn't the brightest crayon in the box, even he didn't miss the obvious display and stopped before taking a healthy step backward. Aiden's possessive posturing pulled up the corner of my mouth in a smirk. The protective gesture made my little heart beat just a bit faster.

"Sorry, it's just good to see you," Jeff responded with a slight quake in his voice as he eyed up the intimidating man holding my hand.

His eyes then raked over me, and I noticed the admiration plain on his face. Thank God Mark had picked out my outfit and played dress-up Barbie with me tonight. Normally when you run into an ex you're in sweats, have a zit the size of Mount Everest on your face, and bags bigger than my Birkin under your eyes. The Murphy's Law of love gone wrong. I thought running into an ex looking amazing with a smoking hot man on your arm was an urban myth. Yet here I was, looking like a million bucks with a man who looked like a Greek God. This really was the best birthday ever.

After a pause, he let out a sigh. "You look amazing, Emilia."

"You look like shit," I spit out, realizing only after it came out how awful it sounded. I didn't even mean it as an insult. He really did look like shit. Jeff wasn't ever what one would call handsome before, but he wasn't a complete troll, either. But not tonight. His long dark hair fell limp, he had bags under his eyes, he'd put on a good twenty pounds, and his skin looked like it had aged ten years. Drugs, partying, and this new rock-and-roll lifestyle had not been kind to him. "I'm sorry, I didn't mean that. You just look tired," I said, cringing at the failed attempt to smooth over my abrupt comment.

"It's... it's a busy life I live now," Jeff said, shifting awkwardly. "I haven't gotten much sleep."

"I bet. You're about to play at Madison Square Garden. It's your ultimate dream." For a moment a sliver of happiness crept in. Why, I couldn't explain. Lord knows he didn't deserve to be here, seizing this opportunity on the back of my support and the destruction of others. My mother always said I was too nice, and this moment was apparently going to be one of them. Perhaps I shouldn't let Aiden stomp Jeff's dreams into the ground. Maybe I just needed to wish him well and walk away.

Be the bigger person. Get my closure without destroying his life. And then...

"Emilia? What the fuck are you doing here?"

A voice like nails on a chalkboard. *Fucking Sheena.*

Aiden and I turned in unison to face her and watch while she strutted up to Jeff's side. She cocked a hip and put a possessive arm around his waist. Though admittedly pretty, I wouldn't call her beautiful. In fact, her lack of model perfect looks pissed me off. If Jeff had cheated on me with someone stunning, his betrayal wouldn't have been as insulting. And she looked exactly the same, except for her new hairstyle. She'd cut her dark brown hair into a trendy bob with chic straight-cut bangs that fell just above her glaring brown eyes.

"Hello, Sheena," I snarled. She flashed a fake smile that showed off those oversized teeth.

Aiden leaned down and whispered, "That's her? I'll admit I thought she'd be much more attractive."

The look on her face told me she'd heard his attempted whisper. I wasn't sure if he'd meant to say it just loud enough for her to hear, or if it truly was an accident. When I caught the look in his eyes, I knew it was the former. God this man was amazing.

"Looks like you've been busy." She eyed up my Birkin bag and the man holding my hand.

Seeing her standing next to Jeff reminded me what a shit he was, and that little bit of pity I had for him fluttered away on the notes of the music coming from the stage behind us. Aiden could have his way with him. Hell, maybe I needed to reconsider the throat-ripping-out thing.

"You're up, baby," Sheena said, turning her attention to Jeff. "You're gonna blow them away, baby! This is it!"

Jeff hopped up and down and shook his head, trying to shake off the nerves. I'd seen him do that same move before many shows back when we were together.

"Emilia? Do I have your blessing?" Aiden whispered into my ear.

I turned and looked him straight in the eye. "Do your worst."

His sinister smile deepened the dimples in his cheeks. He released my hand and walked up to Jeff, catching him as he headed onto the stage. They locked eyes, and I tried my best to read his lips. I couldn't hear the actual words, but Jeff nodded his head. Aiden touched him on the shoulder and stepped out of his way. When Jeff marched onto the stage, I heard the roar of the crowd.

After shooting me a haughty glare, Sheena moved to the edge of the stage, and Aiden waved me forward. I walked toward him at the side entrance and when I peered out at the crowd, the sight of the full house of people screaming Jeff's name amazed me. He'd always dreamed about hearing the roar of the crowd and feeling the adoration of so many fans. I glanced to Sheena who beamed with pride when Jeff picked up the microphone.

"What did you do?" I asked Aiden. His eyes danced with excitement and he looked like a kid on Christmas morning. He slid an arm around my shoulder and pulled me close to his side. I caught Sheena's glance at the impressive man claiming me as his own.

Not this time, bitch. I narrowed my eyes and leaned in closer, pressing my body against his muscular frame.

"Just watch," Aiden said, pointing to Jeff on the stage. I followed his finger and watched the man I once called husband take the microphone in his hand. The crowd roared again while he lifted it to his lips.

"Hello, New York!" he screamed, and they returned the sentiment by screaming back. "I am so thrilled to be here with you! I came here tonight to play you some rock-and-roll! Is that what you want?"

The roar of the crowd reverberated through my entire body, even more powerfully than I could have imagined. Jeff stood in front of them, the blue spotlight beating down on him while the band prepared to count off.

"Before I get started, I have to tell you all something!" he shouted over the noisy crowd.

Aiden's smile grew while he squeezed my shoulder tighter.

"I don't belong up here. I shouldn't be here," Jeff started, the excitement in his voice dissipating as the crowd quieted down with him. They looked as confused. I glanced up at Aiden who waggled his brows and gestured for me to keep watching.

"I don't belong here!" Jeff shouted the words this time, and the crowd fell silent. The musicians behind him shot glances to one another, and I realized this was not part of the show.

This was all Aiden.

"I'm a half-assed musician and the only reason I'm here is because I stole a woman's inheritance after her parents died. I used her to help me get here. I tricked her into marrying me when she tried to take the money and leave. Then, after years of supporting me and taking care of me, after my song became a hit, I left her for one of the many whores I liked to fuck. And I didn't even feel bad about it!"

One of the whores?

The crowd booed, and I glanced over to see Sheena shifting uncomfortably. Perhaps that was news to her as well.

"I left her with tens of thousands of dollars of debt and saddled with a mortgage while I ran off to live this dream! Then, if that wasn't bad enough, I dumped my high school bandmates... the ones who helped me get here. I replaced them with these guys because my manager told me I could go farther without them."

The crowd booed even louder and random items pelted Jeff on stage.

"Then, I slept with the girlfriends of my current band. All of them."

The band glanced amongst each other again before their eyes all narrowed into slits and focused on his back. If looks could kill, Jeff would have burst into flames.

"I destroyed so many lives to get here that I don't deserve to play for you tonight. I don't deserve to have a music career."

"Get off the stage you piece of shit!" a woman screamed and broke the silence.

The crowd joined her in a chant for Jeff to get off the stage. Boos and shouts replaced the cheers that had greeted him.

"Oh. My. God." I gasped, glancing up at a grinning Aiden. "You did this?"

He nodded and flashed a bright smile. "Wait for it..."

I turned my attention back to Jeff. There he stood on stage, thousands of people screaming for him to get off, his music career in shambles, and this would definitely be viral online tomorrow... the new musician who got up on stage and tanked his entire career. I couldn't help but look over to Sheena's ashen face. She looked more than ready to run.

"I need to admit one more thing before I go!" Jeff shouted into the microphone.

The crowd kept up their incessant booing while he stood motionless on stage.

"I just pissed my pants," he said matter-of-factly.

My hand flew to my mouth and my eyes nearly popped out of my head. The crowd fell silent for a moment while Jeff stood in front of them.

"Yes!" Aiden shouted, his rolling laughter following.

"Holy shit." It was still all I could manage to say from behind the hand I still held clasped over my mouth.

The crowd shouted again, and Jeff dropped the microphone and started off the stage, moving toward us wearing an expression filled with horror.

"Aiden... I... I can't believe... Did that just happen? I feel so vindicated." And I did. Watching Jeff blow up his fraudulent career had been so cathartic. He didn't deserve to be there. And now the rest of the world knew it, too.

"What did I just do?" Jeff mumbled when he arrived at Sheena's side. He reached out to wrap his arms around her, but she scoffed and sidestepped his embrace.

"Don't. Fucking. Touch. Me," she snapped. "You and I are done. You are over and the fuck if I'm dating you if you're just some schmuck in a garage band."

"Ready for the rest of your present?" Aiden asked.

My head nodded before giving it another thought. He pulled me to her side and looked her square in the eyes.

"Sheena. Listen to me. You will not leave Jeff. Ever. You wanted him, you got him. You will stay at his side when he is a washed-up musician playing for pennies at dive bars. You will stay at his side even when he cheats on you, which he will, repeatedly. You will sit in misery at his side for the rest of your days because you don't deserve to go off and live a happy life. You're a shitty person, Sheena and this is the life you deserve."

"This is the life I deserve," she responded in a robotic tone.

"Did I miss anything?" Aiden turned to me.

I stood stunned at his side shaking my head before the smile pulled up on my lips. "I'm pretty sure you covered it all. And then some." I chuckled while I watched Sheena and Jeff stand awkwardly beside one another, the wet spot in his pants now impossible to ignore.

"Why did I do that?" Jeff mumbled, searching first Sheena and then me when she didn't respond.

"Was anything you said up there untrue?" I asked him.

"No. It's all true." He dipped his head.

I no longer felt even an ounce of pity for him. There were far more deserving people who could take his place in the spotlight. People who'd earned it and had worked for it. "Then you don't deserve this, Jeff. None of it. Go home to Milwaukee. Try to be a better person."

"I'm ruined," Jeff mumbled.

"Goodbye, Jeff," I said and felt the weight of my anger leave my body. The hurt, betrayal, and humiliation poured off me in waves. For a moment I closed my eyes and relished the sweetness of the release.

"Are you ready to go, Emilia?" Aiden whispered.

I opened my eyes to find him staring at me, his eyes searching my own. Without warning, I flung myself forward and threw myself into his arms. He wrapped his around me and pulled me tight to his chest, pressing his chin to the top of my head and enveloping me in a cocoon of safety and security.

"Thank you, Aiden. Thank you," I whispered.

"You're welcome, Emilia. Happy birthday."

"No girl in the world has had a happier one. Ever."

"Well, then my work is done, and I need to get us home before the sun comes up and I turn into a pumpkin."

"A pumpkin?" I asked, pulling back enough to look up into his face.

"Well, a charred and burning pumpkin."

My face lit up with recognition and I grimaced. "Yeah, that. Then let's go."

I glanced to Jeff one last time. He wore the weight of his choices plain on his face, and the band he'd betrayed now leaving the stage and heading his way only deepened the worry lines in his worn skin.

"Good luck with that," Aiden said to him before slinging an arm around my shoulder and leading me away.

Jeff watched us walk away, and I took a deep breath and left the last of my anger behind me with him. He'd broken me... or tried to, but tonight Aiden had helped me patch up the last of the cracks. When we made it around the corner, I allowed myself to explode with the emotions I couldn't even begin to process.

"Did that just happen, Aiden?" I laughed, hopping up and down. "Did you seriously just mind control him into saying all that?"

Aiden nodded and chuckled. "I told him to walk on stage and admit all the terrible things he did to you and his bandmates to get here. The rest was up to him. Although, I meant for him to admit what he did to his previous band-mates. It hadn't occurred to me he had also wronged his current bandmates. That was just a welcome surprise."

"And the part where he pissed himself? Did that really happen?"

Aiden laughed louder. "That little tidbit was your present from Mark. He insisted I add that in for good measure... to really seal his fate. Mark says I'm supposed to say 'Happy birthday, sweetie. You're welcome.'"

"There is no one in the world who will work with the guy who stood up at Madison Square Garden and pissed his pants." Laughter erupted from deep within me and continued until I struggled to breathe. I kept hearing him say the words, "I just pissed my pants" over and over in my mind and each time it got more ridiculous and hysterical.

"I can't wait to see the YouTube videos of this," Aiden said.

"Mark will *die* when he sees this! We'll be laughing about it for years!"

We reached the exit and Aiden held the door for me while I stepped out into the open air. I felt lighter, and it made me do an impromptu twirl. I caught Aiden's appreciative glance when my skirt flitted up a bit too high. His intense gaze made my cheeks flush and soon I felt my chest follow. Thank God I'd insisted on underwear tonight.

While I smoothed my skirt back down, I looked at Aiden and tried to comprehend how I'd ended up here... on this perfect, amazing, incredible night with a *vampire*. And only one thing could make my night even better. The one thing I knew I shouldn't do.

A kiss.

CHAPTER ELEVEN

Emilia

WE MADE OUR WAY PAST the crew members loading trucks in the lots and Aiden pulled out his phone and texted Cyrus.

Aiden put away his phone. "He's two blocks over. With this traffic it will be faster for us to walk to him. Is that all right?"

"Lead the way!" I practically sang. "I'm so exhilarated I could run ten miles right now. Even in these shoes, and that's saying something."

"This way," Aiden pointed to the alley across the street.

We moved through the traffic to the shortcut that cut across to where Cyrus would be waiting. When we stepped into the dim lights of the alley, it gave me pause, but then I remembered who walked beside me.

"Are you all right? Your heart sped up."

"I forget that you can hear my heart. It's a little strange."

"Sorry, I didn't mean to pry."

"No need to apologize. I don't mind. And yes, I got a little scared coming down here. I'm not the kind of girl who walks into dark alleys. I'm the kind of girl who stays in the lights and the crowds for safety. I've seen the movies. Nothing good ever happens in alleys. Don't run up the stairs when the killer is chasing you, don't yell, 'who's there?' into the creepy room, and don't walk down dark alleys. And never *ever* collapse next to the killer's 'dead' body and sob. That son of a bitch is still alive. It's 'How to Survive a Horror Movie 101'."

He laughed, and I loved how natural it sounded now.

"It's a good thing you've got me, then. Although it sounds like you've got things covered. Since I'm making you break a rule, I'll make sure you make it to the end of this movie."

He stepped closer to my side, and his close proximity caused a wave of desire to move through my body again. "I suppose it's a good thing to have you by my side."

"Did you have a nice time tonight?"

"A nice time? Are you kidding? A nice time is what you have when you go for dinner and a movie. This... this was straight out of a fairy tale. Honestly, Aiden. I can't believe you did all this for me. And on such short notice, no less. There aren't enough words to thank you for this perfect evening."

"Your smile is thanks enough."

Heat flushed back to my cheeks and chest again. Tonight, something had shifted between us, and I found myself even more drawn to him than before. It wasn't just his looks I found intoxicating now... it was him. All of him. Beneath that cold exterior beat the heart of a charming, funny, and even romantic man... vampire. He sucked me in like a vortex I had no desire to fight. In fact, it was all I could do to keep myself from running straight at it and leaping into the depths without questioning where it would take me. All I knew was that I wanted to taste his lips again and feel those cool hands on every inch of my body.

Aiden froze, and it snapped me out of my fantasy of feeling his tongue invade my mouth again. I heard cans clank and I spun to see the silhouette of three men emerging from the shadows.

"Emilia, don't move," he commanded and pushed me behind him.

The men stepped into the dim lights and the gun glinted when the man in front drew it to chest level. "Don't resist and you'll both walk out of here just fine," he said, stepping toward us. His bald head shone bright as he stepped further into the light. "Just give us your wallets, jewelry and other valuables and we'll be on our way."

Aiden lowered his head, blocking me behind his body. "Leave. Now." The primal tones in his growl sent a shiver snaking up my spine.

"Don't be a hero, pretty boy," the short red-haired man said, stepping up beside the man holding the gun who continued his approach. "If you put up a fight, this won't end well for you. Or her."

Peeking around Aiden's shoulder I saw him give my legs a leering glance. I could feel Aiden's muscles twitch as raw power radiated off him. I pressed myself into his back.

His voice deepened. "I said leave. Now."

The bald leader shook his head and pulled back the hammer of his gun. "Listen up, pretty boy. Perhaps this is your first mugging. If so, welcome to the club. But the way this works is we point a gun at you. You hand us your things.

Everyone lives. We leave happy. The other option is we point a gun at you. You resist. We shoot you and have our way with her before killing her. We live, you two die. We leave happy. It's your choice which way this will go. Either way, we're leaving here happy and with all your money."

"There's a third option," Aiden said.

"Oh yeah? What's that?"

I didn't even see him move. I just felt my body slam against the wall that was ten feet away not a split second ago. The power of the blow forced the air out of my lungs and left me gasping while I watched Aiden dart between the three men in a blur of motion. Two fell to the ground in a heap, their necks bent at unnatural angles. In a matter of seconds the blur of movement reformed into Aiden. He stood holding the gun to the head of the bald man who he had forced on his knees. The man stared up into the barrel of his own gun with raised hands and bulging eyes while Aiden stared him down.

"*That* was the third option," Aiden growled.

"Please don't kill me," the man begged. "Please. I didn't mean it. We weren't really going to hurt you."

"Is that so?" Aiden quirked a brow and pressed the gun into his forehead. "Then why did your pulse tell me you were lying just now?"

"What? How? What *are* you?" he stammered.

"I'm the man who would never let you, or anyone, lay a finger on her," he snarled.

Panic inched the criminal's voice up several octaves. "Are you going to kill me?"

I watched frozen from my place against the wall. These were bad men who probably deserved to die, but I didn't know if I could stomach watching Aiden kill a man begging for his life. I held my breath awaiting Aiden's answer.

"No." Aiden lowered the gun and leaned in closer to look the man in the eyes. "You will walk down this alley, go find the nearest police officers and tell them you had a fight with your friends, and you broke their necks. You will then confess to every crime you have ever committed and spend the rest of your miserable life in prison. You will also forget that you ever saw us. Now go."

The man stood up in a trance and started walking out of the alley. For the first time since Aiden spoke, I blew out a breath. With a whoosh Aiden stood in front of me and I sucked that breath back into my lungs.

"Are you hurt?" he asked, the concern heavy in his voice. His hands moved over my shoulders and his gaze scanned my body for injury before settling back onto mine.

I could only shake my head.

"I will never let anyone hurt you. Ever," he said with such an intensity I felt it in the depths of my soul. His hand moved to my face, his thumb brushing against my cheek. Our eyes locked and then mine dropped to the lips that sat parted just inches from mine. The need for his kiss over-whelmed me and I gave in to the carnal urge demanding I submit to it. I leaned forward and pressed my lips to his, closing my eyes when they touched, savoring the softness of his kiss. His tongue slid past my lips, first soft and gentle, but then it grew hungrier as he deepened the kiss. I moaned with the force of his response and savored the sweet taste of him while he invaded my mouth.

My body slammed into the wall behind me when he pushed me back and captured my gasp in his mouth. I left my hands free to explore him, and they traveled to his back, sliding over the shoulders bulging beneath his shirt. Clawing and desperate I pulled him into me, needing him closer, needing to feel his body pressed into mine. He offered no resistance and instead pushed into me, our breaths mingling while I moaned into his mouth. His tongue delved deeper while his hand grasped the back of my head and pulled me in tighter, crushing my lips with the weight of his desire.

His other hand drifted down my shoulder and then slid the length of my side and settled on my hip. A strong pull eliminated any space left between us and I no longer knew where my body stopped and his began. His touch set me on fire and left me burning and writhing, engulfed in the heat of his passion and overwhelmed by the intensity of my own. My hands moved to his chest, and I slid them over the muscles that twitched at my touch.

He softened his kiss, and I whimpered when his lips pulled back from mine. Panting, I opened my eyes to see his own boring into me, heavy with desire. A gentle tug of my hair pulled my head back and my skin ignited when his lips touched my neck. No fangs punctured me, and instead delicate kisses pecked along my skin, leaving a burning trail in their wake.

Savoring every touch, he coaxed moan after moan from me while his lips traveled down my neck. Grabbing a handful of his shirt I pulled him against me. His touch brought me to life and my need to feel it everywhere deepened with each flick of his tongue on my skin. I wanted him inside of me, in every way imaginable.

"Drink from me, Aiden," I whispered, my need for the euphoria his bite brought intensifying with every touch. It wasn't just his fangs I wanted inside of me, and the sound of them popping free fanned the fire that also scorched between my thighs. I could feel his cock press against me, and I pushed my hips into him. Feeling him pressing into my dress and up against the place that needed him most sent a shudder through my body. I waited for the heat that came when his fangs slid inside of me and held my breath while I prepared for the sharp tips to begin their descent into my skin.

"Down here," a voice echoed down the alley.

Aiden straightened with a start and I whimpered when I felt his lips disappear from my skin.

"I killed two men right down here." *Fuck!* The mugger Aiden had hypnotized.

"We need to get out of here. Now," Aiden said, turning back to me. Before I could respond or recover from the touch that still had me sweltering inside, his arm snaked around my waist and I felt my body slam into his. He shot us forward with the power of an explosion and I tried not to choke on the air that filled my lungs from the speed we hit. Everything looked like a streak of colors and lights; we moved too fast for anything to process or take form. Despite only seconds of movement, when we stopped the momentum nearly sent me tumbling to the ground. He caught me by the waist and steadied me while I waited for the world to stop moving.

"Holy shit," I managed to say while it felt like my head swirled and I waited for it to slow down. It reminded me of the feeling I got when I used to spin around as fast as I could as a child, and then try to stand straight. I teetered in his arms trying to make the world stop moving.

"Are you all right?" he asked, his face finally coming into focus as I wobbled in his arms. "I'm so sorry I didn't warn you. I didn't want to risk us getting seen, and I needed to get us out of there. Are you hurt?"

I shook my head but realized the error of that idea when it intensified the spinning. "I'm fine. I think."

"Are you sure?"

"I might be sick," I admitted, feeling the waves of nausea traveling up into my throat.

"I'm so sorry." He took my face between his hands. "Just look at me and breathe."

The back and forth swaying made it hard to focus on his face, but second by second the motion subsided and soon I stood erect staring up into those incredible blue eyes. The nausea dissipated, and I blew out a deep breath. "Whoa. That. Was. Crazy."

The concern on his face softened, and a smile took its place. "It's kind of fun, isn't it?"

"A little warning next time. And maybe some Dramamine. But yeah... that was fun."

A car horn honked, and I looked away from him for the first time. It was only then I realized we were standing on the sidewalk of a busy street in downtown New York. People moved in herds around us and cars buzzed down the busy street. I had been so entranced in his eyes that I hadn't even noticed we were no longer alone.

"Mr. Mackay! Over here!"

Cyrus waved from the limo just a few car lengths up from us.

"Can you walk?" Aiden brushed a hand down my arm.

"I think so." I took a wobbly step. My legs turned to rubber, and I stumbled forward.

Aiden caught me in his arms. "I think I should carry you. It takes a while to get used to the speed and until then, it takes a while to recover from it."

"Good idea." I had no desire to end our incredible night in a heap on the sidewalk with my dress up over my head. Once again, I felt thankful for my underwear just in case I went down.

A gentle scoop pulled me up against his chest. I slung my arm around his shoulder and giggled when our eyes met. "Here I am all 'damsel in distressy' again. It seems I'm making a habit of this."

"It's a habit I'm more than happy to feed." He smiled.

"Do you need help?" Cyrus asked, hurrying to our side.

"Someone had a bit too much birthday champagne," he lied. "Just get the door and we should be just fine."

"Damn bubbly," I said, solidifying the story. "I'm a lightweight."

"I've been there a few times myself!" Cyrus chuckled and opened the limo door, stepping aside so Aiden could lower me in.

Once he'd situated me on the seat, Aiden slid his arm out from under me and scooted to my side.

"Are you heading back to the airport, Mr. Mackay?"

Aiden looked at his watch. "Yes, Cyrus. It's time we got back."

Cyrus didn't hesitate and hopped into the driver's seat and got us underway. We needed to make it home before sunrise. It was time for tonight to end... and I didn't want it to.

I never wanted tonight to end.

I wanted more of everything... but especially more of Aiden. My body still burned where he had touched it, and the places he hadn't touched still begged for his attention. If the divider in the limo hadn't been down, I wasn't sure I wouldn't have thrown myself on top of him.

It had been a year since I'd had sex, and at least five years since I'd had good sex. Jeff wasn't a stallion in the sack to begin with, and the last years together had been the old married couple kind of encounters. A nudge of the elbow to get things started, a few pumps, and a faked orgasm and it was over. Over the past few years I'd begun to wonder if I even liked sex. It became more of a chore than a desire and something that never occurred to me until Jeff would elbow me in the side and say, 'Wanna do it?'. I usually obliged him, but I often wondered if I was defective and that thing that made you want to get it on had left me. When Aiden had touched me, that thing sprang back to life with renewed enthusiasm, alive and well.

Really well.

We arrived at the airport and Cyrus pulled us up to the stairs of the plane. Opening the door, he stepped aside, and Aiden climbed out first, extending a hand and pulling me up to his side. Just the touch of his skin had every nerve in my body on fire again.

"Are you okay to walk?" Aiden asked.

I stood upright for a minute to verify the ground no longer rumbled beneath me. "Yes, I'm good now. Thank you."

"It was a pleasure to meet you Miss Charles." Cyrus folded into a bow.

I stepped forward and threw my arms around his neck. He chuckled his surprise and then patted me on the back. "Thank you, Cyrus. I had such an incredible evening, and it was wonderful to meet you."

"I hope to see you again, Miss Charles," he said as we broke our embrace. I saw the accusatory look he shot to Aiden and struggled to stifle my giggle. It seemed I had won Cyrus' stamp of approval.

The flight attendant stood at the top of the stairs and waited while Aiden and I made our way back up them. I headed back to the private room from the flight out. The elegance of this jet still blew my mind as much as it had the first time I'd stepped onto it. Soft cream leather covered every inch of the furniture and walls, and rich mahogany wood trimmed the small bar and the chairs that sat facing one another. A large couch stretched out the length of the room and a fake fire crackled from the screen on the wall. It was a far cry from the cramped seating and the snoring man beside me the one time I flew commercial before tonight.

"Can we get you anything before take-off?" Sheila asked.

"No, thank you. I'll buzz you if we need anything," Aiden answered.

"Enjoy your flight," she said and pulled the door shut behind her, sealing us into the room alone.

I sat down in the oversized leather seat I had used on our way here. Aiden sat in the matching chair just across from me. The ride in had been unbelievably awkward because I couldn't stop thinking about our kiss, and now it seemed the ride home would be just more of the same. All I could think about was how much I wanted his tongue in my mouth and his hands up my dress. The incessant thoughts left little room for casual conversation.

The engine of the jet started up and the lights in the room dimmed. Flickering flames from the fake fire made up most of the light left in the room. Crossing my legs, I shifted in my seat, and he watched me with a contemplative gaze, resting his chin on his fist. Curious eyes raked me over while I squirmed beneath the intensity of his stare.

The heat raced back to my face and then settled in my chest while I smoothed my skirt for the umpteenth time since sitting down.

Good God, I'm a disaster.

Crossing and uncrossing my legs, I let my eyes dart between him and out the window. A glance outside showed the plane had started its slow crawl toward the runway and my slight fear of flying only strengthened the pulse I could feel thumping through my veins.

Just do it, Emilia. Get up and kiss him. Finish what you started.

I couldn't. I wanted to, more than anything, but fear glued me to my seat and forced my eyes back down to the ground. It wasn't that I didn't think he wanted to kiss me, the passion that exploded off him in that alley washed away any doubt of the intensity of his feelings. But the moment had slipped away, and I wasn't sure how to ignite the fire again. Being ballsy and approaching a man felt strange. Wrong. Not to mention my lack of practice. I'd only been with a few guys before Jeff back in high school. It had been over a decade since I'd been in this situation and I felt like an awkward teenager again under the weight of Aiden's stare.

Closing my eyes, I pushed my head back into the leather seat. *Come on, Emilia. You only live once. And if he isn't into this, just have him erase the memory of the awkward moment away and it will be like it never happened. Just do it. You deserve this.*

With a deep breath I squeezed my eyes tighter.

Fuck it.

I would get up, march over there and plant one on him. But just before I rose from my seat, a brisk wind blew back my hair. I inhaled a sharp breath and snapped open my eyes. Just inches from my face I saw his penetrating eyes locked with mine before drifting for a second to my lips.

"Sweet Jesus. You *can* read my mind, can't you?" I gasped.

A sly smile tugged up one corner of his lips and he slowly shook his head. A cool hand slid across my cheek, stroking the heated skin before sliding through the soft curls cascading over my shoulders.

"Then how did you—"

He didn't let me finish. The force of his lips crushing into mine pushed the words back into my mouth. His hand slid behind my head and drew me into him while his tongue demanded entrance. I submitted to his command, my body no longer my own to control. He captured my moan in his mouth and matched it with his own. Our kiss deepened when he pressed into me, and I felt every inch of my body crackle and explode to life. A shiver traveled down my spine and moved all the way to the tips of my toes.

My pulse raced as the jet engine roared and screamed while we careened down the runway. I wasn't sure if Aiden's touch gave me the sensation of elevating off the ground or if the plane was taking off. Every sense heightened to the point I could no longer distinguish them, a swirl of emotions and senses all colliding into one explosion of pleasure.

The soft caress of his hand lingered even when it left its place on my cheek and slid down the length of my side, moving to the small of my back. The plane's takeoff pushed me forward in my seat and I slid tighter into his body, a wall of muscle that supported me and pressed me back into the cool leather. Our lips moved in sync, our breaths mingling into one while our tongues danced and twirled together, desperation deepening our kiss with each passing second.

Reaching up, I slid my arms around his neck, my fingers raking through his hair. His kiss contained an urgency, an urgency that matched my own. An insatiable desire that only increased with each brush of his lips against mine. I needed him in me, on me, around me. Suddenly, I was in his arms and across the room being laid down on the long leather couch. The gentle way he set me down was a stark contrast to the force of the movement that brought me there. It left me spinning while I struggled to catch my breath, realizing how empty I felt with the sudden absence of his lips.

Searching his eyes, I reached up and slid my hand across his chest before grabbing a fistful of fabric and yanking him back down to me. He offered no resistance, and I moaned when his lips reconnected with mine. It was where they belonged, and I felt empty without them. The weight of his body pressed along the length of mine when he settled on top of me. His tongue resumed the tantalizing twirls that sent my stomach plummeting and tumbling as if I had fallen out of the plane and plunged toward the ground.

His kiss softened, and I stifled a whimper when his lips drifted away. Opening my eyes, I found his searching my own.

"Are you sure?" he asked, his usually commanding voice soft and concerned. "If this isn't what you want, we don't have—"

"I guess you can't read my mind after all," I said, flashing a smirk. "Now stop talking and kiss me."

His lips that had been pressed tight together in concern spread into a wide grin. I watched as they moved back toward me and I closed my eyes, my breath held fast while I waited for their return. Instead, I felt them brush against my neck. My lips parted, and I breathed out a contented sigh when they brushed the most sensitive spot on my neck, just below my ear.

"Oh, God," I moaned while he kissed his way down my neck, his tongue leaving little trails of tingling skin in its wake. Cool fingers traced their way down toward my cleavage and my breath hitched when they moved down the crevice between my breasts. Reaching the fabric pulled tight over them, he traced his fingers over the top, brushing my nipple that strained hard against the fabric. A shudder racked my body, and I held my breath while his hand opened up and cupped the entirety of it, a gentle squeeze forcing my head back into the pillow.

When his thumb traced my nipple, I felt the heat sizzling between my legs. Writhing beneath him, I closed my eyes and begged his hand to move south. The need to feel his touch below caused my stomach to clench in a knot I couldn't unravel. Only his touch could ease the ache.

His lips returned to my neck and his hand drifted from my breast and slid across my dress, following the contours of my figure while it moved down my body. My heart hammered in my chest when his hand moved to my thigh, traveling to the bottom of my dress before sliding beneath it and touching the sensitive skin on my inner thigh. A sharp inhale trapped in my lungs when his fingers moved higher up my leg. Every nerve in my body came alive everywhere he touched. The sensation of his lips moving down to my breasts while his fingers moved up to my heat set my body on fire.

For the first time tonight I cursed the lacy panties that kept his touch at bay. "Please," I whispered when his fingers reached the lines of my underwear and paused. I needed his touch. I needed to feel him inside me. He raised his head from my chest and met my pleading eyes with an intensity that rocked me to my core. Holding my gaze, a single finger slid beneath my panties and I whimpered when it slid inside my folds and moved up the length of me. When he reached the spot that needed him most I shuddered and closed my eyes while his finger played me like a fine-tuned instrument.

Pressing my head into the pillow, he touched and teased the bundle of nerves screaming for release. When his lips returned to my neck, I moaned and writhed as he brought me closer and closer to the edge. I reached forward and grabbed his shirt, pulling him back up to my wanting lips. He indulged my desire and pressed his lips to mine while his fingers continued their brilliant performance below. My lips parted, and his tongue invaded my mouth as his finger did the same, pushing deep inside of me. I cried in pleasure, the feeling of him inside both places left me overwhelmed and spinning with ecstasy. My body tensed and trembled as he brought me to an almost unbearable level of pleasure. Finally, the sweet release exploded from within me and I let the waves of pleasure roll over me like an ocean storm.

Quick breaths shook my body while I panted beneath him. His lips softened, gentle kisses now teasing my swollen lips. My eyes fluttered open and locked with his. Pride swelled from beneath them and a satisfied smile tipped up the corner of his lips.

"Oh, my God," I moaned, gasping to catch my breath. My head still swirled, and the buzzing in my ears almost drowned out the roaring of the jet engine. It had been awhile since I'd had an orgasm, and longer than I could remember that a man had given me one, but what I'd just experienced was more powerful than anything I could remember.

With my senses returning, I let my focus move from the satisfied throbbing between my legs back to the striking face staring down at me. Starting to feel self-conscious lying there like a boneless lump, and nowhere near ready to be done, I sat forward pressed my hand to his muscular chest. Using a little pressure, and with no resistance from him, I pushed him backward. Aiden arched a brow while he settled back against the couch.

Hoisting my dress up, I straddled him and settled down onto his lap. He closed his eyes when I let the weight of my body press down on the cock straining hard against his jeans. His lips parted, and I wasted no time in reclaiming them as my own. When my lips pressed against his, I inhaled his warm breath as he blew out a moan. Squeezing my eyes shut, I savored the taste of him and the emotions ripping through my body every time we kissed.

His hands moved up to my back, and I arched against him, pressing myself even harder against his straining member. A moan of agony and ecstasy slipped out of him and encouraged me on. Tipping my hips again, I pressed against him and took his lower lip between my teeth. He moaned again when I tugged it, nibbling on it before giving it back to him. Having this powerful man melting beneath my touch only encouraged me and emboldened me to continue. I wanted him to experience the intensity of the pleasure he gave me.

Leaning back, I drew my lips away from him. He leaned forward to follow them, but I sat upright, moving just out of his reach. His azure eyes snapped open and the intensity in them nearly sent me tumbling backward off his lap. Passion and power collided beneath the ocean of blue and threatened to explode in a tidal wave of desire.

"Emilia," he whispered, reaching up and brushing a tendril of hair from my face.

He mesmerized me, and I took a moment to stare at him and appreciate the exquisite features on his face. He was beautiful.

And he was mine.

Without warning, I grabbed his shirt with both hands. Clutching the fabric tight, I ripped my hands in opposite directions. His eyes bulged when his buttons flew, and his chest exploded into view. The smooth skin of his impossibly chiseled pecs drew my eyes first, and then my hands shortly after. I slid my palms over the bulging muscles and sat back to admire the view. My fingers traced down the distinctive lines that carved into his abdomen and formed a Photoshop worthy six-pack. The sight of his chiseled body beneath my fingertips sent the heat racing back down between my legs.

He watched me, fascinated, while I explored his body. I took my time and let my hands wander over his flawless skin before letting them descend to the part of him I wanted to explore the most. When my hand slid across the swelling in his pants, his eyes slammed shut and his head flew backward.

"Oh, God," he breathed.

I continued sliding my hand across it, moving it back and forth and up and down the length of him. His hips bucked beneath me and he strained against me, desperate for more pressure. The need to have him inside of me moved my fingers to the fastenings that kept us apart. His eyes opened and locked with mine while I undid his button and drew down his zipper with a long, slow pull. His lack of underwear allowed his cock to spring out uncontested, and I drew a sharp inhale when it burst free and came into sight even bigger than I had imagined.

I reached out and stroked it with a tentative touch. A guttural moan shook his whole body when I took him in my hand. His face twisted in pleasure as I moved my fist up and down, taking a firm hold on the shaft and finding a gentle rhythm that made him squirm beneath me. Sliding forward, I could almost feel him against my own pulsing heat, my thin cotton underwear the only thing separating us. He moved his hips, and it tipped me forward just enough that I brushed against him with my most sensitive spot. A shock of pleasure exploded out of me and I knew I needed more. I needed it all.

His eyes shot open, and I held his gaze while I inched forward. He moved his hands under my dress with blurring speed and I gasped when I felt my panties tear free. Grabbing my hips, he drew me against him. His straining skin slid along the length of me, the wetness my desire for him created allowed me to move against him with ease. Our breathing deepened as I moved closer to the tip, my need to have him inside of me growing to unbearable lengths.

"Condom," I whispered, almost too caught up to care. But in the length of my next breath, his lightning fast movement had produced a condom already in place. With eyes locked, I raised my body until I felt his cock pressing at my opening. His grip tightened on my hips and held me steady, slowly pushing me down the length of him.

Together we sighed as he slid inside, filling me in more ways than I could have imagined. Our moans mingled on a single breath, and I felt our bodies connect and fuse into one. He sat forward, pulling me into his chest and wrapping his arms around me. My arms encircled his neck, and our lips pulled together in a kiss so powerful it stole away my breath and sent shock waves rippling through every inch of my body.

Before I had time to exhale, I was up against the wall on the opposite side of the plane. The force of my back hitting the cold metal side forced the breath I held out with a groan. Aiden's body held me tight against the wall, and my legs lifted and wrapped around his waist. It pushed him even deeper inside of me and it filled the last of the ache that had been building all night.

Our mouths continued their desperate kisses while he moved inside of me. Pinned to the wall, I writhed against him, his passion and power building with each thrust.

"Drink me," I begged. I wanted him inside me in every way imaginable.

His lips left mine and our eyes met for a moment before his gaze fell to my neck. Closing my eyes while he thrust in and out of me, I felt his lips brush against my skin. His kisses trailed up my neck and I inhaled a long breath when his teeth sank into me as his cock plunged deeper inside of me, a pleasure and pain so deep I felt the world around me shift. I rode the euphoric wave his bite induced while his presence inside of me below brought me pleasure so intense I feared my body might explode. With one last powerful thrust, the power of my release sent my mind tumbling into the void, and I screamed his name while my body trembled over and over and the sweet release washed over me.

His own body tightened and then shuddered, his thrusting slowing to a stop as he held me pressed up against the wall, panting.

His fangs retracted and his lips returned to mine.

"Emilia," he whispered, his breath ghosting my lips.

His hands moved to my face and cupped it while I dissolved into his kiss. My body buzzed with a euphoria I never imagined possible. It was more than an orgasm. More than him drinking my blood. It was a connection to him more intense than anything I could have dreamed. If I had a habit of falling for bad boys before, I had flung myself off a cliff when it came to Aiden. And I had no intentions of pulling the parachute.

CHAPTER TWELVE

Aiden

HER SOFT BREATH BRUSHED across my chest while I held her sleeping in my arms. She had dozed off a half hour ago and looked so peaceful curled up at my side. I hated needing to wake her, but as my jet slowed to a stop, I knew Sheila would knock in moments to announce our arrival. I was half-tempted to tell them to leave us here so I could keep her sleeping, but the morning light crept closer by the minute. In less than an hour it would be upon us and I needed to be in the safety of my bedroom or remain trapped here in my light-tight jet until darkness.

I stroked a finger across her cheek, brushing a long piece of hair from her face and tucking it behind her ear. "Emilia?" I whispered, still pained to wake her. "Emilia, we're here. You need to wake up."

Lids heavy with sleep blinked open, and sleepy blue eyes met mine.

"Hi." I smiled while I stroked her cheek again. "How did you sleep?"

"What year is it?" She moaned and stretched in my arms.

"That good, huh?"

"So fucking good."

Now that my greatest need in life was to see her happy, I let my smile grow. "I'm glad to hear it. After such a long evening, I know you needed your sleep."

"Tonight was perfect, Aiden. I feel like it was a really crazy dream."

The whole evening had gone exactly as planned, except for the last part. The best part. Feeling her melt into my touch, and meld with my body... my soul, had been a pleasant surprise I hadn't expected. My desire for her still pulsed through my veins and drove deeper now than carnal pleasures. A need for her burned inside me now, an unquenchable fire I knew would never burn out. It started as a spark when I saw her that first night and flickered and burned brighter with every moment since. Last night the spark had exploded within me and consumed me from the inside, fueling a desire to protect her, care for her, and cherish her. I *needed* her now.

"Did you sleep?" she asked, sliding a hand across my bare chest before stopping and sucking the air through her teeth. "Oh, God, I ripped your shirt. I forgot. I'm so sorry."

"You never need to apologize for something like that. It was hot and well worth the loss of some buttons." I kissed her forehead, squeezing my eyes shut while I savored her sweet vanilla smell.

"Mark is going to kill me. I defiled an Armani. That's a capital punishment-type offense to him."

"I'll protect you."

She giggled and skootched up tighter against me. I let out a long, satisfied exhale. The knock on the door pulled our attention.

"We're here, Mr. Mackay," Sheila called from the other side.

"Do we have to go?" Emilia asked, puppy dog eyes pleading into mine. "Can't we just stay here a bit longer?"

"Well, we either need to go now or I need to close up the plane and hunker down here until tonight. It will be daybreak soon."

"Oh, shit. I forgot."

"The plane is light-tight back here so if you want to keep sleeping, I don't mind one bit."

"No, no. I won't make you sit in your jet all day while I snore."

"I don't mind at all." I stroked her hair again.

With a deep moan she pushed off my chest and sat up, a yawn and a big stretch completing the movement. She looked adorable with her tousled hair and sleepy eyes. I loved how she looked waking up, and then a pain snapped through my stomach, remembering that I wouldn't get to see her every morning. I slept all day and came awake at night. Perhaps I would have to convince her to switch to my schedule. Then I could kiss her forehead every evening when we awoke together.

"Come on. Let's get going before you turn into a human bonfire," she joked.

Together we stood and started toward the door. Before we reached it, I caught her by her wrist, yanking her back into my arms. Her mouth opened when she hit my chest, a breath escaping just before I claimed her lips as my own again. She leaned into my body, her arms encircling my neck while I pressed my lips against hers in a soft and sensual kiss. It was all I could do to pull away and not slam down the blinds and take her again on the couch.

Our lips drifted apart, and she looked up into my eyes. Her own, heavy with desire, seemed to reflect the intensity of the emotions she evoked in me. She smiled and reached down, pulling my hand into hers and leading me out of the plane and down the stairs. I felt physical pain when she released my hand as we got into the helicopter. The absence of her touch left a weight around my heart that smothered me, like being trapped beneath the water unable to come up for air. I reached over and took her hand and inhaled a deep breath when her fingers tangled with mine.

We landed at my estate and Mark waved at us from the ground, his face lit up in anticipation for how the evening unfolded. I knew he and Emilia would have a lot to talk about today while they floated around the pool sipping on Bloody Marys. A pang of jealousy shot through me, wishing I could spend the day with her floating by the pool as well. She and I would need to talk soon about how to figure out our schedules so I could see more of her than Mark. Not that I minded their relationship, in fact I was ecstatic how well they got on, but I wanted more of her time than Mark... or at least as much as she would give me.

The helicopter settled into the grass, and Emilia looked at me with a frown. "I'm not ready for it to end."

"Neither am I."

We had no time to continue the discussion because Mark pulled open the door. He yelled his greeting over the whirring of the blades thumping above us.

"I am *dying* to hear all about your trip, Birthday Girl!" he said, pulling her out of her seat then wrapping his arms around her. I climbed out of the helicopter and stepped toward her unsure of how to end the evening. I wanted to kiss her, to scoop her up into my arms and bring her back to my room, but I didn't know what to say.

Mark jutted an accusatory finger at me. "Aiden! It's almost light! And your *shirt!* What happened to your shirt? That is an *Armani!* You destroyed it!" He placed his hand on his chest and gaped in horror at the ruined shirt.

Emilia shot me a look while I tried to suppress my laughter. She knew Mark very well.

Tossing up his hands, he grumbled. "Ugh! We'll talk about your treatment of exquisite clothing later. You need to get inside. Now."

He sounded like my mother but the glint on the horizon told me I needed to move.

"Aiden! Now!" Mark pointed at the yellow light fighting its way against the darkness. I had pushed it too close today. Emilia gave me a worried nod, and I groaned when I realized they were right.

"Goodnight, Emilia," I said. With the pilots still there I couldn't use my speed to get inside, so I took off at a human paced run to get into the safety of my room. I heard the helicopter lifting off just when I got behind my bedroom doors. If they hadn't been here, I would have grabbed Emilia and whisked her away with me before she could argue. Now the light would be up, and I was trapped inside this room, and her on the other side of the door. I growled my displeasure at the situation and tossed my clothing into a heap on the floor, climbing into bed. When I woke up, we would talk about our situation and I would figure out a way to spend more time with her, because even this one minute without her seemed too many.

MY EYES SNAPPED OPEN the moment the sun disappeared. I couldn't see it, of course, but I could feel its absence. My heart pounded at the thought of seeing Emilia again and I shot out of bed and pulled on a pair of jeans and a loose shirt. Racing to my door I pulled it open to see Mark standing in his usual spot holding my newspaper.

"Good evening, Aiden. I take it you slept well?" He waggled his brows at me. His glimmering eyes told me Emilia had filled him in on the details. Suddenly, I felt nervous wondering what she had said. Mark pushed me back inside my room and closed the door. I furrowed my brow at his emboldened behavior.

"Tell me you really like her," Mark said, flopping down in the chair in the corner.

"I really like her."

"Thank God." He breathed. "If you just fucked her for the sake of fucking her, I would have to kill you myself. She's too good to be treated like a blowup doll. She's special, Aiden."

His concern for her touched me. She had grown on him in a different way, but he felt protective of her as well. I sat down on the edge of my bed and looked him square in the eye. "I'm crazy about her, Mark. No... it's more than that. I... I can't even put it into words."

A little smile pulled up on his lips. "Good. It seems like the feeling is mutual."

My eyes lit up. "What did she say?" I realized I sounded like a teenager, but I didn't care. If he knew something I needed to know. I would compel him to tell me if I needed to.

"Look at you, lover boy!" Mark laughed and slapped his thigh. "I never thought I'd see the day!"

"Mark," I warned. "What did she say?"

"Well, I won't break the bonds of girl talk, but I will tell you that she's into this. A lot. And I'm warning you to be careful with her, Aiden. She's been through a lot and if you're not *sure* about this, then you need to back off before she gets really hurt."

"I'm sure, Mark." The words fell out of my mouth without thought. "I've never been more certain of anything in my life. She's the one."

His hand flew to his heart, and he clutched his chest, big puppy dog eyes welling up with tears. "This is just so incredible. You love her."

I didn't argue, but I couldn't say it out loud, even though I felt it in every inch of my body. It still felt like a betrayal to Isobel to fall in love with another, but there was no denying that my heart had finally healed and opened up to Emilia in a way I never imagined was possible again. I wanted to spend every minute with her for all of eternity. Then, it hit me.

"I'm going to ask her to turn," I said, matter-of-factly.

"What?" Mark shot forward in his chair. "Are you fucking serious?"

"Yes," I said, standing up and letting the decision resonate. "I'm not losing her the way I lost Isobel. I can't go through that again. I'm not spending an eternity alone mourning her after she dies. I won't. I'm going to ask her if she'll turn."

"Whoa, let's talk this over. First, it's a little soon to be proposing eternity. It's more serious than marriage and you guys have had like, one fucking date. Two, there is no way you are turning her before me! I've been waiting *years!* It's not fair!"

"I'm not waiting, Mark. What if she gets hit by a bus tomorrow? Or gets sick? Or gets drunk with you and drowns in the pool?"

Mark shrugged and nodded. "Valid on the last one."

"I'm at least going to offer it to her. If she doesn't want it, I'll wait a little longer and bring it up again."

"This is a big step, Aiden. Huge. Are you *sure* she's the one? I know you guys have some serious sex chemistry, but this is eternity, Aiden. It's more than sex."

"I can't explain it, Mark. It's like she's a part of me I never knew I was missing. I can't breathe without her nearby. It doesn't make sense, I know, but this is how it was with Isobel. Instant, powerful, and all-consuming. It's just how it is when you find your person. There's no rational explanation for it. I need her."

Mark clutched his chest again. "She's your lobster."

"What?" I snapped my brow together.

"Your lobster! It's from a *Friend's* episode but... ugh, never mind! She's your lobster. Your true love."

Love. There it was again. I felt it buzzing through me and compelling me to her side. My world began and ended with her, my need for her, my undoing and my salvation all whirled into one. The spark I'd felt explode inside when we had connected flooded me with feelings so intense, I'd felt I might combust. Now they begged for release, to run wild and free me from the prison of pain and agony I had lived in for hundreds of years. Love didn't ask permission, and it didn't always make sense. When it was true and real it was demanding and unyielding until you submitted to its will. I gave up my fight and sighed.

"I love her."

"Oh, my God." Mark bit his lip. "It's amazing."

"I never thought this would happen to me again. And it's happening so fast."

"I've never made it past lust, so I can't say I have any ideas what you're feeling. The closest I've come to true love was with those fabulous Prada loafers that came out last spring." He closed his eyes and inhaled a deep breath. With a shake of his head he snapped back to reality. "But I do know I can see the difference in you. It's good, Aiden. Really good."

As the truth of his words sank in, I breathed a sigh of contentment. I was different. Happy. I was happy and smiling for the first time in centuries. The betrayal I felt for falling in love with someone other than Isobel faded when I realized she would be even happier for me than Mark was. With her zest for life and love she would have been furious watching me brood my way through the centuries, barely alive. This was the life she would have wished for me, and I knew she would love Emilia as much as I did. I could almost feel her blessing while I closed my eyes and said goodbye to her for the last time. I would always cherish our memories, but it was time to move forward and let go of the life I once had. Isobel was my past, but Emilia was my future.

"Can you—" I started, but Mark cut me off.

"Set up a romantic candlelight dinner for just the two of you? Yes, and it's already done. Emilia will be down soon."

I chuckled and shook my head. "Impressive, Mark."

"Impressive enough to turn me, too?" He waggled his eyebrows.

"We'll talk."

"Yes!" He pulled a fist to his side and followed it up with a clap. "I'm gonna make the *best* vampire, Aiden! You will love having me around for eternity!"

My laugh deepened, and I shot him a staying glance. "We'll *talk*."

"Fine, fine." He tossed up his hands. "We'll talk. Now, get off to dinner and I'll give you two lovebirds some alone time. And you two better not start excluding me all the time. If you won't turn me into a vampire so I can go do sexy vampire things myself, I'm not going to sit in a corner while you two play house. I'm more than happy to be a third wheel, but tonight... tonight is just for the two of you. You have some things to figure out, so I'll keep my distance."

"Thank you, Mark."

"Now, off you go. Her dinner just arrived and yours... well, you can drink her whenever you're ready."

Mark grabbed a book from the table. "By the way, the performance with her shitty ex last night has gone viral. Fucking brilliant." Mark grinned and gave me a round of applause. "That was without a doubt the best use of your vamp powers yet. I've had it on repeat all day."

"Your suggestion at the end really made the whole performance." I smiled back.

"It did, didn't it? We make a good team." He closed his fist and held it in the air, presumably for one of those fist-bumps, but I just rolled my eyes.

"I'll see you later, Mark."

He dropped his hand and smiled. "Go get our girl."

He didn't need to tell me twice. I moved out into the hallway and tried to stop my feet from running, the pull to see her and tell her how I felt drove me forward. I didn't have a plan other than I needed her to agree to become immortal and stay at my side forever. Not exactly a small feat when I let the weight of my request sink in. I slowed down my pace as I started to lose confidence, my mind drifting back to Mark's words. We had only been on one official date.

Sure, I'd spent time with her around the estate and our feelings for each other had grown daily since she'd arrived, including that incredible kiss in the hot tub, but if I sat down at dinner and dropped a lifetime commitment on her head tonight, she could take off and write me off as a lunatic.

I needed to slow down... and not just my pace moving toward her. This didn't need to happen tonight, and even as the thought of her mortality ripping her away terrified me, I realized I should ease her into the idea with a bit more decorum and finesse. Tonight would be about us, and instead of putting so much pressure on her, I would take my time and feel her out.

What happened between us wasn't just sex, and I was certain she had felt the connection, too. This wasn't a fling, or a whirlwind romance... it was a love that could last through the ages and sustain us through eternity. Perhaps it was a vampire thing that made it so instant and intense. It was what I had felt with Isobel, though with Emilia it was even more powerful. My brother, Lothaire, had a similar connection with his wife, Grizella. They had only known each other for two days before she'd agreed to turn and spend eternity at his side. That was over four hundred years ago and their love hadn't diminished in the slightest. Now I just had to hope Emilia felt it, too.

The clicking of Emilia's heels down the hallway pulled my attention from my spiraling thoughts, and I turned the corner and met her at the dining room entryway. She paused when she saw me, and that soft pink color rose to her cheeks and then settled down into her chest. I loved the way she looked when she flushed.

"Hello, Emilia," I said, moving toward her. She wore the black Versace gown I had picked out for her last night. It looked even better hugging her enviable curves than I had imagined. She shifted in front of me, biting her lower lip before giving me a nervous smile. God, how I wanted to kiss those lips.

Take it slow, Aiden.

"Did you sleep well?" she asked as I stepped in front of her. She pressed her back into the door frame, and her lips parted when I stepped closer. Each step I took toward her sent her heart beating faster.

Take it slow, I reminded myself, but when her gaze drifted to my lips, I lost my resolve.

Maybe just one kiss.

I slid my fingers beneath her chin, drawing her toward me. Her eyes danced with desire before closing when I leaned down and touched my lips to hers. Those familiar sparks ignited my skin, and I inhaled the sweetness of her breath as it mingled with mine. It took everything I had in me to pull my lips away and not rip off her new gown and take her on the floor.

"How did you sleep?" she asked between soft kisses.

"I slept better than I have in centuries." I smiled and pecked her lips once more. "Are you hungry?"

She leaned back and quirked a brow. "I'm always hungry. Haven't you figured that out yet?"

I chuckled at her never-ending sense of humor and gestured toward the dining room. "Please, have a seat. Mark has dinner for you on the table."

Pressing my hand into the small of her back, I escorted her to the oversized table. Even though it could seat twenty, it barely filled the over-sized dining room. For someone who never hosted guests, I certainly had the space to hold lavish parties and get-togethers. But tonight the only get-together I cared about was the one with me and Emilia.

After she sat, I pushed in her chair and moved to the other side of the table. She closed her eyes and took a deep inhale of the steam rolling off her plate.

"It smells so good," she said before picking up her fork.

"What is it?" I tipped my head, looking at the pile of noodles in a cream-colored sauce.

"Shrimp fettuccini alfredo," she responded before taking a bite. She made that "mmmm" noise while she ate, and it caused my stomach to flutter. It was the same noise she had made when I'd stroked her to climax last night, answering my question about the noises she made eating being similar to the noises she made writhing beneath me. Hearing her make them again sent my pulse pounding and my heart racing.

"Good?" I asked, leaning forward and resting my chin on a fist. Her eyes bulged while she nodded, her mouth too full of food to answer. I chuckled at her enthusiasm for eating, and once again I wondered what her meal tasted like. I could smell it, but I had tasted nothing with those smells before, so I struggled to imagine what flavors it contained. Dry bread, mutton, potatoes and root vegetables had been most of my meals before blood became my new nourishment.

"What did you want to do tonight?" I asked while she finished chewing her food.

"I'm not really picky," she answered. "I don't suppose shopping sprees in New York and brainwashing my ex into destroying his life are something we'll do every night, so you tell me what's on the agenda." She grinned before taking another bite.

"We can go for a ride. Or perhaps a swim. Or both?"

"That sounds perfect," she answered.

"Or if you prefer, I can call the helicopter and take you somewhere off premises?"

"What, like Paris?" She chuckled.

"Sure. Would you like me to call for a ride and head to the jet?"

She snorted and nearly choked on her food. "I was kidding! Are you serious? If we wanted, we could just... go to Paris?"

I shrugged and nodded. "Of course. I've even got a light-tight penthouse there. We can go anywhere in the world you want, anytime you want to go. It's a perk of having a helicopter and a private jet and a staff on standby twenty-four hours a day."

"Holy shit, Aiden. I was totally joking."

"Just say the word and I'll take you anywhere you want to go."

"That's amazing. Maybe sometime we could go to Bora Bora! I saw a special on the Travel Channel and they had these huts on the water that have glass floors. You can literally stand on the floor of your hut and stare down into the ocean. I have been dying to go! They are supposed to have the most beautiful beaches..."

Her voice trailed off, and I saw the excitement disappear from her eyes.

"I'm sorry. The sun. I wasn't thinking." She dropped her gaze back to her food.

"You don't need to apologize."

"It's going to take me awhile to remember we have to travel and explore only at night."

"Understandably," I agreed. "But never apologize. It sounds like an incredible trip. I'm sorry I can't give it to you. Perhaps I can send you and Mark without me."

Just the thought of sending her away left an emptiness in the pit of my stomach. I never wanted to deny her anything that brought her pleasure, but I couldn't survive in a glass hut, and the thought of her experiencing it without me filled me with a deep sadness.

A noise from the front of the house pricked my ears, and I tuned in to hear the front doorknob turn. Mark was in my room, and I wasn't expecting anyone else. My muscles twitched as I prepared to dart to the door, but a whoosh of air blew into the room and I saw a figure with flaming red hair materialize in the doorway behind Emilia. I blinked and saw her leaning against the doorframe examining her long, sharpened red fingernails.

"Leeya," I ground out after my lip twitched my disgust. "What are you doing here?"

"You don't call, you don't write, you don't return my texts." Her full red lips pulled down into a faux pout. "What else was I to do but come and check on you? I missed you, Aiden."

In a flash she sat on the table beside me. The short nature of her skin-tight mini dress did nothing to hide the long ivory legs she crossed seductively in front of me. She leaned over on an elbow, giving me a front row show to the cleavage pouring out from beneath the plunging black dress.

The horrified look on Emilia's face drew all of my attention and I locked eyes with her, flashing her an apologetic stare before turning my glare to Leeya.

"You need to go," I growled and pushed up from my chair. "You shouldn't be here."

"Ouch," she responded with a scowl. "Is that any way to treat your lady?"

I saw the whites of Emilia's eyes flash from across the room.

"You are *not* my lady. And I've told you many times I don't want to see you again. Now go."

"I flew all morning to be here and got stuck in my stupid jet for hours waiting for sunset. Now I arrive, and you don't even greet me with a kiss?"

She reached out for my shirt, but I stepped just out of her reach. She glowered at me and stood up, smoothing the minimal material of her skirt. "I see." She arched a meticulously groomed eyebrow. "You're still angry."

Rolling my eyes, I pointed to the door. "I'm not angry, Leeya. I just never want to see you again. Now get the hell out of my house."

"Well," she said, flipping her long wavy hair. "If you're going to be such an asshole, I'll just be going."

"Thank you." I breathed a sigh of relief and shot a staying look to my shocked Emilia.

"But before I go, you can at least offer to share your dinner. I didn't get to eat because my fucking flight attendant called in sick and I didn't have time to compel a new one. I'm starving."

Before I could respond she was across the room with Emilia's head pulled back. Her white fangs snapped out and my heart tightened when I saw the fear shoot through Emilia's eyes.

"NO!" I flashed to her side and caught her by the throat as her teeth descended onto Emilia's neck. The wall shook and exploded into rubble when I slammed her against it. "Don't touch her!"

Leeya snarled at me and I tightened my grip on her throat and slid her up the wall, holding her off the ground.

As quickly as they had appeared, she retracted her fangs and replaced her snarl with a sly smile. "Ahhhh," she cooed. "Looks like someone has a little thing for my dinner."

"You will not touch her, Leeya, or I will kill you."

"So you *do* have a thing for my dinner," she said, trying to turn her head toward Emilia, but I tightened my grip on her throat. "Isn't she a little plain for you, Aiden? Perhaps you should let me drink her dry and I'll show you what a real woman can do."

My own fangs popped out, and I snarled at her, pressing her harder into the wall again and knocking down Mark's favorite painting.

Emilia stumbled and pushed up from her chair. Mark burst into the room and skidded to a halt when he saw Leeya in my hands. His face soured, and he put his hands on his hips and glared.

"Ugh, Leech," he spat at her.

"Lee-ya," she corrected.

"Leeya-ch," he said, deepening his glare. "What the fuck is that crazy broad doing here?"

"Leaving," I growled and glared into her mischievous eyes.

"You've still got that mouthy puppy?" Leeya snickered. "I think you should let me go so I can castrate him and make a good little lapdog out of him."

"Bitch," Mark retorted and put a protective arm around Emilia's waist. "Say that to me next year when I'm a vampire! Don't think just because you're a girl I won't kick that perfect little ass of yours."

She shot him a leveling glare and then turned her attention back to me. "Well, since I'm starving and you now have *two* humans in your house I'm not allowed to eat, and your welcome was far from desirable, I think I'll be going."

"Good," I answered. "Now get the hell out of my house and never come back. If you do, I will part your head from your neck. Is that understood?"

I released her and she landed on her stiletto heels and rubbed the red mark around her throat. "Whatever, Aiden. I'm supposed to tell you that the families are convening in Scotland next month. They require your presence."

"I won't go. Now get out."

"Your brother said he won't take no for an answer."

"Well he had better keep getting used to disappointment. I'm not going... but you are. I said get out. Now."

"Fine," she spat. "Have fun with your pathetic little toys. Call me when you're done with her and ready for a real woman." She launched forward and pressed a kiss to my lips before flashing out of the room. I heard the front door slam a second later, and I took a deep breath and turned to Mark and Emilia who shared the same shocked stare.

"What the fuck was that crazy bitch doing here? She is straight outta *Fatal Attraction*. And who knocked down my van Gogh?" Mark released his grip on Emilia's waist and tossed his arms up as he headed for the painting lying on the floor.

"Emilia," I whispered and flashed to her side. "Are you hurt?"

Her mouth kept opening, but no sound came out. The color in her face had long since drained and I worried for a moment she would faint. Finally, words formed though she stammered over them.

"Who was that?" she asked.

"Leeya. A vampire."

"Those two things I put together on my own. Who is she... to you?"

I didn't want to answer that question, but I couldn't lie. "She's part of one of our ally clans." I swallowed and forced the next words out. "And I slept with her."

Though I didn't think it possible, even more color drained from her face. "Oh," she managed to say.

"It happened a few times. It was a terrible idea and she meant nothing to me. I didn't find out she was crazy until after. Now she thinks we're a couple or something and she just keeps showing up. I can't get rid of her."

"Bitch be cray-cray." Mark twirled his finger around his temple, then lifted the painting back onto the dented and cracked wall.

"I need some air," she said and stepped away from me.

"Emilia." I reached out to touch her arm, but she ripped it from my reach.

"Leave me alone."

Tears clouded her eyes, and knowing I'd caused her pain sent agony searing through my gut. She bolted out of the room and I heard the door slam when she ran outside.

"I told you that Leeya was a bad idea. She's cuckoo for Cocoa Puffs. You can tell by her crazy eyes," Mark said, pointing to his own eyes.

"Not now, Mark." I sighed and started out of the room after Emilia. This was not at all how I saw tonight going, and now I needed to find her and make sure she was all right. Not just from her emotions, but also from Leeya who may very well still be creeping around. And now that she knew I held real affections for Emilia, she wouldn't hold back on hurting her if the moment presented itself.

And no one would hurt my Emilia.

No one.

CHAPTER THIRTEEN

Emilia

I'M SO STUPID.

Running through the yard with my shoes in hand, I followed the trail leading down to the stables. I didn't even know where I was going, but I knew I needed to get out of there. I needed space, fresh air, and a place to puke in peace.

So, so stupid, Emilia.

Like dropping an anchor into the ocean, the weight of my reality sank in. The man I'd gone and fallen for was a vampire. A real live vampire! I had thrown caution and my good sense to the wind and fallen for *a fucking vampire*.

That "no more bad boys" rule I made? Not only did I ignore it, I strapped a stick of dynamite to it and lit that sucker up. It exploded, and like most explosions, it hurt like hell when it blew up in my face. I'd made the rule for good reason, and yet I tossed it aside the moment he blinked those arctic eyes at me. How pathetic that I would toss away all sense and reason for a guy. Not even a guy... a freaking vampire. And yet here I was, surprised that he had a psychotic ex-girlfriend vampire who nearly tore my throat out.

Way to go, Emilia.

When I reached the stable, I pressed my head into the cool stones trimming the walls. It felt good to combat the heat scorching through my face. All the blood that had drained at the sight of that cruel creature had rushed back in all at once and it felt like my cheeks were melting off. I stood still for a moment with my eyes closed and let the silence and cool air wash over me while I tried to slow my pounding heart. Crickets chirped in the distance, and the swaying branches in the trees above me rustled and creaked in the breeze. A branch snapped, and I spun around half-expecting to see Aiden behind me, but instead a chestnut gelding stepped toward the fence to examine me.

"Hey buddy. Nothing to be scared of. No crazed vampire bitch named Leeya here."

Leeya. Ugh. Visions of her lethal glare sent a shiver slivering down my spine. That and the thought of that perfect-looking creature tangled up with Aiden in a heated love affair. That movie-star hair, Angelina Jolie worthy lips, and legs that seemed to never end. Not to mention her boobs.

Those things couldn't possibly be real, but then again, I doubted a vampire could get a boob job.

And those eyes. I wasn't sure if it was jealousy, hunger, or both that had produced the blood-chilling gaze she'd used to penetrate me and shake me to the core. If Aiden hadn't stopped her, I would have been a bloodless corpse right now instead of a stupid girl crying alone by the stables.

Another branch cracked, and I spun around again. My heart pounded in my chest, but I saw it was only the same gelding coming even closer for inspection. It was only then I realized the greatest depth of my stupidity... I had run out alone to a secluded place when there was a jealous, blood-thirsty supermodel vampire with a hard-on for my death on the loose.

And I thought age was supposed to make you smarter. It looked like thirty was starting off with a bang in the brains department.

My anger toward Aiden didn't matter, or more-so my anger toward my bad decisions. I needed to get back to the safety of the house. I had a bedroom big enough to cry in and a closet full of clothes to wipe away my tears.

I turned to start back to the house but ran into a wall of flesh blocking my way. A scream started crawling up my throat but stopped when I heard his voice.

"Emilia," Aiden whispered, reaching out and touching my shoulder.

"Sweet Jesus! I thought you were that crazy bitch here to finish ripping out my throat!"

"You shouldn't be out here alone."

"Yeah, I figured that out, too. I may not be making the best decisions these days, but at least I come to my senses. Eventually."

"Emilia, I'm so sorry about tonight. I had no idea she was coming, and I'll make sure we never see her again. You need to know I would never let her hurt you."

His pleading eyes plucked those pesky strings of empathy surrounding my wounded heart. With the shake of my head I silenced their song and dug deep to find my resolve. Those impossibly beautiful eyes staring straight into my soul wouldn't mesmerize me again and send me racing away from my good senses.

Not this time.

"I need to go inside, Aiden," I said, breaking the eye contact in an attempt to break his spell.

"Emilia, please." He touched my chin and lifted my face to meet his. The desperation in his stare tied my stomach into a knot so tight I wasn't sure I could ever figure out how to unravel it. With a deep breath I fought to break free from the invisible tie binding us together. Like a Chinese Finger Trap, the harder I fought the tighter it got.

I made the mistake of glancing at his lips and my own parted a bit in a complete betrayal of the plan I had to end this insanity, to go find a nice boring accountant to marry and end my string of bad boys and broken hearts.

"Please don't be angry with me, Emilia." He stroked my cheek, and I pulled away, not because I didn't enjoy it, but because I did.

"I'm not angry with you, Aiden," I said in exasperation. "I'm angry at *me!*"

When I looked up into his face, I saw the confusion furrowing his brow.

"No more bad boys. That's what I promised myself. And then I had to go fall for a fucking vampire. *Literally* the baddest boy of them all."

"But I would never hurt you, Emilia. I wouldn't—"

"You're a vampire, Aiden. A *vampire*. You drink blood and you've killed people. And you have one vampire ex that I know of, and she's a crazy broad who will probably come back and kill me one of these nights. And that's just one. For all I know you have a harem of angry murderous exes because well... they're *vampires* and they kill people. And I'm a people."

"There aren't more, it's just—"

"Let me finish," I said, closing my eyes while I tried to find the strength to end this right here and now. "I know you won't hurt me, Aiden. I can feel it in the deepest part of my soul. Something awakened in me and came to life with your touch. I know you feel it, too. Something happened, and we're connected. It doesn't make sense, and it's scary, and I have no idea what's happening, but the bottom line is this can't happen. *We* can't happen."

I didn't look up into his eyes. I couldn't. One look in them and I would crumble again under the weight of his intentions.

"It's not that I don't want you, Aiden. Good God, I do. So much. But this life... the life of danger, and darkness, and secrets... I can't do it. I won't. It's too hard, Aiden."

Even though I wasn't looking at him, I could feel the pain radiating off him. It bombarded into me and shook me to my core, my shattered heart crumbling into even tinier pieces with each wave of his pain that washed over me. My own pain threatened to take me to my knees, but I fought through it and steadied my nerve.

"I need you to erase me, Aiden. Erase all the feelings I have for you and make me forget the things that happened between us. Just do it quick and then we can go on like nothing happened."

"What?" he blurted.

"Compel me to not have feelings for you and forget that we are anything other than feed bag and feeder. There is no other way I can stay here for five years feeling the way I feel and not being with you. It would crush me."

"And what about me?" he choked. "I can compel you to forget and feel nothing for me, but what about me? I'll remember everything and sit alone in my pain and agony while you march around my house without a care in the world for me? Sitting outside at sunup would be a much more humane ending for me. I won't do it, Emilia. I can't."

"Then what are we going to do?" I finally looked up and our eyes locked. That magnetic pull between us snapped on like a light.

Shit. I shouldn't have looked at him.

"Emilia." He stepped forward and slid his hand around my waist.

I froze beneath his gaze and not because he compelled me not to move. The connection between us held me fast and commanded me to stay. Powerless to resist him, I tumbled into the depths of those eyes that held me locked in an imaginary embrace.

"I know it's soon. I know this doesn't make sense. But I also know it's real. We're real. What's happening between us is special and we can't throw it away. I love you, Emilia," he whispered, pulling me closer until my body pressed up against him. His soft touch brushed against my cheek and slid through my hair. The weight of his words crushed down on me and ripped open the armor I struggled to secure.

The memory of his lips on mine haunted me. My resistance shattered when he leaned down, the slow descent of his kiss pulling the breath from my lungs until the world shook beneath me when his lips touched mine. I felt him flow through me, a connection between us like two rivers colliding in a violent crash of churning waves before blending into one and flowing together as a single soft, steady stream. He was part of me now, and I was part of him. No amount of resistance could pull us apart again, and I gave in to the power he held over me and embraced it while my arms embraced him. I plunged into his gravity and floated with him in a world all our own.

His desperation pushed into my mouth and I returned it with my own. Our frantic kiss deepened, and I moaned into his mouth, exhaling my fears and constraints, surrendering myself to his will and his life. I didn't know what the future held for us, but in that moment, I knew that we were in this together.

A strong arm swept me even tighter against his chest. I tightened my embrace around his neck while he carried me back to the barn. The cold stones felt sharp against my back when he pressed me up against them, a dull pain eased away by his kiss. I slid my palms across his chest and moved them down the tight abs rippling beneath my touch. Grabbing the bottom of his shirt, I dragged it up, sliding the soft fabric over his head. Watching his smooth, sculpted body come into view sent a shock of heat down my spine that moved through me before settling between my legs. With our eyes locked, I traced my finger along the lines carved into his stomach before spreading my fingers and sliding my palms across his chest. His eyes closed for a moment and he exhaled a contented sigh.

He opened his eyes, and his gaze fell to my breasts that lifted with every eager breath. My skin burned beneath his gaze, and I wanted to feel his hands on me and in me again. As if he could read my thoughts or feel my raging desire, he obeyed my silent command, sliding his hands along the contours of my body until they settled on my breasts. Closing my eyes, I mirrored his satisfied sigh.

When the tight fabric of my dress denied him access, he growled, and with one quick movement he spun me around, pressing my chest into the wall. His fingers traced down my shoulders to the top of the dress binding me in with dozens of small buttons. My skin shivered when his lips brushed the back of my neck. I grabbed ahold of the stones and held on tight while his lips traveled down my spine. Strong hands grabbed at my dress, and in one swift movement I felt the constraints release with the sounds of my buttons showering the ground like raindrops. The breeze blew across my exposed back and my skin prickled from the contrasting sensations of the cool breeze and his hot breath as it worked down my spine.

His hands moved to my hips and spun me around again. Stepping back, he reached up and slid his hands along my shoulders, pushing the cap sleeves of the dress while he smoothed them down my arms. My dress slid down to the ground unchallenged and piled in a heap at my feet. I stood before him in my black lace underwear, my exposed breasts rising and falling with each panting breath. He raked my body with a fiery gaze that seared my skin everywhere it went. When it settled onto my perked nipples, I bit my lower lip and pressed my body deeper into the wall.

He stepped forward and slid a hand behind my head, pulling my mouth to his hungry lips. They didn't stay long, and I whimpered when he moved them down my neck. His hands slid up my sides while his lips traveled down my neck. They met together on my breasts, his hands pushing them up into his waiting mouth. I inhaled a deep breath when his lips closed around my nipple and a gentle pull tugged it deeper into his mouth. A light flick of his tongue sent my body shuddering and then he moved to the other. My head swirled along with his tongue while he sucked and licked my stiffened peaks. When he released it from his mouth, the cold air hit the damp, warm skin and sent another shiver snaking down my spine.

He didn't give me any time to recover. I was in his arms and lowered to the ground before I could finish my satisfied breath. The damp grass cooled my overheated skin, and I relished the way the blades tickled my body while I lay sprawled out beneath him. Aiden kneeled above me, desire brewing like a storm behind his eyes. With just one look I felt my body aching for more, yearning to feel him fill me again.

Pressing my knees open, he moved between my legs while he unzipped his pants. I watched while his cock broke free, hard and straining against him, and in one swift movement he encased it with a condom. He lowered himself between my legs, and I spread them wider waiting to feel him push himself inside of me. He lowered his lips to mine, sliding his tongue into my mouth and tangling it with my own. I held his face in my hands, pulling his lips deeper into mine while I kissed him with a desperation I felt in the pit of my stomach.

The pressure pushed against my opening and I moaned into his mouth, tipping my hips to encourage him in. Slowly he slid inside of me and I ached to feel more of him, my need to have him to the hilt intensified my moan. Inch by inch he moved deeper into me until finally he thrust in with a power that caused me to inhale a sharp breath and hold it while I adjusted to the exquisite fullness. Our breaths mingled into one while he held himself there. I could feel our bodies connecting again, an energy that transcended sex and linked us together in an unbreakable bond.

He began moving inside of me and my hands slid around his back and dug into his skin, pulling him down onto me. The weight of his body pushed into me and I moved my hips to match his. We moved together as one, our bodies melding together while his pace quickened, and our passion deepened. My legs wrapped around his waist and I inhaled the soft moan that slipped past his lips.

The pressure started to build, and my body buzzed and vibrated as I began the climb back to the heights where only Aiden could bring me. His pace quickened, and my body begged for release, the pressure reaching levels that sent my senses to heights I couldn't endure. I screamed out when the release finally came, my emotions colliding and churning in a symphony of pleasure. Our bodies shuddered together as we collided, the waves of ecstasy pulled us under and tossed us around while we clung to each other until the last of the waves had passed.

We lay still tangled together in the grass, our breaths intermingling while we inhaled and exhaled, and the weight of him pressing down on me soothed me and scared me. It wasn't just the weight of his body I now felt on me... it was the weight of our life together, the weight of the decision I'd just made to give myself over to this man and all the challenges we would face. I wasn't sure if I was ready for the weight of us, but I had no choice.

I was his, and he was mine.

"I love you, too," I whispered my delayed response, pressing my lips to his ear.

He wrapped his arms around me and pulled me tightly into his embrace. I felt safe again now that my fight was over. Relief had washed over me when I'd made my choice to cast my fears and doubts aside and throw myself into this, into him, and trust that we would find our way through the confusion together.

A brisk wind blew and cut across my naked body. I shivered and pressed closer to him for warmth, but his cool skin only chilled me more.

"Are you cold?" he asked, propping onto an elbow and running a hand through my hair.

"A little," I admitted.

Before I could utter another word, he disappeared then reappeared in a second holding a thick wool blanket speckled with wood shavings and hay. He lifted me up and lay me back down on it, settling along my side and pulling me into his arms before closing the blanket in a warm cocoon around us. I closed my eyes and snuggled in deeper, savoring the feel of his skin all around my body. I didn't know what lie ahead for us, but if it meant spending my life in his arms, I would face any challenges head on. There was nothing now but this... but him. He consumed me and I would relish every second of it.

"It's all right, Emilia," he whispered in my ear. "We will figure out all the details. All that matters is that I love you and I will do anything for you. Anything."

"And I would do anything for you," I responded.

"Turn then. Become a vampire with me and we will never be apart again," he said, and the weight of his words stole away my breath. "Let me turn you."

He tightened his embrace, and I was grateful my back was to him and he couldn't see the bulging eyes that were my silent response.

Me? A vampire?

"You don't have to decide tonight but think about it." He kissed my cheek.

"I don't need time," I answered, my certainty startling me. "I can't become a vampire, Aiden. Not even for you."

"Oh." I heard the hurt in his response.

I rolled over in his arms so I could see his face. Pain and disappointment were visible in the tense lines that formed around his eyes.

"It's not that I don't think it might be amazing to be immortal, and powerful, and all those things. Trust me, I've already thought about it a lot." I touched his face and tried to soothe the sting from my refusal. "I love life, Aiden. I love food, and sunshine, and the freedom my humanity brings me. I don't want to drink blood and live in the dark."

"But you will die, and I will be left to walk the earth without you," he whispered, and I saw a glassy glare shimmer in his eyes. "I don't want to be here without you, Emilia."

"I know." I ran my fingers through his hair. "But I feel as Isobel felt. I want a human life. One single life filled with joy, pain, and eventually death. I want to savor every bite of my food and run down the beach and splash in the ocean. I don't want to live in eternal darkness, consumed by a need for blood. I don't want to turn into Leeya."

"You could *never* be Leeya," he answered.

"You don't know that. What if I lost my humanity and with it everything that you love about me?"

"I will never not love you, Emilia. Not for a single second of my existence will I not love you."

I felt the intensity of his stare consuming me again, begging me to give up my fight and submit to his desires. And the thought of spending an eternity at his side coaxed me with a crooked finger to abandon my own desires and loves and join him. But I couldn't. Not this time.

"Aiden. I gave up everything for a man once. Literally, everything. My money. My education. My passions. My time. My pride. My life. I won't do it again. I can't. I need to be me, and I need to hold on to the things that make me *me*. I love food, Aiden. Like *really* love it... more than most people. And the sun and the beach. Those things are so important to me. I know you don't understand but I can't give up my humanity for you. What if you leave me? What if you turn me into a vampire and decide it was a bad idea and now *I'm* left to wander eternity without *you?* Then what?"

"I won't leave you, Emilia! Ever!" The force of his words shook me, and I knew he meant it. But it still didn't undo the certainty I felt in my decision.

"I can't, Aiden. If you love me, you won't ask me to do this. You won't ask me to give up myself to fit with you. I can't lose myself again... not even for you. All I want is to be with you, and the rest we will figure out. And yes, eventually I will get old and my tits will sag, and wrinkles will cover my body. I'll be mortified to have you look at me when you still look like *that*." I waved a hand over his perfect physique. "But it's my choice and I need you to respect it. And I need you to love me for me and accept this. I'm going to grow old and die, and you will be left alone, and that kills me, but we will have a long and happy life together until then. It's all I can give you."

He inhaled a deep sigh and his gaze intensified while he searched my eyes. We lay there for a moment, the silence deafening while I waited for his response.

"I'll become human again," he said, his eyes locked tight with mine.

"What?" I choked out the word.

He reached forward and touched my face, lowering down for a soft kiss before propping himself back up again. "I want to be human with you, Emilia. I want to experience everything you experience. To hold your hand in the sun and rush into the ocean. Taste all the foods that draw those cute noises out of you. Let you feel warm when my arms wrap around you. And die when you die, a full and incredible life started and ended together. I won't go on without you and I don't want to miss a moment of your life while I'm locked up in a light-tight room. I want this, Emilia. I want to be human again."

My heart pounded so fast I could hear it drumming in my ears. "Are you sure, Aiden? You'd give up eternity for me?"

"There is no eternity without you." He sighed. "Not one I want to be part of, anyway."

"Aiden, this is a huge decision."

"It's time, Emilia. I've lived for over six hundred years... more than enough lifetimes that I never should have experienced. And you're right. What is the point of living forever if I'm trapped in a world of darkness and solitude? This isn't a life worth hanging on to. It's time for me to live... to really *live*. And now that I know I *can* be human I'm not watching another woman I love fade away without me. You fade; I fade. We do this together. But until then I intend to savor every second on this Earth at your side."

"Aiden," I whispered and leaned up, pressing my lips into his. "I can't believe you would do this for me."

"I'm doing this for you, and for us... and for *me*. I want this, Emilia. It's so clear to me now. You've reminded me how incredible it is to be truly alive. The only question left is... will you still love me when I'm just a human? When I no longer have my powers, my strength, my speed, and my ability to make your ex-husband humiliate himself in front of the masses? Will you still love me when I'm just a man who loves you more than life itself?"

A smile pulled up my lips, and I nodded. I grabbed his face and pressed my lips hard into his. "Yes," I whispered between kisses. "I will love you always."

"Then it's settled. I'll start the transition before the sun comes up," he said and flipped me onto my back. His smooth skin glistened in the moonlight while he towered over me. "But I want to taste you one last time before I go."

A nod tipped my head, and I raised my chin, offering him my neck. He settled between my legs and slid inside me while his fangs pierced my skin. I gasped at the intensity of the feelings and savored every second he was in me while we connected over and over again beneath the full moon until the sun demanded his return. I locked the way he made me feel into my memory while the euphoria washed over me in waves. The next time I saw him, he would be human.

CHAPTER FOURTEEN

Aiden

"YOU'RE JOKING!" MARK shouted, storming around the room. "You can't be serious, Aiden! Just like that? You're going to be human?"

Emilia sat on my lap in the living room in her torn dress. The sun neared its rise, and each second I argued with Mark wasted the time I needed to prepare for my transition.

"You can't just *turn* human! You can't give it all up, Aiden!"

"I'm not giving anything up, Mark. I'm gaining everything." I squeezed Emilia around the waist. "I'm ready to live. To *really* live."

He stopped and placed a hand on his cocked hip. "Do you even know how this works? Have you done any research? Is it safe?"

"It's not like I can Google it, Mark."

"He's right," Emilia said, turning to me. "Are you sure this is safe? Is it really just as simple as not drinking blood for a few weeks? Has anyone ever done this successfully?"

"Yes, remember? That vampire turned human after an extended fast," I said, exasperated after going in circles with Mark for the better part of a half hour.

Mark tossed his hands up in the air. "Yeah, but then what? They decapitated him just a few days later so do we *really* know if this works? Has anyone else done it?"

I shook my head. "Not that I know of."

"So, you're going to starve yourself to death... or to life, or whatever, and then we're just going to cross our fingers that you get to live happily ever after?"

"That's the plan," I said with a shrug.

Emilia tipped up my face and stared at me with worried eyes. "Maybe he's right, Aiden. I think we should wait. Let's take a breath and you can call some of your vampire friends and see if anyone has any other information on this. There must be someone."

I stifled a chuckle. "No other vampire would ever choose to be human, so I'm pretty certain I'm going to be the Guinea pig."

She brushed her fingers through my hair. "Let's just wait a few days, Aiden. There's no rush. Maybe call your family first and talk to them about it."

"I don't want to wait!" I struggled to keep my voice down. Now that I'd made this decision, I couldn't wait another second to start my new life. It would take weeks of excruciating pain to achieve my goal, and the longer I sat here arguing with them, the longer it would be before I could get started. I wanted her. I wanted life. I wanted to taste food and feel the sun on my face again. I wanted this and no amount of arguing would change my mind now. It was worth the risk. *She* was worth the risk. "I'm sorry, I didn't mean to yell."

"We're just worried about you, Aiden," Mark said, taking a seat across from me. "If you don't make it, I don't know what I'll do. You've kind of grown on me."

I smiled and nodded. "I'm touched, Mark, and you've grown on me, too. But I will be all right. I can feel it. It's calling me and I don't want to wait. Calling my family will only drive them straight to our door to rip me out of the room and prevent my change. They can't know until it's over and it's too late. In less than five minutes the sun will come up and I need to be locked in the light-tight, vampire-proof holding cell. And you're not going to let me out until I am human again."

Emilia bit her lip and shot a look to Mark before turning back to me. "I'm scared, Aiden. I don't want to lose you... I *can't* lose you. It's not worth it."

Reaching up I took her chin in my hand. "It's worth it. I'm ready to live for you. And for me."

Mark let out an exasperated sigh. "Well, if we can't change your mind, then I guess I'll go get the room ready. Do you need water? Food? I have no idea how this works."

"Just put in a bunch of bottles of water in case I need it, though the thought of drinking it still baffles my mind. But why not? My hunger will intensify as I starve, and you cannot open that door no matter what." I shot them both a serious look. "No. Matter. What. I'll kill you both in a frenzied state if you open that door before, I'm human again. I'll have no control over it. Do you understand?"

The both exchanged a worried glance and then nodded.

"I'm going in that room with some water and when I come out, I will be human. You can watch me on the video cameras to verify it's safe for me to come out. But you don't open that door until you are *sure* I'm safe. And not a second before... no matter what I say or do in there. Understood?"

"We understand. I don't like it, but I'll do it," Mark said before slapping his thighs and standing up. "I'll get the water."

"Mark," I said, stopping his exit. "I'm going to need you as a human to help Emilia while I transition. But when this is over if you still want to be a vampire, I will have someone in my family turn you. A promise is a promise."

"Well, now that you won't be my vampire side-kick I need to do some thinking on the whole subject. But thank you, Aiden. I appreciate your willingness to hold up your end of the deal and when you come out and things are settled, I will let you know my decision. I do hope that the new human Aiden/Emilia relationship is a little more careful with couture clothes," he said, raising an eyebrow at the state of her dress. "Until then I'm condemning you both to nothing but outfits from Target until you can treat clothes with more respect." He shot us an accusatory glare before walking out of the room.

Emilia giggled, and I stood up, lifting her to the ground. "It's time."

The worry danced across her face and I hated that I'd put it there. But the sun inched closer and closer to the horizon and I only had a few minutes to settle into my cell. I'd built it in case of any rogue vampire problems, something I'd dealt with often in my previous life. A life I abandoned for this simpler one a decade ago. I'd never used the cell in this house, so I could only hope it would hold under the force of my self-imposed exile. When a vampire starved, a frenzy took over, and we became feral. If those five-foot thick metal walls weren't strong enough, I could demolish them and even my love for Emilia wouldn't stop me from sucking her dry. It just gave me more resolve to end this way of life. I was ready to be human. I was ready to be hers.

Together we walked holding hands down the stairs to the basement. I pressed the hidden button on the brick wall. Bright lights illuminated a plain metal room when the door creaked opened. Mark walked up behind us carrying two cases of bottled water. He moved past me and set it in the corner of the room before stepping back out and turning toward me.

"Don't die, Aiden." He threw his arms around my neck and I paused for a moment before returning his embrace. "I'll see you on the other side."

"I'll see you soon, Mark. Take good care of Emilia while I'm in here."

"I've already got the alcohol ready. She and I will need a lot to get us through knowing you're locked in a box in excruciating pain."

"Just don't you open this door, Mark. No matter what. Not until you're *sure*."

"And how will I be sure?" He scrunched his brow.

"Well, for one, if I'm a vampire I can't drink liquids without spitting them back up. Watch me drink water through the cameras. And just use your judgement. I trust you not to open that door unless you're certain it's safe."

"You have my word," he said, and with a tip of his head he turned and headed up the stairs leaving Emilia and I alone in the musty basement.

"Are you sure?" she asked, as she slid her hand into mine. "You don't need to do this."

"I've never been more certain of anything in my life... other than my love for you."

Tears bubbled behind her eyes and burst free as she tossed her arms around my neck. "I love you so much, Aiden. Please, *please* be okay. Don't leave me here without you."

Taking one last inhale of her sweet smell, I closed my eyes for a moment before pulling back and pressing my lips to hers. "I said I would never leave you and I meant it. I will see you soon, my love."

Squeezing my eyes tight, I pressed one last kiss to her lips before whooshing into the room and slamming the door behind me. I couldn't bear to see her cry and saying goodbye for what could be a month caused me more pain than I had felt in centuries. When I slid down the wall, I wrapped my arms around my knees and waited for the pain that might take days to come. I heard the click of the lock and closing my eyes, I pictured her face and remembered my reason for doing this.

I'D LOST TRACK OF THE days a couple weeks ago when the intensity of my hunger had me screaming for release. Mark had come over the intercom and I'd heard the shaking in his voice when he'd told me he didn't think he should open the door. For a moment I'd known he'd considered it but my release would mean their deaths, so even in my state of agony I'd found the will to fight it. Her face flashed through my mind and I'd known I would kill her if I'd made it past those walls. Although every instinct in my body had shouted for me to find a way out, I'd slammed my fists on the wall and pushed back the urgency of my nature and demanded Mark ignore me.

I'd spent weeks in unbearable pain as the need for blood tore through my body. I'd writhed on the floor, crippled by the desire to feel my fangs suck every last drop of blood from someone. The insatiable desire for the coppery tang of blood on my tongue had me questioning if these walls could hold me. Instead of the blood loss weakening me, my powers and strength seemed amplified. A primal urge of survival like an adrenalin boost needed to save your own life. Fighting the urge, I closed my eyes and remembered the touch of her lips and the sound of her laugh. I just needed to fight a little harder... endure a little more.

The pain began to subside what must have been a week ago. My hunger for blood faded each day and for the past several days the need had all but gone. After spending centuries as a prisoner to my lust for blood, I no longer craved it. A foreign feeling I still struggled to process. The last time I'd felt this way was a distant memory I barely recalled. I saw the bottles sitting in the corner and felt a dryness in my mouth. And for the first time since I'd knelt by the stream in Scotland before turning, I wanted to drink water.

Walking over to the corner I pulled a bottle from the case, examining it before twisting off the cap and smelling it. Pressing the bottle to my lips I let the cool liquid fill my mouth before swallowing. It tasted good, refreshing. I waited for my body to reject it like it did when I'd tried drinking after I'd first turned. But it didn't. Not only did I not spit it up, but I wanted more. I tipped the bottle to my lips and guzzled down the rest of it, relishing the taste of something other than blood passing my lips for the first time in centuries. It didn't have much flavor, but it was one of the greatest things I had ever tasted in my life.

Tossing the bottle to the ground I rubbed my finger along my teeth and tried to extract my fangs. Nothing happened when I tried, and a wide grin stretched across my face.

I'm human.

"Mark!" I shouted up at the video camera. "Mark!"

Moments later I heard Mark's voice over the intercom. "Aiden? Are you okay?"

"It worked, Mark!" I shouted my excitement up into the little camera in the corner. "I'm human!"

"Are you sure?" he asked, the doubt thick in his voice. "How do I know you're not lying just to get out and tear us apart?"

I laughed and pointed to the water bottle on the floor. "I drank water! If I was still a vampire, I couldn't do that."

"Do it again so I can see it for myself."

I chuckled and nodded, pleased he took his job of keeping Emilia safe from me seriously. Popping off the cap I hoisted the bottle in a cheers to the camera and tipped it back, guzzling every last drop of the clear liquid before crushing the remnants and tossing it onto the floor. I opened my mouth and showed him that it was gone.

"Interesting," he said.

"And look, no fangs!" I tried to make them pop again and failed.

"You could be pretending," he argued. I couldn't see him, but I could picture his face pulled tight with skepticism.

"Mark, I promise I'm a human. I'm safe. You can open the door."

There was nothing but silence and I called out to him again. "Mark?"

Pacing the room, I waited for him to come back on the intercom. The minutes ticked by and my stomach growled. The rumble inside startled me and I looked down at it and listened again to the grumbling my newfound hunger caused. I wanted food, but it had been so long since I'd tasted it, I wasn't even sure what flavors begged to touch my tongue. I just knew I needed to eat.

The lock clicked, and I turned to the door. It cracked open, and I waited for Mark and Emilia to come in. It sat there unmoving, so I went to it and pressed it open. The darkness of the basement was a stark contrast to the lights in the room I had been under for the better part of a month. Blinking, I stepped out into the musty air and searched the room.

"Hello?" I called, and then my eyes adjusted, and I saw Mark across the room with an old wooden-handled axe in his hand. I stifled my chuckle while he shifted back and forth, ready for my incoming assault. He tightened his grip on the handle and watched me with wide eyes.

"Aiden!" I heard Emilia's voice and she raced down the stairs.

Mark huffed. "Damn it, woman! It's not safe! Get back upstairs!"

"He won't hurt me," she said, and I saw her smile when she stepped into the dim light of the lamp swinging overhead. Mark stepped in front of her and blocked her from my sight.

"Stay behind me, Emilia. We can't be sure." Mark lifted the axe in preparation for what he apparently thought would be my attack. "If he comes at us, just run up the stairs. I'll try to stop him, but if I fail, the sunlight will. Just go into the light, Emilia. And I mean the sunlight... not the ethereal one that means you died because Aiden killed you."

"Mark, I'm fine." I laughed. "I promise."

Her face peered out from behind him, and my heart raced at the sight of her. "Emilia," I breathed, stepping toward her. My arms ached to wrap around her.

"Be careful. It could be a trick," Mark whispered to her. "Don't make me decapitate you, Aiden!" he shouted at me and hoisted his axe higher.

"Aiden," she said, pushing out from behind him and bolting across the distance between us. She launched into my arms and I encircled her waist, lifting her off the ground and spinning her around. I felt her hands on my face and her lips colliding with mine while I inhaled her sweet smell. My body lit up in a way I had never experienced while we melted together, our needs and desires exploding into one.

"Oh, my God, you're okay!" she said between desperate kisses.

"I'm okay," I answered and slid my hand behind her head, pulling her lips in for a kiss so powerful that it brought me a flash of pain. It was a good pain, but the first time I'd felt pain in as long as I could remember. It felt good and made me feel... alive.

"Well, it looks like I won't be needing this," Mark said, and I heard the axe drop to the ground. "I'll just give you two a minute."

My lips were too busy devouring hers to answer him. Her skin felt softer than I remembered, and her tongue tasted sweeter. Every inch of my body blazed from her touch. It wasn't just her absence creating this feeling... it was being human. So many years as a vampire and I hadn't even realized how dull my senses were to her touch. Little electric sparks shocked everywhere her desperate fingers clawed, and I sighed my ecstasy. Every second of agony had been worth it to feel her touch and return to her arms.

"I missed you so much," I said as her kisses peppered my face.

"I missed you, too. That was so awful to watch, Aiden. I almost opened the door. I would rather have you kill me than to suffer that way another second."

"I'm so glad you didn't. I'm human again, Emilia. I'm human."

The weight of my words stilled her kisses and her eyes moved to mine, searching. Searching for the truth, searching to see into my soul, just searching. Her fingers moved to my face, a long slow stroke moved across my skin and I closed my eyes and savored the way it crackled beneath her touch.

"You're warm," she breathed.

"I'm alive. For you."

We locked eyes, and she smiled. A tear welled up and slid down her cheek. I wiped it away with my thumb and pulled her lips back to mine. The soft touch sent shivers snaking down my spine, and I knew in that moment I had made the right decision.

I wanted a life at her side. Every single second of it. I didn't want darkness to hold me captive from her again. The feeling of knowing it would end someday suddenly sank in, but it sweetened the taste of her kiss and intensified the feelings rushing through me. Knowing there was an end, an expiration date, only made each second our lips touched more special... more important. I knew now, really understood, why she wouldn't want to give this up.

"How do you feel?" she asked, pulling back to study my face.

"Better than I've felt in six hundred years." I smiled. "And do you know what I want now?"

"What?" she asked, smoothing a hand through my hair.

"I want to walk out into the sun with you."

Her eyes grew wide. "Are you sure it won't hurt you?"

"No." I grinned wider. "But isn't taking risks what being human is all about?"

She wrinkled her nose. "*Some* risks. But not the kind that cause you to burst into flames and disintegrate into a pile of ash."

"Well, there's only one way to find out." I waggled my eyebrows and took her hand in mine leading her through the dark room to the stairs.

"Are you sure?" she asked, tugging me to a stop before I opened the basement door. "It's noon, and it's really sunny."

"The good news is if it doesn't work, I don't instantly disintegrate. We'll have about twenty seconds of me engulfed in flames and screaming in agony before it happens, so just push me back down the stairs and close the door."

"Oh, that's promising." She huffed.

"I'll be fine. I'm ready." With a tight squeeze on her hand, I reassured her with my eyes.

Biting her lip she nodded. "Okay. Let's do this."

Holding her hand tight, I turned the knob. The door creaked open, and I squinted at the bright light slipping through the crack. It touched my skin, and I felt its warmth without pain. I pushed the door open and felt Emilia's grip on my hand tighten. The sunlight filling the room washed over me and I froze, the air drawn from my lungs in an exquisite release. The warmth pulled me forward, and I moved through the sunny room to the front door. Emilia squeezed my hand while I pushed it open.

Together we stepped outside, and I closed my eyes and let my head fall back while the sun's rays caressed my skin and enveloped me in their warmth. The sensations of the heat and the light were like coming to life again, a spring after a winter so long I had forgotten what it felt like to bask beneath their glow.

"It's incredible," I breathed as she stepped to my side.

"Is it what you remember?" she asked.

"It's so much better." I opened my eyes and squinted against the light. The warmth filling my face only deepened the grin spreading across it.

"Are you okay?" Mark called from behind us. I turned to see him standing with a fire extinguisher at the ready, the little black hose pointed at me while he clutched it tight in his hands.

"Really?" I asked, gesturing to the red cannister tucked beneath his arms.

"I was trying to be prepared. You never know," he argued, and then set it down.

"And the axe? Really?"

"I didn't know what to expect! If you were still a vampire, just trying to trick us, I wasn't going to let you bleed her dry!"

"You do know if I was still a vampire that axe would have bounced off my neck and I would have eaten you both anyway."

Mark rolled his eyes. "I'm pretty strong. I've been working out *a lot,* so you never know. I had to try."

"Of course, you did." I smiled and stepped toward him. "Thank you, Mark. Thank you for taking care of her and protecting her."

I threw my arms around his neck and pulled him in for a tight embrace. He froze for a moment before returning the gesture and wrapping his arms around me.

"Thank you, Mark. For everything. You are the greatest friend I could have ever asked for."

"Holy shit. Human Aiden hugs and is appreciative? This was unexpected... welcomed, but unexpected." He tightened his grip on me. "I'm so glad you're okay. You scared the shit out of us a few times there."

"I scared the shit out of me a few times, too."

We broke from our embrace and he skimmed his eyes over me. "So, this is real? You're a human again?"

I nodded and pursed my lips. "It seems so."

"Holy shit."

"Holy shit," I answered back, and we shared a chuckle.

"So, what now?" he asked, looking over to a beaming Emilia.

As much as I enjoyed these moments in the sun, I craved something else now as a human. "I'm hungry."

They exchanged a worried look and Mark took a step back. I laughed from the belly and shook my head. "No. I'm hungry for food. Human food."

"Oh." He touched his chest. "I thought for a second you were going to 'rarr!'" He lunged toward me with fake claws and a growl.

"No." I laughed. "Those days are over. I want food."

Mark swiped a hand across his forehead. "Phew! What kind of food? I'll call the girls and have them whip up whatever you want!"

"I have no idea," I said, realizing I didn't know what current food tasted like and where to begin.

"I do." Emilia smiled and stepped to my side. "Do we have a car?"

"A car? He's not going to eat a *car*, Emilia."

She laughed and shook her head. "No. I want to take him somewhere. Do we have cars here or only the helicopter?"

"We have cars." I waggled my brows. "Lots of cars."

"Where are you going?" Mark asked.

A coy smile lifted one half of her lips. "We. Where are *we* going is the question. And McDonald's is the answer."

"McDonald's?" Mark shrieked, his voice hitting notes high enough to shatter the windows. "His first bite of food in centuries and you're taking him to McDonald's? That's like shopping at Walmart when you could be at Bergdorf! He can have anything in the entire world, and you want to take him to *McDonald's?* I won't have it!" Mark stomped a foot.

Emilia just waggled her eyebrows and looked to me. "Do you trust me?"

I nodded my head. "Of course. Mark, we're going to McDonald's."

He tossed his hands in the air. "Fine! It's a tragedy to corrupt his tiny little newborn baby taste buds with peasant swill, but if you insist, then let's go."

Emilia squealed and grabbed my hand pulling me behind her through the house. I hated feeling the sun leave my skin when we disappeared into the darkness of my house. "I need more windows," I said before Mark led us through the door down the stairs to the garage.

"Sweet Jesus," Emilia said when we stepped into the garage and Mark turned on the lights. Dozens of luxury cars stretched out through the expansive underground garage, each glistening under the lights suspended from the concrete ceiling. "It's like Grand Theft Auto in here! How in the hell did I not know we had these?"

Mark shrugged. "Aiden collected them, but we didn't drive them much."

"Which one should we take, Emilia?" I turned to her. She scanned the room and then settled her stare into the corner. A big smile stretched across her face as she pointed. "That one."

Mark and I followed her finger to the Hemi Cuda convertible. She pulled me down the stairs and we wound through the endless cars until we arrived at its side. Soft blue paint wrapped around the contours of the classic muscle car, its flawless sheen glistening in the bright lights.

"The 1971 Hemi Cuda," I said, stepping back to appreciate the sleek lines that had first caught my attention five years ago when I'd bought it.

"This little beauty set us back over a million," Mark said. "And he's never even driven it." He rolled his eyes. "I have to hire someone to exercise the cars every few months."

"This is the one." Emilia slid a hand along the shiny metal and peered inside at the leather seats.

"Are you sure you don't want to take the Ferrari or the maybe the Aston Martin?"

She shook her head. "Nope. This one. I want the convertible."

The thought of riding at her side with the wind blowing in my hair and the sun beating down on my face sent my human heart racing.

"Hold on, let me grab something." Mark ran through the cars and up the stairs, returning a minute later holding three sets of sunglasses. "We're gonna need these."

I took the sunglasses from him and examined them. "Never thought I'd be needing these." I laughed.

"I'm driving!" Emilia hopped over the door and landed in the driver's seat. With a grin, I did the same, reaching my hand across the divide and letting it settle on her leg.

"I can't believe we're doing this!" Mark hopped into the seat behind us.

"Ready?" Emilia looked at me and slid the key into the ignition.

Squeezing her thigh, I nodded. "Let's do this."

She turned the key and the Hemi V8 rumbled and roared through the garage. She slid it into gear, and we crept forward to the ramp that wound out from the underground garage. When we reached the top, Mark pressed a button on his phone, and I squinted as the sunlight poured in through the lifting door.

I looked at my sunglasses then slid them on my face, turning to smile at Emilia and Mark as they did the same. Emilia revved the engine and stepped on the gas. We tore out into the sunlight, Mark screaming with his hands in the air as we launched out onto the driveway.

"Whoooo hoooo!" Emilia mirrored his shouts as we skid around the corner.

My grin was so wide I thought my newly fragile human skin might tear. When we spun out onto the road and hit top speed Emilia took her hand off the shifter and twisted her fingers into mine. Our matching smiles lit up brighter than the sun beating down on us. The wind twisted and twirled my hair and I squeezed her hand tight, never having felt so alive in my life. If this was living, I was ready to suck every last drop of joy from this world. And I was going to do it at her side.

CHAPTER FIFTEEN

Aiden

"WELL?" EMILIA ASKED as Mark's stare burned into the back of my head. I closed my mouth around the burger she had given me and felt my human teeth cut through the layers. Warm juice flowed into my mouth and I moaned when it mixed with the other flavors all somehow piled into one bite.

"Mmm..." I mumbled, my mouth full of my first bite of food in six hundred years. "This is amazing."

"See!" Emilia laughed and slapped Mark in the arm. "I told you McDonald's was the way to go!"

Mark rolled his eyes and crossed his arms. "Just wait until he gets his first bite of Kobe beef. Then we'll see who wins."

I couldn't believe the sensations the flavors sent through me. I started making noises that mimicked Emilia when she ate, and I realized now why she made them. "This is so much better than I ever expected food to taste."

Sitting in the convertible outside McDonald's under the baking sun, I devoured the burger and felt the newfound hunger rumbling in my belly subside.

"Here, a milkshake next." Emilia pushed the paper cup with the straw into my hands. Looking it over, I furrowed my brow while I studied it. "Just put it between your lips and suck."

"That's what she said," Mark whispered and chuckled behind me.

Emilia shot him a look and then doubled over in laughter. "Well played, friend."

I wrapped my lips around the plastic tube and drew a long suck. I could feel the resistance at first, and then the cold substance moved into my mouth. It startled me, such a sharp contrast to the hot blood I had consumed all these years. The shock of the temperature subsided, and I got a trickle of the incredible sweet flavor on my tongue. I'd never tasted anything like it.

Closing my eyes to appreciate the incredible flavor, I took another sip. "So, this is chocolate?" I said, savoring the way it tasted on my tongue. "It's better than the burger if that's even possible."

"Our baby is all growed up and drinking a milkshake," Mark teased and touched my shoulder.

"Shut up, Mark. You should try this. It's incredible."

He shook his head violently and sat back in his seat. "Hell. No. I've worked too hard to get my body in 'Forever Vampire Mark' shape before I change. And I won't throw it all away for a taste of that sludge."

I took another sip of my milkshake and turned to face him. "So, you've decided?"

He nodded his head. "I want it. I want to be a vampire."

I don't know why it shocked me as much as it did. This was something he had wanted for so long I shouldn't have been surprised he hadn't changed his mind based on my decision.

"If that's what you want, I'll see to it that it happens."

"Thank you, Aiden."

Emilia's lip trembled, and I saw the pain flash through her eyes. "I don't want you to die, Mark. I just got you both all to myself now. Alive. And now you're going to leave us."

Mark shook his head and leaned forward, touching her shoulder. "I'm going to change, yes. I'm going to be forever frozen in this impressive body with this perfect face." He waved a hand over himself with a smile. "But I'm coming back, Emilia. If Aiden will have me, I don't see any reason he and I can't just swap bedrooms and I'll take the light-tight one and spend weekends and summers with you guys. It will be like summer camp! But with only really cool kids!"

Emilia nodded and took his hand. "You'd better. I will miss you if you're gone too long."

"Oh, I'll be back often. Between compelling people to give me their riches, seducing supermodels and actors, and basically living like a rock star, I'm going to need lots of R&R. And pool time."

"If you leave us, who says I'm letting you come back?" I arched an eyebrow.

Mark lowered his sunglasses and leveled me with a stare. "Oh, you'll let me back in when I use my new vampire superpowers to compel your human ass to do whatever I say."

"You wouldn't dare." I lowered my own sunglasses. We held each other in a frozen stare before letting our fake glares soften into matching smiles.

"Of course not." He pushed his sunglasses back into place. "But you're not kicking me out, though, right?"

Taking another pull off my milkshake I shook my head. "Not a chance. You're stuck with us. And we definitely expect you to push us around in our wheelchairs and change our diapers when we're all old and gray."

Mark's face pulled into a sour pucker. "Eww. For the first time since I met you, I'm not attracted to you. That image will be burned into my brain for eternity." He shuddered.

Plucking a French fry from the brown bag, I popped it into my mouth and smiled while I chewed. Chewing itself was a strange sensation. It was something I'd done countless times as a human without thought. Now I paid attention to every movement of my jaw while I savored the flavors the action produced. "The French certainly do know food it seems."

"These are *not* French food, Aiden." Mark groaned. "We'll go to France and then you can find out what real French food tastes like."

"First, we're going to Wisconsin for fried cheese curds," Emilia said with a huge grin.

"Fried cheese curds?" Mark's voice hit that high note again. "Are you trying to give him a heart attack? You do know he's human again and can die?"

"A few cheese curds won't kill him." She rolled her eyes. "We'll head up to Milwaukee where I grew up. There is this restaurant called Sobelman's that has the *best* cheese curds ever! They even wrap them in *bacon!*"

"Bacon?" I tipped my head.

"Yes. And they put them in the Bloody Marys along with like a whole assortment of crazy garnishes. Like little cheese-burgers, meat sticks, and you can even get one with a whole rotisserie chicken. So good, Aiden. So good."

"A whole chicken? In a drink?"

Mark faked a gag. "I'm going to be sick."

Emilia spun in her seat. "Don't knock it 'til you try it! Sobelman's is famous for their crazy... and delicious creations. I can't wait to take you guys there."

"I vote for France," Mark argued.

Emilia huffed. "They've got a full bar you can get other drinks at."

He pursed his lips. "I do love drinks. Fine. We'll go eat the curds, drink the Bloody Marys, and give Aiden a heart attack. But then... France!"

"Do I get a say in all this?" I asked, glancing between the two of them.

"Do you have any ideas what kind of food to eat?" she asked.

With a shrug, I shook my head. "Not a clue. You're right. You two lead the way."

We all shared a laugh before Emilia turned the key and started up the engine again. "Home?" she asked, and I nodded.

We turned through the town and I stared in wonder at the world basked in light. People walked down the streets with dogs on leashes, pushing strollers in front of them.

Children played in their yards and the sounds of their laughter pricked my ears as we passed them by. You didn't see many children in the wee hours of the night. It was then I realized when I focused, I still had my special hearing. I furrowed my brow and tuned it in, listening to a child giggle as they slid down a slide a block away, but it sounded like it was beside the car.

"Whoa." I turned to Emilia.

"What is it?" she asked, letting up on the gas.

"I think I still have my powers."

"Seriously?" she and Mark asked in unison.

I couldn't feel them as readily available as they were before, but when I closed my eyes and focused, I could feel them crackling beneath my skin, faded now, but still there. They felt exactly as they had when the Picts first bestowed the gift on us. They were there, but not as powerful as they became when we drank blood and transitioned to vampires.

"Yeah, they're there. My hearing is at least."

"Well that's unexpected," Mark said.

"Let's get home and see what else still works." Emilia pressed her foot back onto the gas. We surged forward and turned down the road that led to home. I had come to terms with the loss of my powers and strength, but knowing they were still here sent a warm feeling through me. Was it possible I could have it all? I looked over to Emilia and knew no matter what, with her at my side, I already did.

After we parked the car and went into the house, I stepped out the back door to the pool area and back into the sun. I didn't want to waste a minute without it on my skin.

"Well?" Emilia asked.

I looked at the horse stable down below and clenched my jaw. With a burst I was there, and with another I was back at her side.

"Holy shit," she breathed.

"Holy shit," I responded.

"You still have your powers. How?"

"I don't know. But they're there. They aren't as accessible as they were before, I need to think about it to make them work, but I can still use them."

"That's amazing, Aiden." She reached out and took my hand. "I don't know how it's possible, but it's incredible."

"So, are you still invincible?" Mark asked, stepping into the doorway holding a pair of plain back shorts.

"I'm not sure," I said as I examined my hands. "Bring me a knife."

"Aiden," Emilia said with concern.

"Just a little nick to see if I bleed."

Mark disappeared into the kitchen and returned with a knife moments later. He placed it in my hand, and we all took a deep breath when I pushed it into my skin.

"Ouch!" I grimaced as the skin ripped and blood trickled out.

"Well, that answers that. You're no longer the Invincible Man."

"That was so strange," I said, examining the cut on my hand. I hadn't bled since before I'd turned. "It stings."

"Here." Mark pushed the swim trunks into my arms. "As requested, plain black, very 'Aideny' swim trunks with no pink and no animals. Put them on and take your lady for a swim. I'm taking a nap. Hoisting that axe around earlier took a lot out of me."

I chuckled. "Thanks, Mark."

"And be careful." He shot us a look. "He's fragile now, Emilia. Don't let him do anything stupid."

She nodded and smiled. "I won't."

Mark yawned and sauntered back into the house.

"I'm going to go put my suit on," she said, but I caught her by the arm as she turned to walk in.

"Why?" I asked, raising an eyebrow. "I'm only going to take it off."

The pink flush moved to her cheeks, and it made me smile to see it again. I had been in agony not seeing her face or feeling her touch while I'd been locked in the basement this last month.

She glanced over her shoulder to make sure Mark had gone in, then pulled her pink sundress up over her head. I watched with my heart racing as she undid the clasp of her bra and released the breasts that I wanted to take in my mouth again. My cock hardened against my pants when she stepped out of her underwear and stood naked before me.

"Your turn," she said, arching an eyebrow before diving into the pool.

I threw the shorts to the ground and ripped my shirt up over my head. Hopping on one foot and then the other, I pulled off my pants and jumped in after her. She squealed when the water from my entrance splashed in her face. Giving her no time to recover, I pulled her into my arms and crushed my lips down onto hers. Her body responded by wrapping around mine, and I moaned from the feeling her touch evoked in me. It set my skin on fire and I wondered now if she felt the same way when I touched her.

It wasn't that I didn't enjoy her touch before, God knows it was the most incredible feeling in the world. But this... this feeling was one I didn't even realize was possible. I didn't know her touch could feel any better, and yet now, as a human, I felt every nerve in my body come to life beneath her fingertips. With no desire for her blood dulling my senses, it allowed the rest to spring to life. The need she conjured in me built until I could no longer stand it. I pushed her up against the pool, turning her from me and pressing my lips into the back of her neck. For a moment I waited for my fangs to spring forth, but when they didn't come, I let my tongue trace its way along the length of her neck.

Glad she'd told me she was on birth control and we no longer needed condoms, I pressed her legs apart and grabbed my throbbing cock, plunging it up into her without warning. She cried out, and I wrapped my arms around her and drew her into me while I moved inside of her. Colors exploded in my mind as the intensity of my feelings for her reached impossible heights. Grabbing her breasts, I continued my desperate assault on her body, my need for her increasing with each thrust. The hot sun beat down on my shoulders and only amplified the heat engulfing me from the inside. If my human life ended tomorrow, in this moment I knew it was all worth it, if only for this one day. I felt her body shudder as she whimpered out her sweet sounds, and my own release crashed through me and exploded out of me in a guttural moan. I held her close while my body trembled, the last of the waves subsiding while I held her still in my arms.

"Emilia, I love you," I whispered into her ear. Her quick panting breaths slowed as she inhaled one deep one and pulled out of my embrace, turning to wrap her arms around my neck. Her answer was a kiss, long and slow, filled with passion and love, flooding me with emotions so strong I felt likely to crumble beneath their weight.

"And I love you," she whispered back between soft kisses. "Was it as good?"

"No," I said, and her eyes snapped open. "It was so much better. So, so much better."

A sweet smile pulled up her lips. "It was?"

"You have no idea." I blew out a puff of air.

"Oh, I think I do." She giggled and pecked my nose.

"I feel so alive, Emilia. For the first time, I get it. I understand why you wouldn't give this up and I'm so glad you didn't. All these centuries I thought I was living, but just these last few hours with you have shown me just how much I've been missing. I can't wait to see where this life of ours takes us."

"There's nothing stopping us now," she said, tipping her head and getting a devious glint in her eyes. "I know what I want to do next."

"Oh yeah? What's that?"

"Bora Bora."

I nodded as my smile grew. "Then Bora Bora it is."

She squealed and hopped into my arms. It drew a laugh from me while I closed my arms around her and spun her around in the water.

"I'll have Mark arrange everything," I said.

She pursed her lips and then they slid into a frown. "We're going to need to start doing these things ourselves. Soon Mark will be gone."

The thought of him not handing me my paper when I awoke caused a knot to tighten in my stomach. After all these years together, I couldn't imagine not having him ridicule my outfits and scold me for being too uptight. I was going to miss him more than I'd realized.

"I need to call my brother," I said, knowing that my hiatus from my family needed to come to an end so I could ensure they would take care of changing Mark. "My brother Lothaire will change him for me."

Emilia drew back and tipped her head. "You've never told me why you don't speak to your family. What happened?"

I sighed and slid to the side of the pool, leaning my elbows back onto the concrete. "It wasn't any one thing, really. In fact, Lothaire, my older brother, is the Chieftain of our clan now and has been for six hundred years. Our Chieftain who made the pact with the Picts was my uncle. When he died, with my father dead and no heirs, the role transferred to my brother. With the title comes certain responsibilities, as well as my place in the family as his right hand. I just didn't want to be part of it anymore. I needed a break."

"Be part of what?"

"Our clan are the original vampires, and over the years we've passed on the gift to others. Some of them formed their own clans, and though we worked together for years, eventually a battle for power began and some of the clans have been warring since. Lothaire has been locked in a constant state of battle against the opposing clans for two centuries."

"So you just left them?" she asked, a hint of judgement in her voice.

"I wouldn't say I just left them," I answered, "I was exhausted, Emilia. As Lothaire's right hand, I was forever protecting him or hunting out those who would oppose him. Every time I eliminated a threat, a new one would pop up in his place. Over and over, I would fight each time a new vampire tried to come to power and move in on us again. It was my job to torture them for information and dispose of them when I was finished. There was so much blood, so much death... I just saw no ending in sight. If I hadn't left, I would have spent the rest of eternity removing people's heads and never getting a moment's rest. So, I told Lothaire I was done and to promote someone else to my place. He didn't take it well. We had a blowout fight, he forbade the family from talking to me, I left, and it's been almost ten years since we've spoken."

"You haven't talked at all?"

I shook my head. "Not once. He's reached out a few times demanding I attend the annual clan meeting. No apology or attempt at reconciliation, just a message demanding I show up. Though at this point, I'm not sure who needs to apologize to who. But honestly Emilia, I love the quiet life. It was just me and Mark. No battles, no heads rolling past my feet, and no more fighting. It's just not who I am, and I hate being forced to live that way. Lothaire doesn't understand. Ruling and the clan means everything to him. Well, that and Grizella."

"Grizella?"

"His wife. They've been together for four hundred years and I swear their bond deepens every day."

"Four hundred years? Most couples I know struggle to make it to ten. I take it she's a vampire, too?"

"Yes, though she was human when they met."

"She changed for him?" Her eyes widened.

"On their second date," I said, laughing. "Much like us, their connection was instantaneous, and they were married on their third date. If that's not love at first sight, I don't know what is."

"I'll say. And you have a sister?"

"Yes, Annella, my baby sister. I miss her terribly, but she is a loyal clan member and abided Lothaire's command that no one speak to me. She's also a warrior, though she works in the shadows more than direct battle. She's not the kind of woman you want to bump into in a dark alley. Then there's Thorne. He's not blood family, but we were best friends since birth. After I left, he became Lothaire's right hand... a position he's perfect for."

"Sounds like your family life is complicated."

"Just a little." I laughed.

"At least you have a family," she said on a sigh.

I realized now how much she had lost and how alone she'd been when I'd found her. Her soul had been as shattered as mine. The night we'd met she'd been on her own, battling this world without an ally in sight. Even though complications filled my family and I hadn't seen them in a decade, I knew they would kill for me and stand at my side no matter what. A twinge of nostalgia twisted in my gut while I wished for the simpler days before the clan battles began. I couldn't understand Lothaire's desperate need to remain in power. I just wanted us to walk away and go back to the way things were. Let the others take over, and focus on being a family again just enjoying our existence. He wouldn't listen and eventually it drove a wedge between us too deep to withstand.

"I'm sorry you lost your family." I slid an arm around her and felt her head settle upon my shoulder. "You have me now. For always."

"Perhaps someday I can meet your other family."

"Perhaps," I said, and then realized I needed to break the news I had turned human again. Not looking forward to that conversation, I still knew it would be necessary when I explained to Lothaire why I couldn't fulfil my end of the bargain with Mark. For a moment I felt like a little boy again awaiting my father's temper when he found out I broke his favorite bow. It would be the first time in ten years we talked, and with my news, it would go badly. That much I knew. At least it wouldn't be about returning to war with him. I was human now, and that option was no longer on the table.

Goosebumps prickled my skin and startled me. Looking down I examined the little bumps on my arm, realizing I hadn't felt cold in centuries. I ran a curious finger over them.

"Cold?" Emilia asked, tipping her head.

"I think I am. It feels so strange!"

"How about the hot tub and then we'll go in and I'll figure out our trip to Bora Bora while you call your brother."

"Deal," I said before kissing her nose and swimming toward the warm water calling my name. Lothaire and my tongue lashing could wait a little longer. Right now all I could think about was spending every second of this perfect day in the sun with Emilia.

CHAPTER SIXTEEN

Emilia

I PUSHED THE LAST OF my shoes into the bag and sat on it to help it close. As I struggled to close the zipper, I smiled when I remembered where I'd be taking this suitcase.

Bora Bora.

And I was going to Bora Bora with Aiden... who was a human.

How all of this had happened was still a mystery I knew I would never solve. If anyone had told me that night in the bar that the man in the corner was the love of my life, a vampire, and now a human because of his love for me I would have called the cops and had them lock me away. And yet here I stood pushing the last of my new shoes into the bag I was taking on my vacation with him.

A human him.

"Get your cute ass down here and say goodbye!" Mark called up from downstairs.

My joy wavered for a moment knowing that Mark was leaving and the next time I saw him he would be different. *Very* different. He would be a vampire.

"Coming!" I called back and steeled my nerve to say goodbye. I'd had two days to process his leaving but knowing the time had come only ripped open the wound again. Aiden had called his brother, and after some heated words Lothaire had agreed to fulfill Aiden's promise and change Mark. Secretly, and selfishly, I had wished he'd said no so Mark would remain as he was now. My bestie. My *human* bestie.

When I made it to the bottom of the stairs, he stood in the doorway wearing a pair of Gucci sunglasses and a goofy grin.

"Well?" he asked and did a twirl. "Don't you think all those extra sit-ups and kale smoothies made a perfect vessel to cement me into for eternity?"

I chuckled and nodded my head. "You look incredible, Mark. Perfect. There will be no sexier vampire on the face of the earth."

"Damn straight," he said, and pulled his sunglasses off his face and shot them a look. "I won't be needing these anymore soon. It's too bad, really. I look fantastic in them."

"You might not *need* them, but you can still wear them inside just to make a fashion statement. Are you sure about this Mark?" I stepped to his side and pulled his hand in mine. "This is forever, Mark. Like *forever* forever."

I heard Aiden come up behind me and his arms slid around my waist.

"Well, if I don't like the blood drinking, stuck in the dark for eternity part, I can always turn into a born-again human. I get the all the good powers and none of the downsides. It seems to be working well for, Aiden."

"Just be sure this is what you want. That's all I'm asking."

He squeezed my hands. "I'm sure. This time next week I'll have compelled a few billionaires to share their wealth and I'll be making out with Ryan Gosling in my new penthouse suite."

"Mark," Aiden warned. "We don't compel people to have sex. That's just creepy."

"Puh-lease," Mark said with an accompanying eye roll. "I'm not gonna get all rapey. I only mean that I'll compel his bodyguards to grant me access to him. Once he meets me, there will be no compelling needed... he'll be begging for a taste of all this." He waved a hand over his body.

"Mark, he's straight." I laughed. "And married. To a woman. A stunningly beautiful, uber-sexy woman."

"He won't be after he meets me. Eva's got nothing on me." He waggled his eyebrows and we burst into laughter.

"God, I'm going to miss you." I threw my arms around his neck and squeezed tight. "Don't be a stranger."

"I'll miss you, too, sweetie. And don't worry, you'll be trying to toss me out of here in no time. You're not getting rid of me that easy."

Aiden stepped forward, and I released my grip around Mark's neck.

"Remember, don't agree to join the clan. Just take the blood and go live your life."

He scoffed, pressing his hand into his hip. "I have no intentions of joining some centuries-old vampire war. The only war I intend to wage is against this fucking wrinkle between my brows I will be stuck with for eternity if the Botox I'm getting doesn't survive the transition."

"Take care, friend." Aiden placed a hand on his shoulder and squeezed. "I'll miss you."

"Who would have thunk? Next week I'll be a vampire and you'll be human."

"Not in a million years," Aiden said with a chuckle.

Mark pursed his lips and I could see the quiver in his lip starting. "Thank you, Aiden. It's been an incredible ride. Now take care of my girl, okay?" He pulled me into his arms and squeezed tight.

"Forever," Aiden said as Mark and I broke our embrace.

Mark grabbed him and yanked him in for a tight hug. The two embraced for a moment before Mark pulled away and bolted out the door. I could see the shimmer in his eyes when he cast a last look back. Aiden took my hand, and we stood in the doorway and watched the helicopter take off. Mark gave a wave, and I remembered my Uber driver, Jake, and wondered if this is how he felt watching me flutter away.

"Well, it's just us now." Aiden squeezed my hand.

"I'm going to miss him." Laying my head on his shoulder, we watched the helicopter disappear into the sun.

"I need to get a message to an Uber driver and let him know I'm alive. Remind me to do that when we get back from our trip, okay?"

Aiden arched a brow. "Do I need to ask?"

"I'll tell you on our way to Bora Bora. Are you ready?"

"I'm packed and ready for my first tropical vacation."

I waggled my eyebrows. "You're going to love it."

"Not as much as I love you," he said.

"Well, obviously." I giggled and leaned over to give him a kiss.

"IT'S INCREDIBLE," I said, leaning into Aiden's embrace while our helicopter passed over Mount Otemanu. The green mountain stretched up, towering over the cerulean waters of Bora Bora. The vibrant colors of the ocean collided with the white sand beach stretching around the island. The beauty took my breath away.

"I can see the bungalows." Aiden pointed to the long dock dotted with the thatched bungalows we would call home for the next two weeks.

"I wonder which one ours is?"

"All of them," he said, turning to me with a smile.

"What?"

"I rented the whole strip of them. We need our privacy. I don't want to worry about waking the neighbors." He winked and pulled me tighter into his body.

"You are something else." I giggled.

"Was I wrong?" He cast a quizzical glance at me.

Flashes of the past few nights of our torrid lovemaking flickered across my mind and I shook my head and shot him a satisfied smile. "Not wrong at all."

After our helicopter landed the staff greeted us and we followed them down the long wooden dock to the largest bungalow at the end. We thanked them and stood side by side at the entrance to our private getaway.

"May I?" Aiden asked.

"May you what?"

Without waiting, he swept his arm beneath me and pulled me up against his chest. I tossed my head back and laughed while he carried me over the threshold.

"Amazing." I gasped. The glass floor suspended over the ocean let in a soft, aqua glow and sent ripples of light from the water flickering across the ceiling and walls. Small colorful fish darted beneath our feet and my stomach flipped from the feeling of being suspended over water.

"Okay, over-the-water-bungalow? This might be your best idea yet," he said, staring down at the view beneath his feet.

"Pretty fun being human, huh?" I traced a finger across his neck.

"This is definitely not something a vampire would enjoy."

He carried me across the crystal-clear floor and out onto the private deck that overlooked the ocean and the mountain just off in the distance. An infinity pool stretched out in front of us and reflected the bright sunlight rippling off the soft waves.

"Wow." I breathed. "It's more beautiful than I imagined."

"I never even thought to imagine something this beautiful."

"Not a bad view, huh?"

"I've got the best view in the world."

With one glance, I realized his eyes weren't staring out into the ocean with mine... they were fixated on me. My stomach flipped for the umpteenth time beneath his gaze. His talent in coaxing those little flutters from me was unprecedented, and I hoped they would never stop.

I leaned up to kiss him, but a knock on the door interrupted my attempt.

"Our bags," I said, and he slid me down to the ground.

We greeted the valet and stepped aside while he carried our bags into the bungalow. Another man came in carrying a tray with two glasses of champagne and a platter of sushi.

"Sushi! I love sushi!" I said. "You can put it out on the table on the deck."

They hurried through our bungalow and left after Aiden slipped them a hundred-dollar bill.

"There. Now it's just the two of us until morning." His sexy smiled caused my heart to squeeze in my chest.

"Sushi, Aiden. Your first bites of sushi. You're going to die."

"Isn't that raw fish?" he asked while I pulled him out to the table for two propped on the edge of the ocean.

"Yes, wrapped in rice and nori."

He grimaced while he sat down and stared at the colorful little rolls. "I grew up on lox and I hated it then. I don't think raw fish is my thing."

"This isn't lox. This is sushi. Trust me; you'll love it."

I showed him how to mix his wasabi into his soy sauce and how to use the chopsticks. When he picked up his first piece and dipped it in the sauce, I held my breath and watched while he slid it into his mouth.

"Well?" I asked while he chewed.

"Mmmmm," he murmured and closed his eyes. The happy sound deepened the longer he chewed.

"Good, right?"

After a big swallow, he opened his eyes and nodded. "So good! I had no idea raw fish could taste like that!"

I smiled and grabbed a piece myself. After dunking it in the soy I popped it in my mouth. My own sounds mimicked his while I savored the best sushi I had ever eaten.

"I love when you make that sound," he said before inhaling another piece. "You also make it when I do that thing with my tongue you like so much."

I almost choked on my sushi. With my mouth full, I couldn't respond.

"What? You do." He flashed that sly smile, and I felt the familiar roller coaster drop in my stomach.

I grabbed my glass of champagne and took a sip to wash down the sushi.

"Is this champagne?" he asked, fingering the stem of his flute.

"It is. Haven't you tried it yet?" I was thoroughly enjoying experiencing all these new tastes and this new world with him. Everything was so fresh and new, and it made me stop and appreciate things even more. I felt like I was seeing everything again with fresh eyes.

"When you drank it in New York, I was so curious what it tasted like."

"Well, now's your chance." I held up my glass and clinked it to his. "Cheers."

"Cheers." He took a sip and furrowed his brow before taking another one. "It doesn't taste at all like I imagined."

"Do you like it?"

"I love it."

"And I love you." I smiled and took another sip of my own.

His contented sigh lifted his shoulders and the look I started recognizing all too well crept inside the eyes matching the ocean surrounding us. I gasped when he appeared at my side and squealed as he hoisted me into his arms. Suddenly I was in the bed, and the sheer white scarves hanging around us blew from our speedy entrance.

He was on top of me, greedy hands removing my clothes while I pulled off his shirt. The sight of his smooth skin and rippling muscles still sent shivers down my spine. Sitting back, he let his gaze rake over my naked body. I melted beneath his stare and every nerve in my body sprung to life, desperate for his attention and touch.

The newfound warmth in his hands still shocked me and I moaned when his fingers glided down the length of my body. Sliding back up inside my legs, his fingers continued their way to the place I hoped he'd never stop touching. I slammed my eyes shut with a gasp when his fingers parted me and slid up the silky skin.

His hungry mouth discovered mine, and I inhaled him while his tongue parted my lips and pressed past them. His fingers found their way inside of me and I pressed against him, desperate for more. I reached out and found his hard shaft, gripping it in my hand. He moaned into my mouth and I moved my hand in time with his. My pleasure built, and from the way his body tensed above me, I could feel his own ready to explode.

Releasing my grip on him, I pushed him backward. He gave no resistance and settled back onto his elbows. Ravenous eyes watched me while I climbed on top of him. I met them with my own mirroring his desire as I positioned myself above him. Matching moans rolled out from us as I made my descent.

His arms wrapped around me as he sat up, pulling me deeper into his embrace and further down his cock, filling every inch of me. Holding me still, I breathed, and my body begged to move. I let my hips move against him, rocking my body against his hard chest. His grip around me tightened and held me against him while I increased my speed. He moved below me, his breathing increasing along with my own. I felt the heat building between us while I writhed above him, my arms encircling his neck as I held on tight. My body buzzed and vibrated while I rode him, moaning my excitement as I reached the highest heights. I clung to him and tossed my head back. The electricity crackled between us while our bodies exploded in unison.

We collapsed together in the bed, panting and sweating in a heap of tangled limbs.

"I think I'm going to pass out." I panted. My head swirled, and the humidity wasn't helping to cool me down. "It's really hot down here."

"I think I know how to fix that."

I scrunched my brow and turned to look at him. Eyes filled with mirth met mine, and before I could protest, I was in his arms and we stood on the edge of our deck, his toes dangling over the edge.

"Aiden!" I protested, slapping his chest. "Don't you dare!"

"Don't you want to be with me for my first dip in the ocean?" He arched a brow and peered back down at the rippling aqua water below us.

I groaned and closed my eyes, nodding my approval. Without wasting another second, he jumped. I screamed while he launched into the air. We plunged into the ocean together and the cool water shocked my senses when we disappeared below it. The force of our landing ripped us apart, but we surfaced together, spitting water and coughing. The sound of his deep laughter carried across the open ocean. I wiped the water from my eyes and smiled when I saw the joy that lit up his face like the sun itself radiated inside him.

"This is incredible!" he shouted and spun around in the water, spraying an arc of it along with him. "How have I been alive so long and never done this?"

"Well, you're doing it now." I swam up to him and slid my arms around his neck. His beaming grin closed for just a moment when he planted a kiss on my lips. It grew back to full size when he pulled back and looked at me.

"Thank you," he said.

"For what?"

"This. All of this. For bringing me to life again. For showing me what I was missing. For showing me how to live. And for loving me."

And love him I did. More than anything. I answered him with a kiss. The world around us faded from thought as we floated together on the soft waves of the sea.

CHAPTER SEVENTEEN

Aiden

"I HAVE A SURPRISE FOR you," Emilia whispered in my ear. I blinked open my eyes and rolled over to find her propped on an elbow staring at me.

"Good morning." I reached out, pulling her into my arms. The soreness in them surprised me, another new sensation brought on by two days of wild sex and swimming naked beside her in the ocean. I finally understood why Mark had griped after each of his grueling workouts. My whole body ached, though it wasn't an unpleasant feeling. Just another reminder I was alive.

Kissing her forehead, I closed my eyes and squeezed her tighter. These past two days had been nothing short of magical. The valets left food on our doorstep and we hadn't left the little bungalow except to dive into the ocean surrounding us and paddle around. Last night we had floated together beneath the shooting stars, and I was certain my heart would explode from happiness while we lay there side by side, fingers entangled as the water continued to lift us up over the gentle waves.

I saw the excitement bubbling in her eyes. "Well? What is this surprise?"

"We're going snorkeling."

"Snorkeling?" I quirked a brow.

"Yep. I chartered a boat and you and I are going swimming out in the sea."

"Does that mean we have to leave our bungalow?" I frowned.

With an eyeroll, she snuggled in closer. "We have to leave eventually."

"And see other people?"

"Yes, Aiden. We're going to interact with other humans."

My frown deepened. "I'm not ready to share you, yet. Besides, we have the sea right here."

"Aiden," she soothed. "We are going to leave this bungalow for few hours. It will be worth it. Trust me. I've never been snorkeling either so it will be a new experience for both of us."

"Fine." I sighed, but I knew she could detect the jest in my voice.

We climbed out of bed and she went to the door to retrieve the fresh fruit and juices that the staff left for us every morning. I pulled on the pair of black trunks Mark had gotten for me and felt a pang of sadness that he wouldn't be waiting at the house when we returned. He was likely getting turned in the next few days if it hadn't happened already. I had wanted to be there for him when it happened, but he had insisted he was fine and demanded we let him do this alone. The transition was brutal, and I hoped that he would get through it quickly and with ease. My good friend Thorne would be there, and I knew my brother and sister would look out for him. Still, I worried about my friend.

"The boat will be here in a few minutes." Emilia stepped into the room while she took a bite of the fresh starfruit plucked from the nearby trees this morning.

"What should I wear?" I asked, flipping through the folded t-shirts.

"You're in it," she said, looking at my shorts before quirking an eyebrow and letting her eyes move to my exposed chest.

"Just shorts?"

"Yep. We're going swimming, baby. That's all you need. And I don't want all of that covered up any more than it needs to be." She wiggled a finger at my abs.

"As always, your wish is my command." I laughed as I stepped away from the shirts.

A sheer white fabric covered her suit and left little to the imagination, yet it begged me to tear it off her body. Before I could make good on my idea, I heard the boat putter up to the dock outside.

"They're here!" she squealed and grabbed my hand, pulling me out into the bright sunshine. Two men waved us over, and we made our way to the small fishing boat. I held her hand while she stepped over the side before hopping in to join her.

"Good morning!" the Captain said in his cheery Tahitian accent.

"Good morning!" Emilia chimed back, and I gave him a smile and a nod.

"We have a wonderful coral reef for you two to explore today. It's pristine... the best in the world!"

"We're looking forward to it," I said and followed his first mate to the back of the boat where a bench seat waited for us.

He waved his hand over it. "Have a seat. Enjoy the ride and we'll be there soon."

Emilia took my hand and pulled me down beside her. Her face lit up with anticipation, her smile contagious and coaxing me to join in on the excitement. The boat puttered away from the dock before the captain pushed forward on the lever and sent us surging forward. The salty ocean water sprayed up around us and droplets splattered across my face.

At first, they startled me, and I cringed, closing my eyes against their assault. But then I heard Emilia giggle, and I peeked open an eye to look at her. The sight of her relishing the experience encouraged me to do the same. Tipping my head back, I closed my eyes and let the sun beat down on me. The wind and the water whipped across my face and I delighted in the sensations the warmth and the wind brought. A smile pulled my face up and soon I laughed with her, sucking every last drop of joy from this human moment at her side.

The boat slowed down a few miles away, and I scowled when the ride ended. I was half-tempted to offer him another hundred to take us around again.

"We're here!" he said as they dropped anchor.

Emilia hopped up and her excitement to jump in stayed my hand and reminded me what we came here to experience. This would be my first time snorkeling, so I listened closely while they explained how to put on the flippers and how to relax and breathe through the funny little tube. She slid on her fins and then pulled the blue and white mask on over her head. When she looked at me, the sight of her in the goofy getup sent a roll of laughter shaking through my body.

"Not sexy?" she asked, her voice nasally from the contraption.

"You're *always* sexy," I answered and pulled on my own fins before securing my matching mask.

When I looked at her, I saw the corners of her mouth twitch.

"It's all right. You can laugh," I said, chuckling myself.

She burst out into laughter and almost tipped back off the edge of the boat.

"Not sexy?" I asked with a smile.

"You're *always* sexy, too," she lied.

"Don't go too far," the captain said before sending us on our way.

I took a staying breath and reached out to hold her hand. Together we tipped backward off the boat and the water engulfed us. My grip on her hand never let up and together we surfaced, each sending a spout of water out of our snorkels. Her eyes and a nod of her head beckoned me to follow her, and I had no desire to be away from her, so I obeyed the silent command. Hand in hand we paddled away from the boat and I let my eyes focus on the hidden world around me for the first time. It nearly choked the air out of me.

Colors and lights flickered everywhere I looked. It was like a secret world trapped beneath the cerulean waves. Fish darted in and out of the corals, moving like one... moving like Emilia and I as we twisted and turned together, our bodies mirroring one another while I closed my grip on her hand

and tugged her closer. She turned to look at me, and I could see the smile even with the snorkel in her mouth. It was her eyes that smiled now, and they stole my attention from the beauty surrounding me. Even behind her goofy mask, she was the most beautiful thing I had ever seen.

She gestured for me to follow her through the maze of corals covered in bright plants. We turned a corner, and I saw an eel peek its head out before darting back into the safety of the dark. For a moment I felt sorry for him. I knew what it felt like to live in the dark and I never wanted to go back. But the light of Emelia's love had freed me, and now nothing could force me back into that hole ever again.

A flash of movement caught my eye, and I turned to find it but saw nothing but endless aqua blue. I saw movement again, now on the other side. But once again, when I turned there was nothing there. My stomach tightened, and I recognized the all-to-familiar sense of danger. My instinct to pop my fangs in response to a threat sprung forward, but no fangs responded to my demand. While I still had my powers, I'd forgotten I no longer had my fangs. My muscles twitched while I spun around to find the threat. Emilia looked to me with a puzzled expression. She hadn't seen the shadows and searched my face for answers.

Then I saw it. The gray shape closed in on her and the shark darted straight at her. With a bolt of power, I pushed her back just before the gaping mouth clamped down on her. The force of my blow sent her tumbling in a whirlwind through the water. As I pulled my arm out of the way, the shark's teeth sliced through my skin. Rage exploded through my other arm with a force I had never felt as I slammed a fist into its head. It spiraled and flipped through the water in the opposite direction before righting itself and swimming away.

Spinning around, I searched for Emilia. I saw her kicking toward the top just a short sprint away, so I pushed all my energy to bolt to her side.

But nothing happened.

My body didn't respond, and my speed didn't come. Gritting my teeth, I tried again, but my powers wouldn't answer. I started swimming toward her, panic gripping me that she was so far away, and I couldn't move any faster. I felt powerless while I cut through the water at an agonizingly slow pace, and for the first time I truly understood the vulnerability of being human. It wasn't fear for me I felt, but fear for *her*. Fear that the shark would come back, and I couldn't reach her in time. My heart pounded as I struggled against the water, eyes searching for the reemergence of the fish, only breathing again once I reached her.

I popped up out of the water with her, pulling the snorkel out of my mouth. "Emilia! Are you hurt?" I panted as she stared at me with wide eyes behind her mask.

She spit out her mouthpiece and took a sharp breath. "No, I'm all right."

A full body exhale washed over me hearing those words. I pulled her into my arms and held her tight while we tread water. Not only could the shark have hurt her, but the force of my blow to push her to safety could have broken bones in her fragile human body.

"We need to get back to the boat," she said, gesturing to the boat floating just a short swim away.

I nodded and grabbed her hand, searching the waves for any signs of an attack. I could only hope that my response had shaken the creature and sent it staggering away. The swim back to the boat seemed to take an eternity. Knowing I couldn't protect her tore me apart while I pulled her forward. I tried to use my powers several times on our way back, but nothing worked. My hearing picked up nothing but human levels of sound; there was no speed, no strength... nothing but human responses. I had prepared for this when I'd decided to change, but since the powers had remained even after the change I reeled from the new loss. Knowing they weren't there when I needed them only deepened the dread.

We reached the boat, and I pushed Emilia up over the edge. The captain could see the anxiety in our faces, and he reached over the edge and pulled me up. I yowled in pain when his hand slid across the bleeding gouge in my arm.

"You're hurt!" he said as I collapsed onto the floor. Blood bubbled out of the wound and ran in a red stream across the white bottom of the boat. "Get a bandage!" he shouted to his first mate.

"Aiden!" Emilia dropped to her knees beside me.

"I'm all right," I said, sitting up to examine the wound. "It's just a cut."

"From coral?" the captain asked, pulling out the bottle of disinfectant and pouring it onto the cut.

I grimaced as the liquid deepened the sting the saltwater had already started. "Shark."

His eyes bulged, and he shot a look to the first mate. "Holy shit. That's a first. They never swim around here and the rare ones who wander over never attack."

"Aren't we the lucky ones," I responded and shook my head.

"Let's get you back to shore," he said, finishing up his wrap around my arm. The pressure felt good and the throbbing subsided. I climbed to my feet and took Emilia's hand, giving her a once over before we went back to our seats.

I tried tuning in my powers the entire boat ride home, but like a dead battery in a car they refused to respond. A pang of despair settled deep in the pit of my stomach. Emilia stroked my neck, and I looked over to her, wondering now how I would keep her safe for the rest of our lives without my special powers... if I was just human. If my powers had faltered only seconds earlier, she may have been ripped from my life and I would have been able to do nothing to stop it. The pit in my stomach deepened, and for the first time I questioned my decision to become human again.

The captain dropped us off back at our bungalow after we agreed I didn't need stitches or medical attention. I'd been lucky the shark had only nicked me with a tooth rather than taken a chunk out of my arm. With ample apologies, he bid us good day and drove away. Emilia and I collapsed on the bed side by side, and for the first time since I saw that shark, I took a deep breath.

"Are you okay? Did I hurt you when I pushed you out of the way?" I asked, turning my head to look at her.

"I'm gonna have a pretty sexy bruise on my stomach, and you knocked the wind out of me, but-"

"I hurt you!" I rolled over and examined her stomach.

"*But,*" she continued, "I'm so glad you did, or I would be shark food right now."

"I'm so sorry," I whispered and looked up at her.

"Stop apologizing. Thank you, Aiden. You saved my life."

Before I could answer she had my face in her hands and she pulled my lips down onto hers. I exhaled a deep breath while I dissolved into her kiss. Knowing I had almost lost her intensified the love for her coursing through my veins. I didn't know how I would make it through this life of ours without the ability to protect her, but the taste of her lips reminded me why I had chosen to be human in the first place. I sunk deeper into her kiss and relished the sweetness of her lips.

Her hand moved up my arm and bumped the red-tinged bandage wrapped around my arm.

"Ouch," I grimaced, and her eyes shot open as she pulled her lips away.

"I'm so sorry!" She cringed and drew back her touch.

"I'm fine." I pushed through the pain and leaned back down for another kiss. "It's nothing."

"You're not fine," she argued as she sat up. "You got bit by a shark. A fucking shark, Aiden. That's not nothing."

"It's not a bite. Just a cut. I'm fine." I slid my hand down the small of her back and drew her toward me. For the first time, she pulled out of my touch. My brow furrowed in frustration.

"Aiden, we're not doing that now. You're hurt. *I'm* hurt."

"It hurts?" I asked, my frustration now turning to worry.

"A little. I don't think I have any broken ribs, but I certainly won't be up for any wild sex for a few days."

"I'm just so glad you're all right."

"Thanks to you," she said as she leaned in and pressed a soft kiss on my lips.

I wondered now if I should tell her that this may have been the last time that my waning powers would be used to defend her. I wasn't sure how she would feel about it... and I hadn't even processed how I felt about it. Perhaps they would come back. Maybe they were just on hiatus... I had expelled a lot of energy when I'd punched that shark. It hadn't happened to me before, so this was all new. I took a stilling breath and hoped that maybe this wasn't it for my heroic rescues of the woman I loved. I would wait until tomorrow to see if they replenished and tell her when I knew for sure.

"Do you know what the best thing is for pain when you're human?"

I shook my head.

"Alcohol." She waggled her eyebrows. "Lots of it."

I tipped my head and shot her a look of concern.

"We're getting hammered. Come on." Before I could protest, she pulled me to my feet.

"The brochure said there's a beach-side bar. We're going. And we're getting wasted. We just survived a shark attack. That deserves some serious cocktails."

"I don't know, Emilia." I pulled against her a bit, not sure I wanted to partake in the human experience of getting hammered.

Her lip pushed out in a pout. "If Mark was here, he would get drunk with me. But he's not... you're my Mark now. So that means you have to get drunk with me."

I chuckled and gave up my fight. "Fine. I'll be your Mark."

"Yay!" She clapped her excitement.

I followed her down the docks and we turned onto the beach. It felt spectacular between my toes. The warm white sand moved beneath me, massaging my bare feet with each step until we reached the thatched bar on the side of the beach. The salty air mixed with the fruity aromas of beach cocktails and coconuts. Island music played from the speakers above the bar and blended with the sound of lapping waves and the wind blowing through the palm trees above us.

"Welcome," the young bartender said in his thick island accent when we slid onto the rattan stools. "What can I get for you two?"

Emilia looked to me, but I just shook my head and shrugged my shoulders. "You know better than I do. What are we having?"

She pursed her lips tight and her nose wrinkled while she decided. I loved how her face looked when she was deep in thought.

"We'll do two rum runners, please," she said decidedly.

"Two rum runners coming right up," he said and spun around to go make our drinks.

"Rum runners?" I asked with a raised brow.

"Fruity and delicious. It's like vacation in a glass. You'll love it."

"I'll take your word for it."

When the bartender returned, he placed the two colorful drinks in front of us. A piece of pineapple clung to the rim and a small pink umbrella stuck out of the top of the glass.

"Start us a tab please?" she asked him, and he responded with a smile and a nod before moving off to give us our space.

I started to pluck the umbrella out from my drink, but Emilia stopped me with a look.

"Ah ah! You're my Mark right now. And Mark would *never* take that umbrella out of his drink. In fact, I'm surprised he doesn't insist on one in everything he drinks."

I chuckled and slid the umbrella back into my glass before raising it up to hers. "Cheers. To Mark."

"To Mark." She smiled and clinked my glass before taking a long swig.

When I lifted the cocktail to my lips, I was taken aback by the fruity smells. I took a small sip and my eyebrows shot up to my hairline.

"Bad? Good? I can't tell what's happening in there," she asked, circling a finger at my head.

"Do they make this by the gallon?" I smiled and then took a big drink. "It's the greatest thing I've ever tasted."

"Yay! We're getting drunk on rum runners!"

"I don't think I've ever been drunk."

"Really? Not even before you turned?" she whispered, making sure the bartender didn't hear.

I shook my head and took another sip. "No. We had ale and wine, but I never really drank a lot. It dulls the senses, and I didn't want to get caught off guard."

"So, you were always that serious, huh?" she teased.

"Yep. But not tonight. Today I'm Mark and he is *never* serious." I held her eyes while I downed the rest of my glass, slamming it back on the bar with a long sigh.

"Holy shit," she stammered. "I need to catch up."

I laughed while she slammed her drink and pushed it across the bar clanking it against mine.

"Bartender? Can we have two more?"

"Of course," he answered.

"Wait!" she shouted before he could turn away. "What's your name?"

"Jonas." He smiled.

"Jonas, I'm Emilia and this is Aiden. We almost got eaten by a shark today, so we're planning on getting wasted if that's all right with you?"

His grin grew and he nodded. "No judgements here."

"Good. Then I will need two shots of Jägermeister."

I saw the surprise on his face before it grew into an appreciate nod. "Coming right up."

"Jägermeister?" I asked her. "What is that?"

"It's the absolute best medicine for sore bodies and injuries. After a few shots of Jäger, you won't feel a thing."

Jonas returned with the dark bottle sporting a deer with an impressive rack. He placed the little clear glasses in front of us and poured out the dark liquid.

"We'll need two rum runners to chase this down," Emilia said. "It's his first Jäger," she added in a whisper.

Jonas shot a grimace at me. "Good luck." He laughed and walked away with the bottle.

"Well, are you ready?" Mirth danced behind her eyes when she grabbed the glass and raised it toward me.

"You're making me nervous," I said as I picked up my own. "And why is he looking at me like that?" Jonas eyed me with anticipation while he mixed our rum runners.

"Just drink it all at once."

I started to sniff it, but she stopped me with a stare.

"No sniffing! Just slam it!"

"What have I gotten myself into?" I laughed.

"To us." She clinked her glass to mine and a little of the brown liquid sloshed over the side.

"To us."

Holding her eyes, I tossed the Jäger down my throat. My face puckered and contorted while I spit and sputtered my response. I could hear Jonas laughing from across the empty bar, and Emilia soon joined him.

"Why would you do that to me?" I continued spatting, trying to get the last of the foul-tasting alcohol off my tongue.

"Chasers! Here drink this!" Jonas appeared in front of me, sliding the rum runner into my hands. I tossed it down my throat hoping to remove the bitter taste from the shot. The fruity liquid dulled the taste and by the time the ice cubes clinked that the cup was empty, it had finally diminished.

Emilia bit her lip, her face pulled tight in anticipation. "Are you recovered?"

I set the glass down and gestured for Jonas to grab me another. "Barely," I answered, wiping the remnants of my drink off my lips. "Emilia. That. Was. Horrible."

A laugh shook her shoulders, and she reached out and touched my hand. "It's a rite of passage. Everyone has to do a Jäger at least once in their life and make that face. But don't worry, they get better. It's an acquired taste."

"Again?" My eyes popped with the thought of tasting that horrifying liquid again. "No way. One is enough for me."

"One and done? No way. Mark would *never*. Jonas? Two more?" she called.

"Coming right up!" he answered back.

She waggled her eyebrows. "Trust me. You're gonna be begging for more of them after a few more."

"You're killing me." I laughed, shaking my head. "It's a good thing I love you and I'm powerless to deny you."

Powerless. The memory of being powerless flashed through my mind and I felt that drop in my stomach again. I tried quickly to focus my hearing, but still nothing.

"I love you, too." She snapped my attention back.

When Jonas arrived with the shot, I already felt a little warm buzzing flowing through my body from the first one. It wasn't unpleasant, and it softened my anxiety over my current situation. Perhaps Emilia was right... getting hammered was just what I needed tonight.

We clanked our glasses together and I let the bitter liquid rush through my mouth again. My face puckered, but it was better the second time.

"Jonas?" I called. "Two more."

Emilia squealed her delight and tossed her arms around my neck.

CHAPTER EIGHTEEN

Aiden

THE POUNDING IN MY head drummed me awake. "Good God," I muttered as I fought to open my eyes. It took a second for them to adjust so I could make out the shapes in the pitch-black room. Another strange thing I struggled to adapt to... the absence of my superior night vision.

With a grunt I pushed myself to sitting. Memories of our rum-filled day flashed through my mind and I cringed thinking about how many of those little brown shots I'd had. A half dozen at least. After being so against them at first, in the end Emilia was the one trying to stop me from ordering more. We'd laughed our way back to the bungalow while the sun set, and I'd realized she was surprisingly strong the way she supported my weight as we stumbled back. Her tolerance for alcohol had also been impressive. She'd, as Jonas put it, drank me under the table.

I smacked my lips together trying to rehydrate my dry mouth. Rubbing my head, I turned to check on her before getting up for water. I furrowed my brow when I noticed the place beside me looked empty. Squinting my eyes, I looked closer thinking it was just harder to see her without my night vision. The clouds moved and the full moon lit up the room. Now there was no mistaking it... Emilia wasn't in bed.

"Emilia?" I called out, pausing to listen for her response. Maybe she was just in the bathroom.

I stood up and walked across the glass floor and stopped when I saw the bathroom door ajar and no sign of Emilia inside. My pulse quickened as I looked around the room and then moved out to the deck.

Nothing.

She was nowhere.

"Emilia!" I called again, desperation trembling in my voice.

The weight of the silence answering me felt like a giant hand crushing my heart. I tried to get my hearing to work, focusing all my energy to listen for her.

Nothing.

That helpless sensation I had felt in the ocean consumed me again. I stood alone on the deck, searching the emptiness with only the sounds of my pounding heart and the lapping waves to fill the silence.

Trying to calm myself, I rationalized she likely went to shore for food or perhaps aspirin to combat our hangovers, though I wasn't sure why she wouldn't have just had it delivered. I walked back into the bedroom and saw her cellphone sitting on the dresser. Doom pierced my gut when I saw her Birkin bag propped up on the chair. There was no way she would leave it behind... she loved that bag almost as much as she loved me.

"Where are you?" I whispered as I paced the room. I closed my eyes and pictured her face. Instead of seeing her soft smile and blue eyes lit up with life, a vision of her face twisted in terror flashed through my mind and I snapped my eyes open.

The vision felt real. Like I was seeing her. I closed my eyes again, focusing all of my energy on my connection to her.

I sat back with a start when it happened again. Like the crackling of a fuzzy movie, I saw her face again for only a second. I heard her call out my name.

And there was no doubt in my mind now... it wasn't a hallucination. I had seen Emilia.

Even when I was a vampire, I had never had psychic abilities. But I was sure it wasn't just in my head. It was real and happening now.

Emilia is in danger.

And I had no idea how to find her.

Agony tore through me and I roared as I swiped the empty glasses off the table, sending them crashing against the wall. As that powerful energy pushed through me, I felt the flickering of my powers crackling back to life. My hearing picked up a noise before puttering back out. My breath trapped in my chest while I tried to do it again.

Tried and failed.

"Fuck!" I screamed. It tore through my lungs with such a force that my body shook.

Aiden!

There! I heard her again in my mind. I dug down into the rage and the pain and let it rip through me. As that energy coursed through me, my powers flickered in and out like a broken light bulb trying one last time to illuminate the room. I saw flashes of her face, heard my name, and finally...

I sensed her. Desperate to get to her, I raced to the door, my senses pulling me somewhere, though I had no idea where. I'd never experienced this before, but I knew I needed to follow the powerful pull that would lead me to her.

I ran down the wooden docks, my urgency pushing me forward while my hearing flickered in and out. Listening as I sprinted across the sand beach, I heard her. And not in my mind this time. I *heard* her. I stopped and listened, my hearing focusing in until I heard her begging... begging for her life.

Emilia. I tried to find her, but my hearing gave out again. Closing my eyes, I pictured her face, I smelled her sweet skin, and remembered the taste of her lips and the sound of her laugh. My feet moved, and I let them. This new power guided me, and I followed the pull from her down the beach and through palm trees to a winding trail that led to a small thatched hut on the edge of the ocean. I stopped, listening again.

"Don't!" she cried from inside the hut.

I found her!

A surge of power raced through me as I heard her cry out. My speed flickered on and I used it to crash through the door separating us. Splinters smashed into the walls as I skid to a stop in the small wooden hut.

"Aiden!" she shrieked when she saw me. She was tied to a chair, her hands bound behind her back. A stream of blood trickled down her swollen lip. A growl rumbled in my chest when I saw the fear in her eyes.

"Well, well, well," a sultry voice drawled from the corner. "So, it's true."

I snarled and spun to see her stepping out of the shadows. "Leeya," I growled.

"You're human. I can smell it on you. I can't believe it." Her face puckered in disgust. "How unattractive."

"Let her go," I demanded.

"Well, *almost* human," she continued, ignoring my command. "You're not quite there yet, and you're not going to be."

"What do you want, Leeya?" I glowered and stepped between her and Emilia. My power had disappeared again, and I hoped she couldn't sense it. Leeya preyed on weakness and I was anything but strong at the moment.

"I was in Scotland when your little pet Mark arrived and said you'd gone and turned human again." She crossed her arms, catching some of the long, red tendrils against her body. "I didn't believe him and needed to come see for myself."

I fought to control my panic and rage, keeping my voice calm and even. "Well, now you've seen. Just let her go and leave us be."

"Aiden." She tipped her head, her red lips pushing out into a pout. "I won't let you throw away *eternity* for this pathetic excuse of a woman." Anger flashed like lightning bolts through her dark eyes and then dissipated with a sweet smile. "I get it. I do. You think you love her." She rolled her eyes. "But you don't. And I'm not going to let you throw it all away. Throw *us* away."

Us? My mind drifted back to Mark's words along with his disgusted expression. Crazy. Completely. Totally. Batshit crazy. I just never realized *how* much until this moment.

She stepped forward, and I glanced down at my terrified Emilia before taking one step toward Leeya, hoping she hadn't sensed my weakness.

Leeya stopped her approach and leaned against the wall. "So, here's what we're going to do. You've got two choices. There is enough magic in you that you still have a chance to turn back to a vampire... back to what you *should* be. You don't have much time, but all you need to do is drink some blood and everything will go back to normal."

"I won't," I ground out with force, though her words surprised me.

I can still turn into a vampire again?

"Oh." She smiled. "You will."

"Leeya," I said, trying to soften my voice. "I'm sorry if I hurt you. I am. But I want this. I want a human life. I don't want to be a vampire again."

And I didn't.

I didn't want to slink back into the dark. I wanted the sun on my face, to feel the warmth of the rays on my skin, and hell, the taste of McDonald's in my mouth. The thought of giving it all up sent a wave of pain through me. Now that'd I'd tasted life I couldn't bear the thought of going back.

"You're only saying that because that *thing* over there bewitched you." She glared at Emilia who squirmed against her restraints. "You can either drink her blood and turn back before it's too late, or you can watch me slit her throat, I'll feed you her blood and then you'll turn back again. Your choice."

With a flash Leeya stood behind Emilia. Red nails pressed into Emilia's throat, drawing a drop of blood with the grip she held on her.

"Emilia!" I stepped forward but Leeya stopped me with a stare. I reached inside myself, clawing into my strength to reignite my powers so I could part her head from her neck before she took her next breath.

But they denied me once again.

"Don't," Emilia said, staying me with a look.

Heaving a deep breath, I raised my hands in submission. "Leeya, please... don't hurt her. We don't even know if drinking her blood will turn me back."

"Oh, but we do. It's been done before."

"It has?" I asked.

"Yes. But you don't have much time. Your powers are faltering. And if you don't... you'll die anyway!"

Emilia's eyes widened, and we exchanged a glance.

"You're lying," I said, though I lacked certainty in my voice.

"I'm not lying, Aiden." She huffed. "You'll die."

"You don't know that, Leeya," I argued.

"I do!" she shouted, her hand tightening around Emilia's neck. "I've seen it happen! Someone from my clan tried."

I took a step back when I saw rage flash through her eyes. Leeya was unpredictable at best and I knew her threats weren't empty. Real danger wrapped around Emilia's neck and if I didn't play my cards right, I wouldn't care if Leeya's prediction about my mortality was real... I would want to die beside her.

"Leeya," I said, soothing my angry voice. "Let's just talk about this."

"We don't have time to talk, Aiden. You're running out of time! I won't let you die!"

"Just take a breath, Leeya. We will figure this out. Just you and me. You don't need to kill her for us to do that."

She shook her head and I saw the frazzled tethers of her sanity shredding. "You need to drink her. Now."

"Leeya."

"NOW!"

Her sharp nail slid into Emilia's skin. The pain caused Emilia to cry out and seeing her in pain created a lump in my throat. I swallowed hard to push it back down.

"Okay, Leeya. Okay." I stepped toward her. "I'll drink from her. But you need to promise me you won't hurt her."

"You will?" she asked, surprise shaking her already trembling voice.

"Yes. I will. And it will just be me and you. Okay? Just let her go and you and I will go find someone else for me to drink. I don't want to taste her again."

Leeya raked me over with suspicious eyes. "You don't?"

"No, Leeya. You're right. She's not nearly good enough for me. I made a mistake. Can you forgive me?"

I couldn't look at Emilia. If I did, there would be no hiding my love for her and Leeya would see straight through me. I only hoped that Leeya was crazy enough to believe me.

"Do you mean it, Aiden?" Leeya asked, her grip on Emilia's neck loosening.

"I do. I'm so sorry, Leeya. I don't know what I was thinking."

"Neither do I." She sighed.

Glad my plan had started working, I tried to move toward her, careful not to spook her. She may be crazy enough to fall for my lies, but she also had a set of fangs that could end my love's life in a second if I screwed up.

"When Mark said you'd turned human, and you were in Bora Bora, I had to come see for myself. I just couldn't believe it. I had to save you. I couldn't believe you would really leave me. I thought you were coming back to me. And then you met *her*."

The anger returned to her face and her grip tightened again. I stepped forward once more. "I know, and I was so stupid. All I was trying to do was forget you and it didn't work. I still love you, Leeya. Let's just leave her and go. There's a really nice bartender I would prefer to drink. He smelled delicious. Much better than her." I crinkled my nose.

Leeya cast a hesitant look to me and then to Emilia. "You promise? You promise you'll turn back?"

"I promise," I said, holding out my hand. "Let's go."

Leeya took a happy sigh and let go of her grip on Emilia's neck.

I struggled to hide my relief. "Come on, Leeya. Come with me."

She stepped forward and then stopped. "Before we go, I need to erase her, so she doesn't tell anyone about us. Don't worry, I'll make her forget she ever met you."

My heart plummeted to my feet when she spun to face Emilia, leveling her eyes to meet Emilia's wide ones. Flashes of our time together collided in my mind, and I knew that even our love couldn't protect her from Leeya. With just a few words those memories racing through my mind would be forever ripped from hers. It would be like I never existed...

like *we* never existed. I couldn't let her erase us. No one would take Emilia from me.

The panic surged through me as she opened her mouth to speak. I felt my powers spark and crackle to life as they flooded through me. I shot across the room, my fury channeling into the hands that moved to Leeya's neck. Her eyes shot open as I lifted her into the air.

"I warned you," I growled. "I told you if you touched her again, I would part your head from your neck."

She struggled against my grip and I saw fear flicker through her eyes. "Aiden," she sputtered out. "Please. Don't."

Rage caused my grip to tighten and I choked out the words she struggled to say. Words I didn't care to hear. I'd left the life of death and destruction behind me a decade ago, but I could step back into my old position as judge, jury, and executioner one last time.

Anything to protect Emilia.

"Goodbye, Leeya," I snarled, and I saw the recognition of her impending end register in her wide eyes.

"Aiden! No!" Emilia cried out. "Don't kill her. Please. I don't want to be the cause of someone's death. I'd never, ever forgive myself."

Leeya's eyes shot to Emilia and then back to mine again. Pink hues colored Leeya's ivory skin and deepened to red as I squeezed again and cut off the last of her oxygen.

"Please, Aiden," Emilia whispered, and I heard the tremble in her voice. "She doesn't need to die. I can't watch her die."

"Then I'll do it outside." I leaned into Leeya's face and listened to the hiss of air trying to make it past my unyielding grip around her throat.

"No. Let her go. She won't hurt me again. Will you Leeya?"

Leeya tried to shake her head but I pressed her back into the wall.

"Aiden," Emilia begged. "Don't."

My shoulders lifted with my heavy breaths, and then I felt my powers fizzling out.

No. They're going. Not yet. Not until Emilia is safe.

Before Leeya could become aware of my dwindling powers, I slid her to the ground and pressed my nose against hers, my stare boring through her eyes. "There will not be a third warning. If you come near us again there is no amount of begging that will spare your life. If you or anyone from your clan harms Emilia, I will have Lothaire wipe out every last one of you. We will decimate everyone you've ever known. Is that understood?"

Leeya nodded as best she could within my grip.

Curling my lip, I narrowed my glare. "Now go. And I never *ever* want to see you again."

I released my grip, but not because I had a choice. As quickly as my powers had come, I felt them sputter out again. Leeya didn't hesitate and whooshed out of the hut, leaving me leaning against the wall for balance. The last of my strength gave out and I dropped to my knees. Not only had my powers left, but I felt weak... frail.

"Aiden!" Emilia shrieked while I crumbled into a heap. "Aiden!"

I lay there for a moment, my body trembling as I convulsed on the floor. Pain radiated through every inch of my body and stole the breath from my lungs. It felt like flames consumed me from the inside, a fire raging through my veins and searing through my skin.

"Aiden!" she screamed again, fighting against her restraints.

A powerful release washed over me, causing a violent spasm that wracked my whole body before I went limp.

"Oh my God, Aiden!" Emilia kept screaming.

The ringing in my ears subsided, and I took a sharp breath, struggling to regain my senses. Something happened to me and I didn't understand it, and I didn't have time to. I needed to get Emilia free and get us out of here before someone discovered us. Without my powers I'd have no way to compel this memory away if someone stumbled onto us here.

With a groan I pushed myself to my knees. I looked up and found Emilia's terrified eyes searching my own. The fear behind them pushed me through the ache that tore at all my muscles. I stood up, and moved behind her, fumbling with weak fingers to undo the knots securing her to the chair. The last one finally let loose and she sprang out of it, knocking the chair aside and launching into my arms.

"Emilia," I whispered as she sobbed into my shoulder. I lifted my heavy arms and wrapped them around her.

"I thought you were dying," she cried. "On the floor, I thought you'd died."

"I'm right here, baby. And I'm not going anywhere. And neither are you. I won't let anyone hurt you. Ever."

The fear I had been fighting finally settled in when I felt her lips press into mine. I'd been so close to losing her. So close to watching her die. So close to watching our love wiped away, sweeping my existence from her memory and leaving me alone in the world with her... but without her. Squeezing my eyes tight, I tried to savor every second of her touch and her taste. Twice today I had almost lost her, and I knew if I ever did, I'd plunge into a darkness deeper than I'd ever known. And one I'd never recover from.

"Are you okay, Aiden?" she asked, between kisses.

"I think so," I said, though it wasn't an honest answer. I felt different. Weak. Like something had happened to me when that last surge of power left me, and this time I knew it had gone for good. But I couldn't worry about that now. All that mattered was keeping her safe. "We need to get out of here before someone finds us."

I dug into my resolve and forced my legs to move. Each step out the door got a little easier, but it felt like sand filled every inch of my body. I couldn't let her see me falter, so I forced my muscles to keep moving. We ducked out into the darkness, looking around the empty beach before making our way toward our bungalow.

Reaching the safety of our sanctuary we collapsed on the bed. I lacked the energy to pull her close, but she crawled into my arms. It took all my power to wrap them around her, but I closed her in my embrace and pressed my lips to her head. I held her against me, and for the first time since finding her missing from our bed, I breathed a sigh of relief. She was safe in my arms again... and I'd make certain she remained that way. Leeya may still be lurking around the island, but I knew she wouldn't dare come after us again and put her entire clan in danger... even though she had shown tonight she lacked even a modicum of sanity and common sense.

No. She'd seen the promise in my eyes... the promise of the death I'd wanted to give her. The one Emilia had begged me to spare her. Because of her human nature, I understood Emilia's aversion to murder, but that didn't inhibit my vampire nature to want to finish Leeya off and assure she'd never again threaten what belonged to me.

But I'd let Emilia's pleas stay my hand, and Leeya had been spared a well-deserved death tonight, a death I had no doubt she understood would come swiftly if she disobeyed me again. With Emilia safe back in my arms, I let my concern turn to myself.

Leeya's words about my death echoed through my mind and I wanted to know what she'd meant when she'd said she'd seen it happen before. Though I didn't have those answers, I did know one thing.

Something is wrong... very wrong.

CHAPTER NINETEEN

Emilia

"TRY THIS," I SAID, offering Aiden a bite of my ice cream. He smiled and let me slide the spoon into his mouth. I waited for his signature 'mmm' sound, but it didn't come. Ever since the tragedy two nights ago, it seemed his newfound zest for life had been left behind in that hut.

"Thank you," he said flatly, and his eyes moved to stare back out at the sea.

"Are you sure you're all right?" I asked for the hundredth time in the past couple of days.

"I'm fine, baby."

His answer remained the same, but I sensed the truth. A darkness sat over him now. A sadness weighing him down that seemed to suck the joy right out of his body. It left me in knots trying to figure out the cause. I sighed and pushed my ice cream dish away. "Want to go for a swim with me?"

He scoffed. "And have you get eaten by a shark? I don't think so."

"Aw, come on, Aiden." I reached across the table and rubbed his arm. "I've got you to beat them up if they come circling around. You can wrestle a Great White for my afternoon entertainment."

"We've had enough life and death fun for one vacation, don't you think?" he answered with no hint of sarcasm.

"I was joking," I said, making no attempt to hide the hurt in my voice. "You may be able to knock a shark out of the ocean with one blow, but you bleed now. I don't want you to get in a scuff with a shark, either. But Aiden, the chances of us getting attacked by a shark twice in one lifetime, much less in one week, is literally slim to none. One could argue that we're actually safer in the ocean now than anyone else." I smiled at my own creative logic.

"It's not worth the risk."

The sharpness in his voice stung, and I stopped before I said something else to irritate him. I barely recognized the man in front of me, and even though he sat just a few feet away, loneliness settled over me while I ached for the old Aiden.

We sat together on the deck all afternoon. I read a book on my Kindle and he just continued his silent stare. The silence between us hung like a heavy fog I couldn't see my way through. It'd settled around us when he found me in Leeya's grasp and showed no signs of dissipating soon.

Leeya..

Not only had she tried to kill me, she'd tried to steal Aiden and erase my memory. If that was what female vampires were like, then I was thrilled I wasn't one of them. She was like Annie Wilkes from *Misery* and Alex Forrest from *Fatal Attraction* all blended into a new kind of super crazy. A powerful lunatic vampire crazy. But even still, I hadn't wanted to see her die.

"Are you mad I didn't let you kill Leeya?" I finally spit it out. "Is that why you're angry with me?"

"What?" He whipped his head around and stared at me. "Angry with you?"

His response was the most animated I had seen him in days.

"Well? What else would make you mope around like your dog just died? You've barely said a word to me since that night. Are you mad at me? I mean, the bitch deserved to die, I get that, but it's still murder and I'm not going to apologize for asking you to not kill a messed up chic in front of me."

He shook his head and a softness flickered inside his eyes. "I'm not mad at you, Emilia. How could you think that? Of course, I'd have preferred to kill her and remove any chance of a future threat against you, but I'm not mad you asked me to spare her life. You're a good person and I understand your aversion to violent death. So no, I'm not angry with you. I don't think I could ever be angry with you."

A small smile lifted his lips for a moment. Seeing that smile, even just a small one, sent a shiver of relief through my body. My Aiden was still in there.

"Well, I'm glad you're not mad at me for stopping you, but I need you to tell me what's going on."

His smile faded, and he turned his attention back to the spot in the sea he had been fixated on.

"Aiden." I grabbed his hand and pulled it into mine. "We're in this life together. You and me against the world. We're supposed to be partners. I can't be your partner if you won't talk to me. I can't fix it if you won't tell me what's wrong. You need to talk to me, Aiden. That's how relationships work."

I watched the breath fill his chest, and he held it there for a few seconds before blowing it back out. "I lost my powers."

"What?" I stumbled over the word.

He nodded and finally turned his attention back to me. The truth of his admission weighed heavy in his eyes.

"The day with the shark. It started then. When I punched it my powers seemed to run out. It's why I had to swim to you, and it took forever."

I was so scared that day it hadn't even registered that he didn't flash to my side like he could have. He was right... he had swum. He was fast for a swimmer, a human one, but he didn't appear at my side like Aiden would have knowing danger loomed close by.

"But you had powers when you found me with Leeya."

Shaking his head, I saw the sadness swirl inside his eyes. "They were gone... all of them. Then when I woke up and found you missing, the fear and anger I felt triggered them again, but only in small bursts. And it triggered something else... I could see you."

"You could *see* me?" My eyebrows crept toward my hairline.

"Only for a few seconds, and like a clip from a fuzzy movie, but yes. I saw you. I saw the chair, the room. I saw your eyes. And the fear..." His voice drifted off. "But I couldn't find you."

A sheen coated his eyes, and I realized now just how awful that must have been for him.

"I had no idea," I whispered.

"I was powerless to find you, and knowing you were hurt and scared—"

"But you did." I squeezed his hand. "You did find me."

He pursed his lips and shrugged.

While I tried to process his words, I struggled to make sense of everything. "If you had no powers, how did you find me?"

"You wouldn't believe me if I told you. Hell, I still don't believe it."

"I'm holding the hand of a man born over six hundred years ago. One who, until recently, was a vampire. Try me." I winked.

"I felt you. Not like with my powers or anything... I just *felt* you. You were like gravity pulling me toward you and I just followed my feet. And then there you were."

Though I knew we had a connection, something special and rare, knowing he could feel my presence even at a distance stole the air from my lungs. "You felt me? How?"

"I don't know how else to explain it," he said, his voice soft and unsure. "It's like we're connected, and I just *felt* you pulling me. Like you had tied a string to my heart and reeled me to you."

"And that wasn't one of your powers before?"

He shook his head. "I've never even heard of it as a vampire power before. I don't think it was a vampire power... I think it was just the power of my love for you."

My heart swelled with the admission. "That's incredible, Aiden."

"It certainly was. I still can't quite process it."

"Well, thanks to our love, you found me and saved me. And luckily, your powers came back on just in time. We were so close to Leeya erasing me. How did you get them working again?"

"Rage. Fear. My need to protect you. It just shot threw me like a bolt of lightning and then they left again."

"Was that what happened on the ground when you fell?" I remembered how scared I had been seeing him like that, writhing in agony at my feet and moaning in pain.

"I think so. It was like I could feel the power, the magic, leaving me. Like I was running on an empty tank of gas and I'd used up the final fumes. Now the tank is empty, and they're gone."

"Is that why you're so sad? You miss your powers?"

His jaw ticked and his eye contact deepened. "That's part of it. I hate that I can't protect you anymore. But there's more."

"What?" I said, bracing myself for a blow based on the look in his eyes.

"I think Leeya was right. I think I'm dying."

The world imploded around me. A push and a pull both crushing me and tearing me apart all at once. The air felt heavy and thick while I tried to inflate my lungs and struggled for my breath.

"You're wrong," I finally sputtered out. "You can't be dying."

"I'm weak, Emilia. I can feel myself getting weaker every day."

"Maybe you're sick... like the flu," I tried to rationalize.

"I've been sitting here for two days waiting for other explanations, but the fact-of-the-matter is that something happened to me that night on the beach. I felt it leave, Emilia. The magic. The magic that started this curse in the first place. It's gone. And without it, what happens? I think Leeya was right and I've been trying to figure out how to tell you."

Tears slid down my face before I even realized I was crying. "You're not leaving me, Aiden. I won't let you. We will figure this out."

He shook his head. "I don't think we can, Emilia."

"You're not leaving me, Aiden!" I shouted, pushing up from the table and storming to the edge of the deck. I heard him come up behind me, and he wrapped his arms around me. Closing my eyes, I let the feel of his touch saturate my skin. I listened to his breathing in my ear and savored the sound. "I won't let you die. Please don't leave me, Aiden."

"I love you, Emilia. And even if this kills me, I just want you to know I would make this choice over and over and *over* again. I would choose life. I would choose you. Every. Single. Time. These past days have been happier than any I've had in six hundred years. You were right when you said you'd rather live a short life filled with love and light rather than an eternity locked in the dark alone. You were right. I've lived longer than I should have, and perhaps this is just my time."

"But I just found you," I said with a trembling voice. "And if you leave me, then what is there for me? A lifetime alone in the dark."

"I don't want to leave you. I *want* to stay here with you, but I think the magic is gone and with it, my unnaturally long life is coming to an end."

"So, what? You intend to just sit here and stare at the ocean until you die?" I spun around, my anger now colliding with my devastation. "If you want to *protect* me and take care of me, then you'll fight, Aiden! You'll do whatever it takes to stay at my side!"

"I... I don't know what to do. I don't think there's anything I *can* do!"

"You don't *think?* I need you to *know* there's nothing you can do. And until you *know,* then I won't accept this. I won't accept you just giving up. If you really love me, then you will pick up that phone and call your fucking brother. Leeya knew something about this... maybe they will know something, too. And if they don't know, he's the fucking leader of the vampires. He can find someone who does!"

His eyes were wide with shock when he stared back at me.

"You're not leaving me without a fight, Aiden. Call your brother."

He bit his lower lip and took a breath before a nod tipped his head up and down. "I'm scared, Emilia. I don't want to leave you."

I threw my arms around his neck and buried my head in his shoulder. "Then fight for me, Aiden. Fight *with* me. Let's face this together. And we're not giving up until the last breath slips past those lips I need to kiss."

"Okay," he breathed.

The sound of his agreement forced my eyes shut. Tears pushed through and streamed down my cheeks, pooling on his shirt. He tightened his embrace and pressed his lips to my forehead before pulling out of my arms.

"Where are you going?" I asked, wiping the tears from my cheeks.

"To call my brother."

He walked to the door of our bungalow, stopping and turning to me. "I love you and I will fight for you... for us."

I stood trembling on the deck, a fear I didn't recognize gripping me tight. Aiden reappeared in the doorway his phone pressed to his ear. He held my eyes, and we stood frozen in a locked stare.

"Lothaire? It's Aiden. I need your help."

With those words I closed my eyes and for the first time in a lot of years I prayed.

CHAPTER TWENTY

Aiden

STARING OUT THE HELICOPTER window I felt a sense of nostalgia watching the lush, green rolling hills of my homeland passing beneath us. A green blanket woven by nature and unspoiled by development spread out in every direction, with small creeks cutting across the rugged terrain. Even after the sun had set as we got closer to our destination, to my family home, you could still see the colors and the beauty beneath the bright moon.

"It's beautiful," Emilia whispered, leaning closer to the window. She pressed her hand on my thigh and I stifled a groan from the pain her touch caused. Everything ached. Every bone. Every muscle. Even my skin hurt.

"This is my homeland. Welcome to *Dùthaich Mhic Aoidh*... Mackay Country," I answered, pushing the pain back into the box I had been forcing it into. I wouldn't miss a second of her touch, not even if it brought me agony. Deteriorating at lightning speed, my body might not be able to savor her touch much longer.

"You were so lucky to grow up out here. I can't imagine having that much freedom."

"It was a different time back then... a very different time. But things still look the same. It's remarkable."

"When was the last time you were here?"

"It's been fifteen years at least. Our clan doesn't spend a lot of time here anymore. They are mostly in London, Edinburgh and Norway."

"Norway?"

"They have polar nights there... months of pure darkness. Norway is basically vampire Disneyland several months a year."

"Yikes." She cringed. "And no one knows?"

"We're pretty good at keeping our nature to ourselves... and compelling away the memories to any who discover us so yes... no one knows."

"The things you learn."

I recognized the mountain near our family estate in Mackay Country. My stomach clenched into a ball realizing we'd reached our destination when the helicopter began its descent. Lothaire would be waiting, and from the tongue lashing I'd received on the phone, I wasn't sure what to expect. Even though I had been his enforcer and saturated these lands in blood, he remained my big brother who could make me feel like a small child beneath his disapproving stare.

The stone estate perched atop the tallest hill came into view as the helicopter turned. More of a castle than a mansion, the estate had been in our family now for several hundred years. We'd spent little time here in the past century, but something about it always felt like home.

"We're here," I said with a deep breath when the helicopter settled to the ground. "Are you ready?"

Emilia nodded, but the worry lines creased into her skin gave her fear away. Well placed fear. She was walking into a clan of vampires... pissed off vampires. And I had little doubt in my mind that the fault for my decision would land squarely on her shoulders... though nothing could be further from the truth. Turning human had been my decision but getting them to understand that would be difficult. At least I trusted that they wouldn't hurt her, no matter how angry they were.

The co-pilot stepped out and opened the door. The wind from the blades blew back my hair when we ducked out beneath them. Pulling her out of their whirlwind, I squeezed her hand when I stood up straight. My family stood in a line under the lights illuminating the helicopter pad. A row of fixed eyes bore through me before all turning to the woman clinging to my side. Emilia shrunk a little and pushed in closer. I cringed at the pressure she put on my side but fought through and put a protective arm around her shoulders.

We stood while the helicopter lifted off, the deafening sound of the blades finally thumping away into the distance. I opened my mouth to speak, but before I could, a flash of color exploded and my sister, Annella, appeared in front of me. Before I could breathe, she threw her arms around my neck, a pull so tight I thought my newly fragile bones might break. Her dark hair, the same color as my own but with a slight auburn hue, smothered my mouth when she pressed into me.

"Dammit, Aiden! I missed you, you stupid arse!"

Her excitement at my arrival surprised me. I'd expected anger. It took a moment for my free hand to respond and wrap around her tiny figure.

"I missed you, too," I said, and I meant it. She was my little sister, and we shared a special connection. Tearing myself from the family was hard, but not seeing Annella had been excruciating.

She pulled back out of my grip and looked up at me with those bright blue eyes that looked just like my mother's. The two could have been twins. They shared the same delicate features, including full lips along with ivory skin and wide-set eyes. But though she appeared sweet and fragile, Annella could easily tear apart a man twice her size. Even the strongest vampire foes had proved little challenge for her... and their underestimation of her strength had been the last mistake they'd ever made.

"Ugh," she said, wrinkling her nose. "You even smell human. Yuck."

"Thanks, Nella." I laughed, and she softened her face and joined me.

Thorne walked across the helicopter pad wearing the same goofy grin he'd had since childhood. Blue eyes situated beneath a mop of soft brown hair lit up with excitement as he approached. They looked just the way they had when he'd run to tell me he'd kissed Addie when we were just twelve years old. My oldest friend, and a brother in every way but blood.

"The prodigal son returns," he said, pulling me in for a hug. "Holy shit, you *do* smell human!"

"It comes with the new human territory, I suppose. I missed you, brother." I returned his hug with one arm but held Emilia's hand tight. Her sweaty palms tightened around my hand.

"And this must be Emilia." Thorne pulled back and turned to look her over. "You must be one helluva woman to steal the hardened heart of this son-of-a-bitch." His pursed his lips that were surrounded by his neatly trimmed facial hair, then pulled them into a wide grin. "It's great to meet you, Emilia."

Emilia and I let out our held breaths in unison.

"You too," she said after a deep swallow. "I've been really excited to meet you. All of you." She looked at Nella.

"I'm Annella," my sister said moving in front of her. "It's so nice to have you here. I can't wait to get to know you." Annella pulled her in for a hug.

"Me, too," Emilia answered, and I heard the surprise in her voice. I'd warned her my family may not be pleased to meet the woman I'd turned human for, but so far things were going better than I had expected. But one family member remained. And that one posed the greatest challenge.

Lothaire.

My gaze stretched across the space between us and fell onto the intimidating posture and intense stare glaring my way from my brother. Grizella, his wife, stood at his side wearing the same stoic expression.

His height, and also the rugged beard he'd worn since before our change, gave him an intimidating appearance... even to me. But it was the intensity in his amber eyes that sent most people scurrying out of his way. The raven-haired beauty beside him with the emerald eyes did just as good of a job shrinking people beneath her gaze. Side by side they were a force to be reckoned with... and right now I tried not to crumble beneath their condemnatory stares.

Thorne and Annella noticed the standoff and stepped out of the way, both turning with expectant eyes to Lothaire. The space between us felt like a bottomless cavern that would send me tumbling into the vast darkness if I stepped forward. I did it anyway, one long stride after another toward the brother I had come to blows with the last time I saw him.

But instead of striding confidently to him, my legs wobbled, and pain seared up through them and enveloped my whole body. While I crashed toward the ground, I wondered if I'd actually plummeted into the abyss. I heard Emilia's scream, but something stopped me from slamming into the pavement. When I looked up, I saw Lothaire's face staring down at me and his worry-lined eyes met mine.

My ears screamed with an unyielding ring, my eyes blinking against the impending darkness.

"I've got you, brother," Lothaire said just before it all faded to black.

THE DIN OF MUFFLED voices stirred me. Blinking my eyes open, I looked around. My family crest above the roaring fireplace drew my eye first. The same familiar antiques and plaid colors that had been here since we'd bought the place a few hundred years ago still hung on the walls and perched on the rich mahogany furniture. It didn't take but a moment to acclimate myself. My old bedroom.

"Aiden!" Emilia gasped when she saw me awaken. "I'm right here, baby."

When I glanced down, I saw her fingers interlocked with mine and I wondered how long she'd been sitting here and how long I had been out. Big blue eyes glistening with tears stared down at me. "How long was I out?"

"Only an hour," she answered, smoothing my hair from my face. "You scared me, Aiden."

"You scared me as well." Lothaire's deep voice pulled my attention to where he stood on the opposite side of my bed. "Don't do that again," he warned with an arched brow.

"I'll try," I said between pained breaths as I struggled to sit up. "Lothaire, I'm sorry. The last time I saw you I—"

"Don't." He stopped me with a raised hand. "Don't apologize. You were right. I should have said it years ago when I realized it."

"So, you've still got Mom's stubborn streak?" I attempted a joke.

He smiled, an odd sight considering disapproving scowls and frowns were a more common sight on his face. I didn't blame him, though. As chieftain, he had to carry the weight of the world on his shoulders and it didn't allow a lot of time for shenanigans. His brief smile made me miss the time before everything changed; the time where three brothers would share laughs and get into mischief all along the countryside. We were best friends, all of us. And then our brother and our father died, and in that instant all the fun and games came screeching to a halt. Lothaire had to grow up in an instant.

His smile dissipated but the softness remained in his eyes. "What happened is behind us... not worth another thought." He furrowed his bushy brows. "What needs our attention now is the mess you've gotten yourself into."

His large hand pressed into my shoulder and I cringed beneath it.

"You're getting worse," Lothaire said, removing his hand when he realized it caused me pain. "You're in the final stage."

"You dumb arse," Thorne said, appearing beside Lothaire, and shaking his head.

Annella moved to my other side and slid an arm around Emilia's waist. "What were you thinking, Aiden?"

"It was worth it." I forced a smile and looked up at Emilia.

"Well, let's just hope we can change him back in time." Grizella stepped forward to Lothaire's other side.

Change back. Those words, the same ones Lothaire had said on the phone when I'd called from Bora Bora, sent more pain shooting through me than the physical pain ripping apart my body. I remembered the eel darting back into his hole... back into the dark. I didn't want that. Now that I had lived this life surrounded by light and love I didn't think I could go back. I closed my eyes to the thought, trying to come to terms with it, like I had since I'd first heard it yesterday on the phone.

"We will find a way to fix you, Aiden," Annella said.

"You'd better!" A voice called from the door.

"Mark." I sighed, a smile lifting my weary lips.

In the blink of an eye he appeared by my bed and wrapped his arms around Emilia. "I missed you so much." He hugged her tight.

"Thank God, you're here," she said, returning the tight embrace.

"I came as soon as I heard." He released his grip on her and turned his attention to me. "I told you it was a bad idea. Didn't I? That's right... I did." He narrowed his eyes and pursed his lips.

"You did," I agreed. "Now stop gloating. How are you? How is life as a vampire?"

His eyes lit up like they had alongside the runway that one time I let him drag me to Fashion Week.

"It's. A. Mazing. Why you would want to give this up is beyond me. *Beyond* me." He tossed his arms in the air, finishing with huff.

"I'm so glad you made the right choice for you," I said, not wanting to argue.

"And Emilia, look!" He pointed to the skin between his brows. "No wrinkle! I vanquished that son of a bitch with Botox and now I've got perfect skin for eternity. Boom. And look." He popped his fangs. "I've got fangs."

"Incredible, Mark," she said, but she lacked the excitement in her voice that usually came out when they spoke.

"I'm sorry, sweetie. You must be so stressed out." He noticed it as well and pulled her back in for a hug. "Don't worry, we're gonna fix him. And then I'll go back to hunting down Ryan Gosling. I was literally right there when you called. Just a doorway stood between us."

She chuckled and shook her head. "You'll get him next time."

"You know it." He winked. "Now, where are we in fixing this hot mess he got himself into? You know, the one I told him *not* to." He shot me that accusatory glance I'd grown so accustomed to.

And had missed.

Lothaire straightened up. "We've contacted every clan and still have little to go on. Leeya wasn't lying when she said she'd seen it before. Apparently one of her clansmen tried and several weeks after the transition back to human, he died. But we think we still have time to change him back to a vampire. He cannot survive as a human, so the only way is for him to drink the blood of a vampire, and we kill him. And then... we hope he returns to us a vampire." His voice trailed off at the end.

"He can't just drink human blood and turn back?" Annella asked.

"The change back is complete. He's fully human now," Grizella said. "The only choice we have is to try to change him back the same way we just changed you, Mark."

"Ouch," Mark said, and I knew he remembered well the pain from his transition.

"And hope like hell it works," Thorne interjected, his voice anything but confident.

"And if it doesn't work?" Emilia asked, eyes searching the vampires surrounding her.

Silence settled over the room like a heavy blanket on a winter's night.

"Then he dies," Lothaire said, his commanding voice so meek I wouldn't have known it was him if I hadn't seen his lips move.

Emilia and I locked eyes, words failing us. There were no guarantees I could make her. No way I could erase the pain that welled up in tears behind her eyes.

"I'm sorry, Emilia. Please know that I wanted a life in the light with you. I wanted our freedom and a human life. I wanted it all and I'm so sorry. I tried."

"Don't apologize, Aiden. I shouldn't have let you change in the first place."

"You couldn't have stopped me," I said, squeezing her hand. "So, it looks like you'll be eating sushi and drinking Jägermeister alone and still living as my blood bank. Is that okay? I know it's not what we wanted."

She bit her lip. "That's not good enough for me anymore, Aiden."

"What?" It felt like the air got sucked out of the room. "What do you mean? You're leaving me?"

Her face softened, and she shook her head. A soft smile slid across her face. "No. I'm changing with you."

"What?" The word fell out of my mouth.

"You go, I go." She leaned down and kissed me. The gentle touch of her lips on mine sent a shudder down my spine. When she sat back up, I stared at her face, disbelief still holding my tongue.

"But it's not what you want." I finally found words. "You don't want to be a vampire, Emilia. You want sunshine and food. A normal, human life. I can't let you do this."

"There is nothing I want more than you, Aiden. There is no light or sunshine without you at my side. I don't want a short life... I want a long one. An eternity. I want this, Aiden. I want you."

"Emilia," I whispered, still stunned at the weight of her admission. "Are you sure?"

"Positive," she answered, her voice strong and sure.

"We're gonna make the *best* vampire friends!" Mark chimed, and tossed an arm around her. "I'm so freaking excited."

I wanted to feel excited, to share in the joy. But sadness suffocated me, like a cloak of doom. Sadness for Emelia's sacrifice. Sadness for the life I had wanted for us. Sadness that we'd only had a short time to dance together in the sun.

"I can't let you do this, Emilia. I can't."

"It's not your choice, Aiden," she answered. "I'm doing this."

"I can see why you gave it all up for her, Aiden," Annella said. "You found a good one."

"I didn't just give it up for her," I said, finally acknowledging the difficulty of this decision. "I wanted that life. All of it. And of course, I wanted it with her. This last week has been the greatest in my life. I don't know how I'm going to go back. I don't want to go back."

Lothaire leaned down, and I saw the sadness in his eyes. "I'm so sorry, Aiden. I wish there was another way, but you're dying, and this is the only way we can save you. It's the best we can do. And at least you'll have Emilia at your side... and us."

I nodded, tossing a glance to her before taking a breath. "Okay, let's do this."

"Wait," Thorne said, shaking his head. "What if there's another way?"

All eyes turned to him.

"There is no other way, Thorne." Lothaire turned to face him. "Leave it."

"But there might be. He doesn't want this. Can't you guys see that? He doesn't want this life anymore and if there is even a chance, we need to tell him."

"What other way?" I asked, my eyes darting between the two men in a stare-off.

"The Picts," Thorne said, turning his eyes back to me. "There are still Picts left in our homeland. They are the ones who put this curse on us in the first place. Maybe they can fix you."

"Thorne!" Lothaire boomed, filling every empty space in the room. "We don't have time to go on a wild goose chase! We already discussed this! He's dying!"

Thorne took a breath. "It should be *his* decision... not ours. If Aiden wants to try, we should try."

For the first time in days I felt a glimmer of hope sparking from the darkness enveloping me. "Are you sure? They're still there?"

"No, we're not sure," Grizella said through gritted teeth and shot a glare at Thorne that could have dropped him to the ground.

"But the rumors are that they are there. Just hidden." Thorne resisted her stare.

"It's too risky, Aiden. You might not even make the journey," Annella said, worry shaking her voice.

"If there's a chance, even a small one, that I can live as a human, I'm taking it."

"Aiden," Emilia breathed. "It's too risky. You might die! You promised you would fight and not leave me!"

"I *am* fighting, Emilia. I'm fighting for the life we deserve. The life we both want."

"Dammit, Thorne," Lothaire growled. "We agreed not to tell him about your foolish idea!"

"No, *you* agreed." Thorne argued back. "I'm not lying to him. He needs to decide for himself."

"I'm not losing my brother again!" Lothaire exploded and finally I understood the reason for his hard stance against this. He'd lost me once. We'd both lost our brother, Caleb. All these years I thought Lothaire hated me and really he grieved for me... for his only brother. The only one left. Now he thought he might lose me again.

"Lothaire." I reached out and took his hand. "I'm so sorry for the years apart. I'm sorry about everything I said, and I'm sorry I left you."

The hardened lines in his face softened while he studied me.

"I don't want to be a vampire anymore. This isn't the life I want, and I need you to understand that. If there is *any* truth to what Thorne is saying, I need to take the risk. Can you understand that?"

"No," he answered, but I could hear the doubt in his gruff response.

"You would do anything for Grizella, right?"

"Of course. Anything." He cast her a glance.

"And I would do anything for Emilia. Anything. All these years I have wanted what you have, what the two of you share, and now I have it. She doesn't want to be a vampire, either. If there is any chance I can save her from that life, then I need to take it. I need to save us both from eternal darkness. Can you understand that, Lothaire?"

His lips pressed into a tight white line while he searched my face. "This is what you want? To be human?"

"More than anything," I breathed. "And I want her." I looked back to Emilia who bit her lip and stared at me, the worry lines cutting deep into her forehead. "Please, Lothaire. I need to try."

A faint nod tipped his head. "All right. Then we try it."

A heavy sigh pushed from my lips and I lay my head back down into the pillow. "Thank you, Lothaire. I know you don't understand, but I need to do this."

"I understand," he said, reaching over and taking Grizella by the hand. "I understand."

"Aiden," Emilia said, dropping to her knees at my side. "It's too risky. You're so weak, and there's no guarantee we can get you there... or that they are even there! If we're wrong, you might die. It's too risky!"

"I might die anyway." The pain flashed across her face and I hated being the one to put it there. "There's no guarantee changing me back will work. If I'm going to die, I want to die trying... fighting for the life we both want. I'm fighting for us... just like I promised."

"Aiden, it's too dangerous."

"How about this? If we go looking for the Picts and we can't find them, or if I'm dying, they can turn us both on the spot. Then at least we'll have tried."

She gave me a worried look and then exhaled a deep sigh. "Okay. Let's try."

"Good." I smiled and drew her closer to me. "I'm not ready to give up Jägermeister yet."

She cracked a smile and snickered.

"He did *Jägermeister*?" Mark gasped. "And I wasn't there? Ugh. I miss all the good stuff! When this is all over, I need a play-by-play, Emilia."

"When this is over, I'll let Aiden tell you," Emilia said, shooting me a confident look.

"Aiden, you sleep. The rest of us will go figure out how to find the Picts and get you better. Don't die on us," Lothaire added with a scowl.

"I'll do my best." I chuckled.

"We'll leave you two be." Annella leaned down and kissed my head before pulling Mark out of the room.

"Thorne," I called, stopping him before he left. "Thank you. You're a good friend."

"Just don't die and make me regret it."

They all left the room and Emilia crawled into my arms. Even though my body weakened by the second, all the reason I needed to fight curled up at my side. I kissed her head and closed my eyes, knowing the risk was worth it... that she was worth it.

CHAPTER TWENTY-ONE

Emilia

"I STILL DON'T UNDERSTAND why we couldn't take the helicopter all the way," Mark grumbled and shifted in the saddle.

My horse ambled behind his, and I looked over to Aiden who fought the grimaces from pain the bumpy ride caused him.

"They are an ancient people who have no connection to society, Mark," Thorne answered, the irritation sharpening his voice. It wasn't the first time Mark had complained since the ride started a couple hours ago. "If we arrive to their hidden land in a helicopter, they will be terrified and turn us away. And Aiden is too weak to endure being dragged at light speed by one of us. Horses. It's the only way to get him out here. Now stop complaining or go back."

"Fine." Mark sighed and turned his attention back to the untouched world stretched out in front of us.

They had night vision and navigated the dark with ease, but it made me anxious being out here in the dark, though staring up at the endless stars soothed my worry. It was like time had stopped here, and I admired the serenity surrounding us. Since we had left the small stable where we'd rented the horses, we hadn't even seen a house or a farm. Though it was dark out, the nearly full moon illuminated the lands around us, and I could see the shadow of my horse as we trudged on.

But as beautiful as it was in the dark, I wanted to see this place in the light. I wanted to see the lush green grass and clear blue streams I could hear bubbling just beyond. Like a punch to the gut, the realization hit me that if I had to change into a vampire tonight that may never be possible again. It would leave me in an eternity of darkness, and I appreciated why Aiden wanted a life in the light so badly.

Looking over to him, I realized though that he would be worth a life in the dark. I could find all the light I'd ever need inside his eyes. The love between us could illuminate the blackest of nights, but deep down I hoped that we could find our way back into the light together.

"He's getting worse," Lothaire said, riding up beside me and keeping his voice low.

"I know," I agreed. Aiden barely had the energy to talk now. It had taken all their connections and two days to get a possible location for the Picts. And it was speculation at best.

"I don't want to lose my brother, Emilia. If things get worse, you'll be the only one who can convince him to change. I need your word you won't let him die. I can't lose him again... he's my only brother."

His eyes both warned me and begged me all at once. After spending two days with him I felt more comfortable around him... around all of them. But there was a power about Lothaire that frightened me even when he didn't intend it. He reminded me of a large grizzly bear. And not just the way he looked. Harmless to his cubs and family, caring even, but lethal to any who would threaten those he loved. I took his words, and warning, to heart.

"I love him, Lothaire and I won't let him die. There is no future for me without him, so I will do whatever it takes to save him... and I will make my own sacrifice, if needed."

"I'm glad to hear it." He glanced over to Aiden, who had slumped over on his horse, struggling to stay on. "I wish he'd agreed to ride with me. His stupid pride."

I arched a brow. "He's got your stubborn streak as well it would seem."

Lothaire snorted. "It would seem so. It runs in the family. I think Annella is the most stubborn of us all, though. The deadliest, too."

I looked up to Annella and those words, and the ones Aiden had said about not wanting to meet her in a dark alley, still confounded me. The Annella I admired and felt connected to was full of giggles and smiles. An innocent looking beauty, there was nothing threatening or terrifying about her. Her miniscule size made it even harder for me to picture her tearing through groups of grown men and even powerful vampires. She must have felt my eyes on her because she turned in her saddle and flashed me her wide grin.

"Don't let her looks fool you," Lothaire said with a chuckle.

"What are you two talking about?" Thorne slowed his horse and pulled up on my other side. His icy blue eyes darted between the two of us. Even though he wasn't Aiden's actual brother, they could pass for them with ease. They shared the same strong jaw, light blue eyes, and impressive figure.

His appearance was more rugged than Aiden's, but their features were remarkably similar. So far, my initial thoughts wondering if all vampires were beautiful seemed to be true. Either that or Aiden just had an exceptionally attractive clan before he turned. Every one of them was striking and beautiful in their own way.

"We're talking about Annella," Lothaire said, "and how she could whoop any of us if she wanted."

Thorne blew out a puff of air. "Can and *has*. I've stopped sparring with her... my pride can't take having her set me on my arse again." He laughed.

"Stop talking about me!" Annella called back and flashed a playful glare over her shoulder. Grizella, riding at her side, glanced back as well and shook her head.

Her beauty was otherworldly. I could see why Lothaire had been so taken with her in an instant. Raven black hair and green eyes gave her an exotic and intimidating appearance. Her porcelain skin practically glowed under the moonlight. When her gaze fell to Lothaire, her face softened, and her eyes flickered the same way mine did when I looked at Aiden. Four hundred years later and their love remained just as strong as ours. You could see it anytime they looked at each other.

Aiden groaned, and all eyes shot to him. He slumped even lower on his horse now. I clicked to mine and trotted over the few steps to ride up at his side.

"Hang in there, baby. We're almost there." I reached over and placed my hand on his leg, but he grimaced at my touch. Withdrawing my hand, I took a staying breath. Seeing him this way, in so much pain, felt like a knife ripping me apart in ways I never imagined possible. Being so close to him and unable to touch him and hold him only sharpened the edges of the blade. And it was my fault. If I hadn't met him, he would still be safe. If I'd thrown away that card Mark had handed me, Aiden would still be living his life, not dying next to me, clinging to the hope that he could remain human.

"Stop," Thorne said, pulling his horse to a halt.

"What is it?" Lothaire asked, powerful eyes scanning our surroundings. His muscles twitched at the ready, but Thorne just lifted his hand to stay him.

"We're here."

It was only then I realized we approached the side of a large lake. From what they had gathered from the little available information, the Picts were living here on a hidden island in the middle of this lake. It took me some time to process that a magical barrier concealing an entire village of people was even a possibility, but one look around at the six-hundred-year-old vampires surrounding me and I realized anything was possible.

This proud people, after having their pact with Aiden's clan implode, had taken what was left of their tribes and conglomerated on an island. Instead of having immortal guardians to protect them from the clans slowly eradicating them, they had used their powers to hide away their island. It was invisible to anyone who wasn't a Pict, keeping them hidden away.

Thorne scanned the surroundings again. "This is the lake. They should be in here."

"You'd better be right," Lothaire grumbled and cast a glance to Aiden, who faded fast. "We don't have much time."

"Get the rafts." Thorne hopped off his horse and gestured for the rest of us to do the same.

Mark hopped down and pulled the yellow inflatable rafts out from the bag behind the cantle of his saddle. Annella flashed to his side, and in moments, they had the rafts unrolled and blown up. Watching Mark move with vamp speed still stole my breath away.

"We're here," I said, moving to Aiden's side. His blue eyes blinked open at me and he forced a smile. Lothaire stepped up beside me and put his arms around his brother's waist.

"I've got you," he said, lowering Aiden from his horse and pulling him into his arms. I stayed at his side while Lothaire carried him to the raft now sitting at the lake's edge. Settling down onto the rubber floor first, I waited as Lothaire laid him down, his head now resting in my lap.

"We're almost there, baby. Just hang on," I whispered and brushed a lock of hair from his face.

"I love you," he whispered back, his voice barely audible.

"I love you more. Just stay with me."

Lothaire pushed our raft forward, the gentle waves lifted us as we slid off the beach. He hopped in beside me and Thorne climbed in beside him. Mark, Grizella and Annella climbed into the other raft and pushed off after us. Thorne grabbed the paddles and rowed us out into the lake. We floated across the water, the moon shimmering white over the ripples our boat made while we continued farther and farther from the shore. Aiden rested in my lap, and I watched his chest rise and fall, praying it would continue and that we weren't too late.

A cool mist crept across the water and swirled around our rafts. A shiver of fear slithered down my spine and goosebumps rose on my skin. I wasn't sure if it was the coolness of the fog or the eerie feeling settling into my gut causing them. With each push through the water the fog thickened until I couldn't see Mark's boat just feet away from us.

"We're here," Thorne said.

"Now what?" Lothaire asked, shooting a glance to Aiden. "We're running out of time."

"We wait."

Lothaire growled. "We don't have time to wait. He's dying!"

Thorne glanced at Aiden and nodded, his eyes acknowledging the urgency. "Hello!" he called out into the mist. "We need your help! Please!"

We sat bobbing on our rafts, all eyes searching the fog surrounding us on all sides.

"Please! We know you're there! We need help! We are your descendants and he will die without your help!" Thorne called out again.

Only the slapping of the waves on our rubber boats answered.

Lothaire rose, remaining steady as the boat rocked beneath him. "I am Lothaire Mackay!" His voice rumbled through the chilled air. "Son of Donnghail Mackay and chief of Clan Mackay! You did this to us! It is your curse that brings us to you now. Now show yourselves!"

I held my breath while I waited for a response. A gust of wind blew across the water, sending the mist swirling around us before it pushed apart the fog. A breath trapped in my lungs when the lifting fog revealed the beach of an island just in front of us.

"Holy shit," I whispered. "It's real."

"Come on," Lothaire said wasting no time. Thorne dug his paddles into the water and pushed us forward until we slid into the sand. The other raft glided up beside us. One by one we climbed over the edge and stepped onto the beach, all eyes scanning for life and finding none.

"I've got him," Lothaire said, reaching down and lifting Aiden back into his arms. He looked so fragile clutched against his brother's chest. I didn't know if I could wait any longer before I begged them to change him. But we were so close... I owed him every chance to live the life he wanted.

A small figure stepped out of the trees lining the beach. A long wooden spear tapped the ground with each step as she approached. When she came into full view under the bright glow of the moon, I struggled to exhale the breath trapped in my lungs. Blonde hair cascaded over her shoulders, and several pieces knotted into dreadlocks fell around her tanned face striped with blue paint. Black smudges of paint surrounded blue eyes so light they almost glowed in the moonlight. Worn leather fashioned a bra and skirt but left the rest of her tanned body exposed. She looked as lethal as she did beautiful.

We stood side by side in silence as she approached. Lothaire lowered his eyes and widened his stance when she got closer. I could feel the protective energy for his brother pulsing off him.

"You should not be here," she said. Although she spoke English, her native accent made it sound like another language entirely.

"You speak English. Good," Thorne said, stepping forward.

She lifted her spear and stopped him with the point in his chest.

"Understood." He flashed his playful smile and stepped back. "We need your help."

"Why would we help you?" she snapped.

"Because he's dying," Lothaire's voice rumbled. "You need to fix him."

She glanced to Aiden and then back to Lothaire's expectant gaze. "We do not *need* to do anything. You are abominations. You should not be here. It is good he dies."

Lothaire snarled, and I heard his fangs pop.

"Calm down." Thorne pressed a staying hand against his shoulder then turned his attention back to the Pict woman. "Let's start over. I'm Thorne. This is Lothaire and Annella from Clan Mackay. That is Mark and Grizella. And this is Aiden and Emilia. We are here for your help. Aiden didn't want to be what you made him anymore. He chose a human life to be with the woman he loved and now he's dying. And he doesn't deserve it. He's a good man. Please. Just hear us out."

I watched her face twist while she contemplated his words. She looked over to the other group who stood motionless beside their boat. Even Mark held his sassy tongue understanding the seriousness of the situation.

"Not you." She waved a hand to Mark and Grizella. "You not Pict. You go."

"What?" Grizella stepped forward.

Lothaire nodded his head. "It's okay, love. Clan Mackay is descendants of Picts. You both are not. We'll be okay. Just take Mark back to shore with you," he said, giving her a comforting look.

"Are you sure?" Grizella asked.

"I'll find you when we're done. We'll be fine. All that matters is saving Aiden."

With a nod she stepped over to us and leaned up, pressing a long kiss against his lips. They pushed their foreheads together for a moment before she turned and walked back to her boat.

"Be careful, Emilia," Mark said, coming over and giving me a hug. "And take good care of our boy."

"I will." I closed my arms around him. "I'll see you soon."

"She go too," the Pict woman said.

My head snapped around to see her finger pointing at me. "What? No! I'm not leaving him."

"You not Pict. You go."

"Emilia," Lothaire started.

"No!" I shouted back. "I'm not leaving him. I won't! He goes... I go."

I clenched my teeth and stepped closer to Aiden. No one, not even this little Pict warrior woman was taking me from his side.

She raked me with curious eyes and then looked to Aiden. Her eyes moved back and forth between us and then I saw a flash of recognition in her face, though I wasn't sure why. She looked back to me and then nodded. "Fine. She comes."

Blowing out a breath of relief I looked to Lothaire. He gave me a nod of approval.

"Follow me," she snapped and turned, pushing her spear into the ground as she stepped off.

"I'll see you soon," I said to Mark and pecked him on the cheek.

"You'd better." He winked before turning away.

As we followed the woman up the beach I turned before we went into the woods. Mark and Grizella floated away from the sand. He held up a hand and waved before blowing me a kiss and disappearing into the mist. I turned back and jumped when I saw other warriors stepping out of the woods. The woman had not come alone, and I didn't think even the vampires had sensed them hidden amongst the branches.

They all wore the same war-paint and tattoos, each with different patterns and colors covering their tanned faces and bodies. The men's impressive sizes rivaled Aiden and Thorne, but none stood as tall as Lothaire. Each wore a primitive loincloth made of the same leather that the woman wore, each in various shapes of revealing dresses and outfits similar to our guide. Though their clothing and tattoos varied between them, each one shared one identical trait... menacing stares that sent shivers rippling across my skin.

They followed us as we pushed past them down the trail into the forest. One look at Aiden and I shoved back the fear threatening to send me running back to the raft to leave with Mark.

No. I wouldn't leave his side and these people were our only chance.

We reached a small village surrounded by thatched huts that looked similar to the ones we'd stayed in when we were in Bora Bora. The warriors filed in behind us and we all followed the woman to the last hut on the end. She pushed open the door and turned back, gesturing to us to follow her in.

We exchanged worried glances before following her inside. This was Aiden's chance, our chance, and I wouldn't lose my nerve now. His eyes opened and met mine, and that familiar flutter danced around inside me. There wasn't anything I wouldn't do for him... and now was my chance to prove it.

CHAPTER TWENTY-TWO

Aiden

I STRUGGLED FOR BREATH while Lothaire set me down on the ground of the small hut. Emilia appeared at my side, and I settled my head back into her lap. I was slipping. The small amount of life left inside clawed at me to leave, but every time I felt my body submitting to its demands, I looked at her.

Her face, her eyes, the promise of a lifetime of kisses from those lips and I felt the fight return. I clung to every breath, willing my chest to rise and fall and demanding that my heart keep beating. It beat for her and I didn't want to leave her. I'd just found her, and I wasn't *ready* to leave her.

My eyes moved between Thorne and Annella and finally settled on Lothaire. I'd never seen fear in his eyes until now. He saw me fading, and his desperate expression screamed to change me back before the last ounce of lifeforce slid from my body... before he said goodbye to another brother. But I was so close... I was so close to the life I wanted that I couldn't give up now. I gave him a look and reassured him with my eyes. Told him that he needed to wait. I wasn't going to let go.

Not yet.

Our stare broke when he lifted his head to the movement behind me. I tried to follow his gaze but the pain in my body wouldn't let me turn my head. With a breath I settled deeper into Emilia's lap and waited.

"Who are you?" Annella asked, her eyes fixated on someone behind me.

A woman's voice, shaky from age, spoke in a language I hadn't heard in centuries. It was the Pict language that I'd only heard several times in my life before the change. If the stories were true, then she was likely the matriarch, the one powerful witch amongst them. Legends said one Pict held all the power... all the magic. When they died it passed to the next woman chosen by fate to carry on the magic. The power would transfer at the moment of death, and a new leader would be reborn.

"I'm sorry," Thorne said, looking to the young warrior woman who brought us here. "We don't speak your language."

"Liùsaidh says you are not welcome here," the young woman said.

"Liùsaidh is her name? What is your name?" Thorne said, his naturally charming demeanor coming through.

There was a pause before she answered. "Catrain."

"Catrain, a beautiful name." I couldn't see him, but I knew he showed her the smile that had melted many a woman in our day. "Could you please translate for me?"

Her silence hung over us. "Yes."

"Please tell her we need her help. We are desperate to save him. Please," Thorne continued.

After another pause Catrain spoke in her language, passing Thorne's message to the woman I still could not see. When Liùsaidh responded, she spat out the sharp and pointed words I didn't understand.

Catrain translated. "She says no. You are abominations and should be dead. You go now."

"You need to fix him!" Lothaire stepped forward, but an invisible blast sent him slamming backward into the wall. I couldn't see her, but I knew it had come from Liùsaidh, confirming the rumors I'd heard as a child of the power of Pict witches.

"No! Stop!" Annella shouted, shooting to the space between them. "Please, we mean you no harm."

Lothaire growled and crawled up to his knees, shaking the debris from his hair while he stood.

"This is not productive," Thorne said, trying to calm the tension in the room. "Will you not help him?"

"Please." Lothaire softened his eyes and raised his hands in submission. "He needs your help. He wants to be human. Please... let him."

Catrain translated again. The witch's response held the same anger and condemnation.

"She say no. Now go," Catrain snapped.

"Dammit!" Annella shouted. "Lothaire, we're running out of time. He's dying... we need to do this. Now."

"We have no choice. It's time. We need to change him," Lothaire agreed. His eyes settled onto mine and I could see the regret hanging heavy in them. "We did everything we could, Aiden. I'm so sorry."

"You could have stopped this," Thorne growled at Catrain.

Emilia sobbed and traced her fingers down my face.

"It is not my decision," Catrain answered. "Liùsaidh has spoken." The roughness in her voice softened, and for a moment I thought I heard remorse.

"Do it, Lothaire. Do it now," Thorne said. His words trailed off at the end, and I could hear the defeat in his voice. "Aiden... hang in there. Don't you dare leave us. You'd better come back after we change you."

I could feel my hope slipping and with it my will to live. Emilia fought her tears and I knew they weren't just about the risk of losing me... they were about loss of her humanity when she followed me into the darkness. No matter what, she lost. She either lost me if I didn't survive the transition, or she lost her life as a human. All I ever wanted was to give her everything, and instead I'd be taking everything away. I couldn't bear the thought of being the one to destroy her.

With a groan I willed my body to move. It felt like fire ripping through my skin, but I fought through it and struggled to my knees, turning to see the woman who wouldn't give Emilia the life she deserved. Pale eyes so light they looked translucent stared through me. Weathered skin hung from her gaunt frame and grey hair twisted into knots on top of her head. Worn and faded tattoos covered her face, an array of colors and shapes that only intensified her appearance.

"Please," I begged, crawling toward where she sat in an oversized chair made of sticks and branches. "Don't force me to change back. If I change, she will change. Please don't take her life away. I love her. Please."

Her eyes raked over me and then moved to Emilia. Though she didn't speak my language she seemed to understand my meaning. Catrain whispered in her ear and both sets of eyes settled back on me and then moved in sync back to Emilia.

Liùsaidh crooked a finger to Emilia to come forward. She responded and knelt by my side. Our fingers tangled together, and we looked up to Liùsaidh as one. Those ancient eyes bore through us and I could feel her tearing through my soul, searching and drawing from me. A transcendent power washed over me and for a second the pain subsided. I inhaled a sharp breath and relished the moment before it crashed back down over me and refilled every inch of my body. I collapsed on the ground.

"Aiden!" Emilia screamed and her face was over me. "Please!" she looked up with tear-filled eyes to the woman sitting above us. "Save him! Someone save him!"

Lothaire appeared above me before I could blink an eye. "I'm sorry brother," he said, and bit his wrist. The blood oozed from the wound and he lowered it to my mouth. I used all my strength to grab his hand and stop its descent. "Wait," I whispered.

I moved my gaze up to meet Emilia's. "I love you. More than anything."

"I love you, too," she cried.

"I would choose this... and you every time. Over and over and over again I would choose you. You gave me the happiest days of my life. And I want you to know that you saved me, Emilia. You saved me from a life in the dark and I don't want you to give everything up for me. I love you too much to take away the things that you love."

"Aiden, it's not your decision. I'm changing with you. All you need to do is survive and I'll be there waiting for you. You and me... for eternity."

Tears burned behind my eyes. I swallowed hard. "No, Emilia. You deserve it all. And you deserve a happy life... a human life. I would rather see you happy without me, then live this dark life with me. I need to let you go."

"Well I won't let you go," she sobbed. "You don't get a say. You go; I go."

Her lips collided with mine and I felt all the joy, love, and life she brought me explode around me. I savored her touch, her taste, and the feeling of her love washing over me. Giving up my darkness had all been worth it for her love, even if it was just for a fraction of my life. Even if it meant I died tonight. But I couldn't ask her to sacrifice everything for me.

Our lips drifted apart, and I reached up and touched her face. "I love you, Emilia." I turned to Lothaire. "No matter what happens, I need you to promise me something."

"Anything, brother." He grabbed my hand.

"You'll leave her a human and compel her to forget me. To forget everything."

"What!" Emilia shrieked. "No!"

"Please, Lothaire. Make her forget me. Make sure she's safe and protected and never wants for a thing. See to it she lives a long, happy human life."

His lips pressed together, and I saw the tears building behind his eyes as he started nodding. "You have my word, brother."

"No!" Emilia sobbed. "You can't! I won't let you! I love you, Aiden!"

"I love you more than anything in the world, Emilia. Enough to let you go."

She collapsed at my side and pressed her head into my chest. I slid an arm around her back and pressed my lips to her head.

Annella and Thorne stepped to my side, and I gave them both a pained smile. "It's time."

"I'll see you soon, friend." Thorne gave me a confident nod.

"Please come back to us, Aiden," Annella said, fighting back tears.

The death that came next would either be the end of me or a new beginning. I would either watch Emilia thriving from afar, or I would watch her from above. No matter what, I would watch over her. Even if heaven didn't exist for someone like me, death couldn't keep me away... not even the deepest grave could keep me from crawling out back to her side, even if just to check on her and ensure her safety and happiness.

I took one last breath filled with Emilia's sweet smell. "I'm ready, Lothaire." Closing my eyes, I waited for his blood to pass my lips.

"Wait!" Catrain's voice shook through the room. "Please wait."

My eyes fluttered open, and I saw her staring at us with tears in her eyes. She turned to Liùsaidh and spoke. "They have a soul tie, Liùsaidh. You see it as I can see it. I know you can. And because of this I know you can save them. Please, for me... your daughter, I beg you to save them."

The silence settled over the room and Emilia pulled her head from my chest. Her swollen red eyes locked with mine.

"I see it," Liùsaidh said, her accent thick, but her English clear.

"She speaks English?" Thorne stepped forward.

"Yes, but she does not want to speak directly to you. She thinks you a blight on humanity... a mistake to be fixed and unworthy of her words," Catrain answered.

Thorne looked right at her. "Please, Liùsaidh. I know our people have bad blood with yours. But Aiden is a good man. Save them."

"Mother, I know you see in them what I see with my gift. They are special, true soulmates. It is a bond that should never be broken and a bond that can anchor them. You have the power to save them."

Liùsaidh's eyes roved over Emilia and I, her face stern and unyielding.

"You should not be here." She glowered at me and spoke in even better English than Catrain. "Your people betrayed us and then took our gift and turned it into evil. A blight on humanity we have regretted for over six hundred years. None of you should be here."

"Please," Emilia sobbed. "Please save him."

Liùsaidh drummed her fingers together and looked between us with a contemplative gaze.

"I have searched inside you both and my daughter is not wrong. You are true soul mates. You're connected together. And he was willing to sacrifice his own happiness for your life. It is a noble man who would give up his own desires for that of another... for that of the one he loves."

"Then save him," Emilia breathed. "Please."

"There is only one way to save him," Liùsaidh answered.

I felt my heart clench at her words... there was hope.

She turned her stare to Emilia. "And it is dependent on you."

"Anything," Emilia begged. "I will do anything for him."

"The gift placed upon them that gave them immortality was bound by a powerful magic." Liùsaidh started. "When the gift was removed due to their betrayal, they discovered that feeding on others and absorbing their life force could sustain them. Without feeding on blood, Aiden cannot survive. The magic within him has gone."

"But you can save him?" Lothaire stepped forward.

Liùsaidh lowered her head in a nod. "I can."

"And *will* you save him?" Annella asked, her eyes soft and pleading. "Will you save my brother?"

Liùsaidh looked to Emilia and I held my breath while I awaited my fate.

Our fate.

She gave another slow nod. "Yes. I will try to save him. His actions tonight show me he is a good man. Not a soulless monster like so many of your kind. But whether I save him is up to her." She lifted a crooked finger to Emilia. "You are already bonded by your special soul tie, two halves that make a whole. Because of this I can tie his life-force to yours, and as long as your heart beats, so will his."

"Yes, do it, please!" Emilia begged.

"Wait." I struggled for breath. "Will she be a vampire? Will she have to feed on blood and stay out of the sunlight? I don't want that for her."

"No," Liùsaidh responded. "You will live a human life, though the magic I will imbue you with that bonds you will return your original powers and grant you a long life, much like the original gift we granted your people. And because you are bonded, your powers will become her powers. But since your own heart is too far gone to be saved, it will beat with her heart. Since she is human, you too will be human."

I felt the world around me pick up and spin, and an unbearable weight lifted from my chest. Emilia looked down at me with teary eyes and touched my cheek, a shaky smile spreading across her face.

"Do you agree to this?" Liùsaidh asked Emilia.

She held my eyes and nodded. Tears spilled down her cheeks. "I do. With all my heart, I agree."

"Aiden? Do you agree?"

"With all that's left of mine, I do."

"Then you must know... you will live an eternal life, but like in the original curse, beheading will still take your life. In the event her heart stops, so will yours. If she dies, you will die as well. Do you agree to this?"

I nodded, reaching up to touch her cheek. "I would die anyway."

Liùsaidh pressed her hands together and bowed her head. "Then let it be done."

Emilia leaned down and kissed me. Liùsaidh chanted in her language and I felt our worlds colliding, our hearts joining as one while the magic moved through us. I felt her in my bloodstream, pulsing through my veins while our hearts pounded in rhythm. The pain in my body dissipated as her love flowed through me, bringing me back me to life. An explosion of energy moved between us and I felt my powers surging back through me. It overwhelmed me, and I reached up and clung to her until I collapsed in her arms, the darkness sweeping me away.

CHAPTER TWENTY-THREE

Emilia

I SAT UP WITH A START. Energy surged through me like I'd slammed a gallon of coffee. My body pulsed and tingled, my heart pounding in my chest while I took a sharp breath. Looking around, I realized I was in a small wooden bed in a hut. Memories of Aiden, of the Picts, and of the ritual all raced into my mind. I searched it like I did sometimes when trying to recollect a dream. Was this a dream? I felt disoriented and dizzy trying to sort through the images in my mind. The last thing I remember was kissing Aiden when I felt an explosion, and everything went dark.

Did he survive?

"Hello, beautiful."

I whipped around to see Aiden sitting it a chair across the room. Though darkness enveloped the room and no light illuminated him, I saw him as clearly as if he'd been standing in the sunlight though the colors seemed muted. His head rested on his hand, and he wore that sweet smile I'd missed so much these last few days. Though my new night vision shocked me, I didn't have time to process it because something far more important pushed to the front of my brain.

He's alive!

"Aiden!" I pulled back the covers and jumped up to run to him. My muscles twitched and suddenly I flew across the room into his arms. The jolt from my speed sucked the air from my lungs. I collapsed in his lap with bulging eyes while I examined my legs.

"Careful, love. It takes a little getting used to." He laughed.

"I... did I? Holy shit," I said, turning to him.

"You've got my powers now... and I've got your heart." He smiled.

"Holy shit," I repeated.

"Let's be shocked about your powers later. For now, all I want is this."

Before I could breathe, his mouth collided with mine. I melted into his kiss, my body igniting beneath his touch. Everything inside me burst to life, new sensations flooded through me and crackled beneath my skin. There was no beginning and no end, no time before him and no life beyond him. It wasn't him and me, it was us. Only us. Weightless yet falling, I tumbled over the edge with him.

He whooshed us into the bed and left me breathless beneath him. Giving me no time to recover he tore at my clothes, and I ripped off his. We devoured each other with hungry mouths, hands desperately clawing at one another. With a flash I flipped him onto his back, straddling him with a smile.

"Well, that was new," he said with a smirk.

Impressed with my own strength, I waggled my eyebrows and pressed my lips to his. His pleasurable moan encouraged me on. Pinning his hands over his head I slid down the length of him and paused to savor the feeling of him filling me again. He sucked in a deep inhale before breathing out the sigh that I drew into my lungs. Our breaths mingled into one as I rocked against him, our passions climbing as we clung to each other. I felt my heart racing, and only then realized it was his heart racing too. Together they pounded as one while our bodies connected and soared to unimaginable heights. We crashed over the edge together, his hands grabbing my face and his lips colliding with mine as we floated back down, our hearts slowing to a steady drum.

I collapsed in his arms and pressed my head to his chest. Feeling him wrapped around me soothed away all the fear and pain that had nearly broken me. It was over, and he was mine. Knowing I was so close to losing him only deepened the love for him I didn't think could grow any stronger.

"I love you, Emilia," he whispered, pressing a kiss to my forehead.

"And I love you."

"Good, because it seems as if you're stuck with me for eternity after all."

"I think I can get used to that." I smiled and pushed into his arms a little deeper. "Although, I'm still pissed you almost had me erased." I scowled.

"Only because I love you that much."

"You're lucky I'm in too good of a mood to hold a grudge," I teased.

"I've got all eternity to make it up to you."

I rolled over and brushed my lips against his. "You'd better."

"I'll start with trying to find you some coffee. I doubt they have any, but I know you can't start your day without it."

"Oh yes, coffee..." I pursed my lips and moaned.

Aiden stood and pulled his pants up. I leaned on my elbow and took in the view grateful I got an eternity to admire that impeccable body. "Where is everyone else?"

"Well, apparently the ritual knocked us both out. I woke up when Lothaire and Thorne were carrying us in here," he said. "You've been out for an hour. Lothaire and Annella are waiting for us outside."

"And Thorne?"

"He's still here and trying to convince Catrain he isn't the devil. I think he's a bit smitten with her." He smirked. "He's always had a thing for bad girls."

Shaking my head, I laughed. "Oh, boy."

"Leave it to Thorne to fall for the Pict witch sworn to hate us." He laughed and shook his head.

"How very Romeo and Juliet of him. I hope it works out."

"He deserves to find someone, too."

I nodded. "I like her. She's a badass, and if it weren't for Catrain things would be a lot different right now. I'd be a mind-erased human and you'd either be a vampire or dead. So, she gets two thumbs up from me."

I grinned, but the reality of how close we'd come to losing it all slammed back into me like a semi-truck. Catrain would have my gratitude every single day of my life... no matter how many centuries stretched before me.

"Speaking of Catrain," Aiden said, tipping his head. "I think we should go out and thank her and let everyone know we both came out of this alive. They need to get back to safety before sunup, so I need to get them on their way."

"Good point," I said and stood up. I pulled on my pants and my clothes with speed that startled me. "I'm gonna have to practice moving like a human again before I go back into the world. That. Is. Crazy."

"I'm happy to take them off of you often so you can practice putting them back on." His sly smile pulled up one side of his lips.

"You've got yourself a deal."

We exchanged a smile and headed to the door together. When he pulled it open Lothaire and Annella paced just outside. I blushed a little thinking they must have heard our exuberant reunion.

"Are you okay? Are you two hurt?" Annella asked when she saw us and flitted to my side.

"I think we're all right," I answered.

"Thank God!" She threw her arms around my neck. "We were so worried!" She moved to Aiden and jumped on her tiptoes to wrap her arms around his neck. "Don't ever scare me like that again!"

"I'm sorry, Annella. But thank you for fighting for me. Thank you for being such a good sister."

"I missed you, Aiden. Promise you won't be a stranger anymore?"

"I promise. No more runaway Aiden. We'll visit you often."

"Good." She smiled and kissed his cheek.

Aiden's eyes moved to Lothaire, who stood back with his arms crossed tight over his expansive chest. That scowl he wore still sent a shiver down my spine and I was glad not to be the recipient of it this time. The two brothers remained locked in a stare.

"Lothaire," Aiden started, but he didn't have a chance to finish. Lothaire appeared in front of him and pulled him into a strong embrace. Aiden stiffened for a moment before returning the gesture and wrapping his arms around his brother.

"I thought you were dead," Lothaire said, struggling to steady his voice. "I thought I'd lost you."

"I'm alive because of you. You didn't give up on me. Thank you, brother."

Lothaire clapped him on the back and straightened up. "Well? Was it worth it? Are you human?"

"Can't you smell it?" Annella laughed. "He's human all right!"

"I hope it's everything you want," Lothaire said and let his glance fall to me.

"It is, and it will be." Aiden reached over and took my hand. "I can never thank you all enough. You saved me."

"What about me?" Thorne's voice came from behind us. We turned to see him walking up with Catrain. "I'm the one who figured out that the Picts were here and could save you. Don't I get a hug?" He flashed his mischievous grin.

"What would I do without you?" Aiden said, returning the smile and pulling him in for a brief hug.

"Apparently desiccate and die. At least that was your plan, wasn't it?"

"Something like that." Aiden shrugged.

"Thank you, Catrain," I said, stepping forward. "Thank you for saving us. We owe you everything." Even though she didn't look welcoming to warm gestures, I tossed my arms around her neck and squeezed her tight.

When I stepped back, her hardened face softened, and she tipped her head in a nod. "It was my mother who saved you."

"But she wouldn't have if you hadn't convinced her," Aiden added. "Thank you. You saved us."

"I saw it on beach. Your connection," Catrain said. "I have some of my mother's magic and I saw it. Like a tether tied between you. An unbreakable bond binding you together."

"Is that why I could feel her and find her when she was in trouble?" Aiden asked, his voice softer.

"Yes," Catrain answered with conviction. "You will always feel her and sense her. And she can feel and sense you. Now even more since your immortal hearts beat as one."

"Well, that explains that," Aiden said, giving me a soft smile. "You were pulling me."

"I guess I was. And knowing now we can sense each other there'll be no sneaking off to the bar with Mark and leaving me behind. I'll find you." I waggled my brows. "Seems like you're *really* stuck with me now."

"I wouldn't have it any other way." The adoration in his gaze brought on that familiar flip-flop in my stomach.

Lothaire broke our stare. "Some of us here are still vampires and can't be in the sun, and we don't have much time before it comes up. It will take us at least fifteen minutes to get back to the safety of the house."

"Fifteen minutes?" I opened my eyes wide. "It was over an hour on horseback here and a twenty-minute helicopter ride before that. You're that fast?"

Annella chuckled. "We'll have time to spare before the sun pops up in twenty minutes."

Lothaire turned to Aiden. "I'll see you at home, brother. Take your time," he said, gesturing to me.

"We'll see you tonight. We've got a lot of catching up to do now that I'm not dying."

Lothaire gave him a soft smile. "I like that plan."

"I'll see you both at home! Welcome to the family, Emilia!" Annella said, smiling at both of us. "Ready, Thorne?"

The glimmer in his eye and the smile he fought to suppress told me he had other plans.

"I'm gonna stay here for a little while. I'm pretty interested in learning all about this culture, and there's a light-tight cave close to here I can crash in for the day. Isn't that right, Catrain?"

She rolled her eyes and shrugged. "He won't leave."

We all exchanged a glance and choked down our laughs.

"Well, I guess you stay and have fun here," Aiden finally said. "We'll see you at home... whenever that is." He raised a playful eyebrow.

"I'll catch up eventually." Thorne smiled and turned to Catrain. "Want to show me where that cave is?"

"Not really, but if you insist." She turned and twitched her head gesturing for him to follow.

"Bye, Thorne!" I called after him. "And thank you again. Both of you! And thank your mother!"

Catrain looked over her shoulder and gave me a nod. Thorne looked back and threw us all a mischievous wink. Even Lothaire chuckled as they sauntered off together.

"Well, we'll see you when you get back," Lothaire said, turning to Aiden and then to me. "Take care of him, Emilia."

Lothaire's voice dripped with emotion. A plea and a warning all rolled into one. This time I didn't shrink from his intense stare. Tossing my arms around his neck, I kissed him on the cheek. "I will. I promise."

After I slid back to the ground, he met me with an appreciative nod and a smile.

"Oh, and tell Mark we'll be home soon so not to leave and go chasing after Ryan Gosling until after we get back," I added.

"He's gonna have to fight me for him. I've got dibs on Gosling." Annella smiled and winked. With a flash, they disappeared, and Aiden and I stood alone in the center of the small village.

"Well, it looks like Thorne will have his hands full for a while," I said.

"That is *if* he has hands when she's done with him. I have a feeling if he tries to make a move, she'll more than likely remove them."

We exchanged a glance and a laugh.

"I'm glad you and your brother patched things up. I'm excited to be part of your family. I don't have one anymore."

"You do now. You have all of us. We're your family now."

Just a month ago I had been alone. Now I had Aiden and Mark, a sister, and brothers. My heart swelled at the thought of being part of a family again. It nearly exploded with the realization I had an eternity with Aiden awaiting me.

"I have an idea," he said, pulling me from my thoughts.

"What's that?"

A playful grin lifted his lips. "Are you ready to see what you can do?" He reached out a hand and held it waiting.

I narrowed my eyes and mirrored his grin. With a flash I appeared at his side, our fingers tangled together.

"Ready?" he asked.

"Ready."

We bolted across the village and out into the woods. When we hit top speed it felt like time stood still... like the world around us had frozen. He looked over at me and smiled. The wind whipped through my hair and I could feel the adrenaline coursing through my veins. I marveled at my reflexes while we darted through the woods, and flew through the fields, hands held tight as I stayed at his side. It felt natural, like I had been doing it for years. I wondered if this was how Mark felt when he changed... so invigorated and alive.

We ran through the fields and dashed around the island, laughing and playing as I tried to catch him, missing by inches each time. He gave me a wink and raced onto the beach, flying into the water. I surged after him, slowing when I saw the droplets of water in his wake spraying up around us. When I turned to look at them, they appeared frozen, like I could reach out and pluck one from the air. The soft glow of the orange strip of the rising sun flickered within them. The incredible sight stunned me so much that I tumbled over my own feet. With a shriek, I flew forward, but Aiden caught me in his sturdy arms before I plunged into the waves.

We tumbled onto the sand, our laughs carrying across the water while we collapsed beside each other on the beach.

"Oops." I giggled. "I guess I need some practice. Thanks for the save. I almost got a face full of water."

"I'm always here to catch you." He sat up and pulled me between his legs. I pressed my back into his chest and inhaled a deep breath while he wrapped his arms around me.

"This is what I wanted to do," he said, resting his head on top of mine.

"What's that?" I asked.

"I wanted to watch the sun come up."

"Oh," I answered, realizing the weight of his words.

I settled back against him and together we stared at the horizon, watching the soft tangerine color spread across the lake stretched out in front of us. The colors deepened and swirled together, and I felt his heart, my heart, speeding up at the sight of it. I listened to his breathing while the translucent glow of the horizon burst into a vibrant pink that stretched long fingers in every direction, bathing everything in its light. The orange rays of the sun crept into sight and set the lake and the sky ablaze. My heart pounded with his as the orb slid into sight, illuminating the darkness around us.

"Incredible," he said, and I felt his breath in my ear.

I turned my head back and saw the light behind his eyes as he watched the sun come into full view, its rays washing over us. The light from the sun paled compared to the light radiating from Aiden. His eyes moved to mine and his hand slid to my chin. He brushed his thumb across my cheek and leaned down, touching my lips with the same tenderness as the sun's rays caressing the surrounding lands.

"I hope you like getting up early," he said between kisses. "Because I intend to watch a lot of sunrises in our lifetime."

"I go where you go." I kissed him back.

"Thank you, Emilia."

"For what?"

"For everything. You saved me. You showed me life and love, and you pulled me out of the darkness and bathed me in light. I will appreciate every day at your side and love you until the end of time."

Closing my eyes, I let his words wash over me. We'd both been so broken when he'd found me. Two shattered souls who found salvation in each other. I'd been through so much, and I had been so alone when he'd walked into my life, but he had reached out a hand and pulled me up from the ground, wrapping me in his protective arms and opening the world to me. He had given me everything... everything I never even knew I needed.

"I love you, Aiden Mackay. Thank you for loving me."

"I love you more, Emilia Charles," he said, pressing a soft kiss to my lips. Then he pulled back and that familiar glimmer twinkled in his eyes. "About that. I like the name Emilia Charles, but I'm wondering what you'd think about becoming Emilia Mackay?"

"What?" I almost choked on the word.

"Well, we share a heart and an eternity. What do you think about sharing a last name? Will you marry me, Emilia?"

My heart exploded, a burst inside me that burned brighter than the sun. I nodded while tears welled up behind my eyes. "Yes," I breathed. "So many times, yes."

I threw my arms around his neck and sank into his kiss. I could taste my dreams on his tongue and feel my heartbeat pulsing through his veins. He was my home, my life, and my heart. It wasn't just Aiden who had been trapped in the darkness before we met. It had been me, too. But now I would dance with him, love him, and live with him under the warmth of the sun and together we would walk into the light.

Did you enjoy *Into The Light*? If you want more, we have good news! Two more books are now in the works and will be coming later in 2020/early 2021. The Immortal Hearts series will be a three-book series of standalone, interconnected novels.

Visit my website to sign up for my monthly Enews and get notified when *Awakened Light*, Thorne's story, releases!

www.katherinehastings.com

OTHER BOOKS TO READ

THE BIG ONE
Romantic Comedy
Some flames refuse to go out...
Even after ten years apart, Ellie can't stop thinking about the summer fling she hasn't seen since. With the encouragement of too many martinis and her meddling wingmen, she ends up on the journey of a lifetime in Italy finding out if it was just summer love or if Liam really is "The Big One".

THE OTHER HALF
Romantic Comedy
When a spoiled socialite is forced to live like the other half, will she also find her other half?
When socialite Cassandra Davenport is shipped off to the country to prove herself worthy of the family legacy, she finds more than just the local wildlife to be troublesome. The biggest trouble of all may be the handsome fisherman next door.

A WAR WITHIN

A WWI Romance
Love. Honor. Redemption.
A shattered soldier searching for redemption finds the one thing he never knew he needed.
Her.

THE ARCH PIRATE
A swashbuckling adventure
Part fact. Part fiction. All Romance.
When Captain Avery went searching for riches, he was looking for gold. But that wasn't the only treasure he found. When he discovered the exquisite beauty hiding in a chest, both their lives would be forever changed.

DAGGERS OF DESIRE SERIES
Action. Adventure. Romance.
Read the historical romance series filled with assassins, pirates, and strong heroines. Each book can be read as a standalone, but you'll get the most enjoyment from reading them in order. You can read the books individually, or grab the boxed set that includes all three books AND *The Arch Pirate!*

IN THE ASSASSIN'S ARMS
Daggers of Desire Book One
Passions flare as swords collide.

When two opposing assassins join forces to solve a mystery threatening them both, sparks fly from more than just their swords.

BENEATH THE ASSASSIN'S TOUCH
Daggers of Desire Book Two
Sometimes the safest place is in the arms of the most dangerous man.
As Viktor fights to save Nora from assassins hot on her trail, it turns out they're up against an even bigger battle... the feelings for each other they can no longer deny.

BY THE ASSASSIN'S SIDE
Daggers of Desire Book Three
Gold may not be the only treasure they find.
As they race to find Captain Henry Avery's treasure, Simon and Vivian must fight the men hunting her down... and the feelings for each other growing each step of the way.

Find them all at www.katherinehastings.com

THANK YOU FOR READING

I hope you enjoyed *Into the Light*! The greatest gift you can give a writer is your review. If you enjoyed this book, I would be forever grateful if you'd take the time to leave a review. Find out more about my other books and upcoming releases at www.katherinehastings.com.

You can also get new book releases, sales, and free book specials delivered right to your inbox by signing up for my Enews!

Get social with me and join me on:
Passion Posse Reader's Group: www.facebook.com/groups/
passionposse
Facebook @katherinehastingsauthor
Instagram @katherinehastingsauthor
Twitter @khastingsauthor
Follow me on:
Bookbub
Goodreads